THE RABBI
OF CASINO
BOULEVARD

THE RABBI
OF CASINO
BOULEVARD

A Novel by

ALLAN APPEL

St. Martin's Press
New York

Design by Paolo Pepe

Library of Congress Cataloging in Publication Data

Appel, Allan.
    The rabbi of Casino Boulevard.
    I. Title.
PS3551.P55R3   1986   813'.54   86-3936
ISBN 0-312-66127-4

First Edition
10 9 8 7 6 5 4 3 2 1

For Suzanne, Sophia, and Nathaniel

I want to thank the following people for their help and good cheer during the writing of this book: Paul Bresnick, Rabbi Lavey Derby, Robert Fresco, Eileen Gillooly, Mark Kaminsky, Peter Minichiello, Iris Rifkin-Gainer, and my editor, Brian DeFiore.

I am also very grateful for a grant from the Creative Artists Public Service Program (CAPS) of New York State.

THE RABBI
OF CASINO
BOULEVARD

Let it not enter the mind that anything in the world's system will cease to exist when the Messiah comes, or that any novelty will be introduced into the scheme of the universe. The world will go as usual.

Maimonides

1

Rabbi Arthur Bloom floated in his inner tube on the waters of the synagogue pool. His dark hair lay in curls on his shoulders and back and a copy of *Being and Nothingness* rested face down on his stomach. To an outsider he might have seemed the picture of contentment, a bear that has caught a salmon and made a good meal of it. But this was not the case. Arthur Bloom was preoccupied, even troubled. What was worse—he was not sure why.

He paddled slowly about, slapping occasionally at the water as if he had suddenly spotted his trouble skitting along the placid surface of the pool. He stroked at the water and maneuvered to the corner, near the eight-foot mark, from where he could see down the asphalt driveway of the synagogue and all the way across Casino Boulevard. Today again the young Japanese woman was sitting out in front of Nakazawas' liquor store, with her tanned, shapely legs crossed, the upper one moving slowly, metronomically, up and down. Whatever was bothering Bloom, the instruments of his long rabbinical training, his reasoning skills, and his passionately rational disposition all were somehow unable to get moving on this pleasant, sun-filled spring afternoon.

Had Arthur not kicked occasionally, the undulation of the water would have carried him away from the corner and his view of the woman. Ten minutes went by and he did not take his eyes from her. He stared at her sunglasses, the swath of white cream on her nose, and her yellow T-shirt over white shorts that made her seem to Bloom the healthiest, tannest woman he had ever seen. She recrossed her legs, and now the left one was up, a glistening curvy shin in hypnotic motion.

Before himself, before his own conscience, Bloom was embarrassed. He should be *thinking*, he chided himself, and reading, concentrating on the basic questions that it was his vocation to study. Yet Bloom's philosophy remained on his belly.

Ten minutes later he lifted up the book but did not read it.

Instead he pondered the pale white skin in the middle of his hairy paunch.

The liquor store owner, Ono Nakazawa, whose husband, Akira, had died a month ago, came out and stood over the young woman. Arthur couldn't be sure, but Mrs. Nakazawa looked angry and seemed to scold the young woman as if she were her child. Perhaps that's it, Bloom thought. The daughter! The younger woman seemed to smile, but the eyes remained a mystery behind sunglasses. Bloom continued to watch intently; he hoped she would not get up, but soon she did rise, towering over Mrs. Nakazawa; then she quickly folded her white canvas chair and entered the store.

Arthur stopped kicking. There was a heavy feeling in his stomach. As he paddled away from his corner out into the middle of the pool, he felt as if he had just experienced the best part of his day, even though there was much he had to do, much that he usually looked forward to, and it was barely two o'clock.

So uncharacteristic of Rabbi Arthur Bloom. When Bloom was sixteen years old, he had read H. G. Wells's *Outline of History*. It occurred to Bloom then that if Wells could outline the history of a whole world, surely he, Bloom, could outline his own history up until then and, in addition, could chart his future.

In the pages of a green notebook purchased at the dime store specifically for this august project, Bloom wrote year by year a careful outline for his life. For ages sixteen through seventy he planned where he would be living and going to school, what he would be reading, what languages he would be learning, what books he would be writing. On a separate page, entitled "Summing Up," he planned years seventy-one to seventy-two. On the last sheet of the notebook he wrote the headline "Death," and below it a bold, curlicued question mark that filled up the page.

According to the outline he should by now, at the age of thirty-seven, have learned Greek and Arabic; he knew neither. By now he was also to have written an important biography, a book on contemporary philosophy, and a general history of the Jews. All Arthur Bloom had to his credit, as he moved toward the end of his fourth decade, was a book for children on Jews in sports and half a dozen poems published in *Jewish Currents*, *Ashanta*, *Spirit World*, *Out of Breath*, *Oink*, and some other small poetry magazines—his only copies of which Bloom often searched for in his study but could never seem to find. Instead of being the intellectual and influential spokesman for his people at a distinguished academic institution, Arthur Bloom was the rabbi of an aging congregation in the small town of Gardena, a gambling enclave less than an hour south and east of Los Angeles, and not far from the desert.

Still, Arthur was not unhappy in Gardena, where his life had taken a form far different from that of his original plans. His nearly three years here had so far been pleasant if uneventful, allowing him time to read, to think, and occasionally to write a poem.

Arthur dropped through the inner tube, so that only his arms, shoulders, and head were above water. His feet did not touch the bottom of the pool; he gave himself up to the bobbing rhythm of the water and closed his eyes. No, he thought, he was just fine in Gardena. In Gardena he was no longer struggling and aimless as he had been at his previous pulpits. Here he felt at home, in his inner tube, in his town, among his odd congregation, where he was less the leader of his people than a kind of spiritual handyman that the congregation had kept on—just in case.

Bloom's eccentric flock was made up mainly of gamblers from Gardena's casinos, and particularly the Silver Dollar Casino, which stood next door to the synagogue. It was from this place that the Silver Dollar Synagogue took its name, although every once in a while someone—sometimes even Bloom—in a fit of correctness referred to the shul as Temple Elijah, its given name. The losers and winners, misfits, black sheep, and occasional high roller Bloom prayed with every sabbath at the Silver Dollar had kept a smile on his face these last three years. Yet somehow he felt he should be a little happier; he felt he might be sinking.

He felt no pressure from the congregation. They didn't care if Bloom never wrote the books he had planned, nor did they care if he appeared on television programs during the Sunday morning religious hours, or gave brilliant sermons on Friday night and Saturday morning. The congregants were clearly happy with him as he was, their Bloom, their Silver Dollar rabbi.

He found it difficult to describe his congregation to the seminary

friends with whom he was occasionally in touch. Most of them had
large incomes from opulent suburban temple centers; they had
houses and luxury cars thrown in. All that came along with the Silver
Dollar Synagogue was fifteen thousand a year, the pool, free washing
and drying at the laundromat owned by the temple president and
her husband, and a four-room apartment up the rickety steps above
the garage.

Yet it had been enough to satisfy him. When Bloom, a subway-
riding New Yorker for most of his life, had finally decided to learn
to drive, the congregation was responsive to their rabbi. They paid
for his driving lessons and then bought him a car, the synagogue
Toyota, which now resided in the garage below the apartment.

As Bloom toweled off and went up the wooden steps to his
apartment, he was still thinking about her. After he listened to the
news, ate a late lunch, and began work on a sermon, there she was
still. Bloom sat over his books and visualized the beautiful Japanese
woman, a diminutive version of her astride the alephs and bets, her
gorgeous legs swinging freely from the tops of the Hebrew letters the
rabbi began to study, and continued to pore over, into the twilight.

2

Already by the end of Bloom's first year as rabbi in Gardena he was
developing a reputation for bringing good luck to those who prayed
with him. Nobody ever went so far as to say that Bloom prayed for
his congregants to win at the Silver Dollar Casino and the other
casinos that dotted the town. However, Bloom surely was not praying for congregants to lose, either.

Bloom had come to Gardena after a succession of failures as rabbi
in several large suburban communities. He had even been on the
verge of leaving the rabbinate altogether; his last unhappy pulpit had
almost confirmed in him an early and deep-seated suspicion that it
had been a mistake for him ever to have become a rabbi. But the
crisis did not occur. Successively he had come with small ceremony
and departed with courtesy (the disenchantment both parties kept

to themselves) to and from Valley River, New York, then Ontario, Illinois, and finally Stafford, Arizona. Now he was in Gardena, California, as if he had been consciously, steadily, moving from east to west, toward the desert, and he was now deep in the desert, like the first and only recruit in some rabbinical foreign legion.

Beyond his own private doubts that he simply didn't have the panache and showmanship necessary to preside at bar mitzvahs, weddings, and the dances of synagogue teenagers, Bloom also felt that his shortness, his premature graying and baldness, and his bachelor status all had played their part in the termination of his previous pastoral contracts. Throughout his peregrinations among the suburban tribes of Israel, Bloom had kept as elements of some permanence only his books and his New York Yankees baseball cap, which he treasured from his Bronx youth and still frequently wore over his yarmulkah as he strolled the streets of Gardena.

That their rabbi should occasionally wear a baseball cap did not cause a single strange look among the congregants of the Silver Dollar. Although he was no gambler himself, Bloom took to these congregants' easygoing ways, and they to him, in a manner he had never experienced before.

Not only did he serve them, he was very fond of them as well. The flock was composed of salesmen, bookkeepers, some small businessmen, owners of a newspaper route and of a coin-operated laundry or two, some civil-service workers, pensioners, and some old soldiers. Most did not live in Gardena proper but came only to gamble. They lived north, most of them, in Los Angeles, and many also belonged to synagogues there. But a great love of poker and twenty-one kept them so often in Gardena, where gambling was legal, that over the years a *minyan* had developed for the sabbath. Since Los Angeles was all too often a long traffic jam away, and because to many of the gamblers Gardena had become a second home, it was only natural, after a while, to establish a synagogue formally, and to try to attract a rabbi.

The congregants, however, were a fickle and superstitious assembly, and Bloom was the Silver Dollar's fourth spiritual leader in ten years. But in the current estimate of the gamblers, they had struck gold in Bloom, and to Bloom, too, Gardena was—or at least up to now it had been—just about perfect. The troublesome doctors, lawyers, and successful businessmen Bloom had struggled with at his previous jobs were not numbered in this new, poorer, far more colorful group.

The synagogue building itself was also a far humbler place than any Bloom had been accustomed to. Packed between the casino on the left, a coffee shop, laundromat, and photo/camera store on the right, and directly across the street from the Nakazawas' liquor store, Bloom's religious precinct was really one long rectangular room, with a minuscule foyer in front, and in back, behind the altar, an office, library, and reception hall. On Casino Boulevard, in front of the synagogue, two large willow trees shaded the congregation from the sun as they gathered or, more precisely, straggled in, for services. The willows also were considerate enough, and large enough by now, to conceal cracks and chips on the synagogue's stuccoed walls and the red Spanish tiles of the roof. In fact the Silver Dollar was like a storefront synagogue, where you climbed up no steps but entered right through a door on street level, in the manner of the shuls in Europe; Bloom particularly liked this feature of the synagogue, and over the years had also grown exceedingly fond of the willows.

Shortly after he had signed on at the Silver Dollar—it was around Tisha b'Av, the Fast of Lamentations, that summer three years back —he gave his first sermon, and it was based precisely on those two willow trees. Bloom compared them with the willows of the Biblical psalmist: "By the waters of Babylon we sat down, and, yea, we wept," he had quoted. "We hung our harps on the willow trees and we cried when we remembered Zion."

Bloom told his congregants not only how fond he personally was of the trees, but how appropriate it was that they were there out in front of the Silver Dollar Synagogue. "Under the beautiful, drooping arms of the willows," he sermonized, "cry about your losses and your bad luck and get all that gambling talk out of your systems. On the branches of *your* willows you hang your decks of cards and your dice and your rabbits' feet, so that when you enter the synagogue and put on your skullcap, then you can pray pure of heart."

But the congregants were gamblers through and through, so that even during the services the sanctuary often buzzed with talk of odds and bets and streaks of spectacular luck—and days, even weeks, without drawing an ace. Yet whenever Arthur coughed or ahemmed or went suddenly silent, like a teacher with a class that knows it's naughty, down the volume came. The congregants always paid attention to Bloom.

Very close attention, in fact. During his sermons of the last two years in particular they listened, not just because they at times found Bloom thought-provoking and respected his learning, and not merely because they thought fondly of him (especially the older couples, who considered him a kind of son); the other, more cogent reason they listened to Arthur was that they considered him plain lucky, a charm, a sign for each of them, a gambler's Hebrew oracle.

Notoriously superstitious people, the gambling congregants noted the chapter and verse numbers Bloom used in his sermons, and they stored the numbers in memory for use later at the gaming tables. Those in the congregation who had counting systems for blackjack paid particular attention to Arthur, listening not only to the chapters and verses, but to the sequence in which Bloom called them. Some ambitious congregants even paid attention to how Saturday morning's chapters compared to the Friday night service's, and tried to discover if the numbers formed a pattern with those the rabbi had employed in the previous weeks.

The congregation might be whispering some intelligence about a casino pit boss, but they always had an ear tuned to Arthur's sermon to hear if he mentioned, for example, a name similar to that of one of the casino managers (to be avoided), or one of the twenty-one dealers (to be challenged, perhaps, after the services).

It wasn't that all the members of the Silver Dollar immediately began to win with Bloom at the pulpit. Far from it. Nevertheless, most of the congregants, whether winning or losing, would swear that when they genuinely needed a good run, or needed a sign—some help to decide whether to play on a given weekend or whether to go home to quotidian L.A.—if they paid close attention to Bloom, to which parts of the Torah he quoted (the fourth book, Numbers, was a favorite), to how many times he adjusted the yarmulkah on his shiny scalp (perhaps a useful number at the craps table), the lucky rabbi would always come through for them.

What Bloom knew of this he viewed with good-natured skepticism. From the very beginning of his stay in Gardena he had sensed how the congregants seemed to study his repertoire of gestures and his sermons for their personal gambling guidance. By now he expressed for his idiosyncratic flock an affection that took the form both of amusement—he could kid them as much as they did him —and occasional exasperation. But generally it pleased him that the congregants regarded him not just as a religious resource but as a gaming resource as well. Fate, God, free will and self-determination, skill and luck, divine intervention in historical time, and the religious significance of the dealer's suddenly changing the deck—these themes and more Bloom put into an intellectual Crockpot that he simmered and stirred for his congregants in sabbath sermons throughout the year.

Bloom enjoyed it, and the congregants delighted in his formulations. They sometimes even applauded him (although he frowned on that), and they regularly asked him to suggest books of history and philosophy to read; all of this flattered Bloom. He had begun rabbinical school at the end of the radical 1960s, a period whose forced reevaluations of absolutely everything touched even the training in the Jewish seminaries, and particularly Bloom's in New York City, not a half dozen blocks from that hotbed of revolution, Columbia University. Bloom had learned about obsession, addiction, nonnegotiable demands, unshakable commitments, and about letting it flow. As a student he had been witness to the crazy, random, passionate lives people make for themselves or muddle into and then have to live out. Even if the temple president, Sarah North, or any of the congregational leaders had been interested in reforming the gamblers, Bloom would have chosen not to be the reformer; it was a role for which his personality and background had not cast him. No, the congregants were endearing oddballs, every one of them, and Bloom loved to be among them just as they were.

What Bloom did not fully grasp was the importance to his congregants of his own very quiet style of living outside of the synagogue, his very chaste personal life. Bloom was not married, nor had he actively been dating any woman since coming to Gardena. To the congregants this monasticism, involuntary though it might have been, had a great deal to do with Bloom's aura of luck and good fortune. Unwed, unattached, alone—except for his mother, Nannette—he was their finely tuned instrument, their spiritual surrogate, their lucky rabbi, their Bloom. If the young rabbi ever got together with a woman, if there then were children to care for, with all the *tsores* and heartaches the congregants themselves had, they feared that Bloom would lose, or at least endanger, his powers.

Therefore something of a silent compact had arisen among the congregants through these three years, that they *not* introduce Bloom to any of their unmarried daughters, nieces, or young female friends. It wasn't as if everyone had conspired against the young rabbi; a synagogue style simply developed that had resulted in Bloom's becoming isolated from eligible females of his generation.

To the congregants no harm was being done Bloom; he seemed happy enough. He almost always greeted them with a bemused look on his face, or a smile, or a wry turn of the lips, as if he knew something they did not; as if someone had whispered a funny line or given him a tip that the deck has always been benignly stacked. Bloom, they said, was just fine, and they saw no need for matchmaking or for helping the rabbi alter any part of his life—which alteration might then change theirs.

3

The woman whom Bloom had correctly identified as the Nakazawas' daughter, Dawn, tanned herself for an hour every day in front of the store, early in the afternoon when the sun was at its hottest. From his floating concealment, Bloom watched. He tried to tell himself that this was only a harmless observation of changes in the neighborhood, but soon even he had to admit that he was staring. He was increasingly embarrassed—but the need to continue overcame him. Had she moved herself on the white canvas chair or changed its position even slightly, he would not have been able to see her— certainly not all of her—and he well might have been deterred. But she just sat there, glitteringly bold and constant as the sun above.

Each day Bloom studied her more intently, as if she were an exotic text. By Thursday, he felt she might be aware of him, but not letting on. As he floated in the tube, his mind straying from the composition of a sermon, he realized he could no longer just watch her from a safe distance. He recognized, with trepidation, that he wanted to find an excuse to meet her.

The weightiness reflected in Bloom's reading of late (Wittgenstein, Kierkegaard, medieval commentary on the Book of Leviticus, and a novel by Turgenev for a change) was suddenly lifted. From the mere decision to meet her, Bloom experienced a lightness as if he had suddenly lost thirty pounds.

From a member of the synagogue's hospitality committee Bloom obtained the list of the congregation's liquor needs for the coming month. The next day, with the list in hand, he set out to cross Casino Boulevard and enter the store.

Twice Bloom prepared to cross but did not make it. Once he stopped himself at the mirror because he felt he looked too formal in a dark cotton suit and his yarmulkah. The second time he tried it he decided he looked too informal in his Bermuda shorts, thongs, and Yankees cap. He thought the thongs might be the right idea, properly Oriental, but when he looked at his feet he realized how ugly his big toes were, how square and pudgy. Scrutinizing them, he felt his elation floating away, as if those dull, square appendages were a reflection of all of him, inside and out. He threw the thongs in the closet and stalked around his bedroom in his robe, the Silver Dollar's brief alcohol list still in his hand. As Bloom walked by the mirror above his bureau, he glanced at himself quickly and then accelerated out of reflection's way. Such vanities had not assailed him since he was a precocious and pimply fourteen.

Bloom felt not only pudgy but short, terribly short. He knew the Japanese beauty across the street was not the traditional miniature, but a leggy, full-size woman—at least five feet, seven inches, Bloom guessed. If he fasted for the whole day, if he had a poem accepted in *Jewish Currents,* and if his congregation were drawing aces and beating the house, then Bloom might, just might, rise to five feet six.

He opened his closet and dug around for his pair of ankle-high boots with the good stout heels. He was disgusted at how run down he had allowed most of his shoes to become, and he made a mental note to take in at least three pairs for soles and heels. Now, however, when he needed all the height he could get, his boots seemed lost, and he was able to ferret out shoes that would add to him at most another quarter inch. If the Japanese were wearing any kind of high heels, he would be staring up at her as he ordered the shul's wine and booze.

And yet what was wrong with that? Hadn't he just read in the Sunday paper an article entitled "Tall Girl/Short Guy—It's the Latest"? Well, yes, but so what? Slow down, Bloom. A voice of reason rose above the din in Bloom's giddy brain. It was the resonating voice of the rabbis, Bloom's professional forebears through the ages, who now chanted him a lullaby of *pilpul,* the singsongy logic of Talmudic disputation: If you read last week, or last year, or maybe even yesterday, an article about boys and girls of different heights going out on dates (God forbid they should be unchaperoned!), and then, if you yourself happened to notice a tall girl, a woman, maybe helping out her poor widowed mother in the liquor store, from where you are buying the wine and schnapps for the shul, what conclusions can we draw from such premises? Well, Rabbi Bloom, what conclusions? Come and listen. The answer is: No conclusions. Because the woman is tall and beautiful, and because you are yourself unspeakably runty and unprepossessing, is that any reason to think that you two will a couple make? No! And, if you want wine, and she has wine, and from her you buy wine, what does this transaction amount to? A contract, but a business contract only. Not a marriage contract, not a promise of engagement. Simpleton! Rabbi of Gardena, wake up!

Bloom opened his eyes, relieved that his interlocutors had omitted any mention of the daunting fact that the woman was Japanese. He pulled out the thongs, drew on his jeans and a simple white shirt, and sat down to finish working on his sermon.

Bloom waited until the sabbath was concluded. Then, at eight-thirty on Saturday night, after having said the blessing on the arrival of the new week, he walked across Casino Boulevard, thronged with gamblers, to the Nakazawa liquor store.

Bloom was strangely relieved to find when he entered that the young woman didn't seem to be in. Perched on a stool behind the cash register, Ono Nakazawa was tending the store, like a patient, long-suffering bird. She was a frail woman of seventy, with her hair in a gray pageboy, and sloping shoulders clothed in a crisp imperial-blue blouse open at the collar. In all, Bloom thought, an unlikely progenitrix of the healthy creature he had been spying on for a week.

But the timbre of Ono's voice—she was now on the phone behind the counter, speaking rapidly in Japanese—belied her appearance. Clipped, gravelly sounds emerged through a Salem dangling from her lower lip, as if the cigarette were a kind of skinny smoky mega-phone.

"Good evening," she said to him perfunctorily, without the slight-est smile. "Can I help you?" Bloom was colossally nervous. He regretted that the synagogue had sent a routine store-bought condo-lence card on the death of her husband, Akira. They should have done something more. However, now, as he was on the verge of asking for a date for the first time in years, he found it extremely tongue-tying to switch gears to a belated expression of sympathy. He fingered the liquor list in his pocket; next to it lay an envelope containing a written invitation. He had invested what remained of a box of notepaper composing its three hand-scrawled lines. He had agonized over the words and phrases, just in case she was not in and the invitation, like a calling card of old, had to be left with her mother. Now, how should he present it to Ono? What should he say?

As Bloom pulled out the list, the young woman suddenly appeared at the end of a row of champagnes. Bloom looked up at her smile —she *was* tall—and felt his eyes enlarge. He handed her the syna-gogue's list. She studied it for a moment. "You're Rabbi Bloom from the synagogue?"

"Yes," he said, dry-mouthed with nerves.

"I know your account. I'm Dawn Nakazawa." She extended her hand and they shook. "You're an old customer."

"Yes, the synagogue is." Bloom tried to concentrate on the matter at hand. She guided him to the corner of the store, and he smelled shampoo or perfume on her, the smell of green, new-cut grass.

She praised a Chablis, suggested a substitute for an item on the list. Bloom struggled for wine talk, small talk, any talk, for some charming formulation that would break the tension. But his wit collided with his nerves. "We'll just have to place our palates in your hands, Miss Nakazawa," he said.

Dawn stuck to business; Bloom began to sweat, and the note he had labored over was reduced to an undeliverable crumpled ball under the pressure of his fingers. Then the ringing of the bell on the cash register and Ono's staccato voice arched toward them, "Got it all?"

"Yes, mom."

Speak, Bloom commanded the fleeing troops of his language, and then, quickly, it was out. Between the scotch and rye, he invited her over for a swim in the synagogue pool.

To his delight, she accepted immediately.

4

The next morning, bright sunshine, eighty-three degrees. Bloom sat by his window and surveyed Casino Boulevard. He had fasted through dinner the previous night and breakfast this morning, and now his stomach, unused to deprivation, was a roiling mess. Bloom wasn't sure if it was hunger or pain from the belly-tightening sit-ups he had commenced at sunrise, in anticipation of Dawn. He had decided to stay upstairs in his apartment until he saw her emerge and cross over toward the synagogue.

As he waited, Bloom sensed something more palpable than expectation, a kind of fear he could not locate precisely in his body. It was a fine little fear, and he was enjoying it thoroughly when suddenly the Nakazawas' door swung open and out strode Dawn.

Bloom threw his shoulders back, tightened his stomach, stood up, and pulled a white terry-cloth cabana jacket over his bathing suit. He brushed back the strands of hair that had strayed from their assigned places on his skull, opened the door of the apartment with an unusually forceful yank, and stepped out onto the veranda.

Bloom hesitated before descending the stairs, for he did not want Dawn to think he was too eager. When he saw her crossing the boulevard, however, he bounded down toward the pool. He saw her long legs striding toward him, strong and tan, boldly exhibiting knee and thigh through the slit in the robe she was wearing over her swimming suit. He looked up toward her eyes: she really was a California-Japanese knockout, and he was Rabbi Arthur Bloom. The center of gravity within Bloom's belly shifted; he leaned toward Dawn. Bloom's former girlfriends, those demure future wives of future rabbis, paled in his memory; all seemed to have had a timidity about them that made Dawn's outdoorsy naturalness all the more enticing and new. Dawn Nakazawa returned Bloom's wave and skipped toward him.

Verbal Bloom, who had planned to launch into the dimensions of the pool, how he himself cleaned and chlorinated it, suddenly forgot all his data. In receiving Dawn's "Hi," Bloom realized there was no need for a sermon on pool maintenance, that this rendezvous would be far easier than he had expected; that it would be almost neighborly. Never before had Bloom known anyone like a girl next door, one you could wave to each day without being dressed up or worrying about your belt being too tight. Bloom's was a New York subway adolescence, and his typical romantic adventures had been loud, bumpy, subterranean journeys to meet little-known girls in their far-flung boroughs. His rueful dating history flashed through his brain. He remembered with a shudder the doorjambs he so uncomfortably used to lean against on the thresholds of his dates' apartments; before him, nervous fathers made excuses for their daughters' tardiness and meanwhile suspiciously took his measure, as if Bloom, notwithstanding the decent, studious fellow he obviously was, were a living altar upon which they were about to deliver up their Jewish Iphigenias—their Avivas, Deborahs, Bailas, Hannahs.

Bloom gestured toward the chaises longues he had meticulously arranged, but Dawn preferred to go straight to the water. Immediately Bloom sensed that Dawn belonged around the water. Now, wonder of wonders, she took his hand and led him toward the deep end.

There was a casual firmness to her grip, a directness without premeditation in this holding of hands, that made planning, strategist Bloom (should he try to have his arm accidentally graze her shoulder?) feel very callow. He stole a look at Dawn, Junoesque yet demure, quiet yet strong, her face rounded under dark brown, almost black hair, a curvature of bangs evenly cut, and a touch of deep red on her lips.

As they stood near each other beside the diving board, Dawn unselfconsciously let her white robe slip off and fall on the deck behind her. She was wearing a small blue bikini. She smoothed back the long fall of her hair and took a step forward so that her toes curled around the pool's edge.

What feet! thought Bloom. Not Japanese bonsai feet, but big healthy wonderfully shapely American feet. Dawn's tan, he noticed, extended quite literally down to her toes, which were browned lightly, the color of toast. She was preparing to dive and handed Bloom the sunglasses that had lain, hidden to him, across the top of her head. Bloom felt honored. "I'll hold this too so it doesn't get splashed," he said, scooping up her robe.

She gave him a gracious smile and dived into the blue water of the synagogue pool. With three strokes she had propelled herself to the far end. She disappeared, somersaulting off the wall and gliding underwater back to the five-foot mark, where she surfaced, gesturing for Bloom to join her. "I will, I will," he said, "but don't wait for me. I take my time."

Bloom was a wader and a slow splasher and he meandered, trying to look nonchalant, around to the shallow end to perform his bearish ritual. Whatever dive he might muster he felt sure would be at best awkward; at worst he would injure himself and, Bloom had no doubt, sink to the bottom like a stone. At the steps he sat down and splashed his arms, then his belly and chest, spreading the chill so his body would adjust to it. But all the while he was also watching Dawn, gliding, sailing, cutting onto her back and side, effortless in the water.

When it rippled over her suit, the water at times made Dawn appear naked. She swam the length of the pool, then back; she had done a dozen laps in a perfectly straight line by the time Bloom entered the water and began wading toward her.

She was treading water in the deep end by the board, observing and growing amused at his turtle-ishness. "Get in before the sun goes down," she said, laughing. Then she dove underwater, surfacing inside Bloom's inner tube. Hoisting herself up through it, so that her legs sprawled Bloom-like over the tube, she paddled toward him.

"Come back here with my toy," he yelled. "I have my best thoughts there."

Dawn sank her chin into the palm of her hand. "Let me see if I can get profound here too." She squinted, tugged at her chin, and then shook her head. She paddled toward him, gave Bloom a teasing splash, and then maneuvered away as he lunged for the tube.

He continued wading toward her, timidly but steadily; he very much wanted to reach his inner tube. But Dawn had paddled half the length of the pool and now was splashing in the corner within view of her mother's store. She visored her eyes. "Isn't this where you were staring at me?"

"Oh, not staring," Bloom quickly said, "just looking up now and then to take a break from my reading. I told you that tube's like my outdoor office. That's where I get a lot of work done. Then I looked up one day last week, and there you were, taking a sunbath. You sat in the same place about the same time every day, as though you were on a schedule."

"That's not true, Rabbi," she said, paddling toward him. "You were staring at me."

"Maybe a little," Bloom admitted.

"Come on into the water, Rabbi."

"I'm coming," Bloom said, "and don't call me 'Rabbi.' Call me 'Arthur.'"

"You're hardly wet, Arthur," she said, now a stroke or two away. Then she veered off into a circle around him.

"Hey, you'll get dizzy," he called. "Give me back my tube."

He tried to reach her, but Dawn was easily the superior maritime power. He lunged for the inner tube but lost his footing and only succeeded in pushing the tube, with Dawn still in it, toward the deep end, where she slipped out and began to do backstroke laps. The tube, buffeted by Dawn's kicking, floated farther and farther away from Bloom and came to rest near the eight-foot mark.

Dawn swam underwater toward Bloom, poking at his knees, before angling away. Bloom floated like a jellyfish above her. She surfaced; Bloom picked his head up, and water streamed out of his mouth. His eyes felt like washing machines, he shook his head, flung away the drops from his nose. The water seemed to cling to Dawn's face in neatly shaped pearls while Bloom felt himself soaking, batrachian. "It's colder than usual," he sputtered.

"It's warm if you swim."

"Right."

"The crawl will warm you up very quickly."

"I'm just fine now."

But Dawn had already taken his hand in hers and begun to sidestroke out toward the deep end, with Bloom good-naturedly hopping along in tow. He again felt the strength of her grip—her hand around his wrist this time—but the water was already chest high, nearing his shoulders. Now it lapped about his neck, and the fright, spreading out from the center of him, suddenly overcame Bloom's desire to continue touching her hand.

Yet Dawn must have thought he was being playful as he tried to disengage. She was strong, and Bloom, who had slippery footing, now found himself between the five- and seven-foot marks, with a gulp of water already down his throat. Still Dawn didn't realize it, and Bloom was angry not at her but at himself for not having told the truth. The result of his embarrassment: he was now bobbing up and down with the water over his nose. If he didn't keep jumping, if he went flat-footed, he would sink below the surface. He bounced off the bottom, kicking hard each time he pushed off, in an effort to breathe.

It was only seconds before they were in seven, then seven and a half feet of water, where Bloom had never been without his tube. His coughs turned into a gagging that made him pull his hand violently away from Dawn's and leap up, at his next push-off, with all his strength so that he aimed for, and succeeded in grasping, the edge of the pool.

There Bloom hung, coughing, water streaming from his bloodshot eyes, his body a glistening furry coat, his face pained and miserable, as Dawn, doing an effortless tread, stared at him in compassionate disbelief. "Let me pull you out. And don't worry—I've got my Red Cross senior life-saving certificate."

Bloom wanted no help. He waved her away and with two pumping kicks of his legs pulled himself up over the edge and lay there, panting. His hair was matted all over him, and his mouth, he knew, hung open unattractively as though he were a caught fish displayed on the pier. He tried to apologize, but Dawn told him, "Don't talk." She was on the deck now, standing beside the board. "Maybe I should clear your lungs for you?"

"I went under only once." Bloom raised a finger. "I have two more times to go." He lifted himself up slowly and saw Dawn. He would have liked her to pick up her robe and sunglasses and walk down the driveway back across the street and away from him. He had wanted to show her that he was a capable fellow, one who cleaned and chlorinated his pool, who knew pH, knocked around, just for fun, with an inner tube. And here he had almost drowned in front of her! He feared her gaze would reflect the low self-esteem he was now feeling. He should have invited her to lunch or somewhere to share a glass of tea and some talk. After all, talking, words, ideas, these were areas where he had some prowess. He felt inept—worse yet, a jerk, for having invited her to the pool; he was like an illiterate trying to show off in a library.

"You should learn to swim," she said to him. "It's dangerous to be the only person in a pool and not know how to swim."

"Maybe I'll get a lifeguard," he said.

"You need to learn to swim." She restated the simple truth of it.

"I should," he said, "but that's why I have my floating office there." He pointed down to the tube now making its way placidly toward the center of the pool. "It's pretty safe."

Dawn's long wet body was profiled in the sun. She rolled her hair into a rope, leaned forward, and wrung water from it. Head down, she told Bloom again, "You need to learn to swim. I've taught lots of kids. I could teach you."

He was no kid; he shook his head. His left ear was blocked with water; it irritated him that the damn water wouldn't leave him alone even when he was out of it. Bloom found and put on his cabana jacket and felt better clothed. Dawn was now sitting on the diving board. What was she doing there, this real bathing beauty, with him —overweight, bumbling, the unathletic rabbi of the Silver Dollar Synagogue? And yet she was there indeed, very much so, offering him lessons to keep from drowning.

"Once I tried to learn," he said to her. "I did it my way, of course, which was to buy a book and study the subject. I took the book to the pool in Central Park on 110th Street in New York. I put the book under my towel, got in at three feet, and tried to swim. But it didn't work. I couldn't coordinate a thing; the breathing was especially bad. I can kick all right, because I've got these big legs from doing some wrestling in college, but the breathing is a disaster. Frankly, I don't think I breathe too well out here on land either, but in the water you can forget it. You know the Book of Jonah in the Bible? He's a passenger on a boat in an ocean storm. When the sailors toss him overboard, down he goes, like I did there. You know there's not a single line of text in that whole story that shows Jonah could do the crawl or backstroke or sidestroke. There's nothing in the Jonah story that indicates the guy could even float. At least I float a little."

"Rabbi," Dawn said, "I don't think you understand water. Maybe a rabbi has trouble. You'll pardon me for generalizing, but maybe the Jews don't have a good relationship with water. Wouldn't Jonah have drowned, just like you said, if it hadn't been for the whale? And the waters of the Red Sea would have swept the Jews away too if it hadn't been for the miracle. And if the waters had flowed over them, do you think a lifeguard at the Red Sea back then would have made any difference with all those people sinking at once?"

"No," Bloom admitted, "no difference."

"The Jews in my opinion are an inland, desert people, Rabbi, even though they ended up living by the sea there in Israel. But I don't think they understand water. Irrigation, yes. Swimming, no."

Bloom had listened, impressed, to her sermon on water. "And yet," he said, "the Jews are also a buoyant people." He pointed to the pool. "They have a way of finding what they need to keep them afloat, even when it happens to be a lousy inner tube."

"Water," she said, "doesn't have to be so threatening. It's primordial stuff, you know. The source of life. I could teach you to swim, Rabbi."

"Arthur."

"I could. Believe me when I tell you I could. I spent most of my childhood in it, racing, and training to race. I used to examine my sides right here for the place where the gill slits would begin to form and turn me into a fish."

Bloom followed her finger toward her ribs. It was then that he noticed the scar on her abdomen, and looked immediately back up into Dawn's eyes. She was scrutinizing him now, trying to register his reaction to it. It was a formidable scar, a thin but dark reddish ridge that ran from the tip of the sternum trailing down into the bottom band of Dawn's bikini. "Instead of gills," she said, "I ended up with this."

"Where, how?" Bloom wanted to know.

"A car accident," she said, a studied response. "You can look at it again if you want, Rabbi. You can even stare at it. I prefer you to stare at it now to get it out of your system."

"What's in my system?"

"The need to stare at something like this. It's human."

"It's not in my system, and I consider myself human."

She studied his face for a moment and said, "Yes, you're very human." She smiled. "There's no doubt about that."

"I mean I see it," Bloom said, "and that's that. Lots of people have scars."

"Most people stare."

"I'll admit to staring at you, but not at that part of you."

A warm breeze rippled over the pool water. Casino Boulevard was particularly quiet. The clicking of the roulette wheels, the voices of the dealers and gamblers, all remained insulated behind the double-glazed doors of the casinos. Behind the low, thick hedges of hydrangea that separated the Silver Dollar Casino from the synagogue and pool, Bloom's congregants gambled; nearby the rabbi sat, enchanted with his new Japanese friend, and feeling for the first time in many years that maybe he too was about to take a chance.

Dawn's wet bangs lay in an even line across her forehead. She was sitting up very straight, very erect, a quarter of a head taller than he was. "Let me teach you to swim," she said.

Arthur Bloom reflected, and then smiled his assent.

5

On Friday night Bloom stood at his pulpit and conducted services. As usual, the same group of twenty-five or thirty gamblers had assembled. Eli Ginsberg, at ninety-one the oldest and most Orthodox member, was there first. The others trickled in, weary from a long day at the casinos, with several bent and already dozing in the back row, even before services began. Bloom's cantor was Angelos Panuzzi, a Greek Jew, son of a concentration camp survivor. Angelos had been his friend from seminary days—a cantor who still had aspirations of folksong-writing stardom, or a killing at the dice table.

Angelos performed at the lectern opposite Bloom's, humming and swaying and projecting his big baritone around the rectangular chamber of the synagogue. When they arrived at the central part of the service, Bloom slowly raised his hands, palms skyward. Amid a rustling of garments, the popping of knee joints, some coughs and sighs, the flock stood, and Bloom pronounced with them the

"Shema," the central credo of the faith: "Hear, O Israel, the Lord our God, the Lord is One."

Then with Panuzzi in the lead, came the response: "Blessed be His name, His Kingdom shall live forever and ever."

Bloom led in the next responsive reading; then he asked the congregation to join him in a prayer for the welfare of the country and, as usual, augmented this with a wish for the health and well-being of the Gardena board of supervisors and the county gambling commissioners. Then Panuzzi was called on by Bloom to chant one of the beautiful hymns in honor of the arrival of the bride of the sabbath. Panuzzi complied and with fervor sang the traditional hymn, embroidering it with a melody that Bloom was sure derived from the Beatles. When Panuzzi finished, he looked to Bloom. It was time for the sermon.

"Ladies and gentlemen, dear friends. Gambling, just like prayer, requires a quorum. Eight for low ball, I am told, six for draw poker, and at least four for interesting blackjack. For a *minyan*, of course, there are ten."

There was a quieting down; again he had their attention. "Why deny it? Is not prayer essentially a great gamble too? How do we pray? The answer is easy: Ten of us draw cards and don't know what is going to turn up. All we know is that the dealer is God, the God of Abraham, Isaac, and Jacob. And He is plenty experienced, this Dealer. So what is called for is humility, caution, and reverence.

"What role does your rabbi have in this little paradigm? Ladies and gentlemen, I don't know what the Dealer is up to any more than you do. A rabbi is a gambler, just like yourselves; maybe in the matter of prayers I am also part pit boss, part floor manager. This much is true. My job is to settle disputes on the when, where, and why of prayers. In other words, to make you lay out your cards; if, for example, you say you have an eight-six, you had better have an eight-six. But, unlike a priest among the Catholics, a rabbi has no special angle or prerogative. I couldn't peek at the Dealer's cards if I wanted to—which I don't—because it's the hand of the Almighty I am talking about. In the casinos here, you go up against the house and try to beat it, and that's the law and that's legitimate. But in prayer, dear congregants, you are going up against a different House, and a pretty extraordinary one, the House of the Lord. That's the difference, and, I beseech you, do not forget it!

"Now, let's move to the business of a strong hand, and how you play a strong hand against the House of the Lord, God of Israel. You all know that *knowing* the dealer and his ways is terribly important, especially in twenty-one. There's no substitute for being familiar with his quirks, his facial expressions, the way his eyes communicate the cards. The more you get to know the dealer, the more you know whether he'll shuffle automatically when the deck is rich with tens or let you have a go at it. Knowledge is the key.

"All the more so when you are up against the House of God, which, please never forget, is no ordinary casino, no Silver Dollar. You'll need to know all you can, and the more you pray, the more you know; and the more you know, the better are your chances. Don't get me wrong. God in our tradition does not have a face, a beard—in spite of what you see on mortuary calendars—or any quirks. He doesn't have a tongue that licks the upper lip whenever He deals himself a seventeen so you know it right away. Our God is a non-anthropomorphic Dealer. You learn the quirks of the Jewish God—Who is a universal God—by studying results, by examining patterns, by seeing what's happened in history. Are you following me? You can call it divine intervention in the affairs of men, or you can call it the articulation of a preordained god-like plan through human events. Either way, the Jewish approach, as Jack Kennedy said, is that God's work on earth must truly be our own.

"An object lesson comes from our ancestor Samson, probably the first casino-type gambler in Jewish history. He was a strong man who, like yourselves, probably had no trouble staying up all night at the tables. Big Las Vegas–type wagers, however, were his downfall, as you will see if you turn with me in your Bibles to Judges fourteen, verse twelve. It says: 'And Samson said unto the Philistines, Let me now put forth a riddle to you: If you can figure it out and tell it to me within seven days, then I will give you thirty expensive linen garments. But, if you cannot figure out my riddle, you give me thirty garments.'

"And the Philistines said, 'Sam, you got yourself a wager. What's the riddle?'

"And he said, 'Out of the eater came forth the eats. And out of the strong came forth sweetness.'

"Ladies and gentlemen, this was a strong hand because nobody in his right mind could figure out such a riddle, especially not the

Philistines, who had a well-deserved reputation in antiquity for brawn, not brains.

"Here's what happened: The Philistines tried to figure out the riddle, but they were unable to, and it angered them, and as usual they took it all out on the Jews by burning towns and crops. However, even if they had had antiquity's version of a computer, they could have made little headway because Samson's riddle was so highly personal. In other words, he had a very strong hand to play.

"On the seventh day, an hour or so before the sun was to set—this was the deadline—right at this crucial moment, Samson blew it. He tipped his hand to his wife by telling her the solution to the riddle and by relying on her to keep the confidence—although she herself was a Philistine—that she would not telegraph it to the other players, which she, of course, did immediately.

"One minute before the deadline, the Philistines show up in force at Samson's doorstep and with a smirk on their faces they say, 'What's sweeter than honey, Samson? And what's stronger than a lion?' Which was, as riddles went in those days—the double entendres being pretty untranslatable—the correct answer.

"Samson was furious, for he knew he had been had, and now he knew that his wife had betrayed him. 'If ye had not plowed with my heifer,' he told them, 'ye had not found out my riddle.'

"You might say that now was the time to call the pit boss over —the rabbi, that is—because wasn't Samson's declaration tantamount to an accusation that the Philistines had cheated? The truth of the matter is that had a rabbi been called in (which is unlikely because there was no such thing at the time), hypothetically, had I been summoned, I would have ruled that Samson too was guilty; he had cheated himself. He had tipped his own strong hand and he had no one to blame but himself. This, of course, was the beginning of his downfall that ended with his being blinded and then buried under the rubble of the Temple of Dagon.

"My beloved low-ball enthusiasts! Samson may have been our first Jewish high roller, but the institution of gambling goes back even farther, all the way back to the Torah itself. Was not the flight from Egypt a great gamble? Crossing the Red Sea was an even mightier gamble, one of the greatest bluffs ever pulled off in the whole history of Chance." (History of Chance, Bloom made a mental note, should go on the books-to-be-written list.) He then pitched his skullcap forward onto his forehead and continued. "And what of Moses? Strong, stalwart Moses, a family man if ever there was one, a good husband to Zipporah—although he could have had his pick of Egyptian beauties—a fine father to Gershom, a guy who would always stop short of betting all his money, cautious by nature, like many of you; he would never bet the rent or the family mortgage payment, never return home broke, drunk, or embarrassed. But what did Moses do, as he sat in Transjordan, in the midst of a terrible streak of personal bad luck, having just been informed by the Almighty that he himself would never be allowed to set foot in the Promised Land?

"Well, he sent out twelve scouts to reconnoiter the new place. Of the twelve, ten, nearly eighty-four percent, came back saying that the land was a mess, that it was harsh, unarable desert, full of entrenched enemies and brigands. Don't settle there, they told Moses. Just forget it! But the other two scouts gave precisely the opposite report. Joshua, son of Nun, and Caleb, son of Jephuneh, both said they liked the place. In fact they were crazy about it, and they went so far as to call it a land of milk and honey; they counseled Moses to go against the odds, to go with it. Sure, these two scouts were eloquent and they made a strong emotional case; nevertheless they were only two out of twelve, a mere sixteen percent. But what did Moses ultimately do? He went, of course, with the sixteen percent. The greatest family man in our history, one of the greatest from every perspective—but that's the subject of a separate sermon —took the big gamble, and the rest is history."

Then a sigh like a high note burst forth from Panuzzi, and the cantor waved his wrist toward Bloom and whispered, "Time, time."

"Ladies and gentlemen," Bloom went on, "let me close by reprising briefly what I have said in this and other sermons: Judaism is a gambling religion, it bends, it absorbs, it changes, it keeps as close to its bosom as it can its renegades and its rebellious sons and daughters. It embraces all its gamblers, and, believe me, if it did not, if this were not true, then you would not be sitting out there, nor would I be speaking from this platform this very moment. Nor," Bloom hurried to add, "would we have the services of our singularly gifted cantor, Angelos Panuzzi, who I am glad to welcome back after an illness last week. And now, if you will all rise, I will call upon Cantor Panuzzi to lead us in the concluding hymn on page one fifty-six of your prayer books."

After the hymn, which he embroidered with melodies from the Kingston Trio, Panuzzi cleared his throat, Bloom stepped over next to him, and the two led the procession out to the reception room. When they came to a stop, David Diamond, whom everyone called Black Dave, the sexton of the synagogue, was standing beside Bloom. Black Dave was a big and hulking fellow, a salesman for Bernie Levitt, who owned the Cadillac dealership at the end of the boulevard. As always, Dave sported a great collection of jewelry, including a golden star of David and a silver "mazel tov" that glittered under the harsh lights of the reception hall. Dave was Bloom's Ethiopian, his black Jew from Harlem, Bloom's New York connection. "Shalom," he said, and bowed slightly toward Bloom in greeting.

The reception line moved along, and Bloom shook hands with the temple president and her husband, Sarah and Abe North. In keeping with what Bloom had grown to expect, Sarah wore a sundress with a white sweater thrown over and reaching down to a full skirt. Abe sported his usual string tie and Western-style shirt. Both he and Sarah were friendly, broad, and Californian in their sabbath greetings. The Norths were unusual because they were a genuine native-born couple. However, unlike the easygoing stereotype, the Norths, particularly Sarah, were not casual people. Bloom, in fact, found her very hard to work with. He smiled "Good Shabbos" back to them, thinking, as he often did, standing there rather uncomfortably in this official posture, that Abe and Sarah—both with premature wattles —were a kind of living portrait, California Jewish Gothic.

"You look extremely well today, Rabbi," Sarah said. "You must have been out in the sun. Positively radiant, honey. Don't you wish I had skin like that, Abe? Like a Jewish bride, I would say, if you were a girl."

"He's not," said Abe, and they moved on to get their *kiddush* wine.

During the next few handshakes Bloom dwelled on Sarah's remarks and wondered if she had seen him swimming with Dawn. He realized now, as the congregants gathered around him and Panuzzi for the blessing over the wine, the *kiddush*, that throughout the entire service he had been feeling slightly odd, like a man in a Chagall painting floating up above his little community, still of it but also somehow suddenly separated, as if an invisible mooring had been cut.

Panuzzi raised the silver cup full of Concord red: "Blessed art Thou, O Lord our God, Ruler of the Universe, Who has created the fruit of the vine."

Then came more handshakes and compliments again, and Bloom's arm was pumped, stroked, touched, his elbow tapped, his shoulder leaned on, his shirt buttons shined. He was at such moments both rabbi and rabbi-t's foot to the crowding, pressing congregants. They all jostled about him. A cup of wine spilled and Bloom's arms grew heavy as congregant hands rested upon them like birds on their favorite branches. Somehow each congregant had to have some of him, or get close enough to him to catch his eye, to receive some sort of acknowledgment from him.

Although he thought it no less ridiculous tonight than at other times, he gave himself up to it again. With good humor he squeezed hands and shoulders, he tapped backs, he greeted, and he bowed. It had become, alas, an essential part of his job as it had evolved, and so he summoned up his equanimity and his smile. As Black Dave had told him three years ago when he took the job, the glad-handing and pawing came with the territory.

And yet tonight he felt a little put upon. Somebody's handshake had been so vigorous it left Bloom's knuckles aching; as he bent down to kiss Ethel Axelrod, he received a shove in the small of the back that propelled him forward right into her dentures, luckily without damage.

He was grateful that the congregants began to disperse earlier than usual, trickling back to the Silver Dollar and the other casinos, or moving off to their motel rooms for a few hours' sleep before the next shift in dealers. When most of the congregants were gone, Black Dave helped Bloom move the tables and chairs back against the wall, and then they returned the wine bottles to the refrigerator. These tasks done, Dave, too, left Bloom for the casino, without giving a single hint that he had knowledge of Dawn Nakazawa's visit, although surely, Bloom thought, as he shook Dave's friendly hand, the ubiquitous sexton must know, if anybody did.

Exhausted from the service and from having once again offered up his body to be grazed by his flock, Bloom fell onto one of the folding chairs near the door. Panuzzi, who alone remained in the hall with Bloom, was busy popping squares of honey cake into his mouth and washing them down with generous swigs of sweet wine.

Bloom pushed his yarmulkah forward from the back of his head, so it perched on top almost like a kid's beanie. "Angelos, what if I told you I was"—Bloom gulped in disbelief as the phrase fell out—"that I might be romantically involved?"

"You're too intellectual, Arthur."

"I'm aware," Bloom responded, as Dawn's image floated up to him, "that the origin of the whole idea of romance is back in chivalry, which is one step removed from the worship of the Virgin Mary. I try not to forget that romantic love is Christianity at its worst, Mariolatry in disguise. Nevertheless," said Bloom, "I think I've got it bad."

"You see? You see?" Panuzzi laughed. "I remember when you brought the hooker up to the seminary. I said to myself: Arthur is finally making a breakthrough, but obviously I was mistaken."

"Cut it out, Angelos. We're in the shul. The truth is," Bloom said as he stood and stretched, "that both our social lives are in need of drastic improvement. When's the last time you had a date?"

"A date?" Panuzzi spluttered, with a mouth full of honey cake. "What's that? Never heard the term. You remember," he went on, droll and not a little bitter still about his divorce of two years before, "that last week you had a dream that you were in a love triangle? You, Susan Sontag, and Hannah Arendt? In my book you have been, are, and always will be a victim of *amor intellectualis*. A terminal case. What's so different now, Arthur?"

Bloom sighed. "Maybe you're right. Maybe nothing." They took off their black robes, carefully folded them onto hangers and placed them in the wardrobe to keep them neat and pressed for the service in the morning.

In shirtsleeves they left the Silver Dollar Synagogue and walked out into the jasmine-scented air. They turned beneath the willows, Bloom in a white shirt, Panuzzi wearing a Hawaiian shirt with mixed-fruit designs, and stepped out onto Casino Boulevard. They often walked like this after services on Friday night, Panuzzi chewing on his nails, and Bloom alternately thrusting his hands into his pockets and resting them behind his back in a kind of clerical at-ease.

The rabbi and the cantor turned off the boulevard and onto one of the residential streets. Here in the greater darkness, out of view of the congregants, Panuzzi lit up a joint of marijuana and took a long, deep inhalation.

Bloom put his arm over the cantor's shoulder, and they began to walk farther from the temple. The streets off the boulevard were quiet, and they could hear their own footsteps. They walked two more blocks up, crossed, and retraced their steps on the far side. The smoke from Panuzzi's joint swirled above them and seemed to follow. There was always the slight chance a patrol car might come by and the police would arrest them. Bloom often thought of this, but it never bothered him enough to tell Angelos he absolutely had to stop. For Bloom also understood that Panuzzi, as a child of old Leonidas, a concentration camp survivor, took a kind of pleasure in these risks, in courting danger. He didn't abuse the marijuana, however; he smoked only on Friday nights, in honor, he always said, of the sabbath bride. It was part of their shabbos ritual, the service, the joint, this walking together while singing old tunes remembered from their years at the seminary in New York, this meandering but determined cogitation between them. Their friendship had a style of shared melancholy that expressed itself best at such times.

Half a block from the boulevard Bloom stopped and turned to Panuzzi. "Listen, Angelos. Now that you're inspired, tell me: what's love, anyway?"

"Take it from a formerly and miserably married man," said Panuzzi as he lit his second joint of the sabbath. "Love is heartache, terror, and self-loathing, in equal portions."

"And no joy? Nothing good? You don't believe that, pal."

"Well, maybe a little joy," gasped Panuzzi, puffing in and out at the cheeks like a bellows. "So what woman?" he gasped. "Who's the lucky lady?"

Bloom shook off the question and led them back onto Casino Boulevard and toward the neon illumination of the casinos. Ahead they saw Abe and Sarah North lock up their laundromat and then pause at the curb, talking. Bloom and Panuzzi speculated whether Sarah was still trying to talk Abe into *not* gambling, at least on shabbos. In another minute, Black Dave and Bernie Levitt drove up in their big boat of a Cadillac and the Norths slipped in.

Now, a quarter of a block from the synagogue, Bloom and Panuzzi halted. They were at the edge of a conical beam of light from a street lamp. Panuzzi buoyed by marijuana, and Bloom afloat with his secret thoughts of Dawn, both might have felt then that the little Jewish community of which they were part was so odd, so strikingly out of the mainstream, that their personal lives could not but be alloys of the same strange stuff.

"What woman?" Panuzzi asked again.

"Forget it," Bloom parried with a smile. "I'm not sure the totally miserable can tolerate a ray of happiness in others."

"Sure, come on. I can take it."

Bloom nudged the cantor on past the casino and then the synagogue, with its willows rustling and swaying above them, two more blocks down the boulevard toward the motel where Panuzzi lived with his father, Leonidas. When they reached the motel, they could see the old man, his mane of disheveled hair silhouetted behind the blind, leaning with his elbows on the card table beside the far window. He was listening to the television, with the volume blasting away.

"He just loves those Westerns," said Panuzzi. "'Bonanza,' 'Have Gun Will Travel,' he doesn't miss a rerun. Arthur, do you remember the 'Have Gun Will Travel' episode where Richard Boone defends this rabbi against anti-Semitism in Nevada, and in the process quotes from Rabbi Akiba, Talmud, Mishnah, the works? You'd have thought Paladin had been ordained. My dad fell off his chair. One good man or one good family triumphs over a town of evil men. He's seen *High Noon* six times; he can't get enough of that stuff."

Panuzzi was getting a little shaky now, and Bloom supported him at the elbow. He felt grateful both for Panuzzi's friendship tonight and, paradoxically, for the fact that now he was going to drop Angelos off and be alone. Tonight for the first time in years he would have the face of a beautiful woman to think about. A woman who was not only very pretty but who genuinely seemed to like being with him. Either that, Bloom thought, or she was a magnificent saleswoman of swimming lessons. He eagerly led Panuzzi to the door of the motel. "Give your dad regards from me."

"Hey, wait." Bloom had begun to walk away. "Hey, what's her name, Arthur?"

"Who?"

"Come on! I'll die if you don't say."

Bloom hesitated, and then pronounced slowly, "Dawn Nakazawa."

"As in the liquor store?"

"Yes."

"Oh my," Panuzzi said. "Oh my, oh my." His bitten fingers flew into his mouth as he swayed in the light of the motel's swag lantern.

"Japanese." Bloom confirmed the question in the cantor's hazy eyes.

"And not a member of"—Panuzzi rocked, his eyes only half open now, and he singsonged—"Judah, Levi, Asher, Naphtali, Zevulun, or any of the other of the twelve tribes of Israel, or is it thirteen?"

"Still twelve." Bloom smiled. "It's okay, though, because, as you've pointed out many times, nothing's going to come of it."

"Right," mumbled Panuzzi. He lifted his arms to embrace Bloom, to give him their customary big, smoky, Greek, sabbath hug, and on his shoulder, right into the rabbi's convenient ear, he said, "If the cantor smokes dope on shabbos, why shouldn't the rabbi date Japanese, Chinese, Hawaiian, Polynesian, Mexican, Szechuan, any cuisine he likes?"

"Go to sleep, Angelos."

Just then the door opened, and Leonidas stood near them, with a little glass of ouzo in one hand and a foul-smelling black cigarette in the other. "Come in," Leonidas growled, "come in, you miserable excuse for a son." And he good-naturedly took the cantor out from under Bloom's arm with a yank and a "Good Shabbos."

Bloom turned and moved rapidly back toward the synagogue and his apartment over the garage behind it. But at the first driveway Panuzzi's hoarse voice reached him. "Since nothing's going to come of it, Arthur, maybe she has a friend, a sister I can meet, too?"

"Get in here, you delinquent," Leonidas hollered. "It's time for 'Gunsmoke.'"

6

"Rabbi Bloom? Rabbi Bloom?"

Was that her already? "Yes?"

"Rabbi Bloom, it's Dawn Nakazawa."

He jumped out of the shower, his face and body streaming, threw on his bathrobe, and rushed to the door. There she was, big as life, framed by the screen.

"I think I'm a little early."

"A half hour early." Bloom looked at the digital clock on his bureau.

"I know. I'm sorry. I'm living with my mother across the street; it's kind of a small apartment and, you know, sometimes it's cabin fever for the two of us. I thought I might come early and swim some laps before we get together for that lesson, if it's all right with you?"

"Okay," said Bloom. "Sure. Be my guest."

"I thought I should ask you first."

"Well you have, and it's okay, perfectly okay, Miss Nakazawa."

"Rabbi, you're all wet."

"I was in the shower."

"I'm sorry. You must have dripped all over your floor to come here. I feel I should offer at least to wipe it up for you. It's my fault."

"No, no, no, it's perfectly all right."

"It seems you're always wet when I see you." She smiled.

"You too," Bloom said, toweling off the water in his eyes. "Look, I should invite you in, but the place is a mess and I don't have any clothes on. . . ."

"That's a nice robe, though. Is it rabbinical?"

"Sorry?"

"All the stripes. It reminds me of Joseph's coat of many colors from the Bible."

"Oh no, no, no." Bloom laughed. "It's just on sale, last week, from Sears."

She raised her shoulder and tilted her head then, with a little pert movement that gave him, Bloom thought, a kind of Proustian flash of how she must have looked as a kid, a tall, lanky, perhaps even slightly gawky, young teenager, not the beauty she was to become.

She turned to go. "I am sorry I disturbed you. I won't do it again."

"You are absolutely no disturbance," Bloom said, suddenly nervous. "*I* am the disturbance, standing here in my birthday suit. I'm always up early . . . except for some reason for today. It's funny."

"I'll let you alone, Rabbi Bloom."

"Arthur." She was the soul of politeness, and it augmented his own. "And please don't feel embarrassed about being here early.

Punctuality is a disappearing virtue, and it's good to see somebody trying to keep it with us."

"Well," she said, as she crossed the veranda to the steps, "you come down whenever you're ready and then we'll start with treading water—okay?"

But when she turned to go down, Bloom, in bathrobe, went out and caught up with her at the landing. "You know, Dawn, I intend to pay you for the lessons, and you never said what you charge."

"Charge?" She threw her head back and laughed.

"I thought that might be the case." He smiled along with her. Now he twirled the sash of his robe, caught himself, and stopped. "Now it's time for me to be a little embarrassed. I thought at least I should ask you."

"Well you have," she echoed him, "and it's perfectly okay. It's barter—in return for the lessons you're letting me use your pool."

"It's hardly my personal pool; it belongs to the temple." He felt the imminent possibility of an erection and retreated upstairs. "But for all practical purposes it is private, so you can swim to your heart's content."

At the base of the steps, she looked up to him. He held his robe closed in the front. "Would you mind talking to me a little, too, about—oh, you know—the history of the synagogue? My family's lived across the street for years and I'm fascinated with the local history; my parents never talked about it."

"I wouldn't mind at all," said Bloom.

"See you in fifty laps," and she jogged over to the deck, slipped out of her robe, and dove smartly into the blue water.

Bloom prayed *shacharis*, the morning service, in Olympic time, slipped on his blue bathing suit, the one with slenderizing white stripes up the sides, said "God help me" on the threshold of his home, kissed the *mezuzah*, and went down for his lesson.

7

"What's our spiritual leader doing now?" Abe North asked.

"Nada, señor," answered Black Dave. They were at the little porthole-style window off the lobby of the casino, staring out toward the synagogue pool. Dave, at six feet three, leaned and looked, but Abe North, shorter by a foot, had pulled over one of the chairs from the coffee shop to climb up on; he was sitting on it now, one leg folded over the other, as if waiting for something to happen. Their spying was intensely unabashed; Dave was holding up the shade, and even the panels of glass were slightly misty with his exhalations. It was, as usual, highly air-conditioned in the casino, but Dave and Abe thought it might be getting hot in the rabbi's backyard.

"What's he doing now?" Abe asked again.

"Looks just like swimming lessons look like. She's got him holding on to the side of the pool and kicking. Now he's turning his head and he's learning how to breathe. It don't look like he's doing too well, but, yeah, that's what he's doing, breathing and blowing."

"Breathing and blowing? Now what do we make of that?" Abe puzzled. "Where is she?"

"She's standing in the water near him. Hey, if you're so curious, hop on your chair and look for yourself, squirt!"

Abe lit a tremendously long cigarette and then held his lighter up for Dave to ignite his Have-A-Tampa. Dave let the shade drop. "As I see it, the rabbi's learning to swim, and this is leading to maybe dates with this Japanese doll. After three years, the rabbi is becoming a human person again, the heterosexual we all know he is. It happens."

"Yeah, too bad." Abe crossed his legs, in reverse.

"What's to complain about? Be happy for the kid."

"We're gonna lose, that's what always happens. We're gonna start losing bad. I feel it. Hey, be careful with that cigar." A small epaulet of ash had landed on the shoulder of Abe's leisure suit.

As Dave was flicking it clean, the atmosphere in the casino pit seemed to alter, and the electricity in the air, usually dispersed over all the gambling areas—the dice, the roulette, the card corners, and the slot machine banks—now seemed to center on the poker tables. The card players' antennae went up, fine-tuned. Abe and Dave turned their glance over to the low-ball corner. They heard a tall, gaunt man, dressed like a cowboy, complete with lariat, swear, throw down his cards, and say loud enough for the whole casino to notice, "Shit, my luck's so bad, if it'd rain soup, I'd only have a fork." As he stomped out, Lucy Leonard and Lulu Fineberg came racing over to Abe and the sexton. "Ethel's won six straight hands, six jackpots."

"*Nu?*" said Dave.

"But she can't play. Dave, you know she can hardly count!"

"Look." Abe was pointing back to Ethel's table. "Two more losers are leaving. What's she got, bad breath?"

"What gives?" Lucy motioned to the window above the sexton and the synagogue vice president. "What's going on over there with the teahouse of the August moon?"

"Breathing and blowing"—Abe slapped Dave good-humoredly on the leg—"and that is all!"

"Well, something's got to be going on," said Lulu. A geyser of excitement began to rise again from the low-ball table. Dave went over to look and soon returned.

"She ain't Einstein, we all know that, but she happens to be the only synagogue member at the table, in case none of you noticed. And she's winning over some experienced good players."

As another groan went up from the table and the friends could hear Ethel yodeling with excitement, Lulu climbed up on Abe's chair. But she—like Abe—was too short to see much. Dave quickly pulled back the drape and beheld the swimming lesson still in progress. "Say, she's much closer to him now than before. Yeah, she's standing behind him in the shallow water now, moving his arms to show him, you know—whaddaya call it?—the crawl, the Australian crawl."

"You guys are the temple braintrust on this," said Lulu. "What gives? We shouldn't play, you said, and so we didn't because the rabbi's swimming lesson was going on, and we listened and nobody sat down except for Ethel. We listen to what you two geniuses say and we don't go near the table because who wants a lousy run, and it's supposed to be lousy because of the female company. But you guys blew it this time." Another eruption of excitement from the low-ball table. "That Ethel is not one iota smarter today than when I saw her lose what little mind she has left by folding at draw with four aces! But now she's taking anyone who goes near that table to the cleaners. What gives?"

Abe popped up and said, "Maybe this girl is different."

"Maybe!" Lucy tugged on Dave's arm. "What are they up to now?"

"More polite lessons . . . no wait, she's going for a swim and he's sitting on the board watching her. Hey, man, the kid's enjoying himself. I mean enjoying!"

Lulu, who had gone to the pit, and now returned, had news. "Ethel's finally losing, too."

"Serves her right," said Lucy. Then she turned to the sexton, "I don't think you guys know what's going on. I'm going home, and I think we better elect a new *gabbai* and a new vice president of this congregation, ones who can read the rabbi right!"

"Shalom, sweetheart," said Dave. "Better luck next time."

8

"Oh Arthur, oh Arthur, the fearful trek is done." She was floating toward him in the shallow water on his inner tube. It was their third lesson. "Your tire's weathered every wreck. . . ."

"I believe it's 'rack.' "

"Your old tire's weathered every rack, the prize we sought is won."

"That was very good," said Bloom when she had arrived at the three-foot mark, where he stood, the staging area for his first attempt at floating by himself. "Except I think it's also 'Arthur, *my* Arthur,' not 'Arthur *oh* Arthur,' as in 'Captain, *my* captain!' "

She slid smartly off and fell to her knees in the water; he was still letting the water lap at his wrists. "I'm going to get you to be as adept at swimming as you are at correcting my Whitman, Rabbi Arthur Bloom. Come on now, let's float."

"Wait, I'm not ready. I'm still acclimating. In fact I'll be acclimating, I figure, for about another forty-five minutes."

"How come you never learned to swim, Arthur? You're from Manhattan, or at least you went to school there for many years, and

Manhattan's an island, no? Dangerously surrounded by deep water."

"No Manhattanite is an island unto himself," he said, which was when she splashed him. "Hey, no . . . that's cold . . . owwie. . . ." But she pulled him in, nevertheless.

"That's a little abrupt, I know, but we don't have all day. I've got to get back to the store in an hour." She cupped some water in her hands and tossed it on Bloom's shoulder, and then splashed his face a little more. She rubbed water on his arms, and then sidestroked around him a couple of times until he seemed ready. "All better?"

"Yes, it's not fatal, so far."

"If you have a heart attack," she said, "I can handle that, too. I know CPR and mouth-to-mouth resuscitation. I could bring you back from the dead and still have time to finish the lesson."

"It'd be a way of getting to know you quickly," he said.

"That seems to be happening anyway. Now come on," she extended her arm, "lean forward. Trust the water."

Bloom stepped forward hesitatingly. "I don't trust it. It's cold and wet and never stays in the same place. What's to trust? But I do trust your arm."

"Good," said Dawn. "Very good. Now stretch your legs. Excellent. Now rest on my arm. Put your head in the water."

"But if I do that, I can't breathe, I can't talk, I can't read, or look at you."

"Flattery will only get you more splashes. Come on. If you put your face in the water, keep your ears above the surface, then I'll recite a poem to you. The poem of your choice. Go on and name it."

Bloom thought about the deal. "It's a generous offer, the best I've had today, but I'd be embarrassed to take you up on it."

"Good, then. Dive in there, so to speak." She gently put her hand on the back of Bloom's neck. "Take a deep breath into those lungs, good, yes, and hold it now. Come up whenever you feel uncomfortable. Good. You have a great set of tubes in your chest. I can tell. Good, fine. Now, can you hear me?"

Bloom followed her instructions. He felt good, but suddenly he sucked in some water and came up gasping and coughing.

"Okay? You're okay. No problem."

"I forgot." He coughed.

"You're doing just fine," she reassured him.

"I am?"

"Yes. Just remember, Arthur, water's the mother of us all. We all crawled out of it, ancestrally speaking."

"That's it!" he said. "Mother Water. That's why I have a problem with it."

"Nonsense." She took his hand and moved closer to the wall; she knew it would provide more security. "I have problems with my real live human mother; in the water, it's pure vacation. You were doing just great, Arthur. You can't learn to belly-float by talking about it. You're doing just fine."

He looked at her skeptically. "What's with all the compliments?"

"First rule of teaching swimming: No amount of encouragement is enough, Arthur. In your case, Rabbi, this is exceptionally true."

"Tell me, how old do you think I am, aquatically speaking?"

"Let me see. I learned to do what you're going to learn today, maybe, at the latest, when I was about fourteen months old."

"That old! Very encouraging."

"Come on, Arthur. You can do it. I know you can. I know, for example, that you have already once been a great swimmer, in a previous life, almost."

"Really?"

"Yes, in the uterus. All that swimming, kicking, somersaulting in the warm ninety-eight-degree fluid. That's water, Arthur."

"Obviously you're right," Bloom said, "from a medical-obstetrical point of view. But imaginatively I always thought I've lived in apartments. I used to think of my *in utero* life as something like the Bronx underwater: coming to term, and being born—just a form of eviction, as it were."

She had her arms across her chest now and was simply waiting for him to stop talking. "You mean," he went on, "it should be easy to float now and to swim because I did it in the uterus; all I have to do now is remember."

"That's right," she said, "simple recall."

"Well," he said, ducking a big splash from her and splashing her back, finally getting into the spirit, "if you put it that way, it's something I might be able to handle. Maybe."

"I'm waiting, Arthur. No more delaying tactics, okay? I do not want to stand behind that counter and sell scotch and rye all afternoon without having done some important work today: namely, getting you floating on your belly. Onward to the breach," she said, taking him by the hand. "Or is it to the beach?" And she was now easing him into another part of the pool, not far from the steps, the shallowest part. He leaned forward and she caught his buoyed weight on her arm. He liked lying there, listening to her swimming chatter: her *yesses*, her *okays*, her *that's fines*, all her encouragements. "Now stretch your legs out behind you, Arthur. That's good, now your arms. Okay, time for the old rabbinical head."

"Okay," he said. "Here goes."

"If we can put an astronaut on the moon"—he heard her kind sweet voice bobbing above him—"then we can teach a rabbi to float."

Meanwhile, Dave was pulling the vice president up toward the window. They were balanced precariously on the casino lounge chair. "Look, man," he said to Abe, "she's showin' him some other stroke now. Let's have ourselves a little experiment. You go over there to the blackjack, see, and I'm going to stay here. You got direct line of sight to me from over there. Now I'm gonna open my hands like this when the rabbi and the girl are apart. Got it? I'll close 'em up like this as they get closer until they're smooching right like this together."

"I don't get it."

"Listen, Socrates, you keep an eyeball up here and watch my hands, see? These big black hands are the Bloomometer: If the hands are together, the swimming teacher and pupil are close. At such moments you play the risk, draw the card, even if you got a seventeen; still, go for the twenty-one and see if you bust or not. When you see my hands apart like this, then play the other way, fold and play the caution, and let's track the difference. A controlled experiment, see, in the luckiness of our spiritual guide. Abe?"

But the temple's vice president was already off and halfway to his blackjack table. Dave positioned himself and moved his hands up and back, like an accordion. Abe watched and played and watched, like an instrumentalist following a conductor.

In five minutes Abe had returned, with a stack of red chips—$75 worth—in his hands. "Man alive," he said, "she's good for him. When your hands were together, the deck got rich. Apart, I drew a card and busted every time, with the same hands, different results."

"I see you learned quick." Dave puffed on his cigar, found it had gone out, and relit; he also lit Abe's next cigarette. They were quite pleased with themselves.

"Let me look now," said Abe, "and you can play."

"You sure you wanna stand on your tippy toes that long?"

But just as Abe got into position, one of the casino officials came over, an assistant pit manager, a pest named Kavanaugh. "What are you guys doin'?" he asked.

"Oh just looking out the window at the view," said Dave.

"At what view?"

"Oh, tell the man," said Abe. "What's the big deal?"

"We're looking at our rabbi through there," said Dave, as he stepped aside for Kavanaugh. "We just want to make sure our rabbi doesn't drown. He's not a very good swimmer."

"You guys are very thoughtful," said Kavanaugh. "Such mother hens for your rabbi!" He pulled back the drape, looked, let it drop, and then irritably dragged the lounge chair back where it belonged. When he returned to the sexton and Abe, he said, "I really don't care if it's Jesus Christ out there walking on the water of that pool; I want the drape shut and your commotion to stop. Am I making myself clear?"

"Sure thing," said Dave. "You're the boss." Abe smiled, too. Never mind that it was only $75 for this time around. Still, an important, a great, discovery about the rabbi had been made.

9

"Are you sure I shouldn't go home first and put on a dress?" She was wearing her big white terry-cloth robe and standing with Bloom at the side entrance of the synagogue. "I could run across and change and be back in a minute?" They had just finished the fifth lesson of Bloom's swimming career, and afterwards Dawn had asked him for, of all things, a tour of the synagogue.

"It's really not necessary to dress up," Bloom said. "There's nothing special going on today, and we're very casual here at Temple Elijah, in case you hadn't noticed. Here"—he opened the door—"let me just flick off the air-conditioning so we don't catch cold." Dawn stuck her head across the line of the threshold but seemed to hesitate. "Have you been in a synagogue before?" He continued to hold the door for her.

"You know, I don't think so. Not in a long time, anyway. Maybe with a roommate in college, I think. But lately only to deliver the wine. Are you sure I'm not being disrespectful? Look, my hair is dripping."

"I often come in here with just my suit and robe on," he said, "to get a book I forgot. Believe me, it's perfectly okay. Anyway, you're with the rabbi, and it's a when-in-Rome-do-as-the-Romans-do situation."

"You mean, when in Jerusalem, do as the Jerusalemites do."

"Yes," Bloom said, "that's right. That's much better put." He opened the door wider. "Let the grand tour begin!"

The linoleum floor was cold to their feet, so Bloom quickly led Dawn up and around to the foyer, which, although also cold, had a thick blue runner that led from the main door of the building to the entrance of the sanctuary proper.

When they stood on this, Dawn said, "Look, I'm dripping on your beautiful carpet." She reached over and took the towel from Bloom's shoulder (she had left hers on the chaise longue) and began to wind it around her long, thick hair, which she now let fall so that when she brought her head back up, she was smilingly turbaned. "There," she said, "much better."

Bloom was tremendously impressed with the way she did that— so much hair, so much towel, and then, presto, she had it all done up, a fine artistic package. "Now," he said, "you look absolutely like the illustration of beautiful Princess Muraski on my paperback copy of *The Tale of Genji*. A great book."

"And a great compliment. Thank you, Rabbi."

"Well, anyway," said Bloom, "here it is, Temple Elijah, Gardena, California. The lobby, the foyer, not really exciting, just a little foyer. Over there on that wall is our memorial plaque collection, the members who have died and whose memories live on. Unfortunately there are quite a few. It's an older population I serve here—by and large retired people in their sixties, seventies, and older."

"And what's over here on this wall?" Dawn had crossed the foyer to the benefactors and founders wall.

"Those are recognition plaques for people who give a thousand dollars or more to support the temple."

"There are only three names."

"Right." Bloom was a little embarrassed. "It's not a well-to-do congregation either. What they have, I'm afraid, they often gamble with. But they always manage to pay the mortgage each month, and pretty much regularly they even pay me. It's a very odd group, and the building matches them—it's oddly shaped for a synagogue, in case you were wondering."

"And do you yourself gamble, Rabbi?"

"Me? Oh no," he said. Bloom thought, My only gamble is in bringing you here. He said, "I used to play poker in college, but I lost badly. That was enough for me. But these people, my congregants, do gamble. They more than gamble, they play, eat, and sleep cards, many of them. They're good people, though. I don't think you could call them compulsive, or at least not dangerously so. They're not raising families any more. It's all fun for them."

"Now what's over here?" She had pointed to a little relief of the Ten Commandments that stood to the right of the sanctuary door. He explained the commandments to Dawn, and he was warming, surprisingly, to his subject. After all, he had never given a tour of the synagogue, and the place wasn't exactly a site of historical importance, but Dawn was very interested, and her intense listening had launched Bloom into an activity he had no idea he would be enjoying so much. Soon he was telling her the background of the place as he knew it, the founding and the early years. He knew, for example, that Casino Boulevard had once been a main north–south interior road linking San Diego and Los Angeles, and the synagogue location had probably at first been the site of an inn or early hotel. Some of those pioneering travelers, Bloom suggested to Dawn, might have been California's early merchants—often young German- or Polish-Jewish men—who stopped at this place where they were now standing well over a hundred years ago.

"When cars came in, however, everything else changed. The

building—we know this for sure—was one of the earliest motels. That accounts for the proximity of the swimming pool and the odd shape of this foyer, which was probably the front room and later the office of the motel."

Dawn seemed to be taking everything in. Bloom went on: "It's certainly not the Touro Synagogue in Newport, Rhode Island. That's one of America's oldest, where General George Washington visited."

"Oh I like *this* one just fine," Dawn said. "It's very warm, and you know so much about it. Who needs George Washington!"

"Yes." Bloom formulated it carefully. "Washington visited the Touro, but Nakazawa visited Temple Elijah." He mentioned the nickname of the synagogue—the Silver Dollar—but she had already been aware of that.

"What's all this stuff? You sell candy bars here?" She was standing in front of the old gift and display case. It was on casters, but one of the wheels was broken, so all the contents had gradually slid toward a single corner. Here a handful of golden Jewish stars and silver "mazel tov" medallions sat in a Snicker candy bar box, the twenty-four pack. "Oh, no, no, no," said Bloom, a little embarrassed and reawakened to the fact that his shul was indeed not quite ready for a presidential visit. "I've been meaning to get my *gabbai*—that's the temple official who helps me maintain the place—to get rid of that stuff. It really doesn't belong here any more. The guy's an interesting character; he's, by the way, a black Jew from Harlem."

"You don't mind if I write some of this down, do you?" In a wall box she had found a pencil and some cards with the times for the lighting of sabbath candles, for August, two years ago. "May I?" She turned one of the cards over and wrote on it.

"Dave," Bloom went on—as Dawn took notes—"traces his ancestry back to Ethiopia, to the tribe of Dan, I believe, who came to Africa after the destruction of the Temple in Jerusalem."

"Would that be the First or the Second Temple, Arthur?"

Bloom was pleased. "My," he said, "that's a surprising question."

"Not really," she said with a big look of satisfaction on her face.

"You just don't expect people to even know that there were two. Now let me see"—he was nonplussed—"I of course know, but I seem to be blanking on it for some reason. Let me think."

"That's okay, Arthur." She walked right up to him, turbanned, tall, and impressive. "You know the story of Mrs. Disraeli—Benjamin's wife, the Prime Minister of England? She supposedly didn't know who came first either, but in her case it was the Greeks or the Romans."

"I imagine," Bloom said, smiling at Dawn, "that the First Temple preceded the Second."

"You can't be sure of anything these days."

"Now wait"—Bloom was in thought—"of course it had to be the second destruction. That's right, the destruction by Rome, in 70 c.e., the one led by Vespasian and his son Titus. Dawn, are you really interested in all this?"

"I am, I am."

"How'd we get on this?"

"Your black Jew."

"Oh, Dave, yes."

"You know," she said, walking around by the yarmulkah box, passing the water fountain, circling back and peering into the sanctuary, "I think I've seen him around. He's very big, right, and wears a lot of gold?"

"Right," said Bloom. "He is also fairly strange and fairly typical of this congregation. He once proposed to me that we should improve the congregation's financial position by building on Temple Elijah's origins that I was just telling you about. He actually wanted to build additions around the side of the pool, on two of the sides, and outfit them with rooms, kitchenettes, televisions, the whole thing. America's only synagogue and motel. He called it a 'synagotel.' He said it would be a real draw for the Jewish traveler. Arrive before the sabbath and leave after. Swim right before you pray at the morning service, and no need to drive. You might enjoy talking to him—he's always hanging around here doing something."

"It's a funny place," she said.

"Very funny. Come on," he said as he put on a yarmulkah, "let me show you where we pray." Dawn pulled her robe tight around her, clasped her notes in her hand, and entered the sanctuary with Bloom.

10

"Rabbi Bloom." She was typing two days later. "Rabbi A. Bloom . . ."

Behind the wine freezer in the liquor store, in a small room set off from the main sales area, beyond a curtain of clacking beads, Dawn Nakazawa was sitting at her Underwood. Each time she banged on the keys, the urn containing her father's ashes jumped slightly off the table, as if alive. This was such a pleasurable feeling, this illusion of intimacy and relationship beyond the grave, that Dawn found herself typing easily and vigorously; the urn containing Akira's remains now drew her to her work, on the rabbi of Gardena.

She was very comfortable at the table where she now sat. It held not only drafts of her articles but three squares of wood, each with a long, sharp nail sticking up at a perilous angle, on which were speared dozens of papers: bills payable, accounts due, and credit-card carbons. Beside these was a box with cardboard squares and marking pencils, which Dawn used to write signs for sale items, and on the far corner was a mineral-water bottle sprouting an ailing chrysanthemum. All of these crowded about the urn and the Underwood. She had bought the machine for $20 from somebody's garage on the day she got the job as a stringer at the *L.A. Eye.* She had had it repaired, oiled, and polished, and it now worked magnificently, without a key sticking, as if the machine had been made for her.

Dawn sat in the silence of the closed store, as Ono rested three rooms away in their adjoining apartment, knitting in the easy chair. Through the wall in front of her, Dawn heard the wine freezer's electric hum. "Rabbi Bloom," she tried again. "Rabbi A. Bloom."

Yes, he was to be her first extended story, with at least three articles in the series. She had suggested him to the editors at the stringers' meeting the day after her swim with Bloom, and they had said yes. A rabbi was good, they said, a lucky one even better. There wasn't much on the Jews in the *L.A. Eye,* the Southland's second-best-selling picture newspaper. Yes, the article should provide some balance.

So Dawn was launched. "Rabbi Arthur Bloom," she retyped, "of Temple Elijah, Gardena, California is . . ."

She stopped again, wondering if she had spelled Elijah correctly. Although her spelling had much improved, especially in the years out of Berkeley, the complaint of Miss Satler, her third-grade teacher, still hampered her: *Child, your spelling gives me cramps.*

Dawn got up, and decided that instead of going to the dictionary, she might just as well go to the window: Yes, she had it right. E-L-I-J-A-H. So much for you, Miss Satler!

She resumed her work. *The rabbi of Gardena,* she now wrote, *is a simple, unprepossessing man. But perhaps this is only a surface view, given to non-Jews, to outsiders. To those who worship with and know him . . .*

Just what, Dawn wondered, was she trying to prove with the rabbi of Gardena?

In her late sixties, UC-Berkeley days, Dawn had been something of an underground newspaper groupie, ornamenting the funky offices of the *Berkeley Rat,* the *Telegraph Avenue Tattler,* the *Marijuana Mirror,* and the many other sheets that had come and gone in the political and cultural waves of the Free Speech Movement. After trying out a dozen counterculture ways to earn a living, including renting the trunk of her Volkswagen (and herself as driver) to one of California's biggest hashish distributors (there was an accident, resulting in the scar), here she was, in a way, back at the beginning. Between the *Rat* and the *L.A. Eye,* the two bookends of Dawn's professional life so far, there was also a stint on the *L.A. Times.* But her meandering paragraphs and inventive spelling, as well as her politics and her cultural sympathies for the strange and offbeat—the heritage of Berkeley—had finally tipped the balance against her at the *Times.* Her father's death had made her realize she was a woman of thirty-five with uncertain vocational prospects, to say the least, with a widowed mother, and herself the only child. Dawn wanted back into journalism very much. If she had to start where she had been many years before, on a kind of sensational newspaper, and as a stringer in Gardena, Torrance, and other points south, so be it.

Others might, but Dawn would not berate the *Eye.* She found it amusing, an institution in its own right—and in the way it unabashedly mixed fiction with fact, it was, she thought, far more honest than a lot of the more respected news media where the line between information and entertainment was consciously, deliberately blurred. No, she was not deterred by this paper that headlined astrology, intergalactic sexual practices ("Pilot of Flying Saucer

Raped Me, Declares Local Woman"), and which ran two new exercise and weight-loss programs per issue, each one supplanting its predecessor in effectiveness and painlessness ("Lose Tons Consuming All the Strawberry Malteds You Can").

Nor did Ono's estimate of the *L.A. Eye*—"lowest of the low"—upset Dawn. One had to start again somewhere, and Dawn was grateful to a paper that would take on a thirty-five-year-old at a beginner's job. As a stringer, she wasn't really on staff, but it was a first step, and, as important, it was a connection. It was work that would defuse, also, the tension that developed between her and her mother around the store and their small living quarters, and it would help her structure her week. Her work for the *Eye*, to Dawn, was nothing less than a godsend.

Dawn touched the urn again. She found herself frequently touching it, and always gratefully. What a sonofabitch Akira had been while alive, what a driving, love-withholding father he had been! But now how wonderful he was, just sitting there, blissfully silent, in his urn. Dawn very much sensed his presence—the cool judgments that, in life, he would pass on her so often. Occasionally she would look up from her work, and she would bend slightly toward the urn, softly saying, "Thank you, father. Thank you, honorable father, very much."

She now typed "The Gambling Rabbi" across the top of the page but on rereading realized she would have to change it, for the rabbi did not gamble. So he had said, and he didn't strike her as the kind of man who would lie. Of course, she would have to talk to several other sources. She would first have to interview some members of the congregation, perhaps this Black Dave, and people working at the casino, the rabbi's family, the works! She found herself looking forward to all of this. And, of course, she would have to talk to the rabbi himself again. She would, of course, have to tell him that she was interviewing him for an article. She hadn't so far, and she was not sure why.

"*Rabbi Is Good Luck Charm for His Congregation,*" she wrote. She was pleased that she had finally found the approach. Then Dawn heard her name and had to stop, for Ono was calling her to wait on three customers who had just entered the store.

11

An hour after he finished rereading the Torah portion for the week, Bloom was on Casino Boulevard, on winged—actually they were sneakered—feet and heading west toward the laundromat. Dawn had telephoned and asked *him* out to, of all things, see the grunion run in Long Beach. It wasn't a swimming lesson, she said, but as the grunion are fish and the ocean is water, it was related.

"I couldn't agree more," Bloom had answered. It was as if they were in on a secret together, and maybe the secret was that they liked each other. Then again, Bloom had chuckled to himself, as he slapped his face with Aramis, maybe it was only swimming lessons.

For Bloom, this was to be a night of many firsts: He had never seen grunion run, or do anything else, for that matter. More important, this was the first time a woman had ever asked him out. That Dawn had asked him to see the grunion flail in reproductive frenzy, to view those fish whose mating orgies on the moonlit beaches was a must for any Californian, was for Bloom thrilling and a kind of personal and long-delayed rite of passage; to what, he was not yet certain.

Because the grunion were to hit the beach, laying their eggs, at 9:30, the plan was for Dawn to pick Bloom up an hour earlier. The laundromat had been Bloom's idea. One too many congregants lately had been whispering "Sayonara" to him in the foyer of the synagogue; he had seen one too many looking at him with a troubled glance as he walked down the street with Dawn. Moreover, when he visualized himself waiting in front of the synagogue for Dawn to drive across in her red delivery van, with the bottle-high letters NAKAZAWA LIQUORS stenciled on three sides, Bloom decided to suggest a different pickup location: the laundromat. It was more discreet, he had said.

With her usual directness, however, Dawn had punctured Bloom's euphemism (did all rabbis, she had asked, have a tendency to euphemism?) and had called it by its right name: secrecy. Since she, however, was making deliveries that evening and would have the van out anyway, Dawn gladly agreed to the laundromat.

Bloom was very relieved because his intense interest in her now seemed to be matched by a powerful need also to be cautious. Should he go on seeing her? He needed time, he told himself, to think and to consider how radical an attraction now consumed him.

At times he would even find himself wishing that Dawn would simply not be so available to him. She *was* Japanese. He half hoped that she would solve his dilemma just by doing what the few women from his past had done: simply lose interest and brush him off. It would be so easy.

Instead, what had she done? She had invited him to see the grunion! Indeed, to his alarm—and delight—Dawn's interest in him, he sensed, was genuine, and, like his own in her, more than a matter of swimming lessons. Although he detected in her a shy, even reticent, side, more often than not she kept on asking him these questions, lots of wonderful, sparkling, intelligent questions. It was such a pleasure to explain to her the Jewish concept of luck and fate; he even ran down a short history of gambling in the Middle Ages that at one point—in his third week on the job, but forgotten in the meantime—he had thought he might write something about. All of this was so easy for him, effortless hours of talk, munching away with Dawn on all this fine intellectual junkfood. It was such a pleasure to be in this smart, beautiful woman's company, to be alive, to be thinking, and learning the flutter kick, too.

Now Bloom's bag of laundry dangled in his hand. Like a kid, he swung his small white bundle at the palms, willows, eucalyptuses, and traffic meters that lined the sidewalk.

The laundromat, into the fluorescent-lighted interior of which he now turned, was operated, though mainly in absentia, by Sarah and Abe, as a kind of investment; had they come there often, Bloom would certainly not have suggested it as a meeting place. He was, however, running low on Jockey shorts, and he did need his white shirts and chinos for the sabbath. He stared at the machine that dispensed little boxes of Tide, Fab, and Cheer. He looked up and surveyed the deserted and depressing rectangle of a room, with its washers and dryers, their large doors gaping open and, Bloom fantasized, listening to him as if with elephant ears. "My friends," Bloom declaimed—a meek sermon for machines—"don't forget that throughout history most people, including myself, no matter what trials we go through, prefer to endure them in clean socks and shorts."

He passed the door marked Private, behind which was the Norths' small office, and paused long enough to satisfy himself no one was there. Then he placed the laundry on the nearby table to be done in the morning. (This free laundry service—in Wednesday, out Friday—was one of the small but much appreciated perks the synagogue provided Bloom.) He lingered for a moment and then slipped out through the rear screen door into the alley. Here, between the strong scent of lemon trees from the yards across the alley and the odor of soap from the laundromat behind, Bloom paced and waited for Dawn.

As he walked in the darkness, he thought: I am a rabbi, hiding here in the dark three blocks from my synagogue, waiting for a Japanese girlfriend to come pick me up to go to the beach, where we will drink a thermos of tea spiked with rum (Dawn was to supply this), and I am telling no one, not even my best friend, about it. Either God has great plans for me, Bloom thought, or He has, in the immortal words of John Ehrlichman, left me to twist slowly in the wind.

It was about half-past eight, and still no Dawn. He heard the quiet humming of the crickets. Were there more crickets than grunion? Would the services of the A & S laundromat continue, Bloom wondered, if there was a woman in his life, or would the Norths withdraw his laundry privilege?

The door of the laundromat behind him suddenly rattled. As it swung open, a large flashlight was aimed at his face, blinding him. Bloom, who had been feeling like a lurking criminal, now began to act like one; he took the first step of a run.

"Police," shrieked the voice attached to the light. "A prowler! Help!"

"No," said Bloom, who had gathered his wits enough to brake to a stop, for he now recognized the voice. "It's only me, Sarah. It's Arthur."

Sarah North now came out, with the beam lighting her way. "What in the world!" she said, nose to nose with him. "What are you doing back here, Rabbi?"

"Taking a walk."

"In the alley? At night? People can get shot for loitering. Abe has a gun in the office, you know, in case of robberies."

"I'm no robber, Sarah. What are you doing here?"

"It's *my* place of business, Rabbi. I just came by to do some work in the office and saw your bag. Look, it's chilly, Rabbi. Come in."

Bloom hesitated.

"Am I keeping you from something?"

"No, no, no," he said.

"Well then, come in, and I'll make you some coffee."

Think fast, Bloom told himself. If I am not out back when she arrives, Dawn will probably come inside, where she'll find me and the shul president—a bad time and place to introduce them!

Bloom now thought he heard the whir of a motor. He stopped. Yes, it was becoming louder and mixed with the crunch of gravel. He recognized the idle of the engine; a van now turned the corner. Bloom came inside.

As Sarah put water on the little stove, Bloom stood nearby, one foot in the private office, the other out in the store in front of a double-load washer; should Dawn enter, he could signal her away.

"Sugar? Milk, Rabbi?"

He stuck his head into the private room now, and then ducked out suddenly because the van, he suspected, was right there outside. He had to act quickly. He could not just race out, disappear without saying a word, so he stuck his head in and said, "Sarah, I'm sorry but I realize I don't need any coffee; it'll just keep me up. It's a bad habit of mine to say yes any time coffee's offered."

Sarah scrutinized him.

The engine of the van was running, but Sarah didn't seem to hear it; thank God, Bloom thought, for aging ears. "Really, no thanks for that coffee. I'll take a raincheck."

Now he was out of the private room gesturing frantically and wordlessly for Dawn to stay out, to continue on that way, he motioned, that way, down the alley, west, toward the beach and the grunion, where he would meet her.

"Who's back there?" Sarah stepped out of the private room.

"No one," said Bloom, easing her back in.

"I thought I heard talking."

"Just me talking to you."

"And a car."

"Something did pass by. Say, how about that coffee now, Sarah?"

"I turned off the burner because you said you didn't want any!"

"Can't I change my mind?"

"You're telling a fib, Rabbi. Who's back there?"

"Nobody. Look, if you want. There's no one there."

12

On deception's unreliable scale (one to ten), Bloom's ruse had been at best a five. He was in trouble.

Now, however, as always when he was with Dawn, Bloom's fear somehow was transforming itself, dividing like a marvelous undiscovered cell within him, half into wonder, half into irreverent, insistent arousal.

Dawn drove briskly and silently around the ribbon of freeway toward Long Beach. They exchanged admiring smiles, they seemed to be congratulating each other on the teamwork that had made their escape possible. The engine ran smoothly, a few bottles clinked in their cardboard boxes in the rear, and Dawn had the van up to seventy. The road curved left, and she leaned slightly over the steering wheel, pleasing Bloom immensely, as her shoulder neared his. "Is it attraction between us or just centrifugal force that has brought you here to me?"

She beamed at him and moved back away, as the road curved right this time, toward the harbor. Bloom felt somehow protected by the van; its speed, its privacy, and its driver all seemed to insulate him from the outside. He wanted to compliment Dawn on the fine way she had immediately understood him back at the laundromat, on how she had driven on and waited two blocks down the alley on the dark side of the street with her headlights turned off, and had started up the engine only when he had come trotting by. Everything had gone so smoothly then, the way it was going now.

He reached his other hand across the space between him and Dawn. His forearm grazed the ball of the gearshift, and now he touched Dawn's golden-haired knee.

Beneath Bloom's arm, on the rectangular little table top beneath some coins and an empty cola can, were the latest copies of the *L.A. Eye*, where, in several weeks' time, Dawn's first article on Bloom would appear. I'm going to tell him, she said again to herself, but to Bloom she said nothing, only smiled. Tonight was not to be the night.

Tonight's enjoyment would be ruined, she thought, by an attempt at explanation. Anyway, she was also writing a short piece on the grunion orgy and wanted to pay attention to them, too.

She slowed down to fifty-five as the traffic grew thicker. They were thriving in this unhurried rush to the beach. Bloom, too, felt marvelous. The quietness around them created a kind of decorousness, a touch of ritual to their trip together, and it all made him feel very exotic, as if he were thousands of miles away from a place or person he could call home. When they finally pulled into the parking lot of the harbor, Dawn checked her watch and said, "It's nine forty-five."

"It's late?"

"It's perfect," she answered his worried look, and pulled up the emergency brake, as if she were drawing a line and daring him somehow, luring him, to cross it. "The fish are screwing like mad, Rabbi. Let's not miss it. You take the blankets."

"You brought blankets?"

"You *have* to have blankets, you strange fellow. And a little whiskey. They're in the back."

Bloom found them. "Come, my little rabbi," she said, and she was already out and walking toward the sand, "let's not miss anything."

"My sentiments exactly," said Bloom, and he skipped along behind Dawn toward the water.

13

Two days later Bloom woke up in the middle of the night. He read for a while, and then he watched *Dial M for Murder,* which Bernie Levitt Cadillac ("Luxury Cars at Economy Prices") was sponsoring with thirty-second commercials. When the movie was over, Bloom still could not get back to sleep. He lay there, first on his bed, then moving over to his couch—dragging his sheet behind him. His brain was at odds with his weary body. He felt himself a fatigued D'Artagnan, full of wit and spunk, ready to disarm all who opposed him —and his swimming lessons. He lay there, opening and closing books from the shelf behind the couch, taking on Sarah North and old Eli Ginsberg, even the Panuzzis and his own mother (who might look up from the shabbos chicken this week and say those trite but —to Bloom—foreboding words: "So, what are you doing? Trying to kill me?"). To all, Bloom spent fitful hours lecturing, sermonizing, debating, justifying himself, parrying their accusations, refining his defense of his conduct with the brilliance of Clarence Darrow, Felix Frankfurter, and Muhammad Ali combined. If he did so much fancy footwork now, recalling passages in *halacha*, Jewish law, pertaining to consorting with gentiles, if he did so much spectacular bobbing and weaving in advance of the attacks he expected for his un-Jewish conduct, then when they really came, would he have anything left? No one yet had said a word to him about Dawn.

Dressed in his pajamas, Bloom went to the window and looked across the street. He stuck his head out into the hibiscus-laden air, and his recollections of lunch today with Dawn came rushing back to him.

They had chosen a restaurant at the far end of Casino Boulevard —again, Bloom thought, an act of discretion. There, amid rushing waiters, amid the sounds of others' conversations and clinking glasses and silverware, he had actually put in his order for a lock of Dawn Nakazawa's hair. "I know it's pathetically old-fashioned," he said, "and way out of date—which I am through and through—but I figured I would just ask you anyway."

"It's a first for me, Arthur, and I'm not sure I get it. People used to exchange such things," she said, "when they feared something might keep them apart. Is that your worry, Rabbi?"

"No, no," Bloom lied. He hadn't thought of that, but, as usual, Dawn was so prescient, so in tune with him, he found himself unable to sustain his denials very long or well. "I mean, I hope it's not that."

Her angular face stared at him from across the table, and he said timidly, as if the compliment had been waiting inside him at least a dozen years, "It's just that I love your hair, I really do. I know it sounds dumb, and I feel like a jerk for even saying it because it's a classic case of confusing the religious and the profane, but that hair of yours is just so soft and beautiful, Dawn, it's as soft and silky as the fringes of a prayer shawl."

"And am I one of your prayers answered?"

Bloom thought then he might have a heart attack, a very young man's attack as strong and fatal as youth itself. Rarely at a loss for words, he was then; his mouth opened and he tried to speak. He thought Dawn might see his heart there, that little red animal, unhooking itself and leaping toward her.

"Well, you have so much," Bloom recovered, "so much long, lovely hair, I thought you could spare a little for me."

"I can spare a little, if you can give a lock of yours to me."

"All I have left is a lock. One lock would finish me off."

"Have you given the rest away, Arthur, to your many girlfriends?"

"No man," he said, "has ever received a better compliment for his baldness. What are you writing down there?" he asked, for Dawn had begun jotting in a small red notebook.

She looked up, Bloom thought, a little startled. "Oh, I'm just putting here that you are not only a rabbi and a poet and pool maintainer, but also a romantic, that you have asked for a lock of my hair on this date, in this place, at"—she checked her watch (she was wearing her childhood Mickey Mouse one today)—"exactly two forty-five. Things like that, some of your quotable quotes, Rabbi."

"But why?" He smiled, a little anxious.

"To have them, just to have them." She averted her eyes from his and then returned his gaze with a strong one of her own. "You see, Arthur, I just don't trust my computer"—she pointed her pencil up to her head to a point below those flawlessly tended bangs. "I don't trust it to record everything, and I don't want to forget anything." She paused and checked his eyes. "Women keep diaries, you know, far more than men. I want to make sure mine are complete."

Bloom found all this odd, but also deeply flattering. Here it had been three years with nobody in his life, absolutely nothing, not even anything casual, and now someone was in his life, commemorating each and every hour they spent together! He was certainly making up for lost time. He reached across the table to touch that shimmering hair, but—and it was only because he did not take his eyes off her—in doing so he knocked over the creamer that stood between their plates. The milk flowed out over the Formica table top, lapped at the red notebook, and then streamed down onto Dawn's lap.

"Damn," she said loudly as Bloom jumped up, a clumsy knight

with his rumpled paper napkin at the ready. But the spell had been broken, on this their first lunch date. More than that, Dawn was very mad.

In spite of his apology, which, now that he reflected on it, Bloom thought appropriate and sufficient for what had happened, Dawn had stayed mad for longer than seemed necessary. At first he thought it was simply an expression of the value she placed on those little notebooks where she kept her diary entries, or the points of interest about the synagogue, or whatever it was she kept there. But the real value of the incident, of the accident, was that Bloom had seen her mad, cursing, overreacting. Here was Dawn Nakazawa, finally with a human frailty, pissed off at an ardently, innocently caused accident. As a result, Dawn was now, to Bloom, not only this extraordinary, gorgeous, exotic Oriental woman whom he was in danger of idolizing, she was also a mortal.

He took her out of the restaurant to the nearby five-and-ten-cent store, and here he bought her ten new red notebooks to replace the soggy one. What Bloom did not know was that the store had not been as deserted as it seemed, and that his congregant Lulu Fineberg, who worked in lingerie and housewares, had seen everything —the rabbinical hand on the Japanese shoulder, all the solicitousness, and, of course, the purchase itself.

No sooner did the rabbi and the Japanese girl leave than Lulu was off to the casino—it was her lunch hour—where she ran into Black Dave. They both went straight to the tables and were dealt one ten after another—"Ten, Dave, the number of notebooks the rabbi bought!" The run also lasted, Dave noticed, exactly ten minutes. As a result, Dave and Lulu made a killing that afternoon at blackjack. What was also odd was that Adolph Gruen, who had not been made aware of this rabbinical intelligence, had, for a lark, decided to play red tens at roulette. He had a streak of winning numbers then like nobody's business—the best of his life.

Bloom, of course, could have known none of this. He leaned on his windowsill a few more minutes, looking in the direction where Dawn lived, and now he turned and went back to the TV in the hope that something else had come on that would help him go back to sleep. The second feature was now in full swing, a gangster movie Bloom had never seen before and was not interested in because

James Cagney was not starring. As Bernie Levitt appeared on the screen with a great deal on a red, fully reconditioned and newly painted 1968 El Dorado—easy financing too—Bloom finally began to fall asleep. But he was wondering about those notebooks.

14

The weather had become so surprisingly smogless and pleasant that many of the gamblers who would otherwise have come down to Gardena on weekends went instead to the beach, or stayed to visit with children, or flew off to Vegas for the casinos there, along with the luxurious pools and floor shows, which Gardena did not offer. The temperature hovered in the upper seventies, a breeze seemed to blow in from the harbor every day around noon, and the sun climbed through a sky clear, blue, and pollution-free as the skies of pre–World War II days.

Partly because of these conditions, the news—namely, that Rabbi Bloom had some female company—still spread fairly slowly throughout Gardena. Not all the synagogue members by any means considered their rabbi a charm, or a key factor in their gaming lives; some thought him quaint, something of an old man living in a young man's body; others, mainly the women, thought of Bloom as adorable, and praying before him, with him, on Fridays and Saturdays gave them a bit of the pleasure (attendant without the anxiety) of being with their own children. In fact the number of gamblers who watched the rabbi closely was relatively small, although a far larger number of congregants (and their friends and relatives, in turn) were quick to pick up hints and rumors generated by the synagogue's officers and regulars. It was a grapevine that never worked the same way twice.

Someone who had become most intrigued with the results of the rabbi's new behavior was Bernie Levitt, one of the congregation's wealthiest members and the owner of the Cadillac dealership where Black Dave worked. A short but powerful cannonball of a salesman in late middle age, Bernie did not attend synagogue regularly, but he was always attending to his rabbi, as he was an exceedingly superstitious fellow and, in his own private way, a religious one. Because Dave had kept him informed, Bernie knew all about the rabbi's swimming lessons and Dave's "experiment," as they now referred to it, and the gambling successes of Abe, Lulu, Adolph, and Ethel. In the small date book he carried in his breast pocket, Bernie kept a detailed charting of his own fortunes, those of these other temple members, and a graph of how this information related to the rabbi's activities. For example, whenever Rabbi Bloom took off to visit his mother in L.A., the earnings graph usually showed a blip downwards—nothing alarming, but a pattern nevertheless. Bloom's previous dating activities—those few-and-far-between Saturday nights he shared, usually doubling with the cantor—always coincided with a dip in winnings, and a significant dip, too. Bernie Levitt had often wondered about all this. While the other gamblers were satisfied to know that such patterns existed, Bernie was interested in the why. In the case of Bloom and this Japanese girl, the pattern was striking, and strikingly different, and Bernie's interest in the rabbi's patterns was reawakened—profoundly.

Just this morning his curiosity took a leap when Black Dave informed him that on the previous night several Japanese (who rarely patronized Bernie Levitt Cadillac and rarely bought luxury cars) had been in to browse; two test-drove El Dorados, and a third had said he was going to consult with his bank and then come in to make the down payment.

For a mind like Bernie's, which sought correspondences, these occurrences cried out for explication. He sought some connection between the developments on the casino front and the business front and the role the new woman was playing in the rabbi's life.

As he perused his inventory, touching shiny fenders, checking rear windows for accumulations of grime, reading the script for his new commercial, Bernie couldn't help but look up into the sky and breathe in deeply of the air, and wonder.

To clear his head, he decided he would take his daily walk earlier than usual today. Dave could handle what business there was. Bernie went into the office, took a glass of seltzer from the dispenser, and set off.

In the dazzling light of the early afternoon, Bernie saw that the casino managers finally had gotten someone to shine doorknobs and treat awning poles with metal polish; how he loved polish and shine.

He walked several more blocks and saw that Angelos Panuzzi, too, had climbed into the window of the Duplicating Room and had cleaned the glass until there wasn't a blemish. He did not know how long he stood there, but soon he was moving down the boulevard and, like the needle on a compass, he stopped finally in front of the synagogue. He approached the sign on the door and read:

TEMPLE ELIJAH

RABBI	ARTHUR BLOOM
CANTOR	A. PANUZZ
SABBATH	Fri 8:35
	Sat 9:30

The "I" missing from the cantor's name didn't bother Bernie nearly as much as the green corrosion on the bronze of the sign, which he picked at with his finger. He might sell cars for a living, but his calling was to get beneath the surface of things. In this case, to the bronze. But in the case of Rabbi Bloom, what?

With his nail he chipped at the corrosion to make it lift off, but it resisted. Bernie squinted against the light, moved out of the direct glare into the shade of one of the willows, and now noticed that the Nakazawa women were rearranging the displays in their window. It certainly was a day for windows. Both women wore red kerchiefs around their foreheads as they worked. Bernie doffed his hat to them, but they did not notice.

Meandering back to the dealership on the far side of the boulevard took Bernie twice as long as usual and provided only half the customary relaxation. When he entered the showroom and threw himself into his chair, Dave announced that three more serious shoppers had been in—all Japanese. What was going on?

15

Bloom looked at the foot of his bed strewn with papers. Yesterday, before his swimming lesson, he had pulled out his college and rabbinical school graduation pictures (already yellowing), his senior sermon, and a notebook of bitter thoughts he had kept that last year, when he thought he might drop out.

He cried over himself in college, the friend of any girl who was having troubles with her boyfriend—either known or unknown to Bloom. These girls had felt so at ease with Bloom that they told him in intimate detail their emotional and sexual histories. Bloom always listened intently, sympathetically, offered sensible advice, quoted Emerson on friendship and Freud on mothers and fathers, and always picked up the tab for coffee or beer. It was the bittersweet joke of his college life to be the lay therapist of his crowd, but never to get laid. As he listened to the outpourings of love, jealousy, and sexual experimentation, he came to feel about himself that he had been born out of his time, a zipped zipper in an era of outrageous screwing and emotional entanglement. He felt Kierkegaard and Jaspers, Rosenzweig and Kafka, Tillich and Sartre, Wittgenstein and Heschel would understand, but they were dead or distant. No one living, no one he could call his friend, not even Panuzzi, who roomed with him for three years, could be told how desperate he really was.

Bloom took cold showers, occasionally masturbated, and read voraciously, as if there were somehow a refuge in words. The more he read, however, the more his distraction increased until he realized that the light of a phosphorescent lust had been lit within him and reading Maimonides' *Guide for the Perplexed* was not going to extinguish it. And yet there was no one to confide in, no girl, no guy who might suggest a cure. Bloom's native timidity, his embarrassment at his tardy sexuality, and his reputation for being advisor-to-all-but-partner-to-none added up to one bleak Saturday night after another of no prospects.

And yet when Lust whispers *Thou Must,* the Body replies *I Can.* At the end of his first year of rabbinical school Bloom dreamed that Sartre took him out for a friendly espresso at the bar down the street from the seminary: Bloom, how can you sit there across from me and say you really listen to your friends talk about orgasms and involvement, commitment and cunnilingus, how can you pass yourself off as informed? How can you be of any real assistance to anyone, Bloom, if you are so fundamentally ignorant, still a virgin yourself? Existence precedes essence, I've said, and your case proves it. Without experience you're alive but a fraud. Get authentic, Sartre said, and get laid.

In his second year of rabbinical school, Bloom resolved to take the philosopher's advice.

The woman was short, with rounded features, and coal black. Bloom could fully understand why she was at first nonplussed by the arrangements he suggested: her fee, plus taxi fare to and from the seminary.

Bloom tried to explain to her that he understood, too, her point of view, but he didn't carry money with him on the sabbath. There was, however, plenty in his desk, and if she would only go with him there, he would make it worth the trouble he knew he was causing her, plus extra for the faith she would be showing in him.

"I should put up money for the taxi cab?" She laughed. "*My* money!"

"Please," Bloom implored. He turned the pockets of his denim jacket inside out, affecting such poignant nervousness, while his face radiated both worldly innocence and the prospect of good hygiene. The hooker was touched and eyeballed him up and down once again.

"I'm gonna charge you extra."

"Anything," Bloom said, "and I will be eternally grateful. Anything at all."

"A hundred," she tried.

"Impossible."

"Fifty then."

"Forty."

"You said anything at all, junior."

"Anything within reason, please. I'm a student, on scholarship. I'm not well-to-do."

"Who am I? The welfare department? I'll make it forty-five, and you supply the rubber."

"I'll have to borrow it from my roommate."

"Another scholarship kid? He there, too?"

"No, he won't be. I promise."

"I must be out of my mind," she said. Surveying the street once quickly for the cops, she snapped at him, "Let's go."

Dressing and undressing included, the act itself could have taken maybe eight minutes. Throughout, the prostitute, lying on her back, kept asking Bloom if he had read all the books in the cases that lined the room, floor to ceiling. Bloom plunged and thrust below, cupped a brown breast above, and buried his head in her musky hair.

She said, "I never saw so many books in my life."

Her admiration for his books made Bloom feel he was doing something very wrong. According to the manuals, her eyes should be closed by now, she should be gasping for breath, ecstatic. He plunged at a new steeper angle, he put his hands on her hips and tried to roll.

"They're not even in English some of 'em. What's that funny language on that one?"

"Hebrew," he panted. "A lot are in Hebrew." His penis was beginning to hurt, and still, nothing. He opened his eyes and saw she was scanning his Babylonian Talmud, the twenty-volume set. Then Bloom remembered you were supposed to kiss. Maybe he hadn't kissed her enough. He raised himself up and found her lips, but it was not a pleasure; they were dry and sticky with nicotine and lipstick.

"Whaddaya doing? Get out of my way. I can't see!"

Bloom stopped then. He had worked up a sweat, while she had been calmly surveying his library. The only hooker on Broadway, on all the broadways of the world, interested in the Babylonian Talmud, and he had found her! An intellectual! He collapsed on her stomach.

"Now what's wrong with you? Just do it, will you? I swear all of you students is depressed. I prefer my regular customers, the old men. I really do. Now just squirt, kid. Squirt and get it finished."

Bloom arose from the bed feeling lousy but a little wiser. On his windowsill his sabbath candles fluttered in the wind. The sabbath, supposedly a propitious time for intercourse, traditionally so, but not so for Bloom. The prostitute looked at Bloom's desk, where his Talmud was open to a complex section, *gitin*, divorce law. She was pulling up her pantyhose. "The writing's purty," she said. "Lots of curlicues."

His chief concern now was to get her out, as he had brought her in, undetected. But it was not to be. Although it was past 2:00 A.M. and although they were using the back entrance of the dormitory, halfway down the steps Bloom found himself staring into the portly, bearded face of Rabbi Langsam.

"Good shabbos, Arthur." Langsam's tired eyes seemed instantly to enlarge behind his spectacles.

"Good shabbos, Rabbi." Bloom looked to the prostitute. His eyes beseeched her. "This is my date."

"Doris, baby. Doris."

"Good shabbos, Doris," said Langsam.

"We're in a rush, Rabbi," Bloom said, pushing quickly by in the crowded stairwell. "I've got to get Doris home. You'll have to excuse us."

"I will have to excuse you," Langsam muttered.

"Who's he?" Doris asked Bloom.

"The dean. The boss. Come on."

Beyond the turn at the next landing Doris turned and shouted up, "You be nice to this boy, you hear? He's all right. I saw he was doin' his homework all spread out neat on his desk."

"Doris, please."

"You hear, mister?" she persisted.

Langsam rushed down half a flight. His face was florid. Bloom turned; he didn't want to look any more. "I hear," said Langsam, "and what's more I'll be calling the police if I see you prowling around here any more."

"Man, I ain't prowlin'! I'm his guest. His date, just like he said."

"Good shabbos, Rabbi," Bloom tried once more, with a formidable pull on Doris's arm.

"Yeah, good shabbos to you, too," she said. Then, at the top of the final flight before the door and the street she freed herself from Bloom's hand and shouted up, "You look a little dried out. You wanna be next, grandpa?"

"Get out," Langsam screamed. "Get out of this building and stay out!"

There was an alarm. Bloom went to the door, opened it, and saw a fire engine racing down Casino Boulevard. He returned to the bed, dropped the papers back down upon it. He had always felt Langsam had meant that "Get out" for him as well as for Doris. But Langsam, who could have had Bloom thrown out of the seminary, never reported the incident—to the best of Bloom's knowledge—to the other officials of the administration. And Bloom, after some other misadventures, had nonetheless graduated.

Now he looked at his watch. Five minutes to go and he would descend these stairs down to the street to see Dawn and lead her back to their place, to their water together. He stood over the photographs of his graduating class, his transcripts, his senior sermon, and all these papers now seemed to be distant documents from the archaeology of a previous life. He threw them in the folder, where he was also keeping his poems and notes about her, tossed it in the desk, and left the apartment.

16

Her Flaw-Finder was continuing to give Bloom an impressive rating. He had passed the Scar Test, and the Angry-Mother Test was in full swing, and he still seemed amiable, and generous, and concerned about her life. Always asking questions, too, as if her inquiries unleashed his own; he particularly wanted to know about her parents, college, and so many things that Dawn would really prefer to forget. And through all this he still remained so much fun to be with. She had thought this first spring back in Gardena would be at best dreary, but it had something poignant about it, something special that reminded Dawn of the best springs of her growing up. The spring had Bloom.

What was even more surprising to Dawn was that lately she had begun to look at Bloom's hands more closely. They were strong, with wiry brown hairs that ran like planted crops up from the nail, broke into a clearing at the knuckle, and then continued in their neat rows up to the wrist line. She particularly liked looking at his hands in repose, glistening with water after a swim, the fingers curled in a way that communicated not grabbiness but a kind of contentment. She was beginning to imagine those hands touching her body.

At that moment Ono came into the living room. She sat down quietly opposite Dawn. Her mother's eyes were an odd gray tonight, a hue composed, thought Dawn, half of sadness and half of steel.

"Is there something wrong, mother? You feel okay?"

"Your dutifulness is so new to me," Ono said.

"Nevertheless, it's genuine."

"We shall see."

"Mother, do you ever reach a point in life"—Dawn tucked her legs under herself where she sat on the couch—"where you stop thinking thoughts like I'm having now? When you aren't troubled by all the people who you could be but either chose not to be or could never become because you're not smart enough or rich enough or you went to the wrong school, things like that? Mother, it seems so unfair that we have to make all these choices, and each choice excludes all others. Ever since I came back here, I've been feeling like a kid who wants to fly, who can't accept that the talent was dished out to birds."

Ono nodded, her face expressionless.

"Mother, why are you staring at me that way? Oh, I get it. It's him, right? It's because of him."

"No," said Ono. "I think not of him but of you. I am thinking to myself that tonight you have asked me how I am, and then you proceed to tell me how *you* are. You must learn again to think not only of yourself. You have forgotten a lot. You have forgotten that the Japanese think about their families."

"I haven't forgotten any of that, mother."

Ono handed Dawn an album that she was holding. "I found this yesterday among your father's papers when I was going through them."

Dawn reached out for the album. Among the loose papers were the documents of Akira and Ono's internment—passes, photographs, official Department of the Army memos, a few legal papers as well, all pertaining to the threat Akira and Ono and the hundreds of other Japanese families posed to the security of the United States during World War II.

"I think you have forgotten about this," said Ono. "You were not born when the police entered our house and gave us six hours to leave, when the whites who owed your father money decided then, in 1942, that there was no need to pay it. Dawn, your father and I were in those camps in Utah for two years. When it got cold, the temperature could go down to as much as forty below, and the buildings stood on flat land, near a lake, exposed on all sides to the winter weather. Even with the stove burning, the windows frosted up. Your grandfather died in Manzanar; Wesley Matsumoto's grandmother, too. They might have lived longer, elsewhere."

"Wesley Matsumoto. Always him. You'd think he was a member of the family!"

"You hear only what you want to hear," Ono said.

"I know about this, mother."

"Then why don't you act as if you do. No, I don't believe you have any sense. You say you know, but you don't. You look Japanese, but you do not act it, ever!"

"You and daddy never talked to me about any of this, mother. Never. I have never looked at this material, and you have never shown it to me until now."

"Your father did not die until now. There was no need, and now there is a need. The dead impose a need."

Dawn got up off the couch and went over to her mother's chair. "I know how hard it is for you, mother."

"How do you know?"

"I can imagine, I can try to imagine how hard it is, but why do you drive me away, when I am here to help you, to be with you? I can't help it that daddy died. Sometimes you act as if it's my fault. He smoked himself to death, and you know it. Every time I see you with a cigarette in your mouth, I want to reach over and take it out. Please, won't you try to stop?"

"I'll stop if you will," Ono said quietly, her hands in her lap, still unmoving.

"If I stop what? I don't smoke."

"I think you know what I mean. You are strong. You are not the child you sometimes think you are. You have the patience and the strength of the Japanese in your blood."

Dawn gathered the documents from the couch, returned them to the album, and handed it back to her mother. "You want me to drop my work, my writing, my life!"

"*He* will do for now." Ono took a huge drag on her cigarette and then crushed it in the ashtray by the chair. "If that is my reward, I can try to quit cigarettes. That would be a worthy reward for my efforts!"

"You're joking, mother? I want you to quit. Of course I want you to quit, but I'm not going to give up my life for it."

"And is *he* your life?"

"Of course he's not. He's a man, he's somebody in my life, and I don't see why your chain-smoking should go on one more day regardless. You should stop and take care of yourself and get a little healthier yourself. Then we can sell this store, we can . . ."

"Don't make my plans for me." She stood up and took a half-filled pack of cigarettes from the table and crushed them, brandished them in her hand, for Dawn to see. "I can quit, I can show you self-control. Here, you see, I have it now." She was giving Dawn her hard maternal stare now. "And I expect you to have it, too. Do it, if not for me, then for the souls of your relatives, Dawn, and for your dead father."

17

On Sunday morning, three weeks after he had met Dawn, Bloom rose early and did what he had not done in some time: He said the morning prayers. Wrapped in the *tallis,* the prayer shawl that had belonged to his father, Bloom recited quickly, efficiently. The *siddur,* the prayer book, was open in his hands and he rapidly, lovingly turned its pages, but he knew the prayers nearly by heart, and it continually satisfied him that although he was no longer saying them regularly, he never seemed to forget. He swayed, he listed, he walked about his bedroom as he prayed, he returned to the corner, to the east, in the direction in which you were to try to send the blessings and doxologies. When it came time for the *amidah,* the standing prayer of eighteen benedictions, he walked over to the window, where the morning sun was streaming in.

It was a bright sun, a beach day. But when, between the blessing for good health and the thanks to God for not making him a gentile, Bloom looked up, he was surprised to see that Dawn's van was missing.

Olenu l'shabeach l'adon ha kol, Bloom prayed. It is our duty to praise the God of everything. He was now on the second-to-last prayer and feeling the warmth of morning pleasantly on his arms as he held the *siddur.*

Lo tate gedula la yotzair ha bresheet. To give gratitude to the creator of the beginning (of life). How, Bloom thought, he enjoyed the prayers—for their fine parallelism, for their poetry. But what about their meaning? What about their content? God? Do synagogue rabbis my age all across America on this fine Sunday morning, Bloom wondered, do they all worry what is meant by "God"? By these very fine, remarkable phrases about kingdoms, about lords of everything, creators of creation?

Bloom stopped, puzzled. He realized some new element, some doubt, had entered his feeling about Dawn. It was those notebooks, those questions she'd been asking him—sometimes suddenly out of nowhere.

Bloom kissed the fringes of the *tallis* and placed it back in the soft blue velvet bag. To dispel his mental hoverings about her, he tried writing some verse, but rereading the results depressed him. So he took his pencil and on the back of a menu—it was from Nero's Grotto, a casino (he could not recall how it came to be in his apartment)—he began to draw pictures. Doodads, faces with bangs of hair and dark eyes and pastel-colored blouses and T-shirts with odd emblems; portraits of Dawn. Below these he wrote "Dawn plus Arthur" and drew a heart around it, in the giggly adorational style of ten-year-olds. Was it possible, Bloom wondered, as he put the pencil down and took up instead the mature tome on homiletics—a handbook for sermon ideas—that, through Dawn, he was reliving each and every stage of need, affection, and love . . . from childhood through adulthood? He wondered if all that he had missed out on was now being restored to him.

It therefore did not surprise Bloom that now, as his brain idled away from sermons, he filled up a napkin with drawings again and phrases of poetry surrounding the heart: Dawn and Arthur Sitting in a Tree, K-I-S-S-I-N-G. Dawn N. and Arthur B., spring 1983. An A-R-T-H-U-R-I-A-N romance.

Bloom went back to his homiletics text now and tried to concentrate. He picked a subject he liked—the study of the attributes of God according to, among other luminaries, the famous medieval Spanish commentator and poet, Judah Halevi. Since Halevi often worked in the acrostic form, however, Bloom soon found himself enumerating attributes, characteristics of, alas, not God, but Dawn:

> Darling
> Aware
> Wise
> Nautical

Bloom told himself he should try again:

Demanding
Anxiety-producing

Would Halevi have permitted adjectival hyphenization?

Willful
Nude

Try as he might, Bloom seemed always to be intruding the flesh into what should have been strictly incorporeal assets. He thought he might try again, acrosticizing the surname to see what he came up with:

Natural
Attractive
Knowing
Attentive
Zealous
Agile
Wonderful
Agony

And below this:

Heavenly
Ecstatic
Luscious
Pencil, Pad, Notebook. Those notebooks!

What *was* going on?

18

It was 10:30 P.M. and Bloom and Dawn were at the pool for a night swimming lesson. Dawn liked the idea because it gave her a chance to do one of her favorite things in life: float on her back and watch the stars. And tonight the usual foggy haze had been blown out to sea, revealing Cygnus, the Summer Triangle, and the falling chair of Cassiopeia. Bloom could recognize only the ever-reliable Big Dipper, but he liked night swimming because it gave him the illusion he was being discreet.

"What are you thinking, Arthur?" she said to him as they sat on the deck.

"I'm remembering watching 'Walt Disney Presents' one night when I was a kid, and it was the program about space flight, narrated by Wernher Von Braun. One day, he said, perhaps in our lifetimes, a man will walk on the face of the moon. As soon as the program was over, I remember, I went outside and looked up at the moon. I stuck my hand out like this," Bloom said, "and placed my fingers wide open and lay them flat across the moon as if it were a white plate. I held them there until I couldn't keep my arm up any longer. The moon tonight looks like the moon did then."

"I like the things you think about, Arthur."

"Thank you."

"I like the way you say thank you and don't compliment me back just because I've complimented you. It shows self-control, a commodity in short supply these days."

"I," said Bloom, "like the way you say exactly what you mean, what you just said, for example."

"I like the way you listen, Arthur. That I think I like most of all."

"I *don't* like the way you always cover your belly with your hand. That I don't like; you don't have to do that."

"But the scar's ugly."

"All right, it's not so great, but not terrible either; it's part of you. When I was a kid I used to be called a 'brain.' I hated it. I used to visualize myself walking around the school yard, a cerebrum and cerebellum with little sneakers underneath. That's all, just a brain, because I was smart and always got A's. But I had hands too, see, and liked to play ball and to joke; but to everybody I was just a brain.

You understand what I'm saying, Dawn. You're more than a belly."

He extended his hand toward her abdomen as if to touch her there, but then he withdrew it. Dawn could not get enough of such diffidence. To her Bloom seemed not so much shy, which he was, as gentle and tender, tenderness itself. She basked in it this evening as she did in the starlight. And yet she had resolved to tell him she was writing an article, and then accept the consequences; there was no other way.

"I don't indulge in empty compliments," she finally said, "but I've got to tell you this, Rabbi."

"Somehow," he interrupted, "I don't want you calling me anything but my name tonight, okay?"

"Arthur. You"—she put her finger on his chest—"are one of the world's nicest men. It's a pleasure to be over here, to be teaching you to swim."

"In the top ten?" he asked.

"Certainly the top . . . fifty or sixty," she said.

A smile moved across Bloom's face. "Blessed art Thou O Lord our God, King of the Universe"—he touched her there again, near the scar—"who heals the sick, frees the imprisoned, and makes scars disappear from beautiful bellies. I made that up."

"You didn't have your hat on. Look, that must be why nothing's happening."

Bloom reached for his baseball cap from the nearby table, tossed it on, and repeated the blessing.

Just then, there was a familiar creaking. "What's that?"

"Nothing," Bloom said. "Just the hinge on the gate. It's rusty. Everything around here needs some oiling and fixing, me included."

"You're too modest, Arthur. You strike me as someone who is" —she hesitated—"in good working order."

"I'm just a well-oiled rabbinical machine." Bloom laughed.

"No, you strike me as someone who, well, just belongs here, Arthur, as if you've been here a long, long time. Some people, I guess, are just right for their jobs. I think of you as I do those trees out front there, the willows. Both of you belong. How many years have those trees been here?"

"You're making me feel ancient," he said. "When what I'm supposed to be in your eyes is youthful, muscled, graceful, witty. . . ."

"Supposed to be?"

"Oh, you know, on a date you're supposed to be all things, to feel all these ways, certain ways, to have the sound of certain music in your ears." He laughed.

"I didn't know we had dates, Arthur. I hadn't realized that these are dates, but I suppose that's it, I suppose you have to give it a name."

"What would you call it?" Bloom asked.

"Oh, I don't know." Should I tell him now? she wondered. Is this the opportunity? Yes, she thought, yes. But still she held back. "Maybe what this is is our very own TV talk show but without a host, without an audience, and maybe without a TV. Arthur, did you hear that gate creaking again?"

"I *hope* it's without an audience." Bloom stood, walked over to the driveway, turned, and sat back down beside Dawn. "Nothing but armies on a darkling plain clashing by night."

"Is that your way of saying that only the cat was in the driveway?"

"There is no cat, but I just guess I'm trying to impress you more than anything tonight. I've done my Matthew Arnold imitation, my John Milton, and who knows who's next?" The eruption of quotations, particularly from poetry, had already become something of a piece of private humor for them. What Bloom wanted to do more than anything now was not quote someone else, but simply put his arm around her shoulders. But Bloom didn't feel his wit had yet earned him the right, and lacking that, the gesture would have no grace.

"You impress me," she said, "when you don't try." And she smilingly reached out and chucked Bloom softly on the chin, turning his face toward hers. "Just be yourself, okay? You seem jumpy. You want to try the crawl again, Arthur?"

"Would it be too forward," he attempted, "if I told you what I really wanted to do was to crawl over on the deck here beside you?"

"Be my guest." They slid out of their chairs, mimed a swim stroke, and lay in their robes shoulder to shoulder on the deck. "You forgot to breathe when you were swimming, Arthur. Forgetting to breathe can cause problems. Actually, I'm a little breathless tonight, too." She twisted her body around, stretched, and pulled out a notebook from her big bag on the nearby chaise longue. "I know rabbis don't hear confessions, but I have one anyway for you tonight. Arthur, I'm a journalist. You see this pad? I'm doing a story about you and the synagogue." She paused, hoping he would not ask who for, but that's precisely what he did.

"Well, I'm free-lance," Dawn said. "When I put the articles together I'll try to place them. I'm sorry I took so long getting around to telling you."

"Well, I knew you weren't taking notes for the FBI or the CIA."

"You never know, Arthur." She felt immensely relieved. "The journalism could just be my cover."

"You're not the spy type," Bloom said. "That I knew, but not much more. I'm glad you told me."

"So you don't mind, I hope?"

"Well, I'm thinking about it. I think I should mind, but I don't." He shrugged his shoulders. "I really don't at all. It's funny, I'm even sort of flattered."

"Remember Ecclesiastes, Rabbi: 'Vanity, vanity, all is vanity.' "

"You're not," he said.

"You're not either. Forgive me, but I usually don't do stories like this. I mean right in the old proverbial backyard, or in this case, the front yard. And I don't conceal my work, but then again I rarely have had a subject quite like you. So that's *mea culpa, mea culpa.* How do you say *mea culpa* in Hebrew?"

Bloom laughed. "I think it's untranslatable, but accepted nevertheless."

"Great." She stood and took off her robe. "Now our mutual admiration society can continue." She dove into the water and came up in the middle. "Look"—she was pointing into the starry skies— "Andromeda is visible now."

"I'm afraid that, next to Talmud, my worst subject was astronomy."

"There." She guided his eyes.

"All the galaxies look like smog to me."

"Come on, Arthur. Come in again and see the stars with me from the watery deep."

But he was hesitant, and she set herself doing five straight, smooth laps. Bloom edged over the side and slowly settled into the water, but with his arms on the edge, as Dawn zipped by him. He felt like a pedestrian on the freeway, but he did want to show her what she had taught him. He lunged for her as she glided by, but he missed and began to sink. But this time he did not panic; he remembered what he had learned and waited until his feet touched the bottom. There he kicked off strongly with his wrestler's legs and rose to the surface, where he treaded water to get his bearings, and then reached the side of the pool in two strokes. It was the first time he had ever accomplished such a feat.

Afterwards, as they were drying again on the deck together, Dawn put her slender hand on Bloom's heart and said, "You have very fine lungs there. I saw what you did, and it was all spontaneous. You put it all together, Arthur. You're hardly afraid at all now. Look what you're capable of in the water!"

"Is there some of your stuff I can read?" Bloom asked. "I'd love to look at an article or something."

In her head Dawn heard Ono's low assessment of the *Eye*. "I have this terrible habit," she answered Bloom. "I just don't keep the tear sheets. I know I should, but I don't. There must be some secret urge to self-destruction at work in me, because I just don't have anything, nothing recent." Dammit, she thought to herself, she just didn't want to have to go into a long explanation about the *Eye;* she was not ashamed like Ono, but now was not the time to launch into her speech about the tabloids, and . . . *Was* she ashamed of the paper? Well, perhaps a little. "I used to work on the *L.A. Times,*" she answered Bloom's inquiring eyes.

"*L.A. Times?*"

"Uh huh."

"That's great," Bloom said.

"But I never got a byline," she hurried to add. She pulled him up by the arm, and now snug in their robes, they slowly walked around the pool. His heart beat like a rabbit's in a cage. They circumnavigated once; the moon was now out from behind some small clouds and lit their way. Together they walked over to the two deck lights and turned them off against the bugs. At the chaises longues Dawn dropped her arm and picked up her bag; the pad fell out. Bloom stooped down, retrieved it for her, and said, in the moonlight shadows, "The strangest phenomenon of all is that after all our yakking together, now that you say you're a journalist, I can't think of a thing to say to you, nothing interesting, nothing at all!"

"Me neither," Dawn said, and then gave Bloom his first non-sabbath kiss in nearly three years. It was long, fascinating, and mysterious, like Dawn herself.

"Can we do that again, sometime?" Bloom asked quietly.

Dawn nodded her head, and then they both looked up toward Andromeda twinkling on the eastern horizon.

19

Slowly backing away from the hydrangea hedge where he'd been hiding, Black Dave saw the rabbi and the girl gather their towels and leave the pool area. When he hit the sidewalk, Dave turned right and made for the casino, but then, on an impulse, he crossed over, under the neon bulbs of Nero's Grotto, and continued several more blocks down toward the dealership—and then another two blocks just for the exercise. He felt slightly criminal, having spied on the rabbi, and he felt a need to walk it off. Had anyone other than Bernie asked him, Dave would have declined. But after all, Bernie Levitt was the man who signed his weekly paycheck.

At the corner, Dave stopped, waited for the light, and crossed back over. His collection of jewelry—two bracelets on each hand, and a thick neck chain that sported both a golden Mogen David and a "mazel tov"—clinked pleasantly as he walked. Dave liked the sound. The "mazel tov" was fashioned in silver, made up of small interconnected letters in Hebrew script. The charm had been Dave's own idea, a little income-producing venture for the synagogue. Forty percent for himself—almost entirely for costs—and sixty percent for the shul. Unfortunately, the fabrication of the "mazel tovs" had been done too cheaply, and the "bet", the final letter, had been hopelessly misshapen into a kind of pretzel, giving the distinct impression that if one wore a "mazel tov," which meant, in Hebrew, good luck, what one would come up with would be quite the opposite.

The charms had therefore not done well. Except for a few, which Dave's friends bought, the "mazel tovs"—about three dozen of them—now lay in the rarely patronized, dusty, leaning gift case in the foyer of the synagogue.

In the lounge he saw Sarah North sitting in front of the TV. Wearing yellow sunglasses with lenses the size of eggplants, she was watching the tube, which was blasting "Hollywood Squares"; she did not seem very happy. She barely acknowledged Black Dave's "Evening, babe." There was Leonidas, and there was his son, too, at the dice table. Dave finally located Abe and Bernie at the stud poker table. In front of them were towers of blue chips.

"Good evening, boss," said Dave. "Did you buy those or win 'em?"

Bernie was deep in poker thought and didn't look up, but Abe answered for him. "An incredible run—all within the last hour and a half." Bernie looked up to the sexton for corroboration.

"Check," said Dave. "They were talkin' real seriously. Having some hand talkin' too toward the end. And then a whopper of a kiss."

"And when was that?" Bernie asked.

"The kiss came," Dave checked his watch, "at ten fifty-three, exactly."

Abe looked at the column of numbers he was keeping on an old postcard he lifted from his vest pocket. "That's it: the biggest jackpot of all came at ten fifty-two, gentlemen."

Dave stole a look over Bernie's shoulder. "But now it's a horse of a different color." He saw the small pot, the timidity of the gamblers to continue going up against Bernie, who was doing so well. The others didn't know that Bernie was holding nothing, *bubkes*, garbage.

"Fold," said Bernie. "They must have just separated?" He was looking at Dave for an answer, but his words had the tone of certainty, as if he were not asking but reporting what he now saw in the message of the cards and chips before him.

"Who you talking about?" said one of the players at the table, an out-of-towner. "Who or what is going on here?"

"We're just mumbling," Bernie said.

"If I wanted to hear mumbling, I could have stayed in the room with my wife. I came here to play, so how about some playing?"

"Think of your pressure," said Abe North. "It's not healthy to be upset, sir."

"Come on, shorty," said the man. "You or your friend, or some-body, just shut up and play. Either that or give your chair to someone else. I want to win," the fellow said, "and I don't want to sit around here until dawn to do it!"

The three synagogue members looked at each other.

"Did I say something wrong? What gives with you guys?" Full of irritation, the man stood up and stormed away. The three temple members, seeing that the gambling was slow everywhere, decided to go for coffee. Dave elaborated on what he had been able to see from behind the gate; he had not been able to hear much, but whatever the rabbi was saying was obviously the right thing. "They were pointing up a lot," Dave said.

"At what?" Bernie wanted to know.

"I couldn't tell you," Black Dave answered.

"But I asked you to stay close to them."

"Look, boss"—Dave did not hide a little irritation—"any closer and they would have kissed me, too. But they were speaking softly, in whispers, see?" And he began to imitate the sounds and gestures with Abe North just then, as Sarah walked by their table.

"I hope I'm not interrupting anything, boys?" she said. There was more fatigue than good humor in her voice. "Abe, I think I'm going home."

"Honey," said Abe, stopping her before she drifted off, "you know that money that I asked you to hold for me?"

"Yes."

"The money I asked you to hold and not give to me when I ask you to give it to me?"

"Yes, Abe."

"Well, I really want you to give me that money now, dear."

"Good night, Abe," she said wearily. "Come home and go to bed sometime this week, maybe. Okay?"

"Okay, honey," Abe said, "but I really need it. I'm a little short."

"When you're rich, you're still short." Dave laughed.

Sarah glared at the sexton, reached into her sundress pocket, and threw a small folded wad of money to Abe. "That's the last of it, Abe. If you want to borrow any more, borrow from your friend or your boss."

When she had gone and the bill was paid, Abe said, "It's not me she's angry at, not really, fellas."

"Nothing like that." Dave slapped the table, so that the spoon bounced off his saucer.

"Really, she's upset at what the rabbi is doing."

"She's a short-sighted woman, then," Bernie Levitt added. "You heard what that guy said about 'winning before Dawn.' I say we go back and see if we can't do some of that ourselves."

All three went back to the stud table they had left. As Black Dave slipped into his seat, he felt a lump. He jumped up. "Look at that!" The guy who had left, the guy who had said "Dawn," had left his wallet, and it was rich with bills.

"It's a night to buy a lottery ticket," said Abe. "What's going on?"

"We have to find out," said Bernie Levitt, as he began to deal, "and we will."

Dave turned the wallet in to the management, and a day later, when he came into the Silver Dollar, he was presented by Kavanaugh, on behalf of the lost wallet's happy owner, with a good-faith reward of $350.

20

With the tension between them lifted, Bloom and Dawn spent a fine two days talking—mainly on neutral ground, away from the synagogue, although the swimming lessons did continue.

Never had he felt so relaxed with a woman. Interviewed, asked his views, he decided that this format was the rabbi's version of the perfect date. She would ask and he would answer; it was like a sermon for one, and then it was his turn to ask her about her life, and she would answer.

Dawn asked him what Jewish law had to say about gambling, and he happily told her that, as with most things, the bark of the law was nastier than the bite. "According to the *halacha*, inveterate gamblers are sometimes synonymous with robbers, with a person who doesn't study or engage in an honest trade, someone who fritters away the precious short time God has given, and ignores how he may make a contribution."

"Might the rabbis of the Talmud," she asked him, "have taught differently had they lived in Gardena?"

"Excuse me?" Bloom was a little startled.

"I mean if they numbered among themselves that famous sage of the Southland, Rabbi Arthur Bloom? I mean, how do you feel about it?"

"Oh, I'm a very soft touch, I guess. Far easier than they were." Dawn was listening very carefully. "I guess I let them get away with virtually everything. I say they should pay the rent or mortgage, help their kids in college or business to get established, if that's a problem, and then put something away for a health problem, a retirement trip, stuff like that. With whatever they have left, people should just do what gives them pleasure. That's Bloom's advice. Bloom tries to remind people of the pleasure principle. I urge my people to enjoy themselves, do a good deed now and then, and thank God every morning that they get up healthy and don't have a kidney stone, angina, or any of the infirmities of old age."

"But what about compulsive gamblers, Arthur? You know I've done a bit of research already, and there's a very high percentage of Jewish compulsive gamblers. Also a high percentage of Oriental compulsive gamblers."

"Jews *are* Orientals," he said, "as in Near *East* and Far *East.* Perhaps," he said to her, "that's what accounts for the attraction between us."

They walked along Paradise Street, and then turned down the next road that led around to Los Cienfuegos Terrace, and from there back to Bernie Levitt's end of Casino Boulevard.

"So you don't think, all in all, Arthur, that you have a social problem here in your little community?"

"Social problem?" Bloom laughed. "Absolutely not."

"Well, you might have one tomorrow," she said matter-of-factly, "because I've made arrangements to interview your mother."

"My mother?"

Dawn confirmed what she had said and then read aloud Nannette's address. "I also may be going in the next few days to your Academy of Judaism in Hollywood to read"—she checked her notes —"something from a book, or a chapter in a book, called Talmud Sanhedrin. One of your members came by the other day—Mr.

Levitt—and we were talking in very general terms, and he suggested the library and that book."

"You *are* serious about this!" Bloom said. They were silent a moment now as they walked on.

Dawn was not sure if Bloom might feel betrayed by all this, which was why she had decided to tell him her plans, in advance.

"I haven't even told my mother about you," he said. "Now she's going to find out, and fast! Maybe I should go along?"

"I don't think that's such a good idea. Not very professional, plus I don't want it."

"Are you going to tape her?" he asked. "If you do, promise me I can hear the tapes."

"I am going to do some taping. I always do. But I can't let you hear them. How can I promise her confidentiality and then broadcast them to you?"

"But she's my mother."

"All the more reason for the confidentiality!" After a pause, she said, "Actually, Arthur, if you feel the interview will cause trouble between you, I can cancel it. I know you're a problem for me across the street, so I don't see any reason to spread the joy, if you know what I mean."

"Oh, no," he said, getting more excited about this prospect. "I insist you go ahead. You have all the permission in the world. You're going to be a toleration test for everybody here, and very quickly."

"Not for you, I hope." She closed her pad, and they walked along the sidewalk together. Her hand was free, and Bloom thought of clasping it, but Dawn seemed preoccupied.

"I suppose I shouldn't be telling you any of this either—professionally speaking—but this reporter is having a helluva time with her mother. My mom, Arthur, thinks I'm being disloyal to her and everything Japanese, past, present, including the future souls of all relatives, just by crossing the street and going over to your side. She thinks I can't do anything right, and the harder I try to be pleasant to her, to understand her situation now that daddy is gone, the tougher she is on me. I don't know about you, Rabbi, but I find it hard to scream at a widowed woman, especially one who happens to be my mother."

"I'll go over and tell her that there's a lot you do right," he said.

"She's nisei, Arthur, through and through." Dawn could see Bloom didn't understand the term. "That's second generation in America, first born here. You know, immigrant mentality."

"And vitality, too," Bloom said.

"That's right. They worked terribly hard to make a start in this country, and then they had most of it confiscated in World War Two, and they were sent away."

"Concentration camps," Bloom said. "I know about that."

"Yes, unfortunately we have that in common, too, I suppose." They turned the corner onto Crestwood Street, and he took her hand. "But niseis," Dawn said, "think sanseis—that's my group, second generation born here—are never going to make the grade no matter what. It's a generational thing. We never try hard enough, they say, never work hard enough, we're soft, have had it too easy, and what's more we have forgotten all the Japanese ways. We're too American. You see, they want us to be American and Japanese, looking forward and looking backward at the same time, and we have failed, failed miserably, even the successful ones among us, according to this nisei view. It's a crazy, troubled situation, Arthur."

"You don't indict, by characterization, a whole generation. Not even a mother can do that," said Bloom.

Dawn let go his hand. "I don't know," she said, "maybe in my case my mother is right."

"In my humble opinion, she's not."

"My very being here with you is part of it—proof of the indictment."

"Nevertheless," said Bloom, "I hold you in high regard, and you deserve to be so held. Who knows, perhaps soon I'll be able to hold you even closer."

"You're a clever boy, Rabbi Bloom."

"You're absolutely my favorite sansei in the whole world. And in fact, my favorite Japanese."

"And you're my favorite rabbi, and Jew." She paused. "Are you really a rabbi, Arthur?"

"Are you really a reporter?"

Instead of answering, they stared at each other a long minute before breaking out into smiles.

21

When Dawn called on Bloom's mother and identified herself as a reporter doing a story on her son, Arthur, Nannette did not immediately realize that she was the same Japanese who, Sarah North had told her, had been seen frequenting the synagogue pool with her son. After all, how could a young woman, a Japanese woman, reputedly giving her son, the rabbi, swimming lessons, also have the audacity to interview his mother?

When Nannette saw Dawn, however, standing in the doorway of her L.A. apartment, tall, serene, with a tape recorder in her hand, she somehow knew that here was an adversary. Yet Nannette had no desire, on principle, to be unhelpful or objectionable. Curiosity moved her, and also a certain amount of respect, even if it was involuntary. For Miss Nakazawa was a reporter, a journalist, a member of the press, and Nannette had an inclination to respect and cooperate with reporters much as one did with the police; for someone of her generation, this was simply a matter of upbringing.

It was primarily from the gossipy pages of papers like *The Hollywood Gazette*, the *L.A. Eye*, and the *Tinsel Town News* that Nannette knew how many times Zsa Zsa had been married, where Lawrence Welk learned to polka, and how fared the children—those little satellites—of the stars. Nannette realized such data were not earth-shattering in importance (alas, Bloom often pointed this out to her), but she valued the knowledge nevertheless. She took pleasure in her expertise, and the new connections she sometimes made while she sat reading the paper on the bench in MacArthur Park, while the ducks quacked and Leonidas rowed by her. Such times provided a reassuring sense of continuity, probably not unlike that which comes to the historian, genealogist, or general researcher.

However, Dawn did not specifically say she was from the *L.A. Eye*; for just maybe she would eventually be able to place an article, or a larger story, elsewhere.

She was asked to take a seat on the sofa, with the blue-green lake sparkling beyond the lamp and window behind her. Nannette was happy at the prospect that her son was finally receiving a bit of publicity, and she said, "What mother does not like to see her own flesh and blood prosper? It would be against nature."

"What is your son's nature?" Dawn went right to the heart of the matter. "I mean, is he lucky for the gamblers as people say, or is it unfounded rumor?"

"A lot of people do think he's lucky for them, I suppose. But luck's all in the mind of the player, you know."

"What do *you* think, Mrs. Bloom? You're his mother. You know him as no one else does or ever will."

This was true, and Nannette liked the way she had put it. "Miss Nakazawa, it's awfully lucky for me that I have a son, and one like Arthur. A lot of women my age have no one, no husband and no children. That's a tragedy. I don't know what I'd do without him."

"You're a strong woman," Dawn said. "I'm sure you could get through anything."

"Why, what an odd thing to say, but thank you. Did you have anything particular in mind?"

Dawn thought the better part of discretion was to shift focus. She asked about Arthur's birth and early childhood, whether there was anything unusual in these stages of life.

"Arthur has a big head, if you hadn't noticed, Miss Nakazawa, and it unfortunately got stuck in the birth canal. Nothing serious but the doctor had to use the tongs. Is this exceptional? I don't think so."

Dawn's tape recorder whirred away. She made a special note in a red pad (one of the ones Bloom had bought her): "Forceps delivery.".

"As a result of this," said Nannette, "I've had varicose veins that hurt me so, you don't want to know about it."

"What I mean to ask, Mrs. Bloom, is whether there were any early signs of this remarkable ability attributed to your son. Did he, for example, express an early interest in, let's say, toy dice? Were his first words the usual 'mama' and 'dada,' or did he gurgle 'roll 'em' or 'I'll see your bet and raise you'? Any things like that from the cradle?"

"No." Nannette chuckled. "An utterly normal child in every way, but very bright."

"Very bright." Dawn thought. "And did his birth result in any special good fortune for you, your husband, your family, or close friends?"

"He brought us joy. That's all. Of course financial and other worries galore, but lots of joy, and that's a kind of good fortune, too, isn't it?"

"Yes." Dawn smiled. "But what about all these big winnings? Did any of this happen to him in places outside of Gardena?"

"Oh, wait a minute here. He doesn't *cause* anybody to win anything," Nannette said. "He's a rabbi, after all, not a magician. He's an ordained Conservative rabbi and he doesn't spend his time beseeching God or whoever for any private individual, not even me. He's old-fashioned traditional, I suppose you'd say, in that he moves through the prayer book every shabbos in Hebrew for himself and those who know, and then in English for the others, but he doesn't get involved in the special-prayer department. The Jews in general do not. He's no reader or advisor like those people who hang signs in their front windows—Reader, Advisor, Tarot, Shmarot. *Vay iz mir!* No, no, no. Special private prayers for good luck or to make a quick buck, for anything like that, do not belong in our faith. I'm no rabbi, but that's a lot of mumbo jumbo Judaism is too sensible to indulge in."

Mother, Dawn wrote down a possible headline, *does not believe in mumbo jumbo.* "Would you say," she continued her inquiry, "that no one benefited materially or got rich as a result of the rabbi's activities?"

"Do I look rich? Miss Nakazawa, my husband was not a well-to-do man most of his life, before and after Arthur. He did do a little betting, of course." Dawn put down her pencil and waited. "But they were small bets on the horses usually, and nobody really won much; he was a union man, the fur trade, and we were all poor people. When Arthur was six months old he was so cute we decided we might make some money and put some aside for his college education, so we found a modeling agency. Nowadays every new parent does this, but in our time we were exceptional. Exceptional and stupid! They took one look at him and said he was cute as can be but he didn't have enough hair. When I think what maybe a little bit more hair could have done for Arthur! He still has the same problem."

"I've noticed," Dawn said. She looked up to see Nannette eyeing her. The rabbi's mother's hands rested in her lap, her white sweater was pulled tightly around her breasts. "I've interviewed him several times, yes."

"Then why don't you ask him these questions? Why *me?*"

"Your perspective is as much a part of the story as what he says.

I intend to speak to others in the congregation as well. Perhaps to you again, if you'll allow me. Because you know, Mrs. Bloom, we live in troubled times now, times of religious turmoil. I think there's a lot of interest in a story like your son's. People want identification with the old established faiths, and at the same time there are all these splinter groups, new religions, sects, cults, new ideas, a whole new fundamentalism, too. It's all so mixed up I'm not sure where your son fits in or how to sort out what's going on here. That's the angle I'm working on."

"You're a regular Japanese Barbara Walters."

Was this a compliment? Dawn was not sure.

"Are you planning to interview my son again soon?" Nannette asked. Dawn heard in Nannette's voice, *Are you going to talk to him again while you wear your bikini right there behind the sanctuary?*

"Yes, I believe I am," came the answer. Then, after a pause, "I'd certainly like to."

"What a fine idea," Nannette said; yet she thought: *Not if I can help it.*

22

That afternoon, the phone rang and it was not the man from Cutty Sark, it was not the Majorska Vodka Distributors, it was Bloom. He wanted to know how the interview had gone, because his mom hadn't even called him yet, and he didn't want to call her; it was a telecommunications stand-off.

"I like your mother very much, Arthur. And I'm a connoisseur of mothers. I think she's full of spunk, but I didn't win her heart. In fact, now that I think about it, maybe she hates my guts."

"That won't happen if I can help it," he said. Then after a pause, "Let's call a recess on the mother wars, okay? I wanted to know if you could come over."

"Of course I can, but when?"

"How about now?"

"I'm working, Arthur. I've got two more hours."

"It'll still be warm enough. Come on. I'm desperate."

"For what, my little rabbi?"

"To swim, to swim. What do you think?"

"I think we're both moths in the flame."

"Well then, fly on over as soon as you can. There's a surprise too, there's something I want to show you."

She found him in his cabana jacket, with his back to her, and his yarmulkah on, reading a large book. She put her hands firmly on his shoulders and paraphrased what she had been reading, "According to Talmud Sanhedrin, the inveterate gambler is considered so unreliable as not to be qualified to give testimony in a court of law. However, the professional gambler, a more serious species, is considered such a parasite that he isn't even allowed to participate in synagogue services. You see, Arthur, these kinds of injunctions verify my own research. Enforced or not, you don't have such strict laws on the books unless you have a serious problem. Historical background, you see, to the saga of the lucky rabbi."

Bloom emitted a slow, genuine, carefully acquired California "Wow."

"Are you reading Talmud Sanhedrin there, too?" she asked.

"I'm afraid it's only the current Yankee yearbook. You're shaming me into spending more hours of serious study."

He saw she was carrying something behind her, and he didn't have to wait long to find out what it was.

"Arthur," she said, "I don't know what's going to happen between us, or, for that matter, what is happening to us right now, so I thought we ought to at least celebrate this moment, for whatever it is. This instant that we can arrest in our friendship, our, I can't stand the word, relationship, our whatever it is we've been doing up to now." She pulled out a bottle from behind her now and handed it to Bloom. "It's to celebrate. It's rice wine, Arthur, the best of my parents' lousy selection of sake. I took the liberty of bringing a corkscrew and two glasses."

As Bloom opened the bottle, he felt her beaming down on him like some great Japanese Statue of Liberty, and he a little tug happily tooting by.

He poured, but Dawn beat him to the toast: "Here's to an excellent interviewee, and to his mother!"

"And here's to a reporter who's made an incredible, remarkable study of the Talmud, and to her mother!"

They drank a glass and toasted their mothers again, and their deceased fathers, and all the quirks of life that seemed to have brought them to this town, this pool deck where they were sitting under the May sun. "You know it is common practice," Dawn said, "that when people do business with each other, they also exchange pleasantries or gifts, that kind of thing, at the end of the project or at Christmas time."

"Sure," said Bloom, "or at Hanukah time." He gestured Dawn over to the small wrought-iron table behind the diving board. "Gift exchanges are part of the professional relationship." He smiled. "I understand that completely, Dawn."

"That's why I wanted us to share the wine—in honor of our good working relationship, Arthur."

"I understand," he said. *"L'chaim,* to life."

"L'kayim," said Dawn.

"Ch," he corrected her. "The efficacy of the toast depends on good Hebrew pronunciation."

She nailed the guttural perfectly, and then said, "To paraphrase JFK, who, I understand, you do quite a bit of quoting from in your sermons, a toast's work depends not on pronunciations, but primarily on the toasters themselves. Here's to you, the lucky rabbi, as people call you. . . ."

"And here's to you," Bloom said quickly, "and the good luck that's brought 'the Japanese doll,' as I've heard you referred to, to me."

They paused in their drinking this toast and looked at each other, and then Dawn said, "I believe I can trust you, Arthur."

"And I have a feeling that I trust you too, very much," he said.

They drank their sake, and when Dawn put her glass down on the table, she noticed the package.

"That's the surprise. That's what I wanted to show you. Open it up."

She extracted from the sheaves of tissue a rectangular box, with a silver base, sides like windows, with a rounded top bearing Hebrew letters. It fit neatly in her hands, and she lifted it up, drawn by the sweet smell. "What's inside, Arthur? Apple blossoms? Magnolia? Linden tree flowers?"

"It's a spice box," he said proudly. "It contains frankincense, cloves, and I don't know what else, and it's supposed to remind you how sweet the sabbath is."

"It is you who are sweet, Rabbi."

"No," Bloom said, "you."

"Come smell it with me." When they were close and had inhaled, she said, "We've had our first gift exchange. We were thinking exactly alike, Arthur."

Bloom was nodding.

"That's a very bad sign." She smiled.

"Very, very bad," Bloom agreed. He pulled two chairs out of the lengthening shadows, and he and Dawn sat. The chairs stood a few feet apart. "Now tell me about my mother," he said.

"I will, if you tell me about mine," she said. She stretched out her long legs and rested her feet atop Bloom's thigh. In her lap, in her hands, she cradled the spice box. She brought it to her face and inhaled deeply. "It's better than drugs, Arthur." She leaned forward and kissed him on the cheek. "Anybody who had a part in making you, I was prepared to like very much." Suddenly she pulled her legs back and was full of thought. The way a notion filled her up like this and animated her intrigued Bloom. "Arthur," she finally said, "do you believe in destiny?"

"Depends what you mean. Hillel said everything's determined, but there's still free will."

"That's very tricky," she said. "What he probably means—is he a rabbi?"

Bloom nodded.

"Is that there's this *illusion* of free will, only he doesn't say it."

"Good for you," Bloom said. "You're very sharp tonight. What kind of brain food did you eat for lunch? Hillel's notion is hard to get—the illusion of free will so vivid that it seems real."

"I'm not sure I get it," she said, "but I'm talking more about something else. I mean here we are in each other's lives, I suppose. And how did it end up this way? I mean I could be married and the mother of two by now and living up in Berkeley; I could be a doctor or a computer scientist, too, I suppose, like my bright cousin up in Seattle; and you could be a holy man, with a beard and those little pigtails behind your ears, living in Jerusalem. But I'm not and you're not. Instead of all the millions and millions of choices we could have made but didn't and all the decisions we made the way we made them, we did, individually, separately, without being aware of one another, whatever was required to bring us here this moment, this instant, with this spice box with Hebrew letters in my one hand, and this bottle of sake on the table between us, and your Yankee yearbook in your lap. Explain it, Arthur. Go ahead and explain it to me. I dare you!"

"I've been planning the whole thing," he said. "I've been making the arrangements for years."

"No, Arthur. Listen, why did you stare at me the way you did from your tube?"

"I suppose for the same reason I'm kind of doing it now." The sun had moved toward setting in the west and was stuck temporarily behind a large whale-shaped cloud over the Pacific. "Tell me why you sat in front of the store all those times? Was that destiny?"

"My destiny at the time was simply to spend a precious little bit of time away from my mom. Oh, Arthur"—she stood up now, looking at the sun mounted like a golden red ball atop the building to the southwest—"I think you're talking to one screwed-up woman."

"You've come to the right place," Bloom said. "Spiritual Lost and Found, my department. What I'm trained for. You teach me to swim, and I'll teach you—"He paused and then looked at her lingeringly. "It *is* unusual, Dawn, to be sitting here and talking this way. I mean listen to the way we're talking with each other after knowing each other for how long? How many weeks? Not two months certainly. You know"—he thought the sake might be playing a role in some of this—"I think it's funny that for some reason I'm thinking about some of my previous pulpits where I had to preside over these funerals and I didn't know the people at all, because the temples were so huge, and I had to act as if I knew the deceased intimately. . . ."

"This reminds you of a funeral, Arthur?"

"No, no, no, it's more like the opposite, a beginning. That's the point. I'm getting to know you, so I don't want to act any smarter than I am. I don't want to be this wise rabbi, see? I'm really as dumb as the next guy about destiny, baseball, sake, you name it."

"Or as wise," she said quietly.

"I'll tell you this, Dawn, you don't strike me as a 'lost soul' at all.

Far from it. You're involved in the family business, you're teaching swimming, right? And you're a free-lance journalist. That seems very *unlost* to me."

"Maybe when I'm with you."

"Well, if necessary," Bloom said, "I'm available for spiritual consultation—day and evening hours. For you, no appointment necessary."

"This is one of the strangest conversations I've ever had in my life," she said. "And you are one of the strangest men."

23

Nervously Nannette added cream and sugar to her coffee, dunked her cinnamon doughnut, and smoked. "Honey," she said to Xiomara, the Silver Dollar's Mexican waitress, "please take this bill, get me a carton of True, and keep the change."

To say that people played their cards close to their vests was, in Gardena, no mere metaphor. Nor was this truer than the evening right before the Memorial Day weekend, during the sixth week of the "affair," as it was now being called, when the informal temple board—the only board there was, consisting of Black Dave, Sarah and Abe, and special guests Nannette and Leonidas—met by arrangement at the coffee shop in the Silver Dollar Casino. The agenda: What to do about the rabbi. Nannette said to her friends assembled, "I've begun chain-smoking again."

"Who hasn't?" said Abe, and no sooner were the words out of his mouth than a Marlboro was in and he had lit his own and Nannette's cigarettes.

"Why," Sarah began, "why is he doing this?"

"Just because I'm his mother"—Nannette puffed—"don't expect me to understand him any better than you."

"You're being coy," said Sarah. "If you don't, who does?"

"You know kids these days," said Leonidas.

"That's it," chimed in Abe. "Even when they're thirty years old, their heads are still scrambled from the dope, the records, the stuff they did when they were younger. They go to the other extreme, becoming vegetarians for a year to cleanse themselves, but it doesn't work; their bodies—and minds—are polluted."

"I want to remind you all"—Nannette drew herself up—"that it's your son, Leo, the cantor, who smokes the marijuana. The rabbi does not smoke marijuana."

"Not on shabbos, anyway." Black Dave smiled. He was perching his bulk on a chair by the aisle.

"Please, Dave." Nannette blew a plume of smoke at him. "You're spreading rumors."

"Are we here to talk about marijuana or Nakazawa?" said Sarah.

"They're both attractions for him."

"We're avoiding," said Sarah. "We're all avoiding this because it's so unpleasant."

"Yes, let's keep avoiding," said Nannette, as the cigarette hung between her lips. "I wish I could make believe it's not happening."

"I'll lay you ten to one it's not a dream," said Dave, but there were no takers.

"He's your son," said Sarah. "You've got to talk to him."

"And tell him what?"

Again they were silent: smoke, drink, cream and sugar, more smoke. Sarah's voice, like a sudden gavel, drew them back: "Tell him to dump her."

"Of course," Nannette said, "but you don't tell him that way. You need to use some psychology."

"Dump what?" said Leonidas. "To dump swimming lessons?"

"He should be learning to swim," said Abe. "It's dangerous with him hanging around the pool so much. That's right."

"You should have heard the rabbi go on yesterday," said Dave. "I was talking to him, and he said that he had learned to float and that he was floating around in the deep water for the first time in his life without that spare tire or some other support."

"You could do without that spare tire of yours, too." Leonidas poked at Dave's belly.

Sarah North decapitated her cigarette in the ashtray and stared the men down: "If any of you think the rabbi is doing anything but breaststroking, you're much more naive than I took you for."

"Sarah!" Nannette yelled.

"Well, someone's got to say it. If we can't say it, we can't stop it."

"He's my son!"

"He's our rabbi."

"You mean," said Leonidas, "he's our jackpot."

"Now we come down to it," said Dave Diamond. "We are winning like mad, and what is there new in the picture? I ask you: What is there new?"

"I've got to tinkle," said Abe North.

"Sit down," said his wife. "How can you leave me here alone with everybody calling me a bad guy?"

"Let him go," said Nannette, "so he won't develop prostate problems and have an accident."

"He's lucky he can go at all," said Leonidas. "Which reminds me —did you hear about the three men who had a peeing problem, and they all decided—"

"Leo," said Nannette. "What's with you men? I've never heard such dirty talk from you all, and at the table."

"You're afraid, you're all afraid." Sarah puffed. "Now who's going to talk to the rabbi?"

But Abe drifted off, and taking their cue from him (after all, he was the president's husband), the others followed. When they saw each other separately during the ensuing days, they all agreed someone ought to talk to the rabbi; they all said they would. But days went by, and then a week, and no one did.

24

Ever since he had won at the racetrack with a horse named Sunup (as in Dawn), Bernie Levitt had found himself spending less and less time at his dealership. Ironically, he was hardly needed there because the cars seemed to be selling themselves. To the amazement of Black Dave—but not of Bernie—the Japanese continued to come in and to buy. Bernie knew that the rabbi's connection with Dawn was somehow at the heart of the flourishing sales, and it was also a key to the good luck at the casinos. But why? What was the precise mechanism? Bernie was less interested in sales and money (although he did not turn these down) than he was in answers. Why, for example, was the good luck being triggered and flowing very strongly his way? He had lots of questions and very few answers, but he had some ideas, some hunches, some clues, and to confirm them he was spending long hours lately at the library of the Academy of Judaism in Hollywood; often arriving when the doors opened and staying until they closed, he pored over the books, especially the kabbalistic ones, those containing the secrets of Jewish mysticism.

His first challenge was to find an answer, or at least a lead to an answer, to the basic question on his mind and half the congregation's: What was there about the rabbi specifically when he was with this Japanese woman that seemed to enhance his powers? For many frustrating days Bernie read, but he sensed he was barking up the wrong kabbalistic tree. He had been thinking that Bloom's comparative celibacy had had something to do with the good luck. Although this surely had been Bloom's history with them up to now, the theory no longer seemed valid. The whole world could see the rabbi was quickly on his way to the termination of that state.

If celibacy was not the key to the good fortune about town, then the next natural place to look was the new factor in the equation, namely, Dawn's being Japanese.

Of course, the way to determine whether Dawn's national origin was the element producing the good luck would, to be scientific, require that Bloom date a Chinese on Monday, an Indonesian on Tuesday, a Mexican, perhaps, on Wednesday, a Russian on Thursday, and so forth. By monitoring the results in the Silver Dollar and the other casinos, one could then determine if her being Japanese was the critical factor. And still questions would remain unanswered: Any Japanese girl, or this one specifically, for example?

Bernie suspected that her being Japanese was a red herring, a bad lead, taking him away from the truth. And yet his methodology required that he eliminate it as a possibility. He spent many long hours on Tuesday and Thursday nights, when the Academy was open, doing his research. He discovered that a Scottish missionary in the 1850s asserted that the Lost Ten Tribes of Israel were the Japanese. Was it possible that the sparks of Dawn and Bloom's affair derived from this? The missionary, named McLeod, had been ridiculed for this idea during his lifetime, and almost no one accepted the notion today; however, a lack of popularity never deterred Bernie

Levitt. Indeed, rejection of ideas often struck him as a positive indication.

He read on voraciously: There were Jews definitely documented as having arrived shortly after the opening of Japan; these were Russian and German itinerants, peddlers, with a stick and a sack, who had struck out on a northerly route. But what of all this? Even if Dawn's ancestral line had touched some Mosaic line a hundred or a hundred fifty years ago, what would be explained? No, a theory was only as good as the results that could be produced, the questions answered.

As Bernie sat poring over the McLeod reports, he realized that the only idea he found really compelling was that some of the *kagones*, the family crests of Japanese clans, had design similarities with the Star of David. This was interesting, but it took the dealer nowhere. A chief reason for his difficulty was a personal belief that McLeod was wrong. For if the Japanese were the Lost Ten Tribes, then how could the African tribes, from which Dave Diamond and other blacks traced their origins, be them as well? Bernie was sympathetic to Dave, knew his salesman considered himself a direct descendant of the tribe of Dan, one of the formerly lost ones, and he preferred to continue to think—indeed he believed—that Dan, Issachar, Zevulon, Gad, Menasseh, and the other tribes that Shalmaneser the Assyrian drove out of Israel, had traveled to the West, not to the Far East. If he accepted even a word of McLeod how could he accept what Dave's recent genealogical researches (which he had given the man plenty of time off to do) confirmed? To accept McLeod, he would have to believe that the tribes at some point split up, saying, You five guys go this way, and you five that, and we'll see you in Gardena, California, in about 2,500 years.

Well, if not celibacy and if not being Japanese, what then? What did she have that had enabled the rabbi to pitch his tent on this great newfound land of luck? Bernie needed some clues.

"Library's closing in fifteen minutes, sir"—the words floated over to him. He checked his watch; it was 8:30.

Yes, he would now need to do some new, more intensive research. He would need, it seemed obvious, to find out just what went on with the rabbi and the Japanese when they were together near the bed and in it. Yes, someone had to do it. A lot was riding on what could be found out.

"Sir?"

"Yes?"

"Library's closing."

Bernie had made his decision: He would have the rabbi tailed regularly and thoroughly whenever he was with Dawn.

25

Ironically, Bloom was relieved Dawn was interviewing him because it now was possible for him to feel somewhat less guilty about his own bulging file on her, which he formally labeled "History of Dawn." Into this manila folder he now placed all his acrostics, his ruminations about her, the data he had been acquiring about her parents and her past, and the ridiculous Hebrew haikus that she was inspiring in him. Beside all this stuff he placed the ancient green spiral notebook that contained the outline and addenda for his life. The pile of material on Dawn now was almost as large as that of his whole previous life. Bloom held the two sheaves in his hand, getting the feel of each, weighing, balancing, like a shopper trying to decide which of two melons to buy.

Now as he tried to understand the strange turns in his life, Bloom also gathered the facts about D. (his formal abbreviation for this long-syllabled and long-limbed woman), sorting, analyzing, imagining episodes of her biography where lacunae gaped, preparing for when he would be called to make his case for her, to himself as well as to all the others:

> D. refers to the early years of her life as per previous incarnations—a strange choice of phrase, no?—and there are many of them. As a young teen she evinces such prowess as a swimmer that her parents, Akira and Ono, enroll her in a pre-Olympic program. (Note: her shoulders and upper body are phenomenally developed and strong for a woman.) D. remembers these years of

her life as if she had spent them entirely in the water,
her lips always slightly blue, her fingers wrinkled.
Remembers being wet all the time, tired, driven,
especially by father, even more so than by coach. To
practice more than the other fledglings, to excel even
beyond the ambitious expectations of coach is Akira's
goal for his daughter. (Note: she often starts talking
about father when she is in water, as if wet triggers
recollections.)

Every morning D. rises at 5 A.M., dresses in silence,
while mother still sleeps, gets into car with Akira and
drives to the pool at Los Angeles High School. (Note:
Your only connection with L.A. High was
Anti-Defamation League conference you attend there in
'81. Worth mentioning?) D. practices for full hour
before the rest of the pre-Olympians arrive.

Chain-smoking his Lucky Strikes, Akira coaches Dawn
during this period; D. refers to this hour of work before
others arrive as the Cruel Time (CT). Overseeing her
five laps, crawl, breast, back, and butterfly, he is like
eagle on patrol, walking the deck as she swims the lanes.
Lap after lap, the CT continues as Akira claps his hands
rhythmically so D. can maintain her pace, not lag behind
or waffle in lane; no letup. If she does, his rage seems
instantly ignited.

(Note: When I told her that her descriptions of her
father at CT remind me of Sesue Hayakawa or Toshiro
Mifune, she said, Are all your images of Japanese from
World War II movies? I'm afraid you're right, I
answered. Then she said, Those images are very
unflattering. To men, yes, I respond, but not necessarily
to women, as there weren't too many war movies
portraying women. Then she said, with a smile, I'm no
Tokyo Rose. No, I answered her, and then she added,
Maybe you should think of me as Gardena Dawn.

(In later conversation, thematically connected to this
one, I confessed to having seen *Back to Bataan* and
Bridge on the River Kwai each three times; *Sands of Iwo
Jima* four times. While she has seen these too, D.
cannot recall the sequence I reprise for her from *Sands*,
in which the Marines are struggling against suicidal
Japanese resistance up the slopes of Mount Suribachi.

The green recruits are, of course, being led by Sergeant
Stryker—John Wayne—who gets them within yards of
the top of the heavily defended mountain when they lose
Private Rosenthal, their joking Bronx Jew. Mortally
wounded, he falls into the arms of the sergeant, and
Duke, having recently boned up on his Hebrew,
administers the "Shema"—Jewish credo of the faith, I
explain to D.—before he dies.)

I imagine D. in those years of the Cruel Time, her
slim shoulders shivering in the cathedral-like pool
building, the cold bumps on her body. As the years go
on, however, Akira is driven more than ever by the
prospect that a child of his, a Nakazawa, might, if
properly trained and ferociously motivated, earn a place
on the American Olympic swimming team. As Dawn's
arms churn the blue of the L.A. High pool, I see Akira
watching the Stars and Stripes through the water. All his
interest is focused on the patch on his daughter's suit.
He must remember the American flag that was also
flying above the Manzanar internment camp, where, says
D., her parents and 1,600 other Japanese-Americans, full
citizens notwithstanding, were sent for two long years.
He must remember and he must vow, too (Note: Jews
can understand this well), that his child will be such an
American, a U.S. Olympic competitor, that, even should
history repeat itself, she would be spared what he has
had to go through. And what could be more American
than being a member of the national Olympic team?
Might the Italians, who also were allied against America,
have been driven to the concentration camps had it not
been for Joe DiMaggio?

Can I stop now, father? D. would ask him, a pleading
thirteen-year-old girl, exhausted and clinging to the wall
of the pool.

Five more, he says, and then do another five after
that. Here is where you have to push, here is where you
build up the reserve for the kick to finish. It is a matter
of seconds, tenths, hundredths of seconds. It is a matter
of never thinking, even for a hundredth, a thousandth of
a second, that you are tired.

Please, father. My arms ache, I can't lift them any
more.

I'll fish you out, daughter. Now swim.

I can't. Her lips must be blue; he can't help but see them in the early-morning light slanting through the high, mullioned windows of the building.

Please, father. Please.

Swim, says Akira. (Note: Here, right through the time warp, I come, in cape and tights, with a big "B" on my chest, for Bloom, to stop him and save my D.)

Somehow D. goes on and with five minutes left before the coach and the others arrive for another hour of racing; in this five minutes of grace Akira pulls her out and wraps her in a thick towel. She wants him to hold her, to cuddle her as she would like to think he did when she was a little girl—but of this she's not even sure —but Akira never does. The Cruel Time (CT) is over.

Again D. has done what her father has asked, and she will do so for many years to come. But Akira is paying a price. Resentment is gradually born in D., cold and then bitter as the first chill of diving into that pool each morning. A little fissure for hate is opening up within her sweetness. She is only thirteen. In another six months to a year, she will begin turning on Akira, again and again.

The swimming will be her first means. And she knows even now, while she struggles daily for the extra laps he extracts from her, she knows that she is going to quit, that she is going to fail, deliberately, in the competition. Yet D. maintains her willingness to practice, to swim the endless laps of the pool because it will add to Akira's hopes and his high expectations, and therefore it will make the disappointment, when it comes, all the sharper. (Note: This strikes me as very Japanese, very formal, symmetrical, ritualistic. As in Bushido, the code of the Samurai. Are the Nakazawas descended from Samurai?)

When D. enters high school, she barely makes the swim team, and then loses her early races. In the second year inexplicably she develops a phobia about the water. A psychologist is called in first from the school, and then an outside specialist. This man, with dark glasses, elbow patches, and many degrees on the wall behind his desk, interviews D., Akira, Ono, and soon puts in a recommendation on the side of D. She should not be

forced because to do so might result in serious emotional
damage. So now it is Akira who is swimming the endless
laps of pleading, of cajoling D., of questioning himself
and his lifetime methods with her, imploring D. to talk
to him, to consider and reconsider. Now it is as if D.
were on the deck of the pool watching her father
struggle in the water; now she is the implacable one, the
granite, and she yields no ground. (Bravo! Bravo! Bravo!)

Result: D. and Akira do not talk to each other for
months; it is the first of many such episodes, with Ono
as the go-between.

D. is through with competition and she emerges from
the pool in her fifteenth year with the first blossomings
of a gorgeous athletic body, with fabulously strong upper
arms, a trim waist, and legs made smooth and shapely
from having flutter-kicked an oceanic distance. Her dark
hair falls now in bangs above the eyebrows, and the eyes
themselves are, I imagine, aglow with liberation. I can
see a touch of red lipstick on the mouth, a screen of
rouge on the cheekbones . . . these are all D.'s face
needs to announce to anyone who sees that here is a
great Japanese-American beauty.

In high school D. is a great hit and is asked to join a
sorority that has never admitted a black or an Oriental
before; D. becomes officer and then is later elected vice
president of the student body. She graduates with A
average and delivers a stirring valedictory address in
which she compares L.A. High to a family, a place of
international friendship; is awarded, and accepts, a
scholarship to the University of California at Berkeley.

As if the four hundred miles separating L.A. and
Berkeley were a kind of diving board, whose northerly
end she is finally able to spring from, D., in college, goes
wild. She takes the whole concept of her Japanese
modesty and demureness, her respect for self, family,
tradition, and peels it off, throwing it on the steps of
Sproul Hall, and, to the background of the Free Speech
Movement, she jumps up and down upon it until it is
unrecognizable.

No bra, no underwear, and tight pants. Lots of eye
makeup and sunglasses both day and night. In her first
semester she gets a little tattoo of a yellow pompom

needled onto outside upper thigh. (Note: Although later
surgically removed, there is a slight discoloration in skin
still detectable below left bow of bikini, which must be
the site.)

Such are the gifts D. brings back to her parents the
first Christmas home from Berkeley. Akira demands that
she withdraw. D. calls him fascist. They cease speaking
to each other for the remainder of the vacation. It is a
cold time (to be distinguished from CT, Cruel Time)
and Dawn spends most of the vacation on the sidewalk
of Sunset Boulevard near Pandora's Box, the nightclub
that is an oasis for bikers, drug dealers, and runaway
children. D.'s own back pocket now frequently bulges,
flauntingly, with a nickel bag of marijuana. Shortly after
she returns to Berkeley, Akira has slight heart attack but
refuses to speak to D. over telephone and does not want
her to visit. Her sense is that the attack is for her, and
he would heal immediately if she were to drop out,
return home; she does not go for the bait.

Back at Berkeley, D. decides to wear tall black boots
with jeans tucked inside, stands with hip flung out,
attracts incredible attention. D. devotes herself during
this period to the study of Marcuse, Fanon, and rock
musicians, particularly performers who are also political
radicals. D.'s innocent, ingenuous face, still discernible
even beneath her double coat of Maybelline, makes her
an ideal carrier for musicians who need drugs transferred
occasionally to Los Angeles; D. happily accepts the
opportunity to help out friends. She will visit parents,
too, now living in Gardena, after drugs are dropped off.

In the fall of her third year in college, with U.S. 395
slick with rain, and the windshield wiper dancing far too
slowly to keep up with the torrent, D. jumps the center
divider, overturns three times, and rolls down an
embankment. Had she not been thrown from the car
before it hit the ditch, she would have died. It turns out
she loses only her scholarship—the police pick up a
pound of hash, two kilos of marijuana, and assorted
amphetamines—and it's also goodbye to the perfect skin
on her belly. The operation required to save D.'s life
leaves a thin but risen scar.

(Note: When I said it looks like she could have had a

baby through there, her answer was, Have you ever thought what it must have been like for Mrs. Caesar, as in cesarean section, to have her little Julius? A section scar, she reminds me, is the other way these days. Not vertical, but a bikini cut along the horizontal. Double Note to Yourself: Watch out, Bloom, for your profound inexperience in such matters is showing.)

D. spends three months at home recuperating, where she and Akira resume talk, rapprochement, as if the nearness of death were the cause. Akira makes sure there are fresh morning glories in D.'s room. (Note: These are still D.'s favorite flower. Is it too soon, too old-fashioned to get some for her?) Ono buys D. some new clothes at a new Japanese-owned department store in L.A. called Seibu, on Miracle Mile. All the clothes are simple and conventional; D. refuses to wear them. Ono plays traditional Japanese music on their phonograph. All very soothing; D. cannot stand it, and requests Country Joe and the Fish. A handful of friends from high school visit, but the Berkeley musicians, those for whom D. has risked and suffers, all but disappear. A friend from Berkeley named Shapiro (need I note, a Jew?), who has heard about the accident, is passing through on his way home to San Diego. He comes to visit and stays longer than either he or D. expect. Shapiro is the first Jew in D.'s life; when D. returns to Berkeley to finish up, she and Shapiro commence dating.

Shapiro is a history major and he has made himself over to look like his hero, Leon Trotsky. The rimless eyeglasses, the penetratingly intense look (which actually reminds D. a little of Akira), the instinct to theorize at the slightest provocation (Note: Do I have same or similar traits?), and the studiously maintained worker look all appeal to D. Shapiro is deeply involved in the Berkeley Students for a Democratic Society, and soon D. too is drawn into poring over Marx, Lenin, Mao.

The last evening D. and Shapiro spend together is the night Robert Kennedy is shot. After that things go crazy, and after things go crazy there is, somehow, graduation. Shapiro is off to Florida for training, then the Venceremos Brigade to Cuba. At this period Dawn is

inexplicably drawn back to the water and begins to swim
at the Berkeley women's gymnasium. She writes Shapiro
that she suddenly does not care about Cuba the way she
thought she did, although she certainly cares about him!
He writes back that personal life must take a back seat
to the waves of history sweeping and tossing them. D.
says that Shapiro felt deeply that we are all victims of
history. Shapiro told D. that he will keep in touch but
the correspondence from the beginning turns out to be
desultory, and he soon disappears from D.'s life. . . .

Bloom put down these papers, all these proofs of his obsessive
ratiocination. Then he picked up his pen, and added: *"Enter Arthur
Bloom?"* And then, *"Who is she, and, for that matter, who am I?"*
and *"My God, is she for me?"*

26

Don't bite off his head, Sarah told herself as she mounted the steps
to the rabbi's house. Be gentle, but at the same time persuasive. Be
understanding without giving the impression of being weak. Be
sympathetic yet firm. Yes, above all, she was thinking as she arrived
on the landing and saw on Bloom's veranda table an anthology of
the Noh plays of Japan, be able to put yourself in his shoes.

Then there he was, suddenly, like on television. "Come in,
Sarah," he said, a greeting full of light. "Come in, Madam President,
and have a seat."

Sarah sat and smoothed her white skirt with her hands. She
hoisted up a wan smile, but she thought to herself, With rabbis like
you, do the Jews need enemies? You're not indispensable. A tragedy
in the making, why don't you . . .

"Is something wrong, Sarah?" And he was back from the kitchen
with a little bamboo tray—was it a gift from the Nakazawa girl?—
and standing in front of her, offering refreshment.

"No," she said. But she thought, Temple president or not, I

should not have accepted this assignment from the board by default, or at least I should have made Abe go along with me. "No, nothing's wrong."

"Your hands are white." Indeed she had been pressing so hard on her knees that blood had drained from her fingers. "I know you and the others must be under a lot of pressure."

Yes, okay, she thought, at least he isn't going to conceal and pussyfoot. He still was the nice honest boy they had hired. So, why, why was this happening? "Shall we discuss it, Rabbi Bloom?" she was finally able to say.

"Oh," said Bloom.

"You can't possibly imagine that we haven't noticed."

"You mean Dawn Nakazawa?"

"I do."

"The young woman we buy the liquor from?"

"I'm not interested—are you?—in talking about *kiddush* wine, Rabbi."

"No, of course not," said Bloom. "She's giving me swimming lessons. It's three years since I'm in California, I have a pool to use, so I thought it's high time I learned to swim."

"She's teaching you to swim?"

"Right. I've already got down holding my breath, and treading water, and floating. Soon we're going to be working on the strokes."

"Rabbi, will you put down that teapot? You're sloshing tea out of it while you talk."

"Is there anything wrong with taking the lessons? I'm grateful for the use of the pool, Sarah. You know that. I don't expect the synagogue, in addition, to underwrite swimming lessons for me." He put the teapot down on the table.

"So you've made your own arrangements for swimming lessons?"

He sat down next to Sarah, close enough, as if to deliver a confidence. "That's right. She's a superlative swimmer. She was even being groomed for the Olympics when she was thirteen or fourteen. And she's patient and knows how to deal with a chicken like me."

"A chicken like you?"

"Well, I am. But she's great, just great. I can float now! If some of the members want lessons, I'm certain she could arrange some time to give them. Senior Citizen swim, sort of. I could look into it if you think there's an interest."

"Oh, there's a lot of interest in *your* swimming lessons, Rabbi Bloom. I can assure you of that."

"Well, Dawn feels a lot of goodwill toward the synagogue. She was particularly grateful for the card she got from us. The condolence card on the death of her father."

"I sent it," said Sarah, with a look over her shoulder. "I happen to have liked her father. He was always very helpful to us and fair; he special-ordered the wine for the synagogue, you know, because they don't have much of a demand here for kosher, but he never charged an outrageous or unreasonable price."

"Yes, she has talked about her father. He was her swimming coach."

"And now she's yours?"

"She's my swimming *teacher.* I don't think I'll ever be good enough to be in need of a coach."

"I can't believe we're dancing around this so," Sarah finally said. "Rabbi, let me put it this way. I, as temple president, am your coach around this synagogue."

Bloom smiled. "That's a nice way to put it. I like that."

"Well," said Sarah, warming to her mission, "I think we have to do some talking about what appears to be more than swimming lessons going on between you and Miss Nakazawa. I assume it's *Miss.*"

Bloom took a deep breath and let it out slowly. "Swimming lessons are swimming lessons," he said. Then he stood and walked across to the chair on the far side of the room and sat down. He crossed a leg and then faced her. "What does it appear to be?"

"More than swimming, Rabbi. There's this"—she pantomimed putting an arm around another person's waist, and then patting, stroking, kissing. "I call that more than simple instruction."

"There's some intimacy involved in teaching swimming," Bloom said from his chair. "It's a hands-on job, I've learned. You have to touch. So what?"

"So what?"

"Yes, 'so what?' Am I not allowed to touch and be touched by the person giving me swimming lessons? Should I learn to swim the way I've learned everything else in my life: by reading a book? I tried that and it didn't work."

"Rabbi Bloom, nobody begrudges you wanting to learn to swim.

The way you're going about it makes for a very bad appearance."

Bloom stood in front of his chair now, paced a little, and extended his arms, a supplication. "And whom do I appear before?"

"Excuse me?"

"If I'm making a bad appearance, it's got to be for somebody. I can't be making a bad appearance for nobody. For the back of the synagogue wall, for the fence, the Toyota, the grass, the trees? Just who's been eavesdropping on what I do?"

"Eavesdropping is no crime, Rabbi."

"Neither is learning to swim."

"This backyard is visible to anybody who looks out the window from the casino. It's visible to anybody walking on the sidewalk. It's—"

"Eavesdropping is a crime, Sarah. It's a violation of privacy, civil rights."

"Look, may I have some more tea, Rabbi?" I will try to be more tactful, she thought. "It's good. What kind is it?"

"Japanese red zinger."

Sarah hastily put down her cup. "Let's not snarl at each other, Rabbi Bloom. We have a good relationship with you, a respectful one since your arrival here, and it's been, I trust, mutually beneficial. You've not gotten rich, and neither have we, but we both have an understanding, I think, that money isn't the most important thing in life. If some of us gamble here perhaps too much, we do it not for money but for gambling's sake, for the pleasure of it, for the way the time goes by so quickly when you need it to go by that way. And you, what are you a rabbi for? I have thought, up to now anyway, you're a rabbi because you enjoy it, just as we enjoy you. But this dating of the girl is of serious concern to us, Rabbi. Serious concern."

Bloom sighed again. He paced in front of Sarah, and then he sat down. "Forgive me if you explained already, but tell me, who is 'us'?"

"The temple board."

"The temple board has not met in years. I don't think anybody even knows who's on it."

"We had no real reason to meet until now. You gave us our reason."

"And, forgive me again," he said, "but it is pretty much standard that the rabbi sits on the temple board. Nobody told me about any meeting."

"Though you're on the board, of course, your presence wasn't needed at the emergency meeting we had."

"And can you tell me what the emergency was, since I was not asked to attend?"

"You are the emergency. And I don't see the point in your being coy about this. Evasiveness does not become you."

"Sarah, please, I do not feel as if I am an emergency to anyone."

"You're involved with this girl, aren't you?"

"I deny your authority to investigate me. I happen to be on the temple board, and any decision taken without my attendance, without my being asked to attend, has, by your very own by-laws, no validity."

"We couldn't very well ask you to attend a meeting to vote on an investigation of yourself."

"That's not my problem."

"I'm impressed, Rabbi Bloom, with your talmudic ability to turn the tables on me. But the problem is not me or the board. The problem is you, and your attitude."

"Swimming lessons are not a problem," said Bloom, and he walked to the door and stood by it.

"Hanky panky with the Japanese girl," said Sarah, "by our spiritual leader, by the rabbi of the congregation, is."

"I'm shocked and dismayed," said Bloom.

"As we are," said Sarah. "But it can end here. It doesn't have to go any further."

"I want to learn to swim."

"So we'll send you to Jack La Lanne," said Sarah. "You want to go to Hawaii and learn to surf? We'll send you there, too. But this . . . this fraternizing looks very bad."

"I like my teacher, Sarah. A good teacher is hard to find."

"Look, Rabbi," Sarah said, and then to herself: Be patient, put yourself in his shoes. "Look, can we agree to disagree for now? Can we discuss this later, can we talk about it like gentlemen?"

"And gentlewomen," Bloom added as he swung the screen door open and stepped outside with her. "Good day, Sarah, and I'm glad you came by."

She went quickly down the steps and did not look back, although Bloom stood there, on the landing, waiting for a final shot. "Thank you, Sarah," he said after her. "I mean that."

But for Bloom, who found that lying made him anxious and then miserable, it had not been a good day at all. Fortunately the night would be far better: for the first time, he was going to the movies with Dawn.

27

Although it was quite unusual for the area, the Gardena Cinema was showing a rerun of *The Yankee and the Geisha*, and they were among the first to arrive for the movie. For four days Bloom had had little chance to be alone with Dawn. Thursday he had had to prepare a review of a Jewish cookbook and then do several other administrative chores that Sarah had asked him to handle. (Bloom well knew that Sarah wanted to keep him busy around the synagogue.) Then preparations for the sabbath occupied him, and then, of course, the sabbath itself. On Saturday night Dawn had a bad cold, she said, and needed to catch up on sleep.

But now she was here, alone with him, and it was soon going to be dark. He put his arm across her shoulders, his ear to hers. Her ears were always wonderfully cool, as if they had just come out of the water. She was wearing a pale gray V-neck sweater that made her breasts look gorgeously supple. "Long ago when I was a lonely person," he said to her, "I used to take the bus to the aviary at the Bronx Zoo. For hours I stood in front of the huge cages watching the long-necked birds wrapping around each other like pretzels. Egrets, pelicans, cormorants, all necking away and in love. It's only a vestige now in us advanced mammals," Bloom went nuzzlingly on, "a lost art of necking, unpracticed, unrefined, unappreciated."

"Except by you," said Dawn.

Bloom looked at her fine intelligent eyes. "I love your neck," he said.

"You may do with it what you will." She extended it toward him. "Neck me."

He began but then pulled back. "Have I ever told you that you inflame me, Dawn Nakazawa? I mean really set me on fire—your neck, your tonsils, all of you."

"Have I ever told you the way you talk makes me want to sleep with you?"

Bloom gulped, he ached, he felt like hacking away the armrest separating him from Dawn. Then the lights dimmed, the music came on, and they sunk into their seats. Hands on adjacent thighs, they watched John Wayne aboard Admiral Perry's ship entering Yokohama harbor: It is a brilliant day, with a last trace of winter breeze moving on the spring air and shaking the ratlines of Wayne's ship. Yes, as the schooner slowly glides toward the rocky island, Wayne is posed heroically beside one of the ship's sixteen-pounders, in pea coat and cap like the Old Spice sailor. Above the fluttering ensigns and signal flags, the Stars and Stripes is proudly waving; everything seems perfect.

Yet, it's very quiet, perhaps too quiet. The Oriental is inscrutable; the water in this serene harbor may soon turn red, a bloodbath, an ambush. But wait! Now the harbor is beginning to fill up with junks, sampans, young boys on pieces of driftwood paddling up and waving to Wayne. A whole Japanese flotilla is coming out to welcome the *ha-ka-jin*, the white men!

The sailors break into applause as the small boats near. Hardtack and rice biscuits fill the air, the first Japanese-American gift exchange! The Americans are slapping each other on the back; a reluctant gunner extinguishes the fuse on his cannon. All will be well; ahead lie hot baths, massages, tea ceremonies, cherry blossoms.

At the dock, as the ropes are thrown out, Wayne surveys the small fishing village. Already in his eye there is a prescient twinkle; he knows that from these humble rustic shores—a century and two world wars hence—Toyotas, Hondas, TVs, cameras, stereos, VCRs and precision dental drills will arise. And in parks yet to be laid out, American lawyers will stroll with their children and their Akitas.

Now the head shogun bows welcome.

Wayne, that inimitable linguist, never at a loss for words, bows in return. *"Arigato, arigato!"*

"What's that whispering?" Dawn suddenly asked Bloom.

Turning together toward the back, they saw the theater had filled up. Bloom twisted in his seat, but saw only featureless heads in the darkness. He did not see, a dozen rows behind, a large container of popcorn propped on the top of a seat and the face of Dave Diamond peeking out.

"Nothing," Bloom whispered to Dawn. "Absolutely nothing."

They resumed their necking. Their hands circled around. Bloom said, "May I rest my nose upon your nape?" Dawn bent her head forward so Bloom could apply himself. Then she looked toward him, and raised her mouth to Bloom's mouth and parted her lips slightly. He felt so grateful he began to feel very weepy in the darkness. Dawn sensed his tears and daubed them away with her tongue. Copying his mentor in love, Bloom swooped down upon Dawn's face and lips. He tried to kiss every part of her face, to touch every pore. "My darling," he said, "my darling Dawn."

Saying his *excuse mes* as quietly and effectively as he could, Dave got up and moved closer by six rows. He sat now, leaned forward, and beheld a wonderful sight, as Bloom and Dawn ardently kissed: the rabbi was drawing her close to him, turning her head with his face, exploring her, making catlike noises—Dave thought he might almost be hearing them—as he kissed Dawn again and again, the passionate spelunker of her ear.

"Tongues around each other," the sexton said softly to himself, "tongues around each other like snakes around the caduceus. Go!"

"Oh Arthur, oh Arthur!" she whispered.

"More Frenching," Dave urged. "More kisses, deep kisses," he whispered. "Now show God praise and thanks, Rabbi, for inventing the mouth!"

"Will you shut up?" It was a woman's voice from the seat behind Dave. He obliged and moved away, even closer to Arthur and Dawn.

"Why are you crying, Arthur?"

"For you," he said.

"For us, Arthur? I think I understand. I'm crying too. For us."

"Us," they said, their lips on each other's, forming the sound.

"Deep again, kids, make it a good deep one," Dave cheered them quietly on. "Yes."

Bloom suddenly stopped and looked behind. Dave lowered himself into the seat, the popcorn up, his chin pressed on his tie knot.

"The movie's this way," said Dawn. "Is something wrong?"

On the screen, John Wayne had just won the hearts of the Japanese. He was burning the laundry at the geisha house, thus preventing the spread of the cholera epidemic throughout Kanagawa Prefecture. Now he's waiting, dressed in a flowing kimono, about to finish up the negotiation of the first trade agreement, which will bring Japanese silk to America. And following the silk will come issei immigrants—among them Dawn's grandparents—to mow the lawns from San Francisco to Los Angeles.

Dave, who had seen enough, now hurried back up the far aisle toward the lobby.

Dawn raised her mouth to Bloom's again and entered his, a perfect dive that left Bloom breathless. When he opened his eyes Dawn was curled on the seat beside him, her head on his shoulder; the credits were on the screen.

Bloom looked around again, but he saw no one he recognized.

28

From the Gardena Cinema, Dave walkie-talkied Lucy Leonard at the Silver Dollar, who had carried the signal into the casino: namely that the rabbi was just at that moment engaged in a fantastic French kiss. Abe North and Elsie Brody, who happened to be at the jacks-or-better table, proceeded to win practically every hand. This lasted for perhaps a quarter of an hour, and then the luck again seemed to trail off as suddenly as it had appeared. While the others were content to count their winnings, Bernie lucubrated. Why such good fortune? And what to make of the timing? Was the lesson of this French kiss that you could conceivably lay a bet down at the precise moment that the rabbi's passion was peaking, and if you hit it just right, your winnings could go through the roof, along with the rabbi's . . . Now, wait, Bernie said to himself. Have they done it yet? Have they had intercourse? And, if not, the potential was wild! Absolutely wild, and Bernie was not thinking of money alone. He was by no means even convinced that the key to the rabbi's success was sex and rabbinical sensuality and its timing. Bernie sensed that this view might be too inherently limited, because there was just far more to know. He had to get closer to the rabbi, and to Dawn. He had to know not the aftermath of the rabbi's star performance but its ascendance.

The next day Bernie had Dave close the showroom early and called a meeting at the casino with Ethel, Lulu, and a few others who were particularly benefiting from their insights into the rabbi's new connection. Bernie chose not to share his thinking with them, but instead to suggest that together they set up a special fund—for the purpose of charity. It was something Bernie had long been wanting to do anyway, but until now there was no financial base for it. The resources of the fund would come from a tithe, a Biblical tithe, of ten percent of all earnings, where the earnings were attributable to the influence of the rabbi. At this meeting, the others followed Bernie's lead, kicking in several thousand to underwrite the initial gifts: In the name of the synagogue, it was decided, charitable contributions would soon be made to the seminary in New York; to the United Jewish Appeal for trees in Israel; to Ethiopian Jewish relief; to aid for Soviet Jewish émigrés; to the poor of Jerusalem; to the United Way.

Bernie's aim was not only altruism. He also wanted to placate Sarah North—no easy task these days—and also to please the rabbi. In fact the last thing in the world Bernie Levitt wanted to do now was to anger him, to offend the very source itself. He felt he couldn't tell the rabbi any of his hunches, his surmises, which, with research, were fast becoming far more certain; no, it was too soon to do that. But it was not too soon for such gestures as this fund represented.

"What if I got him to kiss me?" said Lulu, as the meeting broke up.

"What?" Bernie was not sure he had heard her correctly.

"What if I corner him, say, next shabbos, and just throw my arms around him and kiss him up but good, and we set it up so that I do this when you're all playing in a rich game, and—"

"No." Bernie rose and cut her off. "If you kiss him like that, you can kiss everything goodbye. Let's get this straight: the rabbi is not to be attacked; he is not to be exploited, pawed, done the usual things to; he is not to be used without consultation with me. There's a lot you all don't know about him. He's a precious irreplaceable resource. Understood? Now, don't blow it."

29

RABBI IS RABBI-T'S FOOT FOR HIS CONGREGATION

by Dawn Nakazawa

Three years ago when Rabbi Arthur Bloom came to Temple Elijah in Gardena, California, the congregation had fallen on hard times. Membership in the small Conservative synagogue had been declining steadily, sabbath services were being held only intermittently, the roof leaked badly in the rear of the sanctuary, and there was no money to fix it.

"There was a real danger," said David Diamond, an official of the synagogue, "that we would have to close down for a while—maybe even for good."

All of this was reversed, however, with the arrival of the New York–born spiritual leader. In a matter of months, the membership decline was stopped, people who had not attended a sabbath service in years began to drift back in, and thereafter to come regularly.

"Even the roof stopped leaking," testified Abraham North, a vice president of the congregation, "when Arthur joined us. The rabbi used to joke," North went on, "that he climbed up on the roof with hammer and shingles and did the job himself when no one was looking. But we know better. The rabbi isn't handy, he's just plain lucky."

Said Ethel Axelrod, a long-time member of the congregation, "The rabbi's arrival was like a little miracle for us. We stopped losing and started winning."

Axelrod is referring to a unique feature of this synagogue, which is located in the heart of Gardena's casino district: Many of the congregants are regular gamblers. She is not alone in her assertion that Rabbi Bloom's appearance in Gardena has somehow turned the wheel of fortune in favor of those who pray with him.

"The rabbi does not whisper magic words," said Mrs. Nannette Bloom, the rabbi's mother and a respected member of the congregation. "Nor does he use any mumbo jumbo during services. Our services are strictly according to tradition," said Mrs. Bloom.

What is not according to Jewish tradition—or most religious traditions for that matter—is gambling, and heavy gambling as is often the case among synagogue members, and particularly on the sabbath. "The rabbi does not condemn or preach against one of the most beloved pastimes of his congregation," said Ralph Ackerman, another old-timer at the synagogue. "You're not supposed to drive on the sabbath either," Ackerman went on, "but it's done everywhere all across America."

"If this congregation is lucky," said Abe North, who is also the husband of the congregation's president, "it's in that the rabbi has a broad tolerance and acceptance of us as we are. It's a rare gift."

But does the rabbi actually help his parishioners win at poker? "It's just a feeling," said Lucy Leonard. "The congregation feels very affectionately toward Rabbi Bloom and he returns that feeling. If you feel good and have a strong spiritual life, it can't but help your concentration so you draw better cards and play smart."

30

Bloom entered the store brandishing the paper up high for Dawn to see.

"This is a business," said Ono, with an irritated glance at Dawn, who was working the register. A customer turned to see Bloom loudly rustling the pages of the *Eye.* Since Bloom had planted himself in the middle of the store and seemed to be waiting there with a determination whose object was clearly to speak to her daughter, Ono slipped behind the counter and took over. "I am very unhappy about this," she said to Dawn. "Make it very short, please."

Excused, Dawn walked through the beaded curtain into the office. Bloom followed behind, reading headlines aloud: " 'Richard Gere Owns Harem/Proof: Howard Hughes Alive 150 Years Ago/Woman Born in Elevator, Gives Birth in Parking Lot'—and now for the *pièce de résistance,* " Bloom said sardonically, " 'Rabbi is Rabbi-t's

Foot for His Congregation'! Really, Dawn, you owe me an explanation."

"Come on and be fair, Arthur." She took the paper from him. "There's also a feature on sky diving and drunk drivers. It's not all bad."

"But you said the *L.A. Times*. I was expecting the *Times* or something like it."

"You wanted the *Times* and you thought the *Times* and you thought I said I wrote for the *Times*, but I never did say that, Arthur. I said I used to work at the *Times*. I said I'm free-lance now. I'm a stringer for the *Eye*. Why are you looking at me that way, Arthur? I never led you on to think I was writing for the *Wall Street Journal* or for *Commentary*."

"All that talking, all that interviewing, the tour of the synagogue, all your conversations with my mother, with Dave, with . . . all for this and in here?" He held the paper up, reluctantly, by the edges. "You should have told me *where*," and he said the word so loudly that Ono came running through the curtain shouting at him in Japanese and then at Dawn in clipped and hissing whispers.

"What did she say?" Bloom asked.

"A loose translation would be 'Zip it, you ear-breaker.' My mother, if you hadn't noticed, is often very direct. You really shouldn't have come running over like gangbusters. It's only an article, an innocent little article, and I think you come off very nicely."

"Then why do I feel humiliated by the whole thing?"

"Arthur," she said quietly, "if you feel that way, you can join my mother's company; she feels humiliated as well."

"Let's make a distinction." Bloom was very serious. "She might be upset her daughter is working for this rag—yes, I can understand that—but she's not the subject of an article. I am. Me, my congregation, my life."

"Oh Arthur, it's not as if you'd been defamed, libeled, publicly pilloried, or deliberately embarrassed. It's a crummy newspaper, it's a picture newspaper—I don't deny that—for a lot of people who can't read, but it's also a kick. If you think I didn't do your article with a lot of care, then I'm sorry. I'm very sorry."

Bloom was pacing now in the small office, Dawn watching him, sympathetic but on guard. "If you had only told me," he said, leafing through it again, "then maybe I might have been a little prepared. Of course it's not the end of the world, but it's just such a surprise."

She reached out, found his arm, and reeled him in to her a little. When he was standing beside her, so that her presence was speaking, as well as her words, she said, "After I told you I was writing an article, I was so relieved you weren't angry at that, I dropped it there. Leave well enough alone, I thought. I guess I never mentioned to you where the article was going to appear. And, yes, if this was a deception, a little one, I'm sorry, and I admit it. But it is a sin of omission only. I thought you might be upset, and I didn't want that; and you see I wasn't far wrong."

He sat down in her swivel chair. "Is this where you work?" Bloom asked. "Is this where the evil deeds of journalism are perpetrated?"

"That's my Arthur."

"But don't think I'm not upset," he quickly added. "I'd talk to my lawyer . . . if I had one."

"They've been sued by people richer and even more famous than the Rabbi of Gardena. The legal department is bigger than editorial."

"This sheet requires an editorial department?"

"That's below the belt and it's ad hominem, too. I happen to be learning a thing or two in the editorial department."

"Can't you learn elsewhere?" There was a note of pleading in Bloom's voice; it was deliberately there, for he preferred to plead than to be angry with her. "You can work for the temple newsletter," he said. "I'm the editor. I'll publish you."

"I've seen your newsletter, Arthur, gathering dust in the foyer on top of your display case. Your last issue was about two years ago."

"So we'll become more frequent!"

"You're a sweet man, Arthur."

"I can't buy you off?"

"If you were the *L.A. Times* or the *Washington Post*, maybe, but not the *Temple Elijah Examiner*, or whatever it is. Arthur, listen, I couldn't think of where else to send the articles; anyway, I am working for the *Eye*. It won't always be this way, I hope, but for now it's my only outlet." She was happy to see the first indentation of a smile on his face. Now she could ask him what was really on her mind. "Are you upset, Arthur, at what I wrote, or just where it appeared? Isn't that a valid distinction?"

He surprised her by completely ignoring the question. He had found another issue of the *Eye* on her desk, picked it up, and with amusement finally tipping the balance against scorn in his voice, he read the headlines: 'Dr. Says You Can Now Lose Weight by New Anti-Fat Breathing Techniques Even While You Gorge Yourself.' "

"I don't write those," she said. "Granted it's not the greatest paper in the world, but you'll notice, Arthur, my piece sticks to the facts as I determined them, to the quotations as I took them down, word for word. I challenge you to tell me I'm concocting, making things up. Of course there's the paper's wild editorial slant that they try to give to everything, but I took a lot of pains to make sure I stuck to what your president, sexton, and the others told me, and that it would come through the editorial process and be printed. I'm the principled one on staff, the *Eye*'s intellectual."

"Somehow that's not as reassuring as I'd like."

"It would be a worse paper without me."

"I can't argue with you on that; just don't do a lot of this journalistic social work at my expense."

"I take pains with everything I write about you, okay? I really do. Don't you become a pain about this, Rabbi Bloom."

"Please don't 'Rabbi Bloom' me. Is this our first argument? Our first real one?"

"I think so," she said, "and I'd like it to be over with as quickly as possible. Will you oblige me?"

He looked through some more pages: " 'Colonel Sanders Reincarnated as Chicken/Could Elvis Be Elected President Today?' " He began to chuckle. He read a few more out loud: " 'An Elephant Stepped on Me and I Survived/Fireflies Can Ignite Your Lawn.' " He finally sat down, laughing so hard his stomach hurt.

"I find it a kick too."

"But is it good for the Jews?" He giggled, and she began to laugh aloud, too.

"You want something else to laugh about?" she said to him as he sat limply in his chair. "You're a three-part series at least, Rabbi. Maybe more. The type is being set on one right now."

Bloom stopped laughing. "But why more? Can't we minimize the damage?"

"Arthur, darling, it's not damage, it's a story, it's journalism, it's the truth trying to come out even in the pages of this pillar of the press."

"It's a kookie kongregation," he spelled the k's for her. "Don't blow it out of proportion, Dawn."

"I thought I hadn't," and she returned closer to him to sit on the corner of the desk near the chair, a kind of rapprochement.

He threw the *Eye* back on the desk, decisively. "Okay." He stood up and faced her squarely. "Please, one small favor? Don't write about my being a rabbit's foot again. Okay?" Then he told her about "parishioners." "Priests, ministers have them; rabbis do not."

"And what *do* rabbis have?" she asked.

Bloom thought a moment and replied, "This rabbi has Frieda and Ethel, Bernie and Eli, Sam and Meyer, Dave and Lulu, and Isaac Flutterman."

"How you like them," she said, smiling at Bloom. "How you do like them! Chin up, Rabbi. Remember, I also like them, and I like you, too."

"In your arms today," he said dolefully, "in your typewriter tomorrow. I guess it could be worse."

"An awful lot worse, Arthur. It could be—" She could not finish, nor could Bloom stay a minute more, because Ono, fuming, was pulling Dawn back through the curtain. On his way out through the store Bloom saw the counter thronged with customers and Dawn doing her smiling best to wait on them. He said good night to her, but she was far too busy even to hear.

31

Lulu Fineberg sauntered over to Dave's table in the casino coffee shop and sat down without being invited. A halo of smoke surrounded her face. Dave crinkled his eyes in greeting and kept on chewing. "You look like a big black bull, Dave, just chomping away at his cud."

"It happens to be steak," he said, "and it's quite lousy, thanks."

"Well, I'm here," said Lulu, "as requested. Tell me what's on your mind, as if I didn't know."

"I'm thinking very practical, Lulu." He put down his fork and said, "I'm thinking tatamis, kimonos, rice lanterns, and those shades for bulbs. I'm thinking fans, bonsai trees, little purty parasols, twelve varieties of tea, teapots, chopsticks, and an assortment of rice. The works."

"You want me to check you into the mental hospital, David, or you got next of kin you're still on talking terms with?"

"Lulu, honey, you're making fun of the mind that's about to feed you. This could be your opportunity of a lifetime to make some bucks, and I don't mean in this abattoir for bank accounts either. Honey, don't you see what's surfacing here?"

"Yeah, from the looks of it, probably your meal."

"I predict," Dave went on imperturbably, "that we are soon going to have in town a wave of, what do you call it, Japanese-love, Japanese-a-philia, unprecedented in the history of Gardena. The Japs are swamping the dealership, something is going on here that's drawing them like ants to sweets. Now I'm figuring as soon as the whites pick up on this, they're going to want to start Japanese-a-fying themselves, and you and I, Lulu, are going to help them do it."

"I'm feeling poor and hungry just listening to you."

"Heap your calumny high, sister, but facts is facts: As soon as more people begin picking up on this liaison of the rabbi's, they'll all want to hop right into their kimonos and twirl their parasols and fan themselves with those cheap paper fans—you probably can get a dozen wholesale for three dollars and sell them for fifteen—and I'm telling you the place is going to go nuts, and it's an investment opportunity we can get in on early. Lulu, are you with me, honey?"

She was eyeing his baked potato. "May I mooch?"

"Sure, go on. But listen: I am talking about getting our orders in soon, because this crap probably has to come from Little Tokyo via who knows where."

"Probably Hong Kong," she said, with her mouth full.

"I'm talking Japanese, as in Nakazawa, honey. Not Chinese."

"What kind of businessman are you being, Dave? Everybody knows all that stuff comes from Taiwan or Hong Kong, even the Japanese stuff."

"The Japanese stuff comes from the Japanese. Anyway, it's not worth arguing about because the important thing is to pull together a bundle and invest it. I figure we start on the street with tables up and down the boulevard. We get the teenagers to do the selling for us while we do the supplying. We pay top dollar to these kids, you see, at least a buck more an hour than they can get at McDonald's, and we steal the crème de la crème of them Egg McMuffin makers. I know one boy already who'd be happy to hawk for us. All I got to do is give him the word."

"Get the merchandise first, Dave. May I have that garlic bread, too?"

"What's with you tonight, Lulu? Got a tapeworm or something? Anyway, as I was saying, I figure we set up a table in front of the synagogue, one in front of the liquor store, and a couple more here and there at strategic points on the boulevard. I'll keep the stuff at the lot—Bernie won't mind—and I'll resupply the tables between customers, run it over in the car."

"Dave, I've got to hand it to you," Lulu said. She was standing beside him, mopping his gravy with the heel of the garlic bread. "You have it all worked out, don't you?"

"I do."

"Everything except one thing, the most important thing. You saw the girl! She interviewed you! And didn't you see what she was wearing? She don't wear any of that stuff, Dave. No fans, kimonos, or those funny soft thongs. She wears pumps and T-shirts and sneakers. She's as American as apple pie."

"I never thought of that," said Dave.

"Speaking of apple pie, what do you say you buy me some dessert before I faint dead away?"

But Dave, having wiped his mouth with his napkin, was already handing his check and cash to the cashier.

32

The strange phone call came to Dawn when she was sitting at the stringers' desk at the *Eye*. She had just finished knocking off one of several pieces of filler the editor had her working on:

CALIFORNIANS GOBBLE UP 50 ACRES OF MEXICAN FOOD A DAY

In one day Californians consume 38 football fields of Mexican fare—some 2.178 million square feet of enchiladas, burritos, and tacos, according to *American Stomach* magazine.

The voice was low and husky and vaguely familiar, but she could not place it. "You're it, Miss Nakazawa, you're really it." She thought the caller was deliberately disguising his voice, but it was a man. "You're it," he repeated. "You are absolutely on target. Bullseye. Every word you've written about the rabbi, and what you've done."

"Who is this?"

"I'm a source."

"For what?"

"A source for you."

"And what is you want to tell me?"

"That you and the rabbi are quite a pair. You're really it as far as he's concerned."

"You've already said that. Who are you?"

"I want to tell you that even more important than what you write is what you do."

"I don't understand."

"I'll put it this way. When you touch him, it seems as if the sun comes out."

"Arthur, is this some kind of sick joke? Is this you?"

"When you put your arm around him," the voice went on, "the Dealer trembles. That's Dealer with a capital D."

"Just who the Hell are you? That's with a capital H!"

"I can see why the rabbi likes you so much, Miss Nakazawa. Now who can say what will happen when you two get serious! Goodbye, Miss Nakazawa. Sayonara and goodbye."

33

Although Bloom now expected the temple's entire board to descend upon him, his mother arrived instead. "This place is a dump," said Nannette when she entered her son's apartment. Actually it wasn't such a terrible mess, but she said so anyway, because she felt very nervous about her task and thought a critical remark might somehow sustain her. "Aren't you embarrassed to bring a strange girl here?"

Bloom ignored this and tried to clean up. There were books, as usual, everywhere, but Bloom never considered books, no matter where they ended up or how, as elements of a mess; to the contrary, by the nature of their contents, they lent order, even if they were on the floor, under the bed, or piled high on the toilet tank. Still, it was his mother who was visiting him, and he cleaned up.

His sink was piled high with dishes, and the two closets, revealing the messy thrift shop of his wardrobe, were also gaping wide. He scurried to close them, and this did improve the room.

"Does Sarah have a woman come in here to clean once a week? She used to, I know," Nannette asked him.

"Yes, she still does that along with the laundry privileges, but I'm not sure how long it's going to go on. I think she's angry with me."

"I can't imagine why. May I sit somewhere?"

"Sure, I'm sorry." Indeed every single seat was covered with books. There were Japanese anthologies, there was *One Hundred Poems from the Japanese*, there were small paperbacks that swam across the vast rectangular seas of the volumes of Talmud. In the different books that he had pulled out from the bookcase for his sermon work, many socks lurked, red ones, black, yellow, green; these were his bookmarks.

As she sat down next to volume sixteen of the Talmud, with a blue sock marking a page, she said, "Isn't this disrespectful, Arthur? Sacrilege to throw your laundry inside holy books?"

"It's a bad habit, for sure," admitted Bloom. "But there's actually a system to it, and it helps me work. The red socks are for flagging important points, ones usable for sermons, that I can go back to. The yellow is for a major point, but one that has no direct bearing on anything I'm working on at the moment. And the blue is for interesting items, but ones that are ultimately trivial or somehow nonessential. I find it works."

"Couldn't you use a piece of paper like a normal person?" She touched the toe of one of her son's markers. "Are they at least clean?"

"Absolutely," said Bloom.

"You know, Arthur," she said as she settled in and lit a cigarette, "you're lucky you're not married. Your wife would not know what to think, and I would be embarrassed. She would assume your mother didn't raise you right to see the mess you live in."

"You raised me just fine, mom. I'll take all the responsibility for the mess."

"Really, Arthur! Your father, may he rest in peace, would not like to see the way you put *shmattes* in your books. Find another system."

Bloom came over to her and sat down on the rug next to her chair. He could see she was keeping up a front. She had clasped and unclasped her purse twice and had taken nothing out. She was smiling, but she was very tense. Now the purse again. "What are you looking for, mom?"

"I'm looking for an explanation, son." She lit another cigarette.

"What do you mean?" Bloom fudged. "I'm doing fine. I'm happy. Who's asking? Cousin Harry in the Bronx?"

"No, not Harry, but people here. My friends. Your friends, too."

"I don't get it." Alas, Bloom, a child of the televising of Watergate, was stonewalling his own mother. Silence was his friend. In silence there was no dissent, and in no spoken dissent there was refuge. If Sir Thomas More could use it with Henry the Eighth, surely he could try the same trick with his mom. He took her hand. He felt only a desire to be nice to her and not to hurt her. If lying is what it would take, so be it: "She's interviewing me, mom. She's a friend I've made. She's a reporter. You know that. She's talked to you, too. And you didn't even tell me!"

"And why should I? Maybe I never thought for a moment it was mere interviewing alone but I didn't want to bring myself to butt in, like I'm doing now. Maybe I hoped you would come to your senses all on your own. You're a grown man, after all. But you obviously haven't, and here I am."

"I feel I have my senses about me, mom."

"So tell me then, Mr. Senses, what does she have that's so wonderful, that another girl, a Jewish girl, doesn't have? Let me be honest with you, son. You know books, but I think maybe this girl has a lot more experience of the world than you do."

"Is that so bad?" he answered her. "She's a reporter. She's worked for the *L.A. Times,* too. Sure, she's been around. She's mature."

"And why aren't you? If you were mature, you wouldn't be doing this."

"What do you mean by 'this'?"

"Don't make me say it, Arthur. Don't make me spell it out. I just want you to stop it. You're a rabbi, so stop it, and that's the end to this discussion. You're my son and I'm your mother. I'm asking you to stop it and I'm not talking about interviews!"

Bloom stood up now and gathered his books off the couch, slipped on his thongs—he had been barefoot when she arrived—and turned back to Nannette. "This is not New York, mom. This is California, Southern California. This is Gardena. This is a synagogue where we practically have slot machines in the entranceway to the shul. This is a place where things are done . . . well, differently, and nobody in the three years since I've been here has so much as batted an eye. Now, suddenly everybody is noticing everything. I'm not completely blind. But I'm entitled to learn how to swim and I'm entitled to be interviewed by an attractive reporter without it being made into a federal case."

"Swimming, interviewing! Please, Arthur. You're beating around the bush."

"I've been beating around the burning bush my whole professional life. I am not your conventional rabbi, and you, of all people, know it."

"Even an unconventional rabbi, a highly unconventional rabbi, does not date a Japanese girl. It just is not done."

He went and sat down beside her again. "I don't want to make you miserable, mom, but I'm thirty-seven years old, and for the first time in a long while I'm happy. I go to bed at night happy and I also wake up in the morning happy. Your son is happy, and I'd like to be able to think that my happiness makes you happy, too."

Nannette stood up. "I never knew," she said at the door, "that so much happiness could come from learning to swim." She left him there and the screen door slapped behind her. "And interviews."

Bloom listened to his mother's steps receding, and then a different, clickier sound as they hit on the asphalt of the driveway. He stood for a moment in the apartment, in the sanctuary of his chaos, and looked around. Then suddenly, quickly, one by one, he ripped the socks—the yellow, red, and blue ones—out of each book of Jewish laws and customs, out of each biography and homiletical collection, and hurled them across the room.

34

"Angelos, do me and all of us a favor," Bloom was saying to his cantor poolside, "please don't give our favorite journalist a blow-by-blow account of all your cantorial successes—okay?" Bloom was thinking, specifically, of Panuzzi's stint as assistant cantor at a temple in Bel Air. All the congregants were TV and movie personalities, executives from the studios, talent scouts. Panuzzi should have known better, but he sensed an opportunity and was carried away with his own enthusiasm. He got it into his head that he should introduce to the services new instruments and radically different new melodies. One evening he accompanied himself during Friday night services on the lute, another evening he brought in a tambourine; so far so good. It was a liberal group, he felt, and it seemed to Panuzzi they were enjoying themselves. But he carried things too far.

He hit on an idea that he figured, with this congregation, might even open a few show business doors for himself. He chose Hanukah to introduce his new image, as a kind of hootenanny cantor who was going to enhance this year's services during the Festival of Lights with some songs by Bob Dylan, Peter, Paul, and Mary, and the Weavers. Without preparing the congregation for it, Panuzzi embroidered "If I Had a Hammer" throughout the Hanukah services; it appeared everywhere, at every ceremony he officiated at, as a kind of unofficial theme.

But the congregation did not like it one bit and told him to stop.

"Maccabee means hammer," Panuzzi defended himself, "hammerhead. Musically, thematically, it's right for the occasion."

"Listen, hammerhead," said the temple president, "if you bring an amplified electric guitar in again and blast away on it, you're out. This is a house of God, not the 'Gong Show.'"

Panuzzi lasted two more months but then was fired.

"Well, what do you think of them?" he was asking now, arranging sections of the Sunday paper about him—sports, leisure, the books, and there among them were also some issues of the *Eye*. Panuzzi didn't like a lot of sunlight on his skin and now lay one of Dawn's articles across his chest. "This is something!" he said as he closed his eyes, head turning toward the sun.

"What?" Bloom was dangling his feet in the shallow water.

"The exposé, Solomon. Dawn's rendition of life at Temple Elijah."

"I've told her what I think, and now I'm not going to say any more to her, or to you. Done is done. I think she's doing as good a job as she can, within the strictures of the place where she works. There's still freedom of the press in this country, last I checked. Or so she reminded me. Anyway, she has a right—it's her career. So let her do it."

Panuzzi was impressed. Dawn was turning out to be as formidable as he had had a hunch she might. He folded up the *Eye* and a copy of the *Times* and now covered the pale skin of his legs with an article on how a supposedly chic Washington, D.C., restaurateur had been serving his patrons for years with Cornish hens that turned out actually to be local street pigeons he'd shot with an air gun. The cantor let out a sun-induced yawn, and said, "There's some news, Arthur, not great news, that I thought you might want to hear. Actually I don't know if you want to hear it, but you should."

Bloom, who had climbed into his tube, neared the cantor at a leisurely paddle. "Try me."

"Oh, just rumors, at the vague soundings stage, whiffs on the breeze, but still you should know, Arthur. Some people are getting quite upset, man. More upset than they show."

"About me?"

"Of course about you. It's not about me. God knows I wish *I* were doing something outrageous, too. I'm such a well-behaved boy lately I can't believe it."

"I'm not oblivious. What makes you think I'm not aware that people are upset? Why shouldn't they be upset? Being upset is part of human nature. I'm preparing to deal with everything, Angelos. I'm going to turn this all into an educational project."

"Before you launch the curriculum, old pal, are you aware that the idea is afloat that maybe the temple needs a new rabbi? One who is more in keeping with traditional ways, with you know, blah, blah, and blah?"

Bloom stopped paddling and brought his hands up onto the tire, where he rested them. No, he had not guessed this, and he said, "I do have a contract, in case you didn't know."

"Don't tell me. I'm not the culprit."

"Who is, then?"

"Just rumors, Arthur. I think my father dropped it to me so that I would tell you, for your benefit. I hope it isn't true."

"They'll never get another person like me in this place." Bloom paddled around again, buoyed by a rare rush of self-confidence. "Never."

"That's the point. They don't want anyone like you."

"What else?"

"If there were anything else, I'd tell you, wouldn't I?"

Bloom regretted his accusatory tone. He knew very well that Angelos and his father were very much on his side. If getting people to accept Dawn Nakazawa were a campaign Bloom was, deliberately or inadvertently, launched on, then the Panuzzis, and in particular Angelos, were his reconnaissance battalion. Bloom was grateful Dawn had not come between them.

"No question," said Panuzzi, shifting on the chaise, "that you have done something drastic. Ninety-five percent of the people surveyed agree."

"Right," said Bloom.

"But, Arthur, don't you think that maybe you're pushing it just a little? Maybe flaunting it more than you have to? You're not even making much of an effort to hide any more. You're supposed to be at least a little ashamed."

"And what do I have to be ashamed of?"

"A full eighty percent of those surveyed feel that contrition is in order. Murderers, you know, are supposed to express contrition and remorse for their act before they can be paroled."

"And what crime have I committed?" Bloom was getting a little hot.

"First of all, pal, it's the crime of the sudden and the unexpected. Nobody knows what to make of it. People don't like change, especially when it's so sudden. See it from their point of view, too, a little."

"I think about the congregation always. Night and day, Angelos, I am thinking about them. I think about my mother and Sarah. I think about the seminary and what they would think. I think about all of Jewish history stroking its long beard and looking at me over my shoulder. Rest assured, I do my share of thinking of the way others see me."

"Seriously, Arthur. The voice you are hearing is a friend's."

"Sure, I know that." Bloom felt himself drifting, in more than one sense. "Just remind people that I've got a contract and if necessary I can also get a lawyer."

"Don't argue with me. In fact, my advice is don't argue with anyone. Consider what they say—no? What's there to lose, right? Only, let me see, your happiness, your career, your future, your life —all easily replaceable."

"I don't think you missed anything," said Bloom.

35

Late that night there was a knock on Bloom's door. The screen was rattling. His eyes were closed, but instead of sleeping his brain was whirling: What would she write next? It had to be one in the morning, and yet he felt oddly rested; perhaps he *had* slept. And what about that possible replacement for him that Panuzzi had mentioned? Was he already en route? What a mess I am in, Bloom thought. The knock sounded again. Perhaps this is the new rabbi already tapping at my *mezuzah*. He pulled on his robe, smoothed his hair, and went out to open the door. There she was, standing before him, as if his thoughts had somehow summoned her over at the precise moment he was thinking that he had gone too far and perhaps should stop seeing her.

Dawn's expression was disarming and without guile. Bloom felt a great, if temporary, relief at seeing her there, as if her physical presence were substantial enough to stifle his troubled thoughts. "Dawn, my journalist," he said, "please come in."

"You were thinking about me," she said as she entered. He put his hands on her cheeks and moved toward her mouth. "I can tell you were. You're nervous. You were thinking about the differences between us."

Bloom's fears arose again, but he fought them off. "I am always thinking of you. But it's the middle of the night," he said. "Are you okay?"

"True investigative reporters never sleep," she answered. "I was thinking, Arthur, about all we have in common. I believe I've come over to check it out." Then she took his hands and held them both to her lips.

My God, Bloom thought, I'm really in for it now.

"Oh yes," she said quietly.

"Did I say something?" He wasn't aware that he had.

"You murmured 'No,' with these," she said, touching his lips. They're going to fire me for sure, Bloom thought. "But I say 'Yes,'" Dawn whispered to him now. She was looking at him very intently. "Oh yes, oh yes, oh yes." Then she paused. "Did I ever tell you how much I like these hands of yours? That I've been thinking about them since that first afternoon when you came over to the store and gave me the list. That's when I saw your hands and I knew I liked them. I said to myself, Those are hands I would not mind on me. Arthur, you've been accusing me lately of not telling you things. So, now hear this, darling. I want to be very much understood: I think I've come over here to seduce you."

Bloom's heart ascended to his throat. "As part of your investigation?" He swallowed hard. "Would you be here if I weren't a story for you, too?"

She kissed his hands, her face bent into them, as if she were hiding in his palms. "A man's hands are where most of the contact with a woman is. I wonder how many men appreciate that. I think you appreciate it, Arthur. Arthur?"

"Yes?"

"Will flattery get me anywhere tonight?"

"Just talk to me," said Bloom. Standing beside her, still dressed only in his robe, without shirt or underwear, he felt suddenly vulnerable and embarrassed. "I'll just go put some clothes on. You make yourself at home."

"Oh, no need to put clothes on," she said. "Please come back here just as you are and give another of those kisses."

Bloom stopped at the threshold of the bedroom and reapproached her. She was wearing her heels and so he stood on his tiptoes.

"I haven't shaved today. I hope I won't scratch you."

"Oh my little rabbi," she said, sliding from her shoes, "I love it when you scratch me." His heart did a somersault and he thought, If I am to to be fired anyway . . . "Let me feel your cheek."

He sat down then in the stuffed chair and drew her onto his lap. "Are you going to publish any of this? The way we kiss?"

"Would you prefer the sports section?" She kissed him long and beautifully. "That one," she smiled, "deserves the front page."

"Don't take this the wrong way, but I've been thinking about what's happening between us and I feel, well, I have to ask you something ridiculous. I know it's ridiculous, but I want to get it out. It's these surprises of yours—at least that's the way it seems to me —are they part of some design of yours, some web you're spinning to get me in, and . . ."

"So that I can eat you," she said, placing her mock-clenched teeth near his face, nibbling. "I'm used to compliments from you, Arthur. I thrive on them, I need them, and now you're telling me I'm a spider?" She raised her arms menacingly above him. "A horrible arachnid."

"Listen, Dawn, what I'm trying to say is that one of the pitfalls of being so modern, you know, so contemporary, is that we tend to discount all the truths, or at least the paths to truth, in the old myths and folk wisdoms." He tried to tell her how the concept of dybbuks probably derived from some Greek text of Plato or Aristotle on the transmigration of souls.

"I'm not sure I follow you," she said—but she understood enough to get up and sit down, away from him on the windowsill. "A dybbuk is a sort of devil, as you describe it, right?"

"Yes, you could say that."

Their eyes were locked into each other. "Arthur, do you want to know if I'm a devil? Is that it? Some kind of Japanese devil?"

"I wouldn't put it quite that way, Dawn, but what's happening is so sudden, I sometimes feel overwhelmed and carried away by it all, in the grip of this force I'm totally unfamiliar with.

"What force?"

"You," said Bloom. "You're so beautiful and I'm, well, the way I am, and I haven't had a girlfriend in years and I've never been in love. Ever! Then you come along and I have to pinch my cheek to tell myself I'm awake. And here you are tonight! So I wonder sometimes, like now, whether there's this additional element here, some alchemy, or force generated by you. . . ."

"Arthur, a dybbuk? A devil within me? RABBI OF TEMPLE ELIJAH" —she mimed the typing of an article—"IS BELIEVER IN DEVILTRY. Nonsense, Arthur. But this isn't"—and slowly she began unbuttoning her blouse.

"What's going on?" said Bloom.

"You know perfectly well," she said, standing before him. "Don't worry, Arthur. I know it's been a very long time for you. But don't worry." She smiled. "You know what I think? I think you're just very nervous"—there were now just two buttons still buttoned on her blouse—"and sometimes your erudition—your devils and dybbuks and your transmigration of souls and all that—is a way you cope with it." (There was one button left now.) "It's the way your mind stammers when confronted with a new situation. And this is new for you, I know." (No buttons.) "So just relax."

"What's going on?" He gulped.

Her blouse came off, her top jean snap unsnapped. "Arthur, you have just asked one of the great rhetorical questions of all time!"

"I think I need help," Bloom said.

"I know," she answered. "That's what I'm here for. We're friends, Arthur. That's the first thing to remember. Friends are gentle with each other, and thoughtful."

"Yes."

"I think tonight I am the rabbi," she said, "and you are the flock."

"I'm in your hands," he said.

"I long to be in yours, Arthur." She crossed the room now, her arms over her golden breasts, and lowered Bloom's shade. Then she strode back and stood in front of him. "That moment has arrived, sir. Your devil awaits you!"

"I look forward," he felt himself growing, as he watched her jeans inch down over her hips, "with great pleasure to examining you for a tail."

He put his hands on Dawn's hips and excitedly rotated her around, when she stopped him. She put her finger into the air, mimicking one of his pedagogical mannerisms, and standing there, tan and glowingly naked but for her bra and underpants, she lectured him. "Examine me, Arthur, only if I can examine your scalp, while we're at it, for horns. Doesn't it say somewhere in the Bible that Moses had horns, cute little ones, growing up out of his curly hair?"

Struggling with a massive erection, he lectured her back, "How can you believe that stuff! Surely you can't!"

"My tail for your horns, a fair trade." Now her underpants came off.

"Anyway," said Bloom—it was one of the great moments of intellectual foreplay—"it's all a very unfortunate mistranslation. Here, let me show you." He walked across the room to get his Bible, badly concealing his intense excitement, which protruded from his robe as he walked, like a long piece of lumber being pulled down the highway, a red flag flying at the end. "The Hebrew word, here, look, is really 'beams of light,' perhaps conically shaped, but surely not horns. Not little devilish horns. For God's sake, Dawn! Saint Jerome made lots of errors when he translated the Bible from the Greek— not the original Hebrew—and the poor Jews had to suffer from them for generations."

Like a Miss America contestant in the swimsuit competition— but having oddly forgotten her swimsuit—Dawn strode about the room with incredible, brilliant, and naked audacity. "But obviously, Arthur, the Jews are not entirely free of myths themselves, ones which *you* obviously still find credible."

"Did I ever say dybbuks had tails, real physical tails? That's something you suggested. Words you put in my mouth. If I may point it out, the Jews are just as nongraphic about their notion of devils as they are about God."

"Take your robe off, please, Arthur."

"Devils with tails," he went on, "and cloven feet! Why, that's all a lot of Christian hocus pocus. Dybbuk isn't like that, Dawn. Not the kind I'm talking about. I'm talking about a power, something elemental, not anthropomorphic, rather a disembodied voice, an urging that grabs you . . ."

"I'm going to grab you by your urging." She laughed, and lunged for him.

"Cripes," he sidestepped her and raced around the bed, laughing aloud as he went.

"Let's both take two giant steps," she said, "and meet in the middle of the room, with no more chasing, and see what happens."

There, at the spot where they arrived according to Dawn's instructions, they fell to the floor and kissed. "You see how comfortable I am with you, Arthur? How completely open and at ease?"

Then she turned around, controlling the rise and fall of his desire like an engineer a reservoir. "My only tail, Arthur, is my coccyx, the bone at the base of the spine. You see it there, my roly-poly rabbi?"

"Yes, God, I see it."

Four hours later, after first light, Dawn heard a scraping and then what she thought might be quick footsteps on the balcony and stairs. Someone is cleaning was her first thought. Cleaning the balcony, stairs, deck. But it was quite early for workmen to be at it. She was reluctant to get up. But someone was there. Yes, there was the scraping again, but it seemed to trail off, like a receding echo in her sleep, and Dawn dozed.

Bloom's voice awoke her, a mumbling of words in his sleep, individually coherent words, but which added up to no sense. "You know, Arthur," she said quietly to the ceiling, "to imply that a Japanese is devilish and, let's face it, that's what you were suggesting, that's exactly what was said about us during World War Two. What does it feel like to have just slept with the Yellow Peril? To have made love with the inscrutable stereotype herself? I'm a little disappointed, Arthur. You'll pardon me for saying so, but a Jew, especially a rabbi, should know better."

She was not sure Bloom had heard her, and in a way she hoped he had not. Suddenly she wondered if now was the time to mention that mysterious phone call. "Arthur, are you there? Are you awake?"

He said nothing, and he did nothing, except reach up, pull her toward him under the covers, and make love to her once again.

36

The *Zohar* was the key! There Bernie Levitt had finally found the Nakazawa connection. First there was the swimming, then the hand-holding, then the kiss in the aisle of the five-and-dime; then the French kiss at the movies, and now yesterday's night of love, at last! At each instance, the sexuality of the rabbi and the Japanese seemed to coincide with a rich opening into the mysteries of randomness and the secret order of chance. Each time, when he could get to the casino, or Dave Diamond or Lucy had been able to go for him, or another friend, there had been serious winnings. Why were the rabbi's natural powers being so magnified through concupiscence with Miss Nakazawa? And what would be the effect of intercourse between the rabbi and a mythical Miss Stern, or a Miss Christianson, or a Miss Kwan, or even a Miss Murasaki?

Bernie's head was buzzing as he descended into the library of the Academy of Judaism, after having spent an hour on the Nautilus machines. He sat at the tables with his wiry hands palms down on the cool wood, and the *Sefer ha Zohar*, the source of Jewish mysticism, open before him. It was powerful stuff indeed, and he began his readings for the day with careful, paced concentration. Only after having exercised, lifted weights, and then showered and taken a sauna did he feel up to facing this book. He felt he needed to match it strength for strength, for it contained, he now was beginning to understand, a blueprint for the universe. What Bernie looked for was confirmation of what he was launched on, he and Rabbi Bloom.

According to the kabbala, the universe was created when the *Ein-Sof,* the light without end, contracted a little, resulting in a small point of space where the nine *kelim,* or vessels, absorbed the original light left behind from the *zimzum,* this world-creating contraction.

"*Zimzum,*" Bernie said softly to himself. Then he pulled in his stomach very tight: contraction, hardness. He closed his eyes and tried to imagine the great galactic contractions. "*Zimzum, zimzum, zim—*"

"Sir," said a voice suddenly above his right shoulder. "Sir?" Bernie beheld the librarian, his finger crossing his lips.

Bernie sat up straight in his chair; he was doing anything *but* dozing; never had he been more awake.

Of the nine vessels, the *kelim*, six shattered from the pressure and intensity of infinity's light. This second awesome phase of creation, the explosion of vessels, was, then, a cosmic calamity of the first order. The world as we know it was a result, therefore, not of creativity and light but a kind of cosmic spasm, a glitch in the darkness. Bernie knew this only too well; anyone who read the daily newspaper with his eyes wide open did, too. Bernie felt close to it now.

As the vessels broke, certain shards, known as *klipot*, rained down, but each in its place, following, despite the chaos, a divine order; these shards make up the gross material, the physical world. Thus the world as we live in it, know, and experience it, is a ruin, a disaster still quaking in the aftershock of indescribable destruction. In short, the world is a place desperately in need of repair.

No warranty, said Bernie to himself.

His excitement was growing. It was no wonder that a man was supposed to be over forty, married, and well versed in Torah before he was allowed to read the *Zohar*. One had to have the maturity to handle fire. *Zimzum*, breaking of *kelim*, and now the blessed repair work!

Bernie ran his hands over his face, as if to wash up with cold water. He sent his right hand up to reposition the yarmulkah that had slipped too far back on his head. Restoration, known as *Tikun*, or repairing the damages, and particularly the points of breakage, this was the next phase. The most effective means of restoration, he read on, derived from special shards, which contained the traces of the original light that had pierced and broken them. It was this light, the hope of restoration, that might be used as the glue to bond together the weaker light to the stronger, thus creating new constructions which are able to restore the universe to its original state. And what is that? Bernie felt breathless when he read: It was the perfection in the mind of God.

Bonding, coupling, known as *Zivug*, was the way to bring about this universal reconstruction job. He read on, picking his way through quotation after quotation, until he realized that what he was reading, the entire description, was a highly detailed architectural drawing for this very instant of consciousness and every other instant, and, furthermore, that what was going on was not apart from God but within the mind of God Himself.

While the outer world restores itself very slowly—which was why from generation to generation oppression and disaster for Jews and everyone else seemed to continue in spite of individuals' best efforts —the restoration of the inner world was another matter. This inner world is, alas, the only one that man, in his diminutiveness, can really have influence over. And here, now, at the bottom of page 478, Bernie came across what he had been looking for all along. *Zivug*, coupling! Through the activity of man and woman—and what activity might they be speaking about, however disguised, except sex?— the female waters grow turbulent, so that, like a cosmic wave, supernatural couplings occur, which will tickle, arouse, prod, and create the outward *Tikun*, restoration of the universe.

Bernie looked up now at the room he sat in. He saw a table where three students were working, he saw a clerk now sliding a large volume off onto the book cart, and directly across he saw two young men, probably rabbinical students. All these people, if properly coupled, could be the ignition wires, the mechanism for the return of the world to its lost perfection.

Female waters! Of course, waters! And, of course, who now spent so much of his time in the water, and who was, Bernie had heard, a swimmer of prodigious talent? Bloom and Nakazawa! It was no accident, he decided then, no happenstance that these two had been brought to couple together. *Zivug.* No luck at work here, but some fantastic design, a plan, an order, which he now, for the first time, had gotten to the heart of after all these weeks of study. This was only a hint, but a tremendously pregnant hint. Did the rabbi realize any of this? Had he any notion how much was at stake? If I told him, Bernie wondered, would he laugh in my face?

Zivug, coupling, sex! Bernie felt his heart nudge his ribs, he felt too excited to be sitting here in the chair, and he quickly stood, lifted the book up from the table, and placed it, as much surface of the cover as he could, against his heart. The contact seemed to calm him.

I absolutely need to know each time they're making love, he thought. I need to know that moment, that point of connection. *Zimzum*, the breaking of vessels, and then *Tikun, Tikun Olam*, the restoration of the world.

Bernie placed the book carefully on the librarian's desk and went out of his way to thank the man. "You wouldn't have a copy of this that I could borrow, would you?" he asked. No, there was only this, a reference copy. It was just as well, thought Bernie. If he took the book with him, he would not be able to put it down. If he took it with him, he knew he would not be able to work; he would spend so much time studying the text. No, it was a bad idea, and yet, he asked, "You wouldn't know of a bookstore where I might be able to buy a copy, in paper perhaps?"

The librarian answered by writing out the name and address of a store on a small card. Bernie took it and left the library.

He stepped out onto Sunset Boulevard and immediately looked down, away from the light of the sun that leaped off every car and made the grains of mica in the sidewalk glitter.

"*Zimzum*," he said. The contraction of the *Ein-Sof*, infinite light. He put on his sunglasses, eased his car into the gentle traffic, and headed for Gardena.

37

While he sat in his study adjacent to the sanctuary, Bloom heard a stir, a hubbub that was very unusual for the quiet precincts of the shul. He stood, put down the prayer book, and then nervously picked it up again and went toward the lobby. He was sure one of the congregants had dropped with a sudden heart attack, but no. The crowd of people parted as Bloom approached them, and there, beyond a knot of staring congregants, stood Dawn Nakazawa.

She was in a lush black velveteen skirt, with matching jacket, and a crisp high-neck white blouse. She was dressed with perfect beauty and discretion for the sabbath.

Bloom was surprised, enchanted, worried. His first thought was pure fantasy: Their superlative lovemaking had magically made Dawn yearn to become a Jew. It had been so good, here she was eager to *daven* and bone up on her Hebrew.

Then he realized, of course, he should already have asked her to

come to the synagogue formally; he should have introduced her on
the dais:

> Here, ladies and gentlemen, is my friend, my swimming
> instructor, our neighbor and supplier from across the
> street, and last, but certainly not least, the reporter who
> has penned the article all of us have read with such
> interest. Ladies and gentlemen, may I hear a polite
> sabbath greeting for Miss Dawn Nakazawa!

Yes, Bloom thought, it might have defused everything, or, he
thought, as he clasped the *siddur* to his chest, it would have immediately gotten him fired.

Hardly had he greeted her, however, when a man in a gray suit
whom Bloom did not recognize worked his way through the throng
and stood between Bloom and Dawn. He had tired eyes with brows
like black awnings about to fall. "What do you say, Rabbi?" he said,
his shoulders squared with Bloom's, a deliberate obstacle in the
path. "Should I play tonight? Whaddaya think? A little advice,
please?"

"Who are you?" Bloom said.

"A Jew. Who are you?"

"I don't think I recognize you, sir, but I will give you this advice:
Go home, because you don't look well."

"That's because I'm losing, Rabbi." The man grasped Bloom's
hand.

"All the more reason to stop. You'll lose more," Bloom said as he
looked over the fellow's shoulder. Dawn was watching them intently.
"You really should just go home."

The tired man dropped the rabbi's hand, and Bloom's cuff link,
shaken loose, fell off. The man dropped to the floor, ahead of two
others beside him, and scooped it up. He held it out in front of him,
examining the brass cuff link covetously as if he had found a priceless
jewel.

Bloom tried to sidestep the man, to go to Dawn, but the man with
his cuff link solidly prevented his first step. "Could I, Rabbi?
Please?"

"Could you what?" The fellow brandished his find, and Bloom
realized now what the man had in mind. "It was a gift from my

mother." Bloom leaned forward and spoke earnestly. "It has value, sentiment for me. I'm sure you understand."

But the man seemed only more determined. "I'm losing awful badly, Rabbi. Please, would you mind terribly? I could return it soon, when I get a good run. Rabbi?"

The man was lowering his eyes, bowing his head. Bloom was embarrassed by his deference. "Oh take it, take it," Bloom finally said, "for all the good it will do you, but you don't need any talisman," he said, as the man left the lobby, bound for the casino. "You need to sleep tonight!"

As soon as the man had left, the congregants stood staring and Bloom said to them, "Well, what do the rest of you want? The other cuff link?"

They laughed a little, and nervously continued to mill about, pretending to carry on their own conversations as they watched to see what was about to take place between the rabbi and his stunning Japanese.

Bloom had an impulse to lead Dawn into his study then, where he had come from, but he fought this urge because he didn't want to fuel the gossip any more. He led Dawn to an unpeopled alcove, the space between the box of yarmulkahs and the water fountain. "May I have one of these?" She reached into the box.

"Men wear them, Dawn. Not women." She tried it on anyway. "As usual," he whispered to her, "it looks fantastic on you, but everyone's watching."

"That's okay." She smiled. "Look, there's Bessie Preskin, and, yes, hi there," Dawn said to Adolph Gruen and to someone Bloom himself didn't even recognize. "I've talked to a good number of these people, Arthur. It's beginning to feel like home."

If a single word out of her mouth could provide him with a sense of elation, that was it: home. "That's absolutely great," he said. "But really, darling, these surprise visits create such a condition here I wonder if we'll be able to settle down and have services."

"Who was that guy?" she asked. "The one with the cuff-link fetish."

"I have no idea."

"I wanted to see you in action, Arthur, in your natural habitat, and I guess I did. Would you say this is a typical sabbath? Was that man typical?"

"There's nothing typical about it. Look around." Indeed the congregants were still eyeing them intently. What did they want him to do, Bloom wondered. Kiss her right then and there? How Bloom wished that time would suddenly race ahead and this uncomfortable moment would pass, and the sabbath service would be over and he could plant upon her face the world's most wonderful, tender wish for a peaceful sabbath to be spent, so dearly desired, once again in her arms. But all Bloom could get out, while he squeezed her hand, was a wistful *"Oy vay."*

She touched his shoulder and stepped back from someone passing near. When she did so, Bloom was able to discern Bernie Levitt among the new arrivals.

Bernie stopped and gave Bloom a handshake and Dawn a queer little bow, a sort of deferential nod in their direction. Here suddenly were Abe North and Sarah, too. Abe was wearing a bow tie tonight, and Sarah was in the purple ranch dress. But when she saw Dawn, Sarah veered away from her husband and off into the sabbath crowd now filing in through the sanctuary door. Now Black Dave lumbered over to them. "Hey, babe," he said, "how's the apple of the *Eye?*"

"Great, Dave. Thank you."

Then, without so much as considering the hour, or the place, the sexton leaned down and kissed her. "Shabbat shalom, honey. And same to you, Rabbi," he said cheerily to Bloom, "only I ain't kissing you!" His hand swallowed Bloom's in a big healthy grip. "I got to tell him about the new article, Miss Nakazawa, do you mind?"

"Does she mind what?" Bloom asked.

"No, don't," she answered Dave. "Let it be a surprise."

Then they all entered the sanctuary for the beginning of the service.

38

Bloom read the typescript of the article Dawn gave him the next day as if he were reading a last will and testament—his own:

DRIVE N DAVEN
America's First Drive-In Synagogue

by Dawn Nakazawa

The Jewish people have endured a lot throughout their 5,000-year history, but they soon may be facing one of their most peculiar trials yet as the opportunity nears, for the first time, to consecrate a former drive-in movie theater as a synagogue.

The idea—Drive N Daven (the Jewish word for praying) —is percolating at a small Conservative synagogue in Gardena, California—Temple Elijah. An official of the synagogue, David Diamond, recently said in an interview the congregation was discussing the rental, with an option to buy, of the defunct El Camino Real Drive-In movie theater at the intersection of Imperial Highway and Casino Boulevard.

According to Diamond, the plan would proceed to the next stage only if the expected increase in membership at Temple Elijah comes to pass.

Recently the temple has reported a dramatic influx of new members. The temple's rabbi, Arthur Bloom, is reputed to impart good fortune to worshippers. "We may soon run out of space in the shul [synagogue]," Diamond said, "and then off we go to the movies!" Zoning regulations prohibit expansion on the present site.

Drive N Daven is not so unprecedented an idea as it may at first seem. For years synagogues in the Southland have been renting additional space in halls and often also in traditional movie theaters for the spillover crowds, particularly on the Jewish High Holidays.

"Technically speaking," said Rabbi Bloom of Temple Elijah, "there is no prohibition in Jewish law against having a synagogue without a roof."

"The big hitch," said Diamond, who is the *gabbai*, or sexton, of the congregation, "is that, strictly speaking, an observant Jew should not drive on the sabbath. Historically, driving has been considered work by rabbinical authorities, and work is prohibited on the sabbath. But everybody knows," Mr. Diamond went on, "that if people didn't drive to them, the synagogues across America would be empty. So why not come right out into the open about it? That, to me, is part of the appeal of Drive N Daven."

Commenting on this issue, the synagogue's cantor, Angelos Panuzzi, said, "The Orthodox Jewish authorities strictly forbid sabbath driving. The Reform movement accepts it, and the Conservative movement, to which our synagogue belongs, just hopes and looks the other way."

If Drive N Daven comes to pass, it will indeed pose a whole tangle of questions for which Jewish law may have no precedent. Will automobile-bound worshippers, for example, be asked to stand as pedestrian worshippers now are at significant junctures during the service? Will worshippers be able to open doors, get out, get back in, and close doors at least a half dozen times during the course of prayers without becoming upset? And all that noisy slamming of doors! Can an alternative method of showing respect be found? And what about electrically operated speakers hung on car doors? Would these be permitted on the sabbath as well?

Said David Diamond, "Our rabbi will be studying these questions much more and will be in touch with the right authorities before a decision can be reached." In principle Rabbi Bloom is in favor of innovations that bring people to the synagogue and into a relationship with God.

Although Christianity has long had drive-in facilities, they are new to Judaism.

America's first drive-in church was established in Portobello, Ohio, just outside of Cleveland, in 1961. Recently the congregation sold the site, which has now been converted to a miniature golf course attracting families with young children from throughout Cuyahoga County.

39

"Surprise, Arthur! It's April Fool in June! We didn't publish it!"
"Thank God!"
"The editors loved it, though. I had to beg them for it back."

In his relief, Bloom's arms went around her and he was soon carrying her from room to room trumpeting the Torah processional: *Etz chaim hee, l'ma achazikim bo, v'tomchehaw, meushar.* . . . You're the tree of life, Miss Nakazawa, and all who cling to you and support you shall be enriched."

"Quite a compliment, sir, to be compared to your Torah."

He finally set her down on the edge of the bed, and in seconds his fantasy unfurled: "You were in shul. You saw what happens next in the Torah service, did you not, dear, if you really were a Torah?" Dawn shook her head. "Well, we carefully lay you out," he explained, "just like this."

"Arthur," she said, "oh Arthur!"

"I'm just demonstrating. And now we undo this velvet ribbon right here, the ribbon that binds the two halves of your scroll, see? Now we unfurl you, like this, and we take the pointer, the silver reading pointer, place it upon your gorgeous text at the spot marked . . . here, and. . . ." Bloom's head was spinning with excitement, and sacrilege.

"Arthur, you look a little piqued. You want to rest?" She was lying beneath him and he was about to answer *Yes, with you, my darling,* but she stood up suddenly and went into the bathroom, and he heard her peeing.

"I pinned the article to the wall above the tank. Do you see?" he said through the closed door.

When she returned, she asked if the article really bothered him as much as he was letting on. "Do you really see a contradiction between what is just an exaggerated example of adapting to our contemporary culture and the maintenance of eternal Jewish values?"

Bloom thought for a long time. Actually he was looking at her standing there in his room, the two of them alone, she having posed one of the questions around which his entire professional life was organized—and he had to cope with this question now, while he was experiencing a definitely non-philosophical erection? "Speaking of eternal Jewish values, can we talk about converting you—again?"

"Really, Arthur! Some men feel an obligation to marry after they sleep with you. You obviously feel this obligation to convert me. What's uppermost in my mind now is actually my stomach. I'm hungry . . ."

"I know a kosher deli where they make the best pastrami on rye."

"Come on, Arthur. Cut it out!"

"I'm very hungry," he softly said. "For you."

"Later." She kissed him. "But now, in honor of your grappling with such issues, in honor, furthermore, of America's great drive-in synagogue movement, we are now going to drive to L.A. and go to Dolores's Drive-In Restaurant and have some of those delicious fries."

"Not kosher," he said, "but, yes, delicious."

"You call your cantor—I promised we'd take him along, for his helpful interviews, and I'll go get the van."

She was flying, but stopped at the door and said, "My treat, Arthur, because you're such a good sport."

He stood there and said, with his best rabbinical histrionics, "There is only one person in the world who could write this, refuse to be my Torah, take me for French fries, and live another day. And I'm looking at her right now."

But while he called Panuzzi, tried to locate his safari jacket, and washed his face in cold water, he puzzled: Why should a rabbi, who is about to eat thick, crusty french fries from Dolores's—fries that are cooked in lard—and who is also probably going to take a nibble of Dawn's cheeseburger as well, and who has also just slept with this staggering Oriental beauty, why should such a rabbi have any trouble whatsoever with the idea of a drive-in synagogue? But he did, he really did. Was it a matter only of degree or was there a particular line you crossed, a violation you committed, maybe without even being fully aware of it, whose effects were simply irreversible?

Bloom took his *siddur* from the dresser and began to pray. It was neither the morning service nor the afternoon service. He just leafed through the book, free-lance praying, the various Hebrew paragraphs, like snapshots in a well-thumbed album, bringing back to him moments of deep feeling during a religious summer at camp; the kaddish he had said for his father at age nine, even though he had by law—because he wasn't thirteen—not been required to recite it; the morning prayer that always scared him and which to this day he skipped: I bow in thanks before you, Lord, Living King, who has, with great mercy, returned my soul to me in the morning.

He heard them honking for him now, and from the persistence of it, he knew it must be Panuzzi at the wheel; for his cantor had for a long time been wanting to drive Dawn's van.

Vay iz mir, he thought as he flicked off the light and went downstairs.

40

The sabbath after Dawn had appeared, the synagogue was thronged by people in expectation of seeing her again. Bloom and Panuzzi, who usually presided over about thirty people, now beheld a crowd in excess of one hundred. But size was only one of several remarkable qualities of this assembly. As Bloom chanted the sabbath blessing and surveyed his flock, he saw Ethel Axelrod sitting in the front row in a full-dress kimono. Every few rows, it seemed, there was at least one person—usually a woman—displaying a trace of Oriental fashion in her outfit; he spied a bamboo parasol leaning against an armrest in the middle aisle; Shirley Bloomfield sat holding a fan with, Bloom thought, Buddhist temples on it; there were scarves decorated with snow-capped mountains and cranes on several gray heads in the first row, right below his podium.

"All that's missing," Panuzzi whispered to Bloom, as they met center stage and turned, bowing toward the Holy Ark, "is the empress herself."

"I wish she *were* here again," Bloom whispered back.

"She's here in spirit, Arthur. The joint's a regular pagoda tonight." And then, as if to arouse Bloom from his preoccupation, or to provide the right tone for the evening, Panuzzi boomed out, *"Hee nay, ma tovu, ma nayim, shevet achim gam yachad."*

Bloom, back on the job, led in the translation: "How good and wonderful it is when brothers and sisters dwell together." This was a great hymn, one of Bloom's favorites, that was popular not only

in synagogues but in schools and churches across the land. It cele-
brated the universality of Israel, the message of brotherhood and
peace that the history of Israel taught for the world, he told the
congregation. And as he did, how he wanted Dawn to be there in
the synagogue with him, a living example of the spirit of the hymn.

But Bloom knew what the congregants did not tonight: She had
refused to come; she would not come, so that he might introduce
her formally, and begin to inure the congregation to her presence.
No, she would not lend herself to this purpose. She had told him
plainly.

"Hodu l'Adonai kee tov," Panuzzi trumpeted center stage beside
Bloom. *"Hodu l'Adonai kee tov, kee l'olom chasdo. . . .* Wake up,
Arthur!"

"All praise God," Bloom recited responsively, "Who is good,
because Her mercy is everlasting."

"His mercy," whispered Panuzzi. "His!"

"His mercy," Bloom corrected himself with a faint smile. A titter
of recognition rippled through the congregation. "His mercy is everlasting."

"But is hers?" came Panuzzi's private responsive reading, for
Bloom alone.

41

On Sunday when Bloom arrived at his mother's apartment and let
himself in, he saw the kitchen door still slightly swinging. Nannette
and Leonidas were hollering at each other behind it.

The dining-room table was spread with *kugel,* kasha, *kishkeh,*
knishes, and *knaidlach* in chicken soup—every K food from the
formidable arsenal of the Jewish kitchen. It was a shame, too, because no one was eating. Leonidas and Nannette continued to shout.
Angelos, who had also been summoned for dinner, had not arrived
yet, and Bloom, alone now in the dining room with all that food
inspiring in him a terrible sense of obligation, was growing sick to
his stomach.

In all his rabbinical peregrinations Bloom never had assisted, counseled, or officiated at converting anyone to Judaism. But the more he thought about his dilemma, the more he realized that ultimately conversion was a way for him to avoid having to choose between Dawn and the synagogue. Yet at the same time he felt such a novice in all matters pertaining to conversion, he hardly knew where to begin. He knew Dawn would have to go to the *mikveh*, the ritual bath. But where would he find one in Gardena? In fact the only place to take a public bath in Gardena was at the casinos on a day when you were slow and the dealer sharp. Oh, this was really no problem at all; a *mikveh* could always be located in L.A. He began to think about which of the rabbis in the city he might call to get advice on the conversion of Dawn Nakazawa.

The yelling subsided, and out of the kitchen strode Leonidas, his gray hair going off and up in an unruly ascent of cowlicks, and his black glasses, as always, flecked with dandruff. He put his arm around Bloom and lowered his voice: "When your mother heard you were running around with a Japanese, she got an attack of guilt you don't want to know about, son. Here *I'd* been doing most of the cooking happily for these last years. She learned to like Greek food, she learned to enjoy someone else sweating over her. Suddenly—poof! —this morning, because of you, she goes berserk with the cooking. She thinks maybe she didn't feed you well enough when you were a kid. You see? For lack of *kugel* you have the hots for an Oriental. Have you tried the *kugel*? It's really delicious.

"I'm trying to be patient, but we don't think the same on this matter, your mother and me. You understand, Arthur? In Greece there's this saying: In the land of the blind, a one-eyed man is king. All right, she's your mother and says she knows you and what's best for you. I say malarky, and I lose patience. We have to be understanding, Arthur. It's a blow to a mother. With you she's trying not to show it too much, but believe me it's a shot to the chin. So let me lose patience for you, okay, kid? You be Confucius, okay?"

"Confucius and confused," said Bloom. He was feeling vaguely dizzy already.

"By the way," whispered Leonidas, "is she sweet?"

"Who?"

"Who am I talking about? Pat Suzuki?"

Nannette came in then with yet another tray. "You men haven't touched a thing. What's with you, Arthur? Jewish food no longer appeals? Better you like Japanese cuisine? *Tzimis* tempura? Take a deep breath, boys, and come to the table."

"At least say 'hello' first, ma."

"Hello. You could have come in to say 'hello' to me, you know." Bloom tried to delay. "Shouldn't we wait for Angelos?"

"He was born late," Leonidas said, "and he'll be late to my funeral, and maybe even his own, God should prevent it."

"He should prevent a few other things I can name while He's at it," said Nannette. She circled the table, lifting casserole tops, stirring, provoking aromas. To Bloom it was a kind of culinary torture.

"Maybe I'll just open the window wider," he said.

"You want a seltzer, Arthur?"

Nannette glared at Leonidas. "I make all this food, and you offer him seltzer?"

"So he can eat afterwards, darling."

"Open your belt and the top of your zippers, both of you," she said. "I'll put everything back. Maybe you'll eat it later. Maybe you won't eat it at all. Maybe I don't care any more."

She walked back into the kitchen and Bloom, queasy and preoccupied, couldn't think of a thing to say to stop her. Leonidas drank some ouzo and shrugged his shoulders when Bloom looked his way. Bloom put his head out the window of the apartment and drew in some clarifying early-evening air. He felt like Alec Guinness emerging from the sweat box in the Japanese prison camp in *Bridge on the River Kwai*. He surveyed the tops of the palm trees in MacArthur Park and heard the hum of the freeways north of it. He leaned far out, listening intently for the faintest echo of the theme from the movie to come to him over the tops of the ponderosa pines and the eucalyptus trees down below. No matter, he would carry on without any inspirational music; he would not give in.

Nannette reemerged, without the apron she had been wearing (the California coastline). She had on lipstick and, Bloom noticed, a thin jacket with Oriental collar and cherry blossom design. She looked great for sixty-seven. She sat on the sofa next to him, and as the skirt of her sundress rose, Nannette's patellas glistened. Bloom saw Leonidas staring at them over his glass. Between Nannette's knees and her sandaled feet a few varicose veins meandered down each leg. Happily suffering the silent treatment Nannette was administering to him, Leonidas stared with impunity. Her skin was unusually white, her hair thick and red with henna. Strangely she often reminded Bloom of those pretty Irish girls he used to watch marching up Fifth Avenue in the Saint Patrick's Day parade. Their legs short, amusing, thick, and endearing like potatoes.

"Ma"—Bloom turned to her—"tell me, why is everything a matter of 'them and us'? Why is the first question you ask about Dawn *not*, Is she nice? Is she considerate and is she a decent, loving, intelligent person? Why is the first question always, and not just from you: Is she Jewish?"

"Because it's human nature."

"That's not my nature, and I'm human."

"Check again," said Nannette. "It should be your nature, and if it's not, it's not because I didn't teach you what is right. That's the way you were raised, and you're just denying it."

"Hold it, you two." Leonidas raised his hand. Then he spoke quietly. "What's so great about human nature? The Germans' human nature was to ask the same question: Are they Jewish? How much Jewish blood is in their veins? And before them the inquisitors asked the same questions."

Nannette glared at him. "The Germans have nothing to do with the discussion at hand. You ought to be ashamed of yourself, Leon. Anyway"—she turned to Bloom—"just what is so attractive about this girl, Arthur? What is the great secret? That she's Japanese wasn't enough? And the things she's writing! Arthur, you are catching us all by surprise. Everyone's asking me what's got into you, and I can't answer them. Up to now nothing with girls, and suddenly this. Suddenly at your age you get so serious about a strange girl! You think I want to sit here and tell you what's right and what's wrong? The point is you were just fine. I had accepted you, Arthur, and loved you just the way you were. All right, I said to myself, my boy has always been intense, always a little finicky. Maybe girls are not for him. That's okay, I accepted."

"You thought I was gay?"

"Gay schmay, Arthur."

"But you thought so."

She smoothed her dress. "So what if I did? Is that so terrible? That also is human nature to have such thoughts. When everybody else's son gets married and brings pride and pleasure and grandchildren, and yours does not even get married, it's natural to wonder. But you were a boy who had no father after the age of nine years. Maybe I should have gotten married again soon, I told myself. Maybe part of the problem is there. Maybe if this Greek gambler would have come along sooner, maybe; but he didn't. So there was no man in the house, and for this I make allowances. I was in the Bronx, and you kept moving farther away until you got to California, and your business is your business."

"You did think I was gay."

"Thoughts cross the brain like flies through a room," Leonidas pronounced. "Don't analyze your poor mother so."

"No," said Nannette, "not gay, but funny, odd, private, peculiar. When I came out here to be near you, I saw that you finally were at a temple with a job that maybe you would keep for a while. You had a library that you like, you had the little things that I know make you happy. You were respected. What else matters? And so now you have to go and upset the apple cart so that nobody knows what is coming or going with you, Arthur. Do you know?"

Bloom, with his hand under his chin and his head thrust forward, listened, painfully. "He's taking it under advisement," said Leonidas.

"I'm thinking of converting her," Bloom said quietly.

"I want you interested in someone who is a nice Jewish girl already, or nothing at all," Nannette said. "Is it so much to ask? I want that, and Mrs. Nakazawa wants that, too."

"I didn't know," Bloom said, "that she was so interested in my well-being."

"Now is no time to be snide," Nannette said. "What time is it?" she turned to Leonidas, "and where is that son of yours?"

"Maybe Angelos is working for a change. We have a broken machine again and he is impatient about the repairmen. He'll work on it himself until it's done; so we shouldn't count on him to eat."

"I didn't know the cantor was such a mechanic."

After a silence, Leonidas said, "Dearest Nannette, I don't want to intrude between mother and son, but please don't mislead the boy about the right path, perfect things, guarantees. You know as well as I do that no such thing exists. Jews divorce as much as non-Jews. You know what happened to Angelos. There is no guarantee for marriage or for anything else. In your case, Nannette my dear, it was your husband's aorta; in my case the SS. There is always something that can steal away what you love. If it's not health or the Germans, there's always something. Nothing is perfect, because we are not perfect. We're in fact swirling chaoses in bags of skin. We're just particles, we're atoms, discovered, incidentally, by the Greeks. It's physics, electrical charges."

"You're drinking too much." Nannette got up and took the bottle away.

"And," Bloom added, "one of the basic laws is that like particles repel, opposite particles attract. Dawn and I, ma, are opposite particles."

"You're both crazy."

"Take us." Leonidas reached for her hand, but she abruptly pulled it away. "You are fair-skinned and light, the descendant of some well-to-do Russians in Kiev, and I am a dark Greek. We're opposite, we're . . ."

"You're talking too much, Leo, and in front of the rabbi, my son."

"And that's why we attract." He reached for her again and this time caught her and kissed her hand.

She resisted, took two casseroles, piled them on each other, and walked toward the kitchen. At the door she stopped and said to Bloom, "Don't let him drink any more tonight, Arthur, and don't let him take aspirin with that Greek poison."

"Where are you going, ma?"

"I'm going to lie down," she said.

"Okay, ma."

"And drop that girl, Arthur. I'm begging you, before it's too late. Please!"

She went to bed, and Leonidas and Bloom, over several more ouzos each, talked long into the night.

Angelos never showed up.

42

As Bloom raised the prayer shawl to his lips on the following sabbath morning and stepped up to the lectern to begin the services, there before him was gathered a congregation he had never seen before at the synagogue. In addition to the regulars, the place was packed with young Jewish women! Bloom sniffed the air and caught their collective scent wafting up to him: Musk, Chanel No. 5, Youth Dew, Charley, Babe.

Bloom somehow proceeded with the service without a hitch, but never had he had such a gorgeous and attentive group before him. There was the rustle of slips, and starched skirts and blouses; there was the gauzy friction of nylon-ed legs crossing and uncrossing in response to Bloom's instructions to rise and to be seated, please. He felt suddenly, startlingly, the maestro of a whole symphony of female sounds that overwhelmed the chronic whispering, cracking of arthritic joints, and coughs of the regulars.

"What gives?" Bloom whispered to Panuzzi, as he and the cantor stood, between musical phrases, and in front of the Holy Ark.

"You can have your pick," Panuzzi answered.

"Who are they?" Bloom demanded. "What's going on?"

"I won't make a move until you do." The cantor smiled.

"Shut up," said Bloom, "and sing."

"The Torah is a tree of life," Panuzzi belted out across the sanctuary, "to all those who hold on to it." And then, as the congregation sang the refrain, "Listen to all those sopranos, Arthur! And every one of them is tra-la-laing just for you!"

"It's ridiculous!" Bloom was indignant. "Who set this up?" For it seemed to Bloom that suddenly every eligible Jewish woman from San Diego to Ventura was now here, where for three years there had been not a one.

"I've got it on good authority," Panuzzi whispered, "that any one of them would be eager to meet you, Arthur."

"I'm not interested," Bloom said anxiously. "Are you part of this?"

"Me? Never. But I do know that the word was put out, Arthur, that you had the theological equivalent of the sex ray, and here they are to sock theirs right up to you. Man, I can feel it. It's hot as a pistol in here, Arthur."

As he called people up to do the blessings at the Torah, Bloom peeked over the top of the holy scroll on the reading table before him. My, he thought, the congregants have a lot of nieces and young cousins and friends of cousins! He looked, and he instantly understood why he had shunned, in spite of his mother's importuning, every Hanukah and Purim party for L.A. Jewish singles that he had ever been told about. No, he never had allowed himself to submit to being considered a "single," and bus-loading all these women to him was not going to change his mind. He might be full of fear and anxiety about Dawn, but he also felt love for her, and for a change he was not lonely. No, there would not be matchmaking en masse this sabbath. And, furthermore, couldn't all these women out there sense that he was a man already crazed by love?

At his previous posts in the East and Midwest, he had met a Ruth, a Rachel, a Leah, a Judith, like one of these seated before him, with dark hair that fell to her waist. But the relationships had been at best friendly; the young women had been intelligent, even warm toward him. And yet Bloom could not help but feel that these women had been responding not to the man, Arthur Bloom, but the rabbi in him. They admired his book reviews; they would gaze up at him from the rows of seats that seemed to be always before his eyes; but none of this was a turn-on, not for a moment. He had long yearned for something dramatic, some great spark, some thunderbolt of romance, some pulling open the veil of all that polite, warm everydayness. Because shouldn't every person, even a rabbi, be entitled to such an experience? Or, to put it in theological terms, shouldn't the *mysterium tremendum* assert itself through the sparkle in the big eyes of some new haunting face raised up to him, appearing there, somehow, even in the precincts of Temple Shmuel, Ontario, Illinois?

And where suddenly was the *mysterium tremendum* now? As far as Bloom was concerned, she was the one who read poetry and worked at the *L.A. Eye,* the one who was like a dolphin in the water, and she was as near to him as a walk across the street. But, dammit all, she was not Jewish, and they—Sarah, his mother, her mother— were all against it!

As Bloom moved perfunctorily through the service, her image rose up to him and he found himself daydreaming, addressing her with a sermon on conversion which he doubted he would ever be able to say to Dawn's real, unimagined face: *Deuteronomy, chapter 21, verse 10, dear, is a good place to start.*

> *If we put ourselves back a couple of thousand years, it says here that if I, as a warrior of Israel, go out and God delivers your people into my hand and I make you my captive, then there's a good chance that if you find favor in my eyes, you could become my wife—but only providing you pass a number of strenuous tests. First, we have to take you to the beauty parlor and get all that lustrous hair of yours cut off. Completely cut off so you are a billiard ball up there. Then the manicurist would come around while you're sitting, and she would cut off your fingernails. No, not all of them. This is not torture— at least not entirely. She'd cut your fingernails down, so they looked like a butcher's, so that you couldn't wear polish on them; likewise with the toes. Darling, believe me, I cringe too at the thought of that manicurist's scissors slipping, and harm befalling those toes. We'd be very careful.*
>
> *Then there would be other tests required as well. You see, the idea is that you are to be made to look as ugly as possible, which is, of course, impossible in your case. The traditional accessories of female beauty, therefore, have to be cast away—the hair, and the nails, for example, and whatever else can be found. If, after all that, if after you look like Yul Brynner, if even then I can still say I love you and want you, then things begin to look up. It just goes to show that the hoary old authors of Deuteronomy all had the same insight as my mother: they both know that beauty is only skin deep, and that when you are bald and nailless, your true inner beauty, your character, has a better chance of shining through.*

Bloom and Panuzzi finished the Torah reading, and he decided that it would be merciful to all in attendance if he abridged the service. Skipping the *haftorah,* he hoisted the holy scroll on his shoulders, and with Panuzzi behind him he made an efficient promenade down into the audience, in front of the first row. He saw them up close now in their organdy and silk blouses, in their angora sweaters, in their gold jewelry, the turquoise pins, the lace, in the thickness of the alpaca thrown over their shoulders against synagogue air-conditioning, in all their positively daunting shoe, belt, and handbag coordination. A feeling of their expensiveness stole over Bloom, a sense of the burden it would be to support such creatures, a conviction that here in Gardena, far away from Beverly Hills, Westwood, Brentwood, and points north in the San Fernando Valley, these young women, who now leaned toward him from their seats as he passed with the Torah, would surely, like pandas sent to live far from their natural habitat, not thrive. And certainly not on Bloom's $15,000 per year, plus laundry privileges.

During the promenade back up to the ark, the young women reached out to touch the Torah and its bearer, Bloom. A fingertip or two had caught Bloom's hand, his shoulder, the nape of his neck where the hair began. The last touch was a sensual one, and Bloom had picked up a longing stare, but he returned to the podium aroused only by thoughts of Dawn.

The final part of the service wound to a satisfactory conclusion, and minutes later Bloom found himself before the table arrayed with kiddush wine and cookies. As he raised his cup, he became aware of yet another surprise.

"She must be the *pièce de résistance*," the cantor whispered. "A real knockout."

Sarah North was approaching, leading an attractive blonde in a sparkling white skirt and blouse. She had eyes that were haunting, and big and cerulean blue, a pug nose, and clutched to her breast was the *siddur*. Bloom studied her quickly as Sarah surrounded him with introductions: "Brenda Weiner, I'd like you to meet our rabbi, Rabbi Arthur Bloom, whom you'll be hearing from soon, and our cantor, Angelos Panuzzi. Brenda has hopes of joining your distinguished profession," Sarah said, with evident pleasure in this fact. "She's a third-year rabbinical student, and she's a girl!"

Brenda smiled, half with indulgence, half with pleasure, and shook Bloom's hand.

"It's plain enough you're a girl, a woman, I mean," said Panuzzi, as he shook her hand.

"I look forward to learning a lot from you both," Brenda said to them.

"How's that?" asked Bloom.

"Brenda's going to be with us," Sarah said. "I saw to everything."

"I don't get it," said Bloom.

"I'm on the seminary's intern program," Brenda explained.

"I wasn't aware they had one, nor that we requested one."

"It's experimental." Brenda smiled. "You know how slowly tradition gives way."

"Well, here's not the place to discuss it," Sarah said. Her sense of timing was sharp, for a little queue had formed to meet the "new" rabbi. "Anyway, I took care of everything."

"Except consulting me," Bloom snapped.

"Come now," said Brenda as she took Bloom's hand and eased him aside, so a new group of congregants could extend their sabbath wishes. Bloom detected in her voice a very distant Southern drawl. "We're all going to have a very pleasant time together."

As he dispensed his sabbath greetings, Bloom now realized that Sarah had outmaneuvered him. Here he was backed into introducing this rabbi-in-training or assistant rabbi, whoever she was, to the congregants. Before he had time to take steps to throw her out, she was a fait accompli. "Good shabbos," he said to Elise Finkel. "This is our new student rabbi. Good shabbos. Yes, the same to you and your family, Adolph. You're looking well, Isaac." Of course, if Sarah were only out to knock him out of the pulpit, she could have come up with a male student rabbi. He stole a look at Brenda, and at Panuzzi, who couldn't keep his eyes off her, and he realized instantly that he was supposed not only to teach her but, if he were to go along with this scheme of Sarah's and his mother's and whoever else was in on it, to mate with Brenda as well. "Good shabbos, Meyer."

"Well, don't keep our rabbi from us too long," Sarah chirped and moved away from them toward the door.

"I wouldn't dream of it." Brenda laughed, and gave Bloom's shoulder a not unpleasant and public squeeze.

"Our rabbi's been a very busy man lately, but I know he'll find time for you." And then Sarah was gone.

Bloom had not liked the way she had inflected "our rabbi." It sounded all too much as if she had meant "our supposed rabbi" or "our pseudo-rabbi" or "our charlatan rabbi." Patience, thought

Bloom, is a flower that grows not in everyone's garden. But he would try. "Good shabbos, Lucy. Good shabbos, Elaine. Fred and Myra, I'd like you to meet our new student rabbi. . . ."

43

The outsider passing the brightly lit showroom of Bernie Levitt Cadillac would have seen the familiar sight: highly polished automobiles curiously arranged in a circle, a garden party for these metal, rubber, chrome creatures, to display themselves and lure shoppers in to buy them. There were several robust jade bushes, two rubber trees, and a dwarf palm distributed among the vehicles, and along the back wall, beneath large posters of new models in rich surroundings, were three desks for the salesmen. Tonight, with only a half hour until closing time, only Bernie's was occupied.

Bernie was glad there were no more customers—he had sold three cars today—because now it was reading time. Upon the desk covered with manuals, marketing suggestions from Detroit in the form of glossy brochures, and Dave's scratch sheet from Santa Anita racetrack, Bernie's paperback copy of the *Zohar*, the classic of Jewish mysticism, lay open before him.

Last night, at approximately 9:40, Bernie had been in the casino. He had been there, on a strong hint from Dave that around that time the rabbi and Dawn might well be having intercourse of the most personal kind. At 9:43 he had sat down at the poker table. Within thirty seconds he had drawn two aces and two kings. Foreplay, he had muttered to himself. Not too slow and not too fast, he paced himself and played his cards. He threw one out; up came another ace! It was not bad at all, but, he had told himself, keep under control; don't rush; savor and enjoy. It should still be foreplay. Nevertheless, everybody else soon folded, and he won. On the next round, while his eyes never left the table, he saw in his hand, incredibly, three aces and the wild jack: four aces. Orgasm, he had said under his breath. Blast off! Thank you, Rabbi, thank you, Miss Nakazawa.

As a control to his experiment, Bernie had continued to play, and although he also continued to win—he drew a straight and then another full house—the luck left him, the incredible cards of concupiscence vanished. The only conclusion he could draw was that at the moment of consummation for the rabbi and his Japanese woman, great and tremendous sparks of good fortune were unleashed. But generated from what source? In which directions? Why? And then for the most awesome question: What did they mean? "The commandments," he proceeded to read from the interpretations of the mysterious pages of kabbala, "derive from the *Etz-ha-Da-at*, the Tree of Knowledge, and for this reason they contain purity and defilement, that which is permitted and that which is enjoined. However, this is because the Tree of Knowledge is the source only during the exile. At the time of redemption, however, the Torah will be revealed as something totally different, the letters reconfigured to different words, the alphabet changed, revised, totally transformed, because the Torah then will be revealed from a different source, the *Etz-ha-Hayyim*, the Tree of Life. At such a time the *yetzer ha-ra*, the evil inclination, will also be annihilated. And with this inclination eliminated, there will be absolutely no need to check it with the laws and commandments, the rules and injunctions."

"Man alive." Bernie stood up. "Maybe that's what's happening with the rabbi! Maybe it's starting right here, the erosion of the sticking power of rules and regulations, the positive consequences of 'evil' deeds being the sign!" He looked up and out of his showroom to the street. Although he had seen this view, with the traffic light, the drugstore, with its gaudy alternating blue and red neon sign, and the McDonald's, before, he felt as if he were looking at it now as if in tableau, as if for the first time.

"In such a period," he read on, "the mystical Torah, which is the concealed essence of Torah, becomes manifest." Manifest, thought Bernie, to those who open their eyes wide enough to see. "This spiritual Torah, in which the Torah we read each week is really concealed, is called *Torah de-Azilut*, the Torah of the Higher World."

"*De-Azilut*," he said aloud into the shiny silence of the showroom. "Higher World."

It was now not mere reading he was engaged in, but a communication, as if the words were speaking to him of what he'd somehow always known: "As the time of redemption nears, the *Torah de-Beriah*, the Torah in its traditional form, becomes obsolete, the laws contained in it totally abolished, as one now is commanded to live only in accordance with the spiritual Torah, the esoteric Law, the *Torah de-Azilut.*" Is it possible, Bernie wondered, that only Bloom was now living in accordance with *de-Azilut* and that his conduct should be leading the way for others to follow? "In such a world," he read on, "in a state of affairs on the brink of redemption, the role of man must be to accelerate redemption. One does this by converting the sin to the commandment. Doing that which is forbidden now becomes that which is encouraged; the sin is the *mitzvah*. At such a time, all sacrifices will disappear except for the sacrifice of thanksgiving, and all fasts will be converted to feasts."

Fasts? He pushed the brochures off his desk until he came across the Jewish calendar he knew lay there at the bottom of the pile. What month was it? Bernie turned the pages of the calendar: Tishre, Chesvan, Kislev, Tevet, Shavat, Adar, Nissan, Sivan, Iyar, Tammuz, Av, Ellul. Yes, Av was approaching, the month that contained the fast of the Ninth of Av, the fast in commemoration of the misfortunes of war, all the pogroms, expulsions, disasters, the Holocaust, all that had befallen the Jews since the destruction of the holy temples. It was *the* great fast. Was it also just coincidence that the rabbi was falling for the Japanese now, at the time that the greatest fast on the Jewish calendar neared?

Bernie opened his *Zohar* again. "At such a time, all sacrifices will disappear except for the sacrifice of thanksgiving," he reread, "and all fasts will be converted to feasts."

He looked up and said to his cars, as if they were his gleaming listeners, "The rabbi and the Japanese! This place, this town, the Silver Dollar shul . . . might it be?"

44

JEWISH GURU LEADS HOUSE OF WORSHIP NEXT
DOOR TO HOUSE OF CARDS

by Dawn Nakazawa

New religions are a feature of Southern California life as
native as movie stars, gas stations, and smog. In the early
1900s the Father Divine movement took root. By midcen-
tury the influence of Asia—particularly India—was evident
in the appearance of such groups as the Self-Realization
Fellowship of Paramahansa Yogananda, which firmly
planted itself in Hollywood. And more recently the adherents of Hare Krishna, Transcendental Meditation, the Children of God, and Scientology have established substantial,
and often profitable, networks of temples, churches, and
community centers.

Most of these "new religions" have been either a creative
amalgam of the beliefs of indigenous Christian denomina-
tions or mystical imports from the East.

Now the Southland is adding yet a new chapter to its
already colorful religious history, and this time from a most
unexpected source: the usually stable Jewish community.

Rabbi Arthur Bloom, the spiritual leader of Temple Elijah, Gardena, has become the focus of a movement attracting considerable recent attention. Whereas many new religions as well as cults, their less distinguished cousins, offer
adherents grand rewards for devotion, such as proof positive
of life everlasting or dramatically enhanced personal happiness, the followers of Rabbi Bloom derive, they feel, a benefit much more modest, yet solid. They assert that directly
as a result of their devotion they have remarkable good luck
at the dozens of gambling casinos that abound in Gardena.

"I have increased my poker earnings 200 percent," says
Alexander Gluck, a retired small businessman from Thousand Oaks, "since I've been *davening* with Rabbi Bloom."
(*Davening* is the Hebrew word for a particularly deep, emotional style of Jewish prayer that derives from Jewish mystics
of Eastern Europe hundreds of years ago.)

"I never let a weekend go by that I don't come down to Gardena to gamble," says Enid Malkove, a 61-year-old machine operator from the garment industry. "Until I joined the Silver Dollar Synagogue (as Temple Elijah is sometimes called), I had terrible worries about money, about how I would make ends meet. That's in the past now. No more worries, no more being a nervous wreck about retirement. Now I've got it made."

Similar testimonials to the rabbi's uncanny powers to bring adherents good luck are often heard on the streets and at the gambling tables of the casinos. Although no broad theological claims have been made so far, followers of Rabbi Bloom (who is also known as "the Lucky Rabbi") may be beginning to display the characteristic trappings of a devotional community.

One of the most unusual features of this religious movement is the comparative lack of involvement of Rabbi Bloom. Although most new religions differ widely, they all tend to be organized around a single charismatic individual —a yogi, guru, or leader. But Rabbi Bloom steadfastly denies such is the case with him, and it is true that he does not fit the usual description. He is in his late thirties, is slightly balding, and is unprepossessing except perhaps for richly dark, sympathetic brown eyes. A scholar and modest poet, the rabbi is relatively reclusive and is unmarried. He himself never gambles and indeed has never set foot in the casinos of Gardena, not even the Silver Dollar Casino right next door to the synagogue, where many of his congregants are active, and where, according to temple sources, the rabbi's powers are particularly potent.

Although Rabbi Bloom consistently asserts that there is no movement, it is widely believed that such assertions, intentional or not, are part of a complex web of mystery and paradox that the rabbi's lieutenants are weaving around his persona.

In spite of their leader's denials, members of the rabbi's religious community continue to bet heavily on numbers and combinations of numbers (in poker, blackjack, roulette, and dice) derived from such sources as the number of quotations Rabbi Bloom incorporates in his sermon, the dates of his birthday, circumcision, bar mitzvah, and rabbinical ordination.

A manager of the Silver Dollar Casino, who asked not to be identified, said he was aware of the mystique many of the gamblers expressed with regard to Rabbi Bloom. "Nevertheless," said this official, "we're not worried about it a bit. Anybody over eighteen can come here. We don't discriminate," he continued, "based on religious persuasion, country of origin, citizenship, sex, or race. Actually there's just one color—green—that unites us all.

"They can count the numbers of hairs left under his beanie," this official went on, referring to the rabbi's skullcap, "and come up with any personal system they want, so long as when they sidle up to the tables, they don't cheat. And we have never had any problem with cheating here at this casino, from people associated with the synagogue or, thank God, anywhere else. We're all good neighbors, and that's the way we want things to stay."

Whether they will continue to be good neighbors, if Rabbi Bloom's adherents begin to break the house—as many contend will eventually happen—remains to be seen. Furthermore, as claims for the rabbi's extra-gambling powers increase, the effects are liable to be felt throughout Gardena, and beyond.

45

Because Bloom continued to go out with Dawn, Sarah North took extraordinary measures, all the prerogatives of her office, to anchor Bloom to the temple as much as possible and to keep track of his whereabouts. She had Abe hustle up a *minyan* for prayers, morning, afternoon, and evening. Between prayers, Sarah had Bloom at book reviews or representing the Silver Dollar on panel discussions at other synagogues in Los Angeles. She was tireless in her campaign to re-Judaize the temple and to surround Bloom with activities, and alternatives to Dawn. In this effort Brenda Weiner, rabbi-to-be, was the beautiful and kosher hub. She was at every function, on every panel, in every audience Bloom addressed. He never had to look far to find her staring up at him, her blue eyes almost translucent, and the kidney bean nostrils of her pug nose turned upwards as if, Bloom felt, she was about to sniff him in.

"Don't you take classes somewhere?" he asked her one afternoon.

"It's summer vacation. Anyway, I'm on an academic leave," she answered. "Independent study of Jewish institutions."

"And what specifically are you studying?"

"Trends, new trends, like what I represent in contemporary Jewish life," she gushed.

"Alas," he said, "you've been delivered to the right place."

Bloom also became saddled with administrative duties of the kind he thought he had jettisoned by coming to a place like Gardena. Twenty-five new people wanted to become members. The temple board suddenly began to call meetings.

Nannette, at the first meeting dealing with new applications for temple membership, demanded to know just who the aspirants were. Abe obliged by reading a dozen names, half of which did not even seem Jewish. "As a minimum requirement," said Sarah, "I don't believe we should extend membership in a temple to those who are not Jewish."

"Pardon, Madam President," said Dave, "but every name on that list is either a Jew or willing, even eager, to convert. They even ask for our distinguished rabbi to teach them about Judaism and to perform the appropriate ceremonies."

They all looked toward Bloom. Sleepily he eyed them back. "The Talmudic sage Simeon ben Gamliel," Bloom reminded them, "said, 'When a prospective proselyte shows an interest in Judaism, extend to him or her a hand of welcome.' I see no reason to disagree."

"I do," shot back Sarah. "These people are not prospective Jews but card players looking for an angle, and brought in by those articles. If the rabbi were not"—she struggled for a word—"collaborating so openly with the staff of the *L.A. Eye,* do you think any of this would be happening? We don't need more gamblers, we need more Jews."

"Begging the president's pardon," said Leonidas, "but anybody crazy enough to want to become a Jew is entitled."

"How do you measure a person's sincerity in such matters?" Bloom quietly asked.

"At any normal temple," Sarah spoke without taking her eyes off him, "the rabbi makes such decisions based on conversations with the convert!"

Old Eli Ginsberg rose solemnly. He got the board's attention. "Since there is so much discord right now, I suggest we close membership temporarily. We accept no one, but at the same time we turn down no one. Those genuinely interested in us, well, their hearts will just grow that much fonder. The others will drift off. Anyway, Sarah is right. This board has other matters to consider. For example, there is the matter of the rabbi's relationship with Miss Nakazawa. It's a *shanda*, Rabbi. It's a shame! She is a sensational reporter, and Japanese! A terrible shame!"

To Bloom's relief, Dave spoke up. "With all due respect to our elder statesman, we absolutely cannot close membership, not temporarily, not even for another week. We've got pressure building in this community, and on each one of us. I know I feel it, and so does each one of you. We've got a flow toward us here, a stream that we really can't stop even if we wanted to."

No one had ever heard Dave speak quite this way. Bloom's momentary relief evaporated.

"I predict," Dave stood and not so much spoke as orated, "that the interest will force us to deal with it sooner or later, and it may as well be sooner. Why, if you look at the addresses on that list that Abe has, you'll see we have people from Ventura and Cucamonga, from Thousand Oaks and La Puente, from one corner of the Southland to the other. Don't you see this groundswell of interest in our community is unprecedented? This is a revival of interest in Judaism, on a potentially huge scale. There was even a couple in from Nevada this morning that bought an Eldorado and said to me afterwards, 'Dave, sign us up at that little church of yours while you're at it, would you?' Sure, they don't know much about us, but, I ask you, how did they hear about the rabbi all the way in Nevada? And I also ask you this: What are we here for? Aren't we here to teach people, to help others learn, to conquer prejudice and ignorance! I say that the People of the Book got no business closing the book on anyone, I mean anyone, interested in our faith for whatever reason. I predict that soon Gardena will become a place of pilgrimage!"

"Jews don't go on pilgrimages," said Bloom.

Sarah, Abe, Eli Ginsberg, Nannette, and the other board members were silent. They could hear the cars accelerating down Casino Boulevard. Chair legs scraped, and then the scratch of a match perforated the air, as Dave slowly lit up one of his Have-A-Tampas.

Oh no! Bloom thought. Something is coming. And the soothing words of Buson came to him—the great haikuist, whom he'd been reading with Dawn:

> To cherry blossoms I come,
> And under blossoms go to sleep—
> No duties to be done.

"Madam President, Rabbi," Dave said, "I feel the solution is not to close the membership, but on the contrary to open it as wide as we can. Why not make public what we have here!" Then he paused, as a smoke ring floated out among them. "I think we all should start considering the possibility of launching our very own, very special Jewish ministry of the air. . . ."

46

"Paramahansa Yogananda? Extra-gambling *powers?* I don't need any of this," Bloom said. "I don't need new religions, gurus, strange forces!" He held the *Eye* up against the sea wind. Dawn sat on the hood of the Toyota next to him. She was wearing a T-shirt with a slice of pizza silk-screened on it, and jean cutoffs. The car, with both of them atop it, was pointed out at the big red ball of the sun setting in the Pacific.

"You should have published the Drive-In Synagogue," Bloom said dejectedly. "That was child's play. This time you've gone too far, Dawn. What movement are you talking about? What telltale trappings of a devotional community? What lieutenants? I think you're selling papers this time, not the truth."

"And what is the truth?" Dawn sat up, looking straight ahead. She had asked the question of the sun, but it was Bloom who answered. "My congregation is not a devotional community. They are what Voltaire said about the Holy Roman Empire—neither holy, nor Roman, nor an empire. And that's the truth about Temple Elijah—not very devotional and in fact barely a community."

"I think you're not being honest, Arthur."

"Well, okay," he said, "maybe they're devoted to poker and a little to me. But you're teasing readers in this piece about theological claims and nascent movements, and Father Divines and who knows what!"

"It may not be good for the Jews," she quoted Bloom affectionately, "but I hope it's good for you."

"Pardon, but I am a Jew too, last I checked."

"Pardon me, also, Arthur, but I guess I'm just a little frustrated with a few things around here. If you were, for example, to spend just a fraction of the time you spend on trying to convert me rather to listening to what your own congregants are saying about you and to watching truly how they regard you, we wouldn't be sitting here arguing, which gives me not one ounce of pleasure!"

"I don't like it either," he said.

"Arthur, may I read you some of my notes, some of the stuff that's never going to make the paper?"

"Sure. If it will get it out of your system, go right ahead."

"Out of my system," she said as she hopped down and took her bag from the car seat, "and, I hope, right into yours!" Sticking out of the purse was a yellow legal pad, which Dawn carried in her hand, while Bloom held a copy of the *Eye* with the latest article rolled in a tube under his armpit. They walked across the still warm sands. "May I?" Dawn unfurled her pad.

"By all means," said Bloom.

"If congregants' grandchildren have a drug problem that the parents are mishandling, congregants sometimes talk to the rabbi about these matters. At least two parishioners—oops, congregants—contend that shortly after pastoral counseling with the rabbi, their grandchildren shaped up, and all was well."

"Really?" said Bloom.

"Yes, now listen to this: One congregant, Lucy Leonard, had a son-in-law who died, leaving three children soon to enter college, without funds for this having been provided by the deceased. After talking to the rabbi, Lucy, a dice player, won $12,000 in one long weekend of betting, which was enough to launch two of the three into their freshman year, tuition paid. Up to the weekend in question, Lucy had never cleared more than about $600. She attributes the dramatic change in luck to the rabbi."

"Nonsense," said Bloom. "I talked to her the way I would anyone. It was sheer coincidence; she got lucky."

"Precisely when she needed to, says this witness."

"Witness? Witness to what?"

"Let me finish," said Dawn. She leafed through until she came to another page covered with script: "Does the rabbi know a lot about financing a college education for one's grandchildren? IRAs? Trusts? Does the rabbi impart some of his insights that alter the mental makeup of the congregants he deals with, so that when they gamble something is unleashed within them, some heretofore unknown acumen or quality, some insight transferred from the pastoral session to the gambling sessions? Precisely what occurs?"

"Are you asking or telling?"

A seagull swooped low over their heads.

"No, no, no," Dawn answered him. "It's the journalist musing to herself. I'm just asking questions. Don't you ask these questions of yourself, Arthur?"

"Did you write that?"

"Of course."

"Keep reading," said Bloom.

"By all reports, Rabbi Bloom's pastoral conferences are not brilliant. He is not up to date on the above. Rather the sessions are characterized by attentive listening, sympathy, and real warmth."

"How nice."

"It's too early to congratulate yourself, Arthur." Dawn looked up at him. The wind had blown her hair into a swath of black about her face. Bloom removed it slowly, a handful of strands at a time, and then kissed her. "The congregants report that the sessions were short on detailed, practical advice. However, this deficiency has never kept them away from their rabbi, and they seek him out formally and informally, before and after services, sometimes on the sidewalk, or occasionally to discuss a matter over lemonade beside the pool, where the rabbi spends a considerable amount of time. Sounds like a very cushy deal you have here, Arthur."

"They really said all that?"

"Absolutely. You want more?"

They reached the old pier, and there, amid the barnacled pilings, she enumerated: "First, foiling the repossession of a Lincoln Continental—Benjamin Gerber's; second, the reclamation of a life-savings account in the amount of $7,256 from a phony investment operation in Arizona that had hooked a congregant—Rhoda Sinefeld—and her unmarried daughter; and third, successful referral to a psychotherapist who saved Victor Singer's suicide-prone son, after his vinyl seat-cover business went belly-up."

"I'm impressed," said Bloom.

"That's what I'm worried about, Arthur."

"Don't misunderstand. I'm not all that surprised; I'm impressed with all you've been able to find out and in so little time."

A discarded can of motor oil washed up to them. "You haven't heard anything yet." They retraced their steps. "In addition to these highlights," she read, "an atmosphere of steady good fortune seems to surround the congregants in their gambling activities, in particular. Only on three occasions," said Dawn with a quick glance up at Bloom, "has there been a dramatic downturn in the good luck. You see, Arthur, they keep a sort of scratch sheet on you, as if you were a thoroughbred. Your wins, places, shows, your misses, and by how much. I wouldn't be surprised if they had it all on somebody's computer, too. You're not aware of this, are you? Why, I wonder?"

Bloom stared at her fixedly without providing an answer.

"The following incidents stand out in the memory of congregants: On May 4, 1981, when you double-dated—Panuzzi and his then wife, you and a girlfriend of hers named Rita, a medical student at UCLA—on that night for some reason, a number of people around here lost a bundle."

"Maybe they just played stupid." Bloom kicked irritably at the surf.

"What was Rita like?" asked Dawn.

"Couldn't hold a candle to you."

"Good," she said. "If you'll give me a kiss"—he did—"I'll go on. Second incident occurred on December twenty-first of last year, when Lucy Leonard gave you an afghan she had crocheted to thank you for helping her send her grandkids to college; she came up to you, you'll recall, and told you details of how your tête-à-tête with her had resulted in her winnings. Well, in the next two weeks, she had the worst run of bad luck ever seen here. Third incident occurred on February sixth of this year, when, you'll remember, you ran after Sarah North to tell her something, some synagogue business, and in catching up to her, you entered Nero's Grotto, the casino, at midday. Again there were unusually uniform losses for synagogue-affiliated people. You had one member who was an unusually high roller?"

"Yes, Reuben Miller," recalled Bloom.

"Well, that was goodbye, Reuben. He never showed up again."

"You learned all that?"

"Lucy showed me a chart she carries in her purse. It's about you, Arthur. She said it was nothing compared to the logarithms and calculus some of the others do."

"I stimulate their minds to mathematics," he said. "I'm a force for keeping them young." He was very impressed with what she had found out, but he did not want to show it, not too much.

"Lucy calls her graph Bloom's Curve. For many of them, Arthur, you're the goose that's one day going to lay the golden egg."

"Unflattering," Bloom said, pulling in at his belt. "I am a rabbi, not a piece of poultry."

"Tell it to them, Arthur."

47

"Dawn," he said to her in his kitchen, after another article had appeared, "if you want to lecture my congregants on the evils of gaming, go right ahead." They clinked glasses and drank, without a toast, a red California wine. "Just don't do it in the paper. Come to the synagogue again. Give a lecture. I'll start an adult education series. You can be the featured speaker. I'll write an eloquent introduction for you. I'm sure the house will be packed and people will be respectful."

"It's not the point either," Dawn said. "From what I gather, coming from me, advice about gambling wouldn't go over."

"From me it doesn't either."

"So you deny you have an influence over these people?"

"Absolutely. Judaism doesn't rest on mystery-supported authority. It doesn't have an elite group of priests. You can conduct services with the rabbi or without him. If you convert, sweetheart, you can learn all about it. All you need is a *minyan,* any ten men bar mitz-vahed and willing. A rabbi is strictly frosting on the cake."

"You're not frosting on this cake, Arthur. You're not just another bar-mitzvah boy. You're being cute, but at the expense of the truth."

"Tell me then what I am, in their eyes."

"Some sort of magician, that's all."

"The only trick I'm any good at is making you angry at me."

He proceeded to embrace her and she closed her eyes. He put his fingers under her chin and pulled her face toward his. "Jews are commanded," he said, "to love their neighbors as themselves. Never was I happier than the day I found out you were a neighbor. I'm only fulfilling a commandment, Dawn."

"Fulfill away."

"Not only," he said, "are we commanded to love our neighbors as ourselves, but we're advised not to waste time about it. For, as our teachers said back in the second century, 'If not now, then when?' How about now, Dawn?" he murmured, with the slightest note of pleading in his voice.

"I came to castigate you," she said, "and I end up making love."

" 'Tis a consummation,' " said the rabbi, " 'devoutly to be wished.' "

"Shut up." She laughed. "I'd rather consume first and consum-mate next. I'm awfully hungry."

"You're always hungry when I want to make love."

"You can't do something so strenuous on an empty belly."

"May I think of you as dessert?"

"You may think anything you want as long as you get the barbe-cue going right now."

" 'You're the cream in my coffee,' " Bloom sang as she helped him tie his Bronx apron around his middle, " 'I'm the milk in your tea. . . .' "

He got the food out of the refrigerator, went out to Dawn on the veranda, and placed the hamburgers near the barbecue. Then he made the strategic error of reminding her that the meat was kosher.

"Darling Arthur"—she cupped her hands and megaphoned him her message across the veranda, where he was tending the fire— "Now hear this: *I do not want or need to be constantly reminded of such differences between us. Isn't it enough others do?*"

"Yes," he said quietly, "you're right."

"Don't look so sad." She went over to raise Bloom's fallen face with a deep and undulating kiss that made him forget all the craziness. "You're a lousy proselytizer, Arthur, but a great cook, and kisser."

48

The kiss on the veranda was twenty-six seconds long, according to Lucy Leonard's stopwatch; it was only eighteen seconds long by Meyer Briskin's timing, but that's because with his opera glasses trained on the veranda he detected a pause, during which Bloom turned his head away from Dawn—to check the fire?—and then returned to her waiting mouth. But because Arlette Rosenberg had also timed twenty-seven seconds and Meyer did record an after-kiss of about ten seconds (making his a total of twenty-eight, which was close enough to the findings of the others)—twenty-seven seconds, and a very passionate twenty-seven, was finally agreed to as the consensus number for the kiss.

Because they didn't want to waste any force generated by this longest rabbinical osculation on record, the little crew of observers, having convened to share intelligence, now went quickly skipping past the hydrangea hedge and into the casino. As soon as they entered the lobby, they whispered "Twenty-seven" to Black Dave, who was waiting just outside the pit for the information.

When the sexton got the word, he sent his runner, Betsy Levine, and she reached all the craps-playing temple members; Morris Brenner ran to the poker table, and Yvonne Schwimmer circulated with the number among the ladies of the slot machines.

Within minutes the place began to hum. Sheldon Freeman, who had arrived in time to get chips, watched breathlessly as the bones rolled down the greensward of the table. The dice banked off the side, and careened down to the far end, where he could not see, but then a shout filled the room, for two sevens had turned up. Hoots and cheers erupted at various places on the floor as Adolph Gruen, the retired pharmacist, came running back with news that the winning number on the roulette wheel, to his delight, had been twenty-seven, two out of three spins—a most unusual occurrence. Shirley Bloomfield, the hairdresser, who still worked part time, came up to Black Dave. In her hands were $400 in blue chips, winnings from blackjack. The dealer there had just been replaced, but before his removal the house had lost twice, each time with two kings and a seven.

"Shall I tell you something about that dealer?" said Lucy Leonard to Dave. "I joke not, but the kid is twenty-seven years old, today. He told me."

The floor manager, Kavanaugh, came rushing up to Dave. "How'd you all know that number? How come twenty-sevens are breakin' out like a rash here?"

"You noticed?"

"We ain't blind, Dave. What's up?"

"The rabbi told us, the rabbi conveyed it to us."

"I don't see any rabbi." Kavanaugh looked around the room. "But I did see one of your little friends, Mr. Gruen, with this." Kavanaugh now showed the binoculars to Dave—he had had them behind his back. "You know this ain't allowed. No equipment, Dave, except a butt and a brain. Okay?"

"Sure," Dave said confidently. "No problem."

"You can tell Mr. Gruen he can pick his binoculars up on the way out," and Kavanaugh left Dave thinking to himself that lucrative as these surveillances had become, maybe the time had arrived to make money another way. He had been uncomfortable about it all for a while now, although he hadn't yet mentioned it to Bernie. But now Kavanaugh was obviously doing surveillance on the surveillance.

Shirley Bloomfield came up to Dave. "Does the pest think we're cheating?" she asked.

"*Vay iz mir,*" said Dave with a sigh deep enough to be heard all the way around in the poker corner, "weren't we? The rabbi's powers are strong. I'm telling you it's like Superman's x-ray vision, it's like seeing right through the cards!"

"Seeing through is not the same as liftin' 'em up," said Adolph Gruen, who had joined them. "It's not the same as crimping or bending. It's not so bad, Dave. Nobody's accused you of anything. Come on, the coffee's on me."

*   *   *

When they came back from their break, Lucy Leonard awaited them, and Dave said to her, "I'm beginning to feel real crummy doing Bernie's dirty work. I know you all are doing it too, but making money's one thing. That's respectable, but all this spying on those sweet kids! I mean snoopin' and maybe even getting in nature's way, that's different. They're going to have plenty *tsores,* too, if we don't draw the line. Mark my word, it's not a good thing to be doing."

"Tell it to your boss," Gruen said.

"Na." Lucy dismissed Dave's worrying. "Dave doesn't want to stop any more than the next one of us," she said skeptically to Adolph. "It's just his way of asking for a loan. He gives a sermon, like the rabbi, he sounds off all noble about the poor kids and everything, and he expects to be paid for it, for his laudable sentiments. It's just Dave's way of asking for credit."

"*Nu?*" said Adolph.

"Watch," Lucy challenged. Then she turned to Dave. "How much you need, you big *schvartze,* you? How much? Fifty? A hundred?" Lucy already had her pocketbook out. "Answer, Dave, my hemorrhoids are bothering me and, what's more, I got to use the ladies' room."

Adolph Gruen looked back and forth between the two of them, players in a tennis match.

"Well." Dave slowly rose to his full six foot three. "Now that you put it so kindly, two hundred and fifty dollars will do just fine."

Lucy handed him the money.

"*God bless,* is all I can say to you," he said. "You're a good woman, and a good woman is very hard to find, and get a loan from."

"I want it back next week, no delays." She began walking toward the bathroom.

"You got it," Dave said softly, out of earshot, "if I win."

49

It was small, Leonidas told him, with some speech slurring that, thank God, should only be temporary. It was like a dizzy spell, but between turning off Johnny Carson and the bathroom, Nannette had hit the deck.

In the hospital elevator Bloom was thinking of Nannette's blood vessels. He visualized those sturdy Russian legs of hers, and the veins in them that went wiggly and varicose from the pressure of giving birth to him.

Fourteenth floor. The door opened and Bloom got off. In something of a daze, Bloom wandered down the corridors. He looked into the rooms: here an exposed haunch seemed to be watching TV; in the next room a hushed groaning; here a skinny emaciated arm with the white skin dangling from it like strange laundry. No one bothered him. He found a nurse and asked for Nannette. "Strokes," she said, "are one floor below."

A white solution dripped through a tube into Nannette's arm. Her lips were parched, and her mouth seemed gathered to one side of her face. The indentation between the top of the upper lip and base of the septum seemed very pronounced. This depression, according to an old *midrash*, a rabbinical story, was left by God when he breathed life into every human being, his lips leaving a hollow in the still-soft clay. Bloom moved a chair over near his mother's face, reached out, and touched her there. "It's me, mama."

She opened her eyes, full of tears and redness. "I talk funny."

"That'll get better soon. Don't worry."

"I worry. About you and thish woman." Her natural directness was augmented, Bloom thought, by her brush with serious impairment or even death.

"Mama, mama, don't argue with me. Now's the time for you to relax and get stronger. That's all that's important."

"Baloney and bull you-know-what. God hash not brought me through all thish"—she tugged at her IV—"to live to shee funny-looking grandchildren!"

He reached out and touched her face tenderly. He tried to divert her, but it didn't work.

"How long shince I've sheen you? At leasht now I get to shee you,

Arthur." She spoke in a faint voice that frightened him. "I don't minsh wordths: Like should be with like. You're a rabbi, Arthur. You know the shtory of Noah. Elephantsh with elephantsh, catsh with catsh, fish with fish." (He considered pointing out to her that fish would not have been on the ark's manifest, but he decided this was not the time.) "Japaneesh with Japaneesh, Jewsh with Jewsh."

"Rabbis with rabbis?"

"Yesh, whatsh wrong with Brenda Weiner? A beautiful girl. A cute figure. Alwaysh clean and well-dressshed with the fashionsh. With her I can shee you hand-in-hand under the *chuppa,* breaking the glash, making the shongs and danshes. A regular Jewsh wedding. Ish it sho much to ashk for?"

"Let's not fight, mama. I want you better again, good as new."

"To be healthy? Why, what for? To attend a wedding at the Kabuki theater?"

"Stop it, mama."

Bloom heard the adhesive tape on Nannette's arm tear a little. "Do you think you can be anybody'sh friend in the Jewish community if you keep on going with her?" Nannette was waving her arm in front of her, the bottle was swaying. Bloom feared an accident. "Arthur, have you thought about the conshequenshes? How could you remain a rabbi? And what elsh would you do for a living? You're not equipped to do anything elsh."

"That's true," he said, happy to have finally found something to agree on. "That's very true. And it's one reason why I intend to remain rabbi here, or try as hard as I can. I'm going to convert Dawn, and that'll make all the difference." Bloom tried to ease Nannette back against her pillows. But she was holding him now with both her hands, and the tube of glucose was strung out to its limit over and across the bed. "You'll see, it will all work out fine."

"No, it won't. You can convert her to kingdom come, but she'll never be a Jew. Not inshide her, where it countsh."

"I don't believe that, mother. Now try to rest, please."

"Believe it! Before you leave, Arthur, I want you to shwear to me you won't do it. Shwear!"

"Mama, look! Your needle's coming out."

"I don't care."

"It's ripping. Look, there's blood!"

"Arthur!"

"Nurse," Bloom cried. "Nurse!"

"No," she held him, as the tape tore and the solution oozed onto her skin and dripped onto the sheet. "Promish me, promish on your ordination."

"That's cub scout talk, ma."

"Promish, shon." She held him there.

"Mama, can't you see what you're asking is unfair? On a hospital bed, after you've had a stroke, when you're so weak. It's extortion!"

"Good."

"Mama, no. Nurse!"

"Promish me, Arthur, at leasht that before you take another shtep, you'll shee shomeone, talk to shomeone. Talk to a rabbi!"

"Mother, I am a rabbi."

"I almosht forgot."

50

Even as they offered their solicitations for Nannette's quick return to health, many of the congregants, Bloom now felt, no longer trusted him. Their eyes seemed to say to him, You're killing your mother, and we'll soon be next. Eli Ginsberg and a few other members with Orthodox leanings were now keeping their distance from the synagogue, and Bloom even heard a rumor that services were going to be held at some undisclosed location, without him. With his mind on his mother, and a schism within the congregation fast developing, a short leave might be just right for him. And yet when the Norths made this suggestion to him over lunch, he firmly declined. Sarah retorted, "Brenda Weiner will handle things nicely in your absence, Rabbi. There's nothing to worry about."

Bloom smelled a design, a calculation to get rid of him. "This synagogue needs another rabbi, even a girl rabbi, about as much as the human face needs another nose. Things are confused now, there's a lack of symmetry. The temple needs me and, frankly, I need the temple. I don't see how Brenda fits in at all."

"Young man," she said with unusual calm, "don't let anyone persuade you that you're indispensable. Personally, I don't care what kind of luck you bring to others, I don't care if you're a walking crystal ball, or if you could tell me right now who's going to win next year's Derby. I've got obligations as temple president and so do you as our appointed rabbi, and in my opinion you are not holding up your end. That's all that counts with me, not what you do to the cards and dice. We've spoken to you calmly, sympathetically, urgently, and you're still running around with Miss Little Tokyo of 1983. If you were Abraham, Moses, Moshe Dayan, and Jimmy the Greek wrapped into one, and if you still carried on as you have been, I would consider replacing you."

"Arthur, Arthur"—Abe tried to moderate his wife's charges— "you are a model, after all."

"I am a man," said Bloom, "not an Oldsmobile."

"If we can't live up to the example you set, that doesn't mean we shouldn't still have a good example." Sarah spoke strenuously, with her neck elongated, and her face seemingly never at rest. "Gardena is not New York. Here the Jews are outnumbered and outgunned. When a rabbi crosses the line as you have, and when the news gets out and the papers get hold of it as they have, and when the girl herself is writing the articles, who can say what the consequences might be? With church-synagogue relations in Gardena, with the attitude of youth!"

"Sarah"—he tried to be reasonable—"we've been over this before. We have no youth here. I'm an example for no one. For myself alone."

"Does the world end at the Gardena city line? Wake up, Rabbi. People look from all over. You know who wants to join this temple!" She leaned over toward him now and, with a gesture that Bloom did not object to, straightened his shirt collar. "Just drop this girl, Arthur. For your mother, for all of us. All can still be forgiven, and we'll resume as if nothing has happened. At this point no mistake has been made that can't be corrected."

Sarah asked for the check from the waitress and lit two cigarettes, one for herself and one for Abe.

Bloom looked into Abe's weathered face. "I don't think I'm going to be making any mistakes," he said. "I hope not, and I pray not. But tell me this: Are you asking me to resign?"

Sarah and Abe exchanged a glance. "No, we are not," she said emphatically. "We are asking you to think and to consider as you have never before had to do here, or probably at any point in your life. You're a young man, you have a whole life ahead of you. Don't ruin it."

"Do you love her?" asked Abe, quietly.

"Love has nothing to do with it," Sarah said. "Remember, Rabbi, that when you lie next to her, it is as if the body of the future of the children of Israel were lying there next to her, not just your body."

Bloom thought she was sounding awfully goyish with all this talk of "body." But he stifled an impulse to point it out, or to get up and storm out of the restaurant, which is what he really wanted to do, for he felt she was trying to humiliate him. Instead he stayed and told himself to try to understand her as much as he could. "I know girls," she went on, at the edge of control, "who ask me where are all the eligible Jewish men in California? Attractive women, smart women, college graduates, and pretty, too, who wonder when the telephone is going to ring, or wonder when they're going to meet a suitable man. An eligible, interesting man of the Jewish faith, I might add. Not Mr. Right, not Mr. Perfect. There are Jewish women out there who are worried because, let me be blunt, the Jewish men, they fear, are either all spoken for, are homosexual, or —and here's the part that hurts worst of all—they are chasing *shiksehs*. A sickness in the rest of the country, this is terrible in California, an epidemic.

"The Jews are not reproducing themselves, Rabbi. And in so doing, or so *not* doing, they are accomplishing exactly what Hitler could not accomplish. The Jews are committing slow genocide upon themselves through chasing and marrying *shiksehs* and through becoming *fagelehs*. The net result of both activities is the same: no more Jews, a world without the Jewish people."

"Nobody wants that," said Bloom.

"Good," said Sarah, breathing heavily. "I think you will soon be in a position to act on your conviction."

51

Two days later a special delivery letter arrived at Bloom's door. He noted the return address—Rabbinical Association, Theological Seminary, New York—and slowly, deliberately, slit the envelope. He thought of the old Spanish-Jewish proverb Leonidas had quoted him just the other day: Befriend the hangman until you are over the bridge. Then he read:

> Dear Rabbi Bloom:
> Members of your congregation have strongly indicated they think you are in need of some guidance in the fulfillment of your rabbinical responsibilities as well as in the conduct of your personal life. It is in the hope of assisting you that we urge you to fly out as soon as your schedule permits.

It was signed with a large "Yours Truly" by none other than his former advisor, the dean of students at the seminary, Rabbi Albert Langsam. A round-trip ticket was attached, with the date and flight number left open, made out in the name of Arthur Bloom.

Immediately he called up Dawn and told her. She answered calmly, but with a dreadful new remoteness in her voice, "I'm glad that other people are finally going to be talking to you, too. I hope they're strong and persuasive. I hope they scare and cajole you, Arthur, and bring you to your senses, by the time you come home."

"Bring me to my senses about what? After all we've been through already, you want the seminary rabbis and the Rabbinical Association to convince me I have to stop seeing you?"

"I didn't say that!"

"Then what should they convince me of?"

"To see how you are—in danger of exceeding what a rabbi should be doing. Arthur, don't you understand your congregation thinks you lead a charmed life? Some of them don't care about me at all. Some like me, want you to continue with me precisely because I'm not Jewish. This is an extremely screwy situation that you've let brew up under your roof. Arthur, are we speaking the same language? You're so focused on me, Arthur, you don't see the hole you've fallen into. And won't hear me when I talk about it to you."

A hard fistful of panic swung wildly about his insides. "Will you please go with me?"

"I can't think of a worse idea."

"Nevertheless, will you go?"

"Absolutely not."

"Will you be here when I get back? It'll be only a few days."

"Of course I'll be here," she said.

"Will you be waiting for me?"

"Of course I will."

"That's all I need to know."

52

Bloom hung up and slowly forged his anguish into action. He organized his books and papers. He called the airlines and secured a flight out on July 5; he wired Langsam of his arrival. He didn't bother to call Sarah. The synagogue would take care of itself. Brenda would cover all services for him, and the Norths—Sarah, for sure—would be delighted.

As he packed, it occurred to him the trip would buy valuable time. He called Nannette at the hospital. While dialing, he realized that if he were looking for the perfect excuse not to go, Nannette was it: How could he leave his sick mother? He was her only child, and she was still in intensive care, and under close observation by the doctors! He could not have invented a better reason, he told her on the telephone. Yet it was pusillanimous not to go and respond to charges against him; it was an admission, a running away. And Nannette agreed with him. "If you don't go," she said weakly, "I'll have another shtroke. Go and lishen and do exactly as Langsham tellsh you!"

"Ma, how did you know it's Langsam I'm going to see?"

"I'm on the board of your shynagogue, Arthur, in cashe you forgot. But everyone knowsh. Unfortunately, everyone! Fashe it, shon. You've made the temple into an aquarium and you're the biggesht fish. I am the fish's mother. I want you to behave yourshelf in New York, Arthur, and don't embarrassh me further. Remember on my father'sh shide you have rabbishe going back two centuries, and I'm sure they're all watching."

"I like to think that in heaven they have something better to do with their time."

"Arthur, remember to talk with respect."

"Your lisp's getting better already. I'm very happy about that, mom."

"No arrogansh, remember!" She paused, and Bloom could hear Leonidas whispering for her not to get excited, to get off the phone so she could eat his baklava and then rest; she was telling him to mind his own business. The sparring was a sure sign of Nannette's recovery. "No sharcashm, Arthur."

"Tell me, ma, what you think I should say to them."

"You can plead temporary inshanity—that's very popular these days. Then you're going to ask them to forgive you and give you another chance. Then you're going to call up Mrs. Levin, Mrs. Epshtein, and Ida Fine for me. After that you fly home, Arthur, and forget you ever met this *shikseh*. Arthur?"

"Yes, mama, right here, listening away."

"Be sure to take handkerchiefs and clean socks and a shweater, and remember that I love you and Leo the pest loves you, too, and wishes you, he says, a good flight. Arthur, can you also look up Gilda Fingerote's number, on Jerome Avenue?"

"Yes."

"Call her, please, in the Bronx, to see maybe she's still alive."

Trying to sleep that night, Bloom several times imagined how the jet would swoop up out of L.A. International and bank slowly over the Pacific, south over the ocean for at least a dozen miles, before it pointed its nose toward the east. He imagined that at just at this instant, as the aircraft hovered between east and west above San Pedro Harbor, two engines would suddenly explode and it would fall flaming out of the sky.

That also would be a solution.

53

The news that the rabbi was about to be called on the carpet by the authorities in New York made Bernie Levitt very excited. This was another sure sign. First, flagrant intercourse with a Japanese; now defiance of rabbinical leaders was surely in the offing. Moreover, the rabbi's mother had had a stroke; a stroke was suffering, and suffering must always precede redemption. Bernie felt that before the rabbi left, the moment should be seized and the circumstances created for Bloom to sin. Even a little sin, a moderate violation, would do; if it could be arranged, it might reveal a lot, for the time was very propitious.

Early on the morning of his departure, as Bloom went out on his veranda to water his poinsettia enough to last until his return, he saw sitting there, beside the plant, a large white bag. From the logo— a large smiling sombrero—Bloom knew the bag contained a take-out order from Rosita's, the tastiest Mexican restaurant in the area, and definitely not kosher.

At first Bloom thought there must be some mistake. He looked around for the delivery kid, but no one, positively no one, was in sight at this early hour. It was so early, in fact, that it puzzled Bloom how this food could be delivered by the restaurant, when the restaurant surely was not even open yet. He bent down to examine the bag and smelled the savory aroma of enchiladas, or maybe it was burritos —it was hard to tell. He found now on the other side a card: "This is to give you strength to tell the truth in New York. From an admirer."

Bloom stood up and looked around. Was it from Dawn? It was definitely not her style, and she would know that this kind of food at this hour might not so much give him strength to tell the truth as give him gas and a bad attack of indigestion.

Bloom picked up the bag, set it on the wrought-iron table, and opened the containers inside. There was a large helping of enchiladas, one of chicken tacos, and some guacamole. And, ah yes, a large order of the soft tortillas that he loved. He was hungry and was about to raise one of them to his lips, when he stopped suddenly and looked around. That feeling again. He surveyed the pool, the roof of the casino with its dish antenna; he even looked carefully in the thickly leaved branches of the trees, but he saw no one. Nevertheless, the order, the timing, all of this was tremendously peculiar. He put the enchiladas and the tacos back in the bag, and, reluctantly, the soft tortillas as well. It was his policy not to bring nonkosher food into his apartment, and the veranda still counted as his apartment. He was glad he had caught himself. He decided to put the bag back down on the veranda, so that whoever left it there—surely it was a mistaken address—could pick it up later. He folded down the flap of the bag firmly, went into the apartment, found a rubber band wrapped around his History of Dawn folder, and returned to the bag, which he secured with the elastic. Then he went back inside and finished packing.

Bloom had no idea that concealed behind the far wall of the synagogue, with a camera and zoom lens aimed at the veranda, was Adolph Gruen, placed there by Bernie specifically to document if and how the rabbi would bring the forbidden foods to his lips. Although Gruen had clicked away, and one of the shots did show what looked like the rabbi tasting a tortilla, there was nothing that seemed a real violation of *kashrut* that Bernie could determine, when he looked at the photographs some seven hours later. "Something strange did happen, however," Gruen told him as he left, "when I parked at the drugstore to pick up the pictures."

"Yes?"

"On my way back to the car," Gruen said softly, "I am about to open the door, and there, next to the left front tire I see a money clip. Just a clip, with no name on it, no ID, no way to return it to whoever dropped it."

"What makes you think," Bernie said with satisfaction, "that any*body* dropped it?"

"Excuse me?"

"Maybe it was placed there, just for you."

"Placed there? Who by?"

"By the Maker of us all."

"Come on!"

"How much was in the money clip?" Bernie asked calmly, as if he already knew.

"There were just some hundred-dollar bills," said Adolph.

"You can tell me how many," said Bernie. "I don't want any myself, why should I?"

"There were thirty of them. Thirty hundreds."

"I think you owe ten percent of that to the rabbi's fund, don't you? Your tithe?"

After a slight hesitation, Adolph Gruen agreed and handed over the money.

"Why be reluctant?" Bernie said, with a smile. "How else could this have been left in the parking lot?"

"Somebody could have lost the clip," said Adolph. "A simple accident. It could have fallen out of someone's pocket, that's how."

"If someone lost that much, there'd be a sign up somewhere. Wouldn't someone have put the word out? Wouldn't there be a reward, even a modest one? Have you heard anything, Adolph?"

He had not, which was unusual.

"And I assure you," Bernie went on, "you won't. Tomorrow either, or the day after. This is a gift to you, to us, my friend. This is the reward of your belief!"

That night Bernie Levitt decided to stay away from the casino and, instead, to read *Zohar* through the night and into the morning as the rabbi would be meeting the Rabbinical Association. A time of boldness was definitely at hand.

54

Panuzzi drove Bloom and his one suitcase, a distinguished and dilapidated Gladstone that had belonged to his father, through a rare smogless L.A. morning. They were doing sixty-five on the Santa Monica Freeway, bound for the airport. Cirrus clouds streaked the sky above the downtown skyscrapers, and a large orange sun was rising behind them like a backdrop for the slow drama of rush hour on the interchange.

Panuzzi turned the radio on and off and bantered but Bloom was lost and distracted in the fresh new beauty of the view. "Did you hear me, Arthur?"

"No."

"I said I think I'm falling for your colleague, Rabbi Brenda Weiner."

"Good," said Bloom absently. He found the tall palm trees that seemed like sentinels lining the freeways very appealing this morning. It was as if the road were a gauntlet, guarded by these old skinny trees, all the way from Gardena to the airport. It was a fitting way to be leaving town.

"Since she's sort of meant for you, Arthur, I thought it was only right to clear it."

"Go right ahead and fall, Angelos."

"She's as cute as a bunny."

"Have you gone out yet?"

"No."

"I suggest you look in the almanac to find out when the grunion are running again. An excellent early date."

"You're so suave and experienced now—especially for a rabbi!"

When they pulled into the treadmill lanes of the airport departure zone, Panuzzi said, "Everyone's watching you, Arthur."

"I know. It disappoints me, Angelos. I much preferred when they ignored me. I respected that in them."

Bloom, who did not like the awkwardness of long goodbyes, jumped out quickly and received the bag Panuzzi pushed toward him. He was eager to get checked in, get his seat in the nonsmoking section, buckle up, and begin to cry.

"Give 'em hell for me, too," said Panuzzi. "Sayonara, old friend."

Bloom later would think of the trip to New York, the days at the seminary, as a turning point, a kind of protracted crash that delivered up to him dream-borne recollections of his tortured rabbinical education, the grounds of his beliefs. Each day he wandered down the hot, somnolent halls of the seminary buildings—it was July and the school year was over—reliving the ridiculous contretemps of a student life which is supposed to be preparation for service to God and man. So much had happened right here, Bloom would realize, right here in the linoleum-lined halls, with their slightly ammoniacal glow of too much Janitor-in-a-Drum, their image-less walls, and the musty smell of well-thumbed and well-loved books behind every door.

Only later would he understand that in the remembered indignities of a Talmud student, exiled forever below C-plus, was a lesson about good luck, and its necessity, valuable to Bloom for Gardena and beyond. Only later would he realize that right here, on the training ground for the God of Abraham, Isaac, and Jacob, right here his youthful praying to a personal God had been somehow supplanted by lackluster entreaties to a kind of Jewish To Whom It May Concern.

Now Rabbi Albert Langsam sat across from Bloom in the seminary lounge. His hair was nearly all white and his face more aged than Bloom expected, but the cheeks were still florid with spent capillaries. He was warm and friendly. "Arthur," he said, "we always expected the unexpected of you, but maybe this time"—he laughed —"it's a little too much." The dean's joviality simmered pleasantly, but Bloom fidgeted, waiting for the *J'accuse*, for which he had prepared.

Instead he got pleasant old anecdotes, gossip, and finally the key to what turned out to be his very own old dormitory room. Langsam guided Bloom to Room 221, where he said simply that *mincha* was to be at 4:00, *ma-a-riv* services at 6:00, and dinner at 7:30. Bloom could come to all or none depending on how he felt, and then, on the following morning at 10:15, Langsam said, "You can have your little schmooze with the Peer Review Committee."

"Schmooze?" Bloom sleepily inquired, kissed the *mezuzah*, and went in.

He attended no services, slept through dinner, and did not wake up until 8:30 the next morning. He lay in bed—was it the same noisy metal bed where he had lost his virginity to Doris?—and thought he saw Dawn's face perched in the morning shadows like the bust of Pallas in the Poe poem upon the highest bookshelf. The subway rattled outside the window, the Broadway Number One line, which descended from trestle to tunnel at the seminary, and Bloom closed his eyes. He was not eager to greet the day; he pulled up his blankets, and allowed himself to wake more slowly, picking his way, like a man barefoot on glass, through the debris of last night's fitful dreaming.

Panuzzi, who had shared the room with him for two years, also floated up to Bloom. It was no dream but history recollected, the winter of 1971. He had been in a state of lethargy, caught up in the great secular sin of boredom: It was Friday, an hour when he might have gone in to prayers, but all the fervent supplications of the other students would, he knew, only make him feel worse. So he looked at the refrigerator in the corner of the room, and he knew he was going to give in. It was a time when hallucinogenic drugs could be bought on the streets as easily as pretzels and hot dogs. Bloom had done it through a connection at Columbia, a graduate student enrolled with him in a course on myth, metaphor, and symbol (at least a quarter of the class, Bloom now figured, maybe even a third, must have been high for each lecture).

Bloom had bought the cube a week before and placed it in his refrigerator. On this night he had approached it slowly and ceremoniously—this was to be his religious service for the evening —as if he were opening the door of the ark, only with more excitement because he had no idea what he would find. He had been reading Suzuki, Alan Watts, and Buber's *Tales of the Chasidim,* how these men lost themselves in extracurricular joys, in ecstasies of religious transport. Bloom could have justified himself then, he could have answered any question of Panuzzi's or Rabbi Langsam's or anybody's had they walked in and found him on bended knee about to open that cold white box, but nobody came in. So, alone, in the sixty-watt shadows of the shabbos lights he had left on in his room, Bloom reached his slightly jumpy hand into the refrigerator, and there he found, between the small-curd cottage cheese and the box of Goodman's matzoh left over from last Passover, the cube of LSD wrapped in glimmering silver foil. He peeled it back, carefully put the drug on his tongue, washed it down with a half-quart of grapefruit juice (Tropicana), and lay down on the bed to await inspirations, partings of the veil, illumination.

Bloom did not know how long he had been lying there when a rattle at the door was followed by the entrance of Panuzzi. Bloom saw the cantor-to-be as he had never seen him before—a dark elongated spheroid shape with a large mouth and a mustache above it that seemed so big as to possess a spidery life of its own. "Watch out," Bloom cried, "your mustache is trying to wind around your neck, Panuzzi!"

"Hey, knock off the nut talk. I need to borrow your Dubnov *History of Polish Jewry* and your *Playboy.*"

Bloom leaped off his bed and began to ransack the dresser. From beneath pajamas and shirts, and a muffler knitted by Nannette, he extracted the magazine. "Filth," he began to shout, "disgusting pornography, abominations!" Before Panuzzi could stop him, he threw the magazine out the window onto Broadway, two stories below. He stood panting at the window, with his hands timidly touching Panuzzi's mustache, murmuring "Sacrilege! A stench in the nostrils of God!"

"Aw, Arthur, it was the current issue."

Now Bloom's pulse had begun to beat at his temple like a piston. Panuzzi's mustache was winding itself around his neck, but there were other mutations now too; objects were losing their moorings. Bloom tried to locate the cantor somewhere in the whirling phantasmagoric contents of the room, among the papers and books, and the sabbath candlesticks that flew as in an accelerated Chagall painting across the room. Suddenly Bloom found the cantor, fell on him, and cried, "I am high, Angelos. I am ripped, I am higher than a fuckin' kite."

"Why don't you just sit down and take it easy, Arthur." Panuzzi was leaning out the window. "I'm going down to find the *Playboy*."

"Look at your mustache! It's stuffed in your mouth!"

"I'm just fine, Arthur."

"Don't leave, Panuzzi." Bloom shook him. "Promise me you won't read any filth anymore. Promise me you'll change your life just as I'll change mine. Angelos, don't read *Playboy*. Study Torah!"

"You're really a mess, aren't you?"

"From today on we'll reform?"

"Not me." Panuzzi smiled.

"Don't leave."

"Then come with me."

Bloom groped for the hand that was offered. He didn't take a coat, not even a sweater, but went in his thin white T-shirt into the December night. Because they couldn't find the magazine, Bloom wanted to go down to Forty-second Street, to Times Square, and overturn the racks full of dirty books and magazines. He wanted to storm into the adult book shops and throw the displays to the ground. Above all, Bloom wanted to keep moving, to keep walking. So Panuzzi followed, his arm around Bloom, whistling or singing songs, Jewish liturgical melodies, Beatle tunes, the Israeli national anthem, Song of the Palmach, "Come on, Baby, Light My Fire," "Rock of Ages," and the "Grace After Meals"—anything to keep Bloom a little anchored to the planet. In the thirty-degree cold, pushing through the flickering neon, on past the Manhattan facades that seemed to Bloom as thin as stage props, they breasted the wind, marching shoulder to shoulder like a hallucinogenic David and Jonathan, on toward the confrontation with the Philistines at Times Square.

It never occurred. At Fifty-fourth Street an arctic gust blew them into the lobby of the Ziegfeld Theatre. Without knowing what was playing, they bought tickets and entered. They ate popcorn and watched the hot dogs sizzle on the rotisserie. They went into the movie and left before it was finished, and Bloom did not remember a single frame. By the time they stepped off the 104 bus in front of the seminary, it was five in the morning and the LSD was wearing off; Bloom knew he would come down.

"That's very good," Panuzzi said to him back in the room, "because I just read the schedule in the hall, Arthur. Do you know you're supposed to deliver the sermon this morning?" He checked his watch. "In about four hours."

At the moment Bloom happened not to know even what year it was, let alone the week and the *parsha*, the Torah chapter that was to be read. But somehow he rallied. He had come through the trip, and his lethargy and his ennui began to melt away. He was full of the thrill of just being alive. He sensed the palpable beauty of existence, and if he couldn't fashion a sermon around such stuff, regardless of what was being read in the Torah, then to hell with homiletics and he would never make the grade as a rabbi.

So still half dazed, and with Panuzzi, that comforting mustachioed presence, sitting enfolded in his prayer shawl in the front row, Bloom began that sabbath sermon twelve years before: "I was high, and now I am low. I was humiliated, and now I am exalted. Sing God's praises on high." Bloom sermonized vividly; his oratory was sparkling. On and on he went, pursuing the theme, with the double entendres and the quotations coming effortlessly. Exaltation lit up his face as he tied in the upcoming holiday of Hanukah, with its soaring military victories for the Jewish people over impossible odds. He left his congregation of student rabbis and cantors speechless at his delivery—a combination of passion, profundity, and incoherence (the congregation was not sure in what proportions)—as if they had just been privy to the utterance of a Hebraic oracle among their own number.

A week later it was common knowledge that Arthur Bloom had delivered his first student sermon ripped on acid.

*　　*　　*

Bloom opened his eyes and pulled down the covers. His watch on the nightstand told him the interrogation would soon begin. He got himself out of bed and showered. He padded through the room, over the coolness of the uncarpeted floor, the utter strangeness of it in the very heart of its familiarity. Where was the sunshine? Where were the lovely yellow and purple bougainvillea, the Japanese, the Mexicans, the barbecuers, and the pools he had grown to love? Where was the spiciness of existence, the life lived in sharp relief that he had experienced on acid that long-ago night? To have once felt at home here, in these halls, seemed to Bloom quite incredible.

By the time he finished knotting his tie it was 10:20. Since the elevator seemed slow or out of order Bloom raced up the steps to the fifth-floor office where the representatives of the Rabbinical Association were to convene. He got there, stopped for an instant to push his hair back over his bald spot, grasped the knob, and pushed the door open.

From behind a huge pier table the august committee beheld him. To Bloom they seemed like a kind of living Jewish Mount Rushmore. Of the three men, Bloom knew only the figure in the middle, Rabbi Abraham Moses Karpf, an English scholar and Talmudist, noted for saintliness and for a teaching style that posed cryptic question upon cryptic question. The men on either side of Karpf were also bearded and seemed to defer to him. Luckily none had been Bloom's teacher during his years as a seminary student.

"Rabbi Bloom," Karpf began, "step in and tell us why you seem so out of breath."

"The stairs," Bloom panted.

"And the lift, it wasn't working?"

Bloom shook his head.

"Strange, but it operated for us. I wonder, Rabbi, would you describe yourself as an impatient person?"

Bloom shook his head again.

"Please be seated, Rabbi."

Bloom did so, slowly.

"Would you say you are a person who refuses help?"

Again no.

"Well, I hope you are right. I hope you will let us help you, young man."

"But I'm doing fine, thank you."

"But if that is the case," Karpf said with a pull at his beard, "why are we gathered here? And why have you come?"

Bloom shrugged, he feared, with a little arrogance.

Forgive me, mama, he thought.

"I see," said Karpf. "But the question before us, Rabbi, is whether *you* see?"

"See what?"

"What we all of us see!" Karpf smiled.

"I might and I might not, Rabbi, depending on what you're talking about."

"My dear boy"—Karpf kept up his smile—"I understand you write some poetry. We have some copies here in your folder, and I quite enjoyed one or two of them. You might know John Donne and Shakespeare, of course. That is the kind of seeing I'm talking about. Sight as in *King Lear*. When Donne and Shakespeare wrote about sight, about the eyes, they were talking not about eyes, you know, not about twenty-twenty and all that, but eyes, windows to the soul."

"They were talking about *in*sight."

"Precisely, my boy. So now let's talk about you, with some insight. Do you remember Talmud Nedarim, sixty-six, column B?"

Alas, Bloom did not. Karpf reached on the shelf behind him for a large volume and opened up to the column of Hebrew he had marked, and read:

> A certain man said to his wife, "I vow that you will derive no benefit from me until you show me that there is something beautiful in you."
>
> But the man could find nothing beautiful about his wife, so he came before Rabbi Ishmael ben Rabbi Yossi, who said to him, "Perhaps her head is beautifully shaped?"
>
> The man said to the rabbi, "No, it is round."
>
> "Perhaps she has beautiful hair?"
>
> "No, it is like stalks of flax."
>
> "Perhaps her eyes are beautiful?"
>
> "Goggle-eyed," said the man.
>
> "Perhaps her ears are beautiful."
>
> "They are doubled over."
>
> "And what about her nose? Is it not beautiful?"
>
> "It is swollen."

"Her lips, then?"

"Thick."

"Her neck?"

"Sunken."

"Her belly?"

"Distended, Rabbi."

"Her legs?"

"She waddles like a goose."

"Perhaps she has a beautiful name?"

"She is called Muck."

"Aha!" said the rabbi, "the vow is fulfilled. Her name suits her beautifully."

"Why quote this to me?" asked Bloom.

Karpf looked in the dossier before him. "Because I take it your Dawn Nakazawa, as you see her, also suits her name beautifully. The dawn of some kind of new life for you, a departure, another beginning for Rabbi Bloom?"

Bloom embraced silence; the silence was his friend.

"The question is: Beginning of what?"

Bloom remained silent.

Karpf closed the Talmud and took the folder that was in front of the rabbi to his left. "Speaking of beginnings, do you happen to recall your interview here, for admission to the seminary? Let me jog your memory. You were asked, among other questions: Suppose you were going to Antarctica and the conditions of your travel were such that in your backpack and survival gear there was room enough for only your *tallis* or your *tefillin,* but not both. The question is, Which would you take? Your answer, according to the record here, is that you would take neither. Considering the climate, you said you would use the space for an extra down parka or pair of socks. You said you would stow as much extra survival gear into the available space as possible. Then Rabbi Langsam, the admissions interviewer, asked if you considered your *tallis* and *tefillin* to be of less importance than a pair of thermal underwear. Your response was that in an absolute sense, as he was posing the question, there were really no grounds on which to compare underwear with a prayer shawl, or parkas and tinned food and bandages with *tefillin.* Under extreme circumstances, such as survival in Antarctica, the value of all things is subject to change, relatively, you said. Then Langsam went on to question you, Rabbi Bloom, if you thought there were not indeed some basic, minimal survival rations for the Jewish soul, the Jewish religious spirit. He asked you if you were hungry, even starving, and the only thing you could find to eat was pig, for example, would you eat it? Your answer to him was, and I quote, 'Sure thing.' One of the other interviewers, I see, made a notation, Rabbi, in which he says that he sensed in the tone of your 'Sure thing' that you had insufficient appreciation or perhaps knowledge of all the Jewish martyrs, who had given their lives rather than answer 'Sure thing' to precisely the same question put them by kings, princes, bishops, inquisitors, and tormentors throughout the ages. Your response was to quote the brilliant but ambiguous rabbinic dictum that the purpose of life was to live and that therefore staying alive is a person's first duty. Then Rabbi Langsam asked if you meant staying alive at *any* cost. And to that question," said Karpf, finally looking up to Bloom's eyes, "there is no indication in this record of your answer. I ask you now, Rabbi, whether what you are doing is worth the cost."

"But it is not a matter of life and death," Bloom protested.

Here Karpf raised a finger to stop him. "We understand from your congregational officers that you are seriously involved with Ms. Dawn Nakazawa and that she is not of the Jewish faith. This *is* a matter of life and death, I submit, as regards your professional life, and perhaps your religious life!"

"But I'm working on converting her," Bloom said.

"Bravo, my boy. If you convert her, then fine, you can go back to your business and we'll go back to ours. It's not an ideal solution, but still a solution. The question is what you intend to do if you fail to convert her. What if she does not want to become a Jew? Is there any sign that she does? How far along are you on this project?"

The room went suddenly silent. The rabbi to Karpf's right put his hand on the side of his nose and stared down at the table top. Now Bloom's time had come. It was his turn. They had asked about intermarriage, and he would tell them what he thought. He was prepared. From the moment he had laid eyes on Dawn he had been thinking about the issue; even when he wasn't thinking about it, he was thinking about it.

Up until now he had kept it almost all to himself, but they had asked, and he would tell them. For these rabbis before him, in the ivory tower of Jewish life, just did not know how very often every practicing synagogue rabbi has to grapple with this issue, in all the cities and especially in the smaller towns of America. Bloom saw no reason to obfuscate—and yet, he caught himself as he was about to begin. Why hand the rope to the hangman?

"We haven't discussed marriage," he calmly said.

"And if you did, and the young woman refused to convert, would you still marry her, under those circumstances?"

"I would," Bloom said slowly, "I would marry her, assuming she would accept me. Then through me she would get to know Judaism. Because I'm a rabbi, she would get a kind of behind-the-scenes look, and eventually, I feel certain, she would convert. Eventually, Rabbis, a matter not of principle but of time."

"My dear young man"—the rabbi to Karpf's right stirred—"may I quote you a few statistics? Between 1966 and 1972, thirty-one percent of Jewish marriages involved a partner not Jewish, and seventy-five percent of these spouses did *not* convert."

"Dawn," Bloom said proudly, "will be among the twenty-five percent who do."

"What makes you so certain?"

"Because she would be marrying me, a rabbi, a practicing Jew, someone who lives and breathes Jewish life! To you this might not seem to be the case, but I assure you it is. Night and day she would be, through me, involved in Jewish life and soon she would grow comfortable with it. Jewish books and Jewish styles, food, jokes, holidays, celebrations. As she absorbed it, she'd grow more knowledgeable and comfortable."

"She might go the opposite way," said Karpf's other colleague. "Rabbi Bloom, she might feel surrounded by it all, it might be too much for her, too different and too suffocating. This has happened before."

"Highly unlikely," Bloom said, with assurance. "She loves Jews. She's really hooked on us. There are Christian Zionists, you know. There are some non-Jews who just can't get enough of the Jews, and I sense she may be one of them, although she might not admit it. You'll pardon me for saying so, but you gentlemen should be as lucky as I am. She doesn't talk much about it, but I know she thinks Jews are a race of geniuses. Of course when she marries me—if she does —she'll quickly be disabused of the notion. But she believes that the pivotal characters of our times are Marx, Freud, and Einstein. At

Berkeley she had a professor who told her that the gathering of
Jewish scientists and intellectuals in America, as a result of the Nazi
persecutions and the expulsion from Europe, rivaled in brilliance the
two other greatest periods in Western civilization—the Athens of
Socrates and the High Renaissance in Europe. Gentlemen, I ask you,
can a woman with such thoughts in her gorgeous head ever, ever,
be considered a bad risk?"

"Yes." They shook their heads in unison. "Yes."

"Look at intermarriage, gentlemen, from a fresh point of view.
Instead of seeing it as a source of problems, think of it as a source
of challenge. I'm sad to say that people in mixed marriages are often
more interested in and sympathetic to Jewish lifestyles and culture
than born Jews themselves. They're doing something on their own,
a natural outgrowth of their situation, that we throw away millions
of dollars trying in vain to do in all the Hebrew schools across the
country: They're actually looking for, seeking out ways of being
Jewish, struggling to find equations that make their personal life and
Jewish life agree. They're often creatively Jewish, Rabbis, and they
don't take for granted the things that born Jews do take for granted
and let wither away or slide out of consciousness. They're the fastest-
rising minority in the Jewish community—intermarried couples.
Why shouldn't intermarried people have a rabbi of their own and
a congregation of their own? If Ashkenazim do and Sephardim do,
and the gays do here in New York, and feminists do, why shouldn't
the intermarrieds? If it comes to this in my life, why shouldn't I be
the rabbi that intermarried couples in southern California come to
to talk things over? Why shouldn't they come to me to explore?
There's incredible potential religious energy here. You can either
harness it and turn it into a great religious reservoir for ourselves and
future generations of Jews, or you can ignore, or worse yet, reject
intermarried couples, and the thing will blow up in our faces. But
we all agree on this much: that the intermarried couple is here to
stay."

"Is this a prepared statement, Rabbi?"

"I guess it is."

"Alas," said Rabbi Karpf, "maybe the intermarried couple is, but
the intermarried rabbi is not only not here to stay, it is to be avoided
at all costs."

Thus ended the first session.

55

Although the moment was not yet propitious to make revelations to Bloom, Bernie Levitt seized the rabbi's absence to appeal, for the first time, directly to Dawn. He called her at the paper. After some hesitation, she agreed to have lunch with him. He picked her up and they drove to a restaurant on North La Cienega Boulevard in L.A., where they sat in a dark booth in the rear.

"Look at that," he began after they had ordered, "all that frenzy, all that hectic energy! And for what? For love and money!"

"Is that so bad?" she asked him, "especially if it's for love?" She was still very much on her guard. Down the aisle from them people sitting on bar stools were energetically body-talking and drinking.

Like a play-by-play commentator on life, Bernie dissected: "Yes, you need love and money, but people live for something else too, Miss Nakazawa, something far beyond this bar and grill—"

"Run that by me again."

He stopped and clinked glasses with her, taking the measure of her interest. "Listen, all people, yourself included, want to leave a mark, right? The best of them, those who do things to help their fellow man, even they wonder about their contribution, what they leave behind. Can I make a difference? they ask."

"Mr. Levitt," she said, "I've got a deadline to make tonight. What is it you want to tell me?"

"I've got a deadline, too. The world has a deadline." He unfurled the *Times*, which he had folded into a tube in his pocket. "Look, tensions in the Middle East, the big face-off coming between the Russians and us. Read, look! There's this kid who suddenly snaps, goes up the tower and shoots up all those people at that school in Texas. Look! Genocide in Cambodia, massacres in Guatemala, violence all over Africa, the poor rising up and soon to cut the throats of the rich for food, for fuel, for who knows what. Miss Nakazawa, you know politicians can't fix things up, and people alone can't fix things up so they stay fixed. Yesterday's demonstrator is today's senator, and what fundamentally changes in the process? What the world needs . . ."

Dawn checked her watch. "What the world needs is people who say what they have on their mind and get on with it."

Bernie sat back and smiled. He liked her, he understood why the rabbi liked her. "Listen," he said, "you're right, absolutely right. I'm here to tell you this: We, that is, you and I, are in a position to make a difference in the world, a real difference. We can help pave the way for a time when the world will not only be improved but maybe perfected. A golden age, Miss Nakazawa. A perfect planet, a place of peace and contentment, where nation shall not lift up sword against nation. I'm telling you, Miss, Arthur Bloom, our rabbi, well may be the way. Don't ask me to explain everything because I can't, but rest assured he is on the inside . . ."

"Inside of what?"

"Miss Nakazawa, Rabbi Bloom, in our estimation, is not only a man of God, he is God's personally picked man. He's the guy God has been dealing all the high cards to lately, and in so doing, they have been falling to us here. Forgive me—I don't want to use old-fashioned words and phrases, trite jargon—I don't want to invoke anything from the past to compare the rabbi to. This man has great reticence and humility that are beguiling, as you well know, but he also possesses powers that are unique. Although he hardly believes it himself yet, he's the source of our movement, one that is growing here. You and I believe in Bloom; we know he's the real McCoy. I want you, I need you, to join forces with us."

"Does this movement have a headquarters?"

"Rabbi Bloom is its name, and you and he, wherever you are, are headquarters."

Dawn sat straight up in the booth and looked squarely at Bernie. "Arthur Bloom," she said calmly, "is a flesh-and-blood man. He is a person like you and me. Nothing less but nothing more."

"Hey, no argument," Bernie said quickly. "None whatsoever, but the man has a track record of being able to help people, in providing good luck when only good luck can salvage a situation. It starts with gambling, sure, but it goes way beyond. Look, you've been out of town for a long time. You don't know what he's done, what he's meant to us. We've got concrete, observable, documented evidence that this man is on top of something, that he's mining a vein, that he's keeping watch at the gate, that he's the toll collector on the highway to powers beyond. I kid you not, Miss Nakazawa. I know I sound daffy to you, but believe me I've had to pinch myself, too, to make sure I'm awake. The kind of information I'm talking about, the knowledge we have, now inspires in us a sense of responsibility. We need to study him more, we need to harness his powers, to use it to unite all peoples, to bring together all souls of all races—yours, mine, David Diamond's—to end the madness of the world, with its sorrow, war, and degradation. The prelude is here, the first act is in Gardena, the first of the birthpangs of this new phase is upon us. We're the midwives, Miss Nakazawa, and I wanted to ask you to help us because the contractions are coming faster and faster."

Dawn slowly finished what was left of her beer. Here, she thought, someone else is out to convert me! She didn't want to be here, story or not. She didn't want this man to buy her even a beer. She decided to cut it short, but found herself asking, "What's being born?" She covered her face with her raised mug, and then pressed the cool glass against her cheek.

"The harbinger," he answered in a whisper, "the first bloom before harvest."

"Indeed."

"Yes." He went on, ignoring her irony, "Since the rabbi found you, it has become clearer and clearer."

"What has?"

"That whenever he does that which he should *not* be doing, whenever he, in short, sins, our luck goes through the roof, and potentially that good fortune can spread out of Gardena, like ripples in a pool where a stone has been dropped, to unlimited points beyond."

"I want to make sure I understand what you're saying. Are you predicting the imminent arrival of something like a messiah?"

"I believe I am."

"You *believe?*" she asked. "Do you have by any chance a specific date, time, or place, Mr. Levitt?"

"Well, we can't be as precise as the people who predict when the grunion are going to run."

Dawn hardly blinked. Carefully, calmly, she let that pass.

Bernie went on, "For all I know"—he laughed, warm now to his pretty listener—"the messiah could arrive in a Cadillac."

Dawn smiled back at him.

"And here in Gardena, too. Why not here? It's got to be some-where. It's easy to joke about the *mashiach*, Miss Nakazawa. That's what we call him in Hebrew. But what's absolutely no joke at all is the arrival."

"You're certain?" she asked again.

Bernie talked to her then in a hushed, whispered voice for several minutes. "We need a test," he concluded excitedly as he buried her hand between his. "We need a big test, really hard evidence. We need you to help us make our case so that it is unmistakable."

"Please be specific."

"We need you to help the rabbi do that which is just about the worst thing a rabbi can do. If we're right—forget the thousands we'll make—the man's powers will shine forth for all to see beyond refutation. We're way beyond money."

How she now wished that she had a tape recorder with her to pick all this up. Though no crime was being committed by Bernie, she wanted to have a record of his words; she wanted, above all, to be able to play them back to Arthur loud and clear. "What is it you had in mind for me to do?" she asked cautiously.

"Help the rabbi do that which he would never think of doing himself. Help him do that which is anathema, which every moment and impulse of his life and training have made him find evil and repulsive. Help him do this so that, like scientists probing mysteries, we can monitor the results!" He paused and she waited silently for the kicker. "Help him to convert! Make him become a Christian, a Hindu, a Shintoist—whatever you are. To get immersed, to be baptized, the whole *megillah.*"

She took out two dollar bills to pay for the beers and laid them on the table. Without a word, she slid out of the booth, into the aisle, and walked straight out.

Bernie followed her out and down the steps, calling, "Let me drive you back."

She stopped and whirled around toward him. "I would never do what you say, never. You're a madman! Do you hear? A madman." Then she rushed down the street into the thick noon crowd.

As Bernie drove back over the freeways to Gardena, he felt satisfied with his effort. He knew she might not agree. In fact, he had expected it. It was sufficient that he had told her, because he knew she would write about it in her paper, which is precisely what Dawn did.

56

As the second session began, Rabbi Karpf drew a long, sibilant breath. "Tell us, Arthur, what you think about children in a mixed marriage. Jewish identity is transmitted, as you know, through the mother."

"And why not through the father?" answered Bloom in a voice that was bolder than he intended. "Fathers are taking a growing role in child-rearing. It only seems right to consider it, sir."

"And what of the fact, Rabbi, that Jewish identity has passed through the maternal line for some five thousand years? Five thousand years, Rabbi Bloom." Karpf held up his fingers. "Five thousand years is not to be sneezed at."

"Yes," Bloom said, far more quietly this time, "but that argument is a weak one, if I may be permitted to be critical. Longevity does not equal authority."

"The tradition is not ignorant, Rabbi Bloom," said Karpf. "The tradition is matrilineal, young man, because it can always be established who a child's mother is, while fatherhood remains elusive."

"Nevertheless," Bloom answered, "if a kid is being raised by a Jewish father and a non-Jewish mother . . ."

"Such as a child of yours, should that come to pass," said the rabbi beside Karpf.

"Yes," Bloom answered, "if I should be so lucky. If such a father comes to me in Gardena and says, 'Teach my kid Hebrew so he can have a bar mitzvah,' I will never turn such a family away." The rabbis on both sides of Karpf looked at each other disappointedly. "This is strictly theoretical for me, of course," Bloom added, "because there hasn't been a bar mitzvah of any kind in Gardena in six years, and that's likely to stay the case."

"May God keep it that way," one of the rabbis mumbled.

"You see," said Bloom, who had heard this, "you see why the trouble continues. The much vaunted and genuinely laudable making-you-feel-at-home style of the Jews goes right out the window when it comes to converts and to intermarriage. I've seen it in all the pulpits I've served in, across the country, and now, today, this minute, I see it here, right here in this room, at the source. When you gentlemen turn up your noses at the convert

and the intermarried couple, noses turn up at every synagogue in
America."

"It is Rabbi Bloom of Temple Elijah, Gardena, California, we are
discussing," Karpf reminded him, "not our generation of rabbis."

"Nevertheless," Bloom said, "it is my humble opinion that what
is endangering Jewish life today is neither me nor intermarriage. The
problem with Jewish life today is the problem with life in general:
Marriages are dissolving, rapidly. What's the point in having a lot
of Jewish marriages, or any marriages for that matter, if they all fall
apart? What is the Jewish community after, I ask you, Rabbis? Are
they after quality Jewish marriages or quantity? Do they want Jewish
marriages by the bodycount, so that the statistics-keepers will be able
to sleep nights? In California people of all religions are divorcing like
traffic accidents on the freeways, by the day, by the hour, they go
crash, and other people drive by and look out the window and they
say, 'Thank God that's not me.' And while they're looking in the
rearview mirror, boom, they go crash, too. And the result is a lot of
unhappy Jewish people, and damaged, screwed-up kids, and creepy
singles clubs and health clubs sprouting up on every corner. Jewish
married life—like all married life these days—is benefiting only one
group: the psychiatrists and the psychologists. What are the statistics on divorce among intermarried couples? Is anybody keeping
those numbers? And if it turned out that such marriages, united by
the magnetism of opposites attracting, turned out to be far more
durable, would we as rabbis have to rethink our position? Rabbi
Karpf, you know as well as I do that good old American Judaism
today needs a tremendous helping hand, and from everyone. For
twenty years the picture has been falling into place: the school
system is a disaster, the synagogues are empty, the—"

"Enough, Rabbi, enough." Karpf was on his feet. "I believe we
have heard enough. I think I speak for the entire committee when
I say you have abused the forum we have given you. Your thoughts,
Rabbi, are discomfiting, but not nearly so much as is the frenzied
manner of your presentation. Is this your usual homiletical style? If
you sermonize this way, is it any wonder, Rabbi, that at your synagogue chaos reigns?"

Bloom thought it best to end positively. "As I've said before, my
intention is not to sow discord. I think night and day about converting Dawn. I am, as you well know, a rabbi."

"You are, at least for now. We'll adjourn and meet again this time tomorrow. Between now and then," Karpf said in a hushed voice, "I urge you to think carefully, Rabbi. Pray a little, too. It won't hurt."

57

CAR DEALER PREDICTS
MESSIAH WILL ARRIVE IN CADILLAC

Gardena, California: "The Messiah will be arriving soon, and probably in high style," said Bernard Levitt, the owner and operator of Bernie Levitt Cadillac.

Mr. Levitt, who is an active member of Temple Elijah, an eccentric Jewish congregation here, recently said that he has had a series of communications with messianic messengers, one of whom appeared to him last week right on his lot.

"He wore a suit, blindingly white, so that it was difficult to make out any facial features. I was on the lot, on my way into the showroom, and the force of this presence stopped me, reached out from the white silver fog that had descended over the area. Then a voice, speaking in Hebrew, said, 'Soon, soon, I am coming soon.'"

When the vision ended and the fog lifted, Mr. Levitt asserted that the used Cadillac he had been standing in front of had been transformed into a shining white model, 1983 Coupe De Ville. "I have no other explanation," said Levitt.

David Diamond, the sexton of Temple Elijah, and an employee of Mr. Levitt, was on the lot at the time of the messianic sighting. He said he saw nothing, although he admits that he was in the back room of the office area at the time. "Bernie is well-meaning," said Mr. Diamond, "but also a little *meshugeh* these days."

Meshugeh is the affectionate Yiddish word for crazy.

DN

58

Bounding out of the interrogation chamber into the corridor, in need of fresh air, Bloom walked down the dozen steps of the seminary and eagerly dived into the noisy anonymity and déjà vu of Broadway.

From 114th Street up to 125th, the forbidding beginning of Harlem, Bloom walked north and south, up and back, touching the trunks of trees of his student years, thicker now by twelve rings. He stopped in front of a plaque on a Columbia University building marking the site of a skirmish where General Washington's irregulars ran into British troops pursuing their advantage after their advance through Long Island. Right here, a block from what is now the site of the best meatball hero on the West Side, the colonial troops had traded volleys with the British and then run. Was he, Arthur Bloom, in spite of all his tough talk, preparing to retreat as well?

There was something in his sneaker, and Bloom took it off. As he stood there on one foot, he imagined that God Himself (I will now indulge, Bloom thought, in a little friendly anthropomorphism) must be on the verge of tears as He stared down at His Jews, His blacks, His Orientals, His cops, garbagemen, dope pushers, hot-dog vendors, taxi drivers, that idle professor, the harassed businessman yelling at the bicycling boy who almost hit him, or this California rabbi with one sneaker off—all the ridiculous Broadway of His creation. To Bloom it was all so terribly moving and so incomprehensible, but to God, that First Brain of brains, it must be a cinch. Bloom found the stone in his sneaker, flicked it out, retied the lace, and walked on.

He had coffee in the same restaurant catercorner from the seminary where he had gone for his surreptitious cheeseburgers during his first year at rabbinical school. The fry cook was a different man, but the steamy place was filled up with that same cheesy, oniony odor. Later, at his pulpits, whenever he read in Exodus and Deuteronomy, the foundations of the Jewish dietary laws—"Thou shalt not cook a kid in the milk of its mother"—he did not think about Canaanite rites but of this cheap, redolent greasy spoon.

Bloom returned to the seminary. Beside the antique switchboard, on the board for notes and messages, he found that someone had called him from California. On the orange slip where she had left no telephone number, the seminary secretary had written the name of the caller: Dan Menachem Zower.

59

Not Dan Menachem Zower, but Dawn Nakazawa, called again at midnight New York time, as Bloom was drifting off to sleep. She told him about her beer with Bernie Levitt, and waited. Bloom was so perplexed by her businesslike tone—she had barely asked him how his interviews had gone—that his tongue froze in long-distance silence. "Why don't you know these things, Arthur? Doesn't anybody talk to you?"

"Of course they do."

"Then why don't you know this stuff? Why does it come as such a surprise to you when I tell you that people are talking about you in crazy, scary ways? Wake up, Arthur. Rub your face with cold water and look around you. Levitt's calling you his leader, and a helluva lot more."

"These notions are silly," he finally said. "They get bandied about. Of course I've heard of them. Nonsense. Anyway, it's just a few people. In any large group—"

"It doesn't take many."

"What doesn't?"

She said, "All it takes is a few, and then it grows. Before you know it, there'll be a cult built around you."

"There's no cult."

"The fact that you're unaware of one doesn't mean it doesn't exist. Don't you see? Don't you understand, Arthur? No one talks to you. That's the point. It's all kept from you. You're kept above it, beside it. You're the holy, the lucky rabbi. You operate on a plane above. Others are supposed to concern themselves with plans, with the details."

"I beg your pardon, Dawn, but there is no cult. The congregants are not adolescents searching for answers or highs; these are grown-ups. These are people who have worked and struggled all their lives. They go to the casinos for socializing and to make some of their tough days pass more quickly. They come to me, I think, for a reminder that there's something even more important than cards, and, maybe, I hope, they also get some peace of mind."

There was a long pause. "I beg your pardon, Arthur, I don't like speaking harshly to you, but now you're acting not lucky but schmucky. It's just as I told you when you left, and before that a dozen times. It starts with gambling, but if they believe you can intervene in blackjack, why not in real estate, in life, in love, in politics, in the affairs of the Gardena City Council, the state of Israel, the world? This is the implication, the logical place it can lead. Have you ever, Arthur Bloom, in a moment of reflection, asked yourself where all of this can go? Where it *is* going?"

"Yes, a few of them have superstitions," said Bloom. "I don't deny that. But I want them to keep coming to the shul. If I reform them, I'll reform them away from attending, and then what have we accomplished?"

"QED," said Dawn. "*Quod erat demonstrandum.* You're casualizing it all, you refuse to take it seriously, even though they are taking you *very* seriously. This is bad faith, Arthur. When eight people call you a horse, consider the possibility that you're a horse—okay?"

"What's happening to us?" Bloom asked shakily.

"Nothing's happening to us. We're fine, Arthur. It's this lucky rabbi, this third party, that I'm worried about."

"Please don't worry," he said, at last encouraged by the return of the voice of the Dawn he knew. "I'm holding up my end here, if you're interested."

"Of course I'm interested, but, Arthur, I want you to focus on yourself now, on your congregation, not just on me. Okay?"

"I am no guru."

"But, Arthur, this cute little lucky gift of yours, as they call it, the knack people believe you have, is becoming a dangerous thing. Gurus often speak of themselves as teachers and among other things as rabbis, as Hassidic types. The last thing in the world I want is for that to begin happening to you."

"And you think it is?"

She hesitated and then said, "At times, yes."

"At times you're paranoid."

"I don't like the way you attack me every time we discuss this. Am I hitting a nerve? Arthur, you're allowing yourself to be manipulated and used. Your innocence is wearing thin."

"I am not innocent, and you are overdoing it. William Randolph Hearst provoked the Spanish American War with his articles, and you're provoking all of this with yours."

"I can hear you, Arthur. You're calling me a yellow journalist." She was silent and then added, "I need a man, Arthur, with his feet solidly on the ground."

Bloom put his hand out, palm to heaven. "What's happening here? Is all we can do insult each other?"

Her only answer was that she would pick him up at the airport, if he still wanted her to.

60

The next day, an unusually fine morning for July in New York, with a bright sun and brisk wind, the proceedings of the Peer Review Committee continued, with the third and final session. They had mulled over his remarks, they told Bloom, and while the future directions of American Judaism were indeed open to question, it was not the committee's intention to debate these issues, especially with a mind like Bloom's (he took this *not* to be a compliment). They told him they had reviewed his grades, his official record, and his teacher's judgment of his character, and had concluded that the skein running throughout the record was that in the case of Arthur Bloom there was something important left unsaid, infractions that were not fully reported or investigated. Even beyond that there was a puzzling rabbinical *je ne sais quoi.* They described 1967, the year of Bloom's admission, as one full of pressure and confusion at the seminary; the several years afterwards only became more difficult. Perhaps admission standards should have been more rigorous, perhaps in Bloom's case the seminary had been too uncritical.

"What are you getting at?" Bloom wanted to know.

"Perhaps," Karpf told him, "it was a mistake to let you into rabbinical school. Perhaps, however, we can also offer you now a long-overdue opportunity to consider whether the rabbinate is truly your calling. Maybe your activity points to an interest in a career teaching philosophy or poetry, a profession you can practice outside of the Jewish world and in a secular institution. Normally, of course, we do not urge rabbis as far along in their careers as you are to consider such decisions, but in your case, Rabbi Bloom, we are prepared to admit error and make an exception."

"You want me out?" Bloom asked plainly.

"Yes," Karpf answered him. "If you can't stop the shenanigans you've begun in California, then, yes, you should seriously consider packing it in."

Bloom listened in silence; he was thinking of Dawn.

"And," Karpf finished up his task, "may we wish you a safe and pleasant flight back to—how do they so charmingly refer to it?—the City of the Angels?"

61

After having waited three-quarters of an hour, Bloom finally saw Bernie approaching, and he intercepted the car dealer a block beyond the synagogue. The two men walked into the empty sanctuary and sat. Bloom looked nervously into Bernie's eyes, but the car dealer scrupulously avoided the rabbinical gaze. Instead he clapped his hands curiously together and said, "My, my, Rabbi, I feel as if I'm about to be called on the carpet by you, but, you know, it doesn't really trouble me; it just gives me pleasure. Your simple presence gives me pleasure!"

"I'm sorry to hear that," said Bloom.

"But no, Rabbi, no! When I look at you, I am looking at a man I believe in. That's why. It's no mystery."

"I don't like that word, *believe*, Bernie, at least not in this context."

"You don't have to like it, Rabbi, although I, of course, wish you did. But don't make fun of it, please. I've been looking forward to speaking with you for days, ever since your return to us."

"Now you have me," Bloom said quietly, reasonably. "Tell me what you're stirring up."

"You know where I am headed this morning?"

Bloom did not, obviously.

"I am on my way to say congratulations to Elsie Heller. You know her?"

Of course Bloom did; she was a regular at the synagogue.

"Well, sir, she believes she is now, at the age of fifty-one, and after many operations, tests, and years of trying and frustration, pregnant. She's going to have a baby, Rabbi, and she swears it couldn't have happened without you, without being near you *shabbat* after *shabbat*."

"And her husband, I suppose, had nothing to do with it?"

"You're overly modest, Rabbi!"

"Why do you believe"—he could hardly get the words out—"that I am lucky, Bernie? Why do Elsie and Lucy and all the rest? What's the bottom line on this, Bernie? I think it's time we were honest with one another."

Bernie smiled his knowing smile. "You're the bottom line, sir. You are helping us win the race, Rabbi."

"One minute I believe I understand you," Bloom said, "and the next you drift out of focus. Look, we both are involved in Jewish life. It's a big part of yours, I know, and I'm proud of that in you. And it's pretty much all of mine. What race are you referring to? I don't know of any Jewish concept that says anything about a race."

"Noah's generation, Rabbi. We were all involved in a major race back then because except for Noah everyone struggled, raced, and lost. He won then, and we are all racing not to drown again, Rabbi. We're all of us latter-day Noahs, racing against destruction. You know what it says in the Book: 'Always, a few, always a remnant will survive.' You're our rabbi," Bernie went on. "You're the rabbi of the remnant, whoever we will be."

Bloom thought earnestly about Dawn's accusations, and yet as he listened to this man, he heard Bernie's seriousness there too, integrity amid the nutsiness. It seemed to Bloom colossally academic to call Bernie's attention to the fact that Jews are not descendants of Noah, Noah being not Jewish, pre-Abrahamic.

"You're exaggerating, my friend."

"Oh, no, Rabbi. Everyone can make a contribution. But not every man's contribution is the same. You can deny and deny and deny your way up and down Casino Boulevard, but I will still know what my eyes have seen."

"Which is?"

"Rabbi"—he was up now and talking to Bloom from the aisle—"what year did the Bomb first go off? What year?"

"Nineteen forty-five. What's that got to do with anything?"

"And when were you born?"

"Nineteen forty-five."

"Well?"

"Well what? Millions of other people were born then, too."

"Who's to say, Rabbi, that had you not been among them, or if one little molecule of you, one particle of air, one leaf on a tree, one sentence uttered by someone now long forgotten, one thought, one incident, one birth—yours, for example—hadn't happened or had happened differently during these thirty-eight years, then, might not this alteration, like dominoes falling crisscross over all the patterns of chance, have resulted, effect after cause, in a changed world? Maybe even an annihilated world, like Noah's. Maybe even worse. Maybe vaporized, obliterated, smashed into light fading throughout the solar system."

"Tell me one more thing." Bloom now stood, and paced, with the dealer, down the aisle and around in front of the first row of chairs in the sanctuary. "Tell me, why did you ask Dawn Nakazawa to try to convert me?" He saw Bernie stop suddenly, his back to him, and then he rocked slightly, ever so slightly. Bloom had saved this for last. "Why, Bernie?"

Bernie's face flushed and he turned away from Bloom. "Did I do that?" He took a step toward the dais. He saw the holy ark and above it in Hebrew letters: Know Before Whom You Stand.

"She says you did."

"We were having some general discussion, Rabbi. You know how she's interviewed me before, for her articles. Maybe she misunderstood."

"What if she didn't misunderstand?"

"Let me put it this way. Did it ever occur to you as significant, Rabbi, that Dawn is not just any old Oriental? That given the wide variety of people in town, residents *and* visiting gamblers, you could have fallen for anyone, a Mexican, or another Asian type, a Korean, a Malaysian, a Chinese, you name it; maybe even a Vietnamese out of perhaps guilt motives your generation has about that war? But you most definitely did not. And that's the point. You fell for a Japanese, a representative of the only nation on earth that has been nuclear-bombed, that has been threatened, like the Jews, with extinction. You see, Rabbi, you and Dawn are not two people alone in this. I see your affair as much more significant than a private carrying-on. Personified in you two representatives are the two great modern victim nations, *the* victim nations, a romance of history. Rabbi, this is a great cautionary tale. Great forces are at work through you and Nakazawa to try to express themselves. Those that were down and almost out, almost annihilated, shall rise again. Your union, your *zivug*. Rabbi, you've got to take the long view. 'Every one of us wise, every one of us powerful, every one of us a king,' " Bernie softly quoted the Passover Haggadah. "Only in your case, Rabbi, it is more than poetry, more than prayer."

"Too much," said Bloom, slumping back into a chair. "Too much."

"Have I, have we, ever asked you to carry any burden? Don't feel burdens, please. Just be yourself, enjoy yourself, do as you feel, do as you decipher your heart, and what you choose will be right. Through you forces can pass without you even being aware of them, just as there can be wind without our seeing it."

"Through me," Bloom sighed, "pass lower-back ache, anxiety, and a fugacious sense of happiness. That is all, Bernie. That is all!"

62

The Jewish calendar was being of no help to Bloom, because a particularly onerous time was approaching—the Fast of Lamentations, Tisha b'Av, and not very long afterward Rosh Hashanah and Yom Kippur, the holiest period of the year. Because much work and preparation were required for these holidays and because the question of the direction of Temple Elijah, and in particular, its rabbi, was still up in the air, the temple board convened yet another meeting.

In a spirit of magnanimity, Sarah offered a compromise: Bloom would not be forced out of his post—not yet anyway—but he would co-officiate or alternate officiating at all services through the High Holidays with student-rabbi Brenda Weiner. Bloom would suffer no loss of pay or benefits.

Bloom also felt so weary, drained of the physical and spiritual energy the holidays required, that he gratefully accepted. What's more, he was terribly worried about a rift developing between himself and Dawn. The appeal of the compromise to Bloom was that it would keep the congregation together, for now.

In fact everybody seemed happy as they left the meeting at the temple. Abe North had a big smile across his face, and Panuzzi was particularly delighted, because the rabbi he would be working with most on the preparation of services—Brenda—had recently become his girlfriend.

Only Nannette, who attended on the arm of Leonidas and Bloom, left unhappy. "It's a demotion," she said to Leonidas.

"One he has worked very hard to earn." The Greek winked.

"Think of it this way, mama," said Bloom. "I'm on my way to becoming the world's youngest emeritus rabbi."

The aftermath of the meeting was a moment of repose, the first in a long time at the synagogue. The tranquillity, however was to be short-lived, for on the very next day these separate, but, Bloom could not help but feel, related, developments occurred: Celeste Fried, who had never had bacon in her life, went to the Casino Coffee Shop and ordered a BLT; Adolph Ginsberg, Eli's only son, and a bachelor, felt obliged to reveal to his aged father that he had chosen not to marry and have children because he was a homosexual; somebody spray-painted across the sidewalk in front of the synagogue under the willows, *The End of Days Has Arrived*"; and the pool in the back of the shul became strewn along the bottom with hundreds of pennies, a floor of copper, for to throw in a coin, it was said, could bring the thrower benefits ranging from a run of flushes at poker to eternal life.

Bloom decided it was time for him to speak to Bernie Levitt again.

63

"Sit down," Bloom said to the car dealer as Bernie entered the rabbi's study. "I'm glad you could come so promptly. And I'm going to come to the point just as quickly. I'm offended by what you are doing. It's wrong, false, misleading, and I am not lending myself to deceptions."

"Rabbi, Rabbi," Bernie tried to mollify him, "how can you sit there and say to me you haven't brought us grand good times here, and much more?"

"That's not the point. The point is what you're making out of it. This is the classic mountain out of the molehill. This place is a molehill, I am a molehill of a rabbi, I am not a lucky anything. A few dollars won at a slot machine because some woman notices I tug at my chin three times and she taps the side of the machine three times before cranking, this amounts to nothing. It justifies none of your claims. Why are you doing this?"

"Rabbi, Rabbi! Don't deny the signs. The more you see her, the better it is. Wrong is right, Rabbi, and you are antinomianism personified. There has never been anything like it."

"Antinomianism, sir, is a Christian term and has nothing to do with me, or with reality here in Gardena. Now I am prepared to believe that you *did* urge Dawn to convert me. To convert me, your rabbi!"

Bernie listened intently, silently.

"If I see you wearing a crucifix in the shul, or if you scrawl eschatological graffiti on the synagogue grounds, or act in any way deliberately offensive to our traditions, I'm going to ask you to leave the congregation. I don't want this to happen, and I don't want to embarrass you, Bernie, but be warned."

"I'm listening to every word you're uttering, Rabbi."

"I bet you are."

"What you say matters to me, to us. We'll try to improve. We're just borne along by you, to wherever you're taking us."

This was very frustrating to Bloom. He had wanted to refute, deny, shoot down, and admonish—but his volleys, caught by this car dealer, were turned into signs and symbols, omens, prophecies. He was sick of it, angry at always finding himself outmaneuvered and

outplayed. "If you don't stop," Bloom said, "my next move is going
to be very serious." Bloom had no idea what that move might be,
but he felt a threat was in order. "Very serious."

"Whatever you wish, Rabbi."

"Don't you understand it can't go on like this? What will it take
you to stop?" Bloom pleaded. "A miracle?"

The dealer rose in front of the rabbi's cluttered desk. His heart
accelerated. "Precisely," he said, "a miracle."

64

In form it was an ordinary-looking 8½-by-11-inch piece of paper,
hand-lettered in black, that came fluttering into the synagogue in
the outstretched fingers of Angelos Panuzzi. Bloom, who was on the
dais rolling the Torah into its proper place for the sabbath reading,
looked up. The ark of the Torah was open behind him and he turned
to close it when his yarmulkah fell off his head. He bent, picked it
up, and habitually kissed it before replacing it.

"You're not going to believe this, Arthur." Down the aisle came
the paper, and behind it came Panuzzi, as if the paper were pulling
the cantor.

Bloom sat down, dangled his legs over the edge of the stage, took
the paper from his cantor, and read:

THE END OF DAYS MAY BE AT HAND

Time:	Monday, July 18, the eve of the fast of the Ninth of Av
Place:	Ted Kasuyama's Japanese Garden 11403 El Segundo Blvd.
Entertainment:	Immediately after a traditional sushi dinner we will go by chartered bus to Santa Anita for an evening at the racetrack
Reservations:	CRestview 4-3546, Bernie Levitt Cadillac

"Where'd you get this?"

"I found this one tacked to a telephone pole. When I was at the store this morning, I saw that one had been put on the bulletin board, too. It's something, isn't it?"

"He's organizing a sushi and gambling party on one of the strictest fast days of the Jewish year!" Bloom was shaking his head. "What the hell has gotten into him!"

"I don't know," said Panuzzi. "What are we gonna do?"

The answer came to Bloom easily. "I'm going to observe the fast and celebrate the day right here, with you and Brenda, just as it should be done. What more can I do? I can't call the police."

"You've got to do something, Arthur. It's a challenge, man. He's throwing down the gauntlet."

"I know, I know." Bloom was up on the dais now, pacing, an expectant father waiting for resolution to be born. "I've been worrying about this for weeks, I've been dreading something like this, Angelos. I've been hoping and praying that I could keep it together. Dammit. Dammit all!" He took the yarmulkah off his head, smoothed the lining, and replaced it. "Listen, every time you see one of these around, anywhere, at the laundromat, the coffee shop, anywhere, you tear it down, okay? You discourage everyone from going, everyone you run into from even thinking about attending something like this."

"Got it."

"You tell them, anyone you run into . . . in fact you write up a counter notice and put it up at the store. No, no, that'll just play into his hands. No, you tell everyone that we, the temple leadership, frown on this activity. No, more than frown, you tell people they are in violation of one of the most important of Jewish practices."

"They'll all say back to me, 'So's the rabbi.' "

"Then you tell them there's no comparison. Tell them the rabbi is a serious, committed, believing Jew, who happens to have fallen for a Japanese woman, and that Bernie Levitt is—"

"What is he?" Panuzzi interrupted. "What's he after?"

"He wants to turn everything on its head for some reason. I don't know what he's after. Believe me, I don't, but he wants to involve me, force my hand, make me do something I don't want to do." Bloom's eyes slowly began to close and his shoulders hunched up and shook. A sigh came out of Bloom that echoed through the empty sanctuary.

65

On Shabbat Hazan, the sabbath before the Ninth of Av, Bloom stood behind his lectern and beheld his beloved congregants, a fractured flock. Merely from where people were sitting he could tell that cliques had been established, God forbid, sects within his own synagogue. In the front sat Sarah, with Brenda Weiner and Abe flanking her (Brenda was off this sabbath) and behind them the more conservative members of the congregation. Brenda smiled up to him and he down to her, the woman waiting to take his job.

"Mi kamocha," sang Panuzzi, *"ba-elim, Adonai!"* He translated, "Who is like you, O Lord, among the mighty!"

Bloom could not help but notice, as he looked now beyond Sarah's group, five rows of completely empty seats. The seats, by informal arrangement or by chance, were like a buffer zone. Beyond them sat Bernie Levitt surrounded by Lucy and Ethel Axelrod, and in the row behind them Leonidas slumped. Bloom's mother was absent today, and regardless of what the congregants were saying, Bloom knew it was not strictly for reasons of health; she had said to him just yesterday she found the services too painful to experience.

The service stalled now during the *"Mi kamocha,"* and Bloom raised his hand: " 'Who is like you, O Lord, among the mighty,'" he repeated, "is actually a very poor translation. The Hebrew, I want to point out to you, really means, 'Who is like you, God, among the gods?' " Attention tightened in the sanctuary. "I point this out only to show you that our religion originated and grew out of, in fact distinguished itself from, primitive forms of polytheism. We have developed and matured from a time when our forefathers didn't believe in one God but in the Jewish God as simply the foremost of many. I point this out so that we can see together where we have come from, so that we can appreciate where we have arrived, or should have arrived, today. I urge you to remember that in this synagogue, in this community, we have one shul, we have one God, and we have one style of worship. I shudder to hear myself saying this," Bloom said with a nod to Panuzzi, "but the flagrant violation of the fast of the Ninth of Av that some of you may be considering participating in is a serious error. I urge you all to be here next week with Rabbi Weiner and myself as we celebrate this important holiday. I urge you to remember this holiday is a remembrance of catastrophes that have befallen our people, and to be at a Japanese restaurant stuffing yourselves on tempura, then gambling immediately afterwards, while we are here reciting *kinot*, the dirges in memory of the destruction of the Temples, the expulsion from Egypt, Spain, France, England, from"—Bloom paused dramatically —"to do this will separate you from this synagogue." And then he stopped.

The silence was loud, palpable. He had not wanted to say that, to talk of separation, of division, of schism. This was what he had been laboring precisely to avoid. He stopped abruptly and continued with the responsive reading, confusing Panuzzi, who, however, recovered, and moved the service on to the Torah reading.

He and Panuzzi now promenaded with the two Torah scrolls down the aisle, and Bloom went out of his way to hold the scroll out in front of each group of congregants he passed in the circuit about the sanctuary. He held it out to Sarah, who extended her fingers to the brocaded Torah cover and then kissed her fingertips. He held it out to Abe North, who whispered to him, "Attaboy!"

The procession slowed. Brenda looked into Bloom's eyes, offering to help him in any way; he nodded and walked on but then stopped and turned to see Panuzzi behind him, moving right in front of Brenda. Panuzzi also held out his Torah for her. As she kissed it Bloom saw his cantor gaze longingly at her. Bloom hoped Angelos wouldn't suddenly extend his arms out to her and in his eagerness drop the Torah as they embraced.

Now Bloom heard, to his great irritation, the sound of change jangled in pockets, fingers full of silver. He turned and saw that the sound was coming from Bernie Levitt's section of the synagogue. Bloom had heard this jangling before, the shaking of loose change, but now he approached Bernie and held out the Torah, offering it and its power for uniting people to him, so that the dealer and his little group would desist from this stupid, petty, deliberate violation of the sabbath. "Please, for God's sake," Bloom said quietly as he passed. Nonetheless, he held out the Torah to Bernie just as long as he had held it out to Sarah and the others. Heal, Bloom heard himself thinking, heal the sick.

Then he and Angelos moved back down in front of the other side of the sanctuary, where people who had not made up their minds to join either faction seemed to be gathered, with their relatives, friends, and even a number of strangers whom curiosity had brought to the temple this sabbath. He held the Torah out to all who reached and wanted to touch it, to the women with their handkerchiefs, to the men who touched the fringes of their prayer shawls to it, so that this great book, which had kept the Jewish people together through thousands of years and thousands of miles of dispersions, might, Bloom hoped, work a little of the same magic for him, here in Gardena this day.

Bloom distributed the *aliyahs*, the honor of reciting the blessings up at the Torah, in an effort to head off schism and defuse the feast on the day of fasting next week. He wanted to use this service to bring all the different people together in one unified shabbat service, one Torah reading, for one synagogue. The first *aliyah* went to Abe North, who came up the steps to the right of the reading platform and perfunctorily read his blessings, as Eli Ginsberg, the reader, chanted the Torah portion in his low sing-songy voice. Bloom wanted really to call up the temple president, but Sarah felt women should not be called—even though, paradoxically, she much approved of Brenda.

After Abe, Bernie Levitt was summoned to the Torah. A murmur rippled through the synagogue as the dealer moved quickly up the carpeted aisle and took his place next to Panuzzi beside the lectern. Bernie made no trouble and chanted the blessings in his impressive bass voice, then stepped aside. Eli Ginsberg, who had come to think of Bernie as the devil himself, stood to the side, when he neared, as if, Bloom thought, to protect the holy parchment of the Torah scroll from Levitt's direct gaze. The tension on the dais grew in proportion to the proximity of these two men.

Now Brenda Weiner was called to the Torah. Bloom had thought this would really be a coup: In a single gesture he would demonstrate his magnanimity, his willingness to embrace this woman on the synagogue staff, if that's what was wanted, and in so doing he would be providing an example for all of the congregants to follow: an example of open-mindedness and tolerance. As Brenda walked up, a pleasant little hum seemed to rise from the people sitting closest to Sarah's camp, while the jangle of change—only a small clinking but audible and irritating to Bloom—still floated through the sanctuary. When Brenda ascended, Abe North, as was the custom, descended to make room for her and went back to sit next to Sarah, which left Bernie standing next to Bloom.

Now, to Bloom's horror, Levitt reached his small hand across the vellum of the Torah, and whispered, but loud enough to be heard by all at the reading platform, "The words written here are only the *letter* of the laws, Rabbi. Beneath the words there is the fire, the spirit, the red letters, the white-hot letters in which the real Torah is written. I can feel the heat beneath my hand."

"Get it off," hissed Eli Ginsberg.

"Please," said Bloom, "not here."

"If not here, then where?" said Bernie. "And if not now, when?" Then he smiled. "I don't mean to disrupt, Rabbi."

"Get your hand off," Eli shouted, and everybody in the sanctuary not only heard the old man's anguished voice, they saw the cords in his neck go taut. "Or I'll stick it." Eli threatened the dealer with the silver pointer.

"Please step to the side," Bloom urged. "Please do it now!"

Although Bernie did step aside, he was still able to keep his hand on the scroll, stuck, as a hand in a plug, rigid with electricity. The jangling in the back of the room now increased. Bloom leaned against Bernie's body to move it, but to no effect. "May I ask the congregation to be quiet," he said. "And keep your hands out of your pockets, back there!"

As the tension and confusion mounted, and the shoving continued on the dais, threatening not only decorum but frail Eli Ginsberg as well, Brenda Weiner, the smallest figure there, simply walked around the lectern, took her hand, and lay it across Bernie's. As if in obedience to her touch, he removed it slowly, almost theatrically, from the Torah. Bloom felt like kissing Brenda there, in public, for gratitude. After a hushed moment, the Torah reading continued, and Bernie and then Brenda, in their proper turns, rotated around the reading lectern and went back to their seats.

Afterwards Bloom tried to launch his sermon. Everything he had discussed with Panuzzi, however, seemed to fail him, seemed to be beside the point in the light of what had just happened. He held his notes above him so that the congregation could see, and then he said, "I would tear up these papers if today were not the sabbath, and tearing, defined as a form of work, is not permitted." He waited to gauge the effect of this, but he could not be sure what it was.

"Some laws might strike you as ridiculous on an individual basis, but Judaism is a religion of laws. All religions are. There is no religion without them, and there is no freedom without order." He paused and then went on, "Ladies and gentlemen: I am not going to read any of this sermon today. I am putting it aside, and I will say only this: We none of us can ignore what you have just seen happen up here, where Jew is turned against Jew, brother against brother. This cannot go on much longer at this, or at any, synagogue. It cannot. As Lincoln said in 1860, as the Civil War neared, 'A house divided against itself cannot stand.' How much more so a house of worship, a little synagogue in a little town, at the end of the diaspora, where we all must help each other and not be at each other's necks for petty reasons. Please, I urge all of you: Consider this day, the sabbath before the Ninth of Av, to remember the disasters of Jewish history, large and small, and please do not act in such a way as to bring another disaster upon us here in Gardena. And now, for the service for returning the Torah to the ark, please stand."

But that service, like the rest of the morning, Bloom knew, had been a failure.

66

The days leading to the fast of the Ninth of Av were full of anxiety for Bloom. The general rule of thumb for this period was that one should observe all the mourning rites that apply in the case of the death of the next of kin. It was not that Bloom feared any next of kin were dying (although he was troubled by the way his mother had been looking and he feared a relapse), but he felt death around him. He understood that in a sense he might be preemptively mourning the demise of his synagogue as he had known it, or of his role in it, or perhaps he was mourning his last job as a rabbi.

He also missed Dawn's company. She was happy to speak with him on the phone but she was not able to see him much. She was spending a week of very long hours at the paper because, she said, it was undergoing a change of editors and she was getting many new assignments. She had also told him, happily, that she was going to have lunch with a few friends from the *L.A. Times* to see if there might be an opportunity for her. It was a first step, that important one Dawn had been hoping for, and he was happy for her.

As busy as she was, Dawn did, however, promise to join him on the night before the holiday. Bloom was devoting himself to studying about mourning and fasting, and the subjects were well suited to his mood. Although you had only to refrain altogether from meat on the day of the fast itself, Bloom didn't have meat or even fish for four days. He lost three pounds. "You're fasting not only for yourself," Dawn said to him over the telephone from L.A., "but also for all those people who are going to Ted Kasuyama's. I have to tell you, Arthur, Ted Kasuyama's is a lousy Japanese restaurant."

The more Bloom studied, the more he realized how congenial this fast was, how appropriate to Southern California lifestyles. On the Ninth of Av, one was not to wear leather shoes or belt, or leather —an item of comfort—anywhere. Well, in California everyone wore rubber anyway—sneakers, thongs. No problem on that account. Also one was expected on this holiday to sleep not in the comfort of a bed with mattress but on the floor, on something hard, to remember the hardness of destruction, and the rigors of persecution, and flight. As Bloom prepared for Dawn's visit, he pulled out the tatami, the thin bamboo mat, from under his bed, and readied it for use. Yes, this also was right.

All that bothered Bloom was that among the forms of pleasures to be denied on this holiday was sexual intercourse. Since he had not been with Dawn for more than a week, this was going to be a difficult commandment for him to fulfill. Perhaps, he thought, this was the reason he was fasting for three people, foreswearing leather and other comforts, observing all aspects of the law above and beyond the call of the law, just so that he could sneak in an act of love and still be in compliance, somehow, with the *mitzvahs* he was supposed to fulfill.

Bloom knew that in actuality such pettifoggery with the *mitzvahs* had been his way of life for many years. He had not until now been so self-conscious about his juggling, and now in fact he wondered how much his laxity about personal observance of the sabbath, dietary laws, and so forth, as well as his toleration of the gambling of the congregants, had contributed to the mess he was in today.

As he showered, powdered, and threw on some cologne in expectation of Dawn, Bloom decided that changing the habits of a decade did not have to begin tonight. Just to right the balance that he knew his hoped-for, yearned-for lovemaking was going to throw out of kilter, he went downstairs, walked across the pool deck and beyond the back gate. Here, behind a bush of thorny beach roses, he found a large stone. It was not as flat as he wanted it to be, but it would be, yes, just about the size of a small pillow, and he hoisted it onto his shoulder and carried it upstairs to the apartment.

When Dawn arrived forty minutes later, Bloom was in the kitchen. She entered quietly, without knocking, and came up behind and cupped her hands over his eyes. "Who am I? Three guesses."

"My mother."

"No."

"My esteemed colleague Rabbi Brenda Weiner."

"Guess again."

"Elijah the Prophet."

"You lose." She took her hands away.

"You're here," he said, "and therefore I win."

She was ebullient, full of energy. "I've been working for six hours. What's to eat?" she asked. "I'm starving." She made fun of his apron—it was one he had taken from Nannette, and above a design of the New York City subway system were the words EAT IN THE BRONX. "There's nothing cooking here, Arthur. What's it going to be, take-out?"

"Oh no, no." Carefully he scooped out two grayish smelly boiled eggs and balanced them on spoons. "Here's your dinner," he said with a smile.

"This is it?"

"It's customary to eat a boiled egg at the last meal before the fast, as a symbol of mourning. Come sit down with me." He led her over to the place on the floor where he had cleared a space and set up two green milk crates (emptied of his complete works of Mark Twain, which he had taken to his study in the synagogue) to be their table. "You're supposed to sit low to the floor, another symbol of mourning," he explained.

They sat, but Bloom suddenly jumped up. "Excuse me, I forgot something." He returned with an ashtray, which he placed on the table between their boiled eggs. "Sprinkle a little ash on the egg, okay?"

"Yummy," she said. "Is this another symbol of fire and destruction?"

"Yup. I've got lots of things I want to show you tonight. Wait till you see the rock."

"The poor Jews," Dawn said, as she bit into her dinner. "The poor, poor, Jews."

He looked up into her eyes. Her face was beautiful but, yes, also slightly mournful, as he had wanted it to be.

"I don't want to feel poor and sad and hungry when I'm with you, Arthur."

"But it's Tisha b'Av. It's the holiday."

"It's the way *you've* made the holiday, Arthur. It doesn't have to be so bleak as all this. What is it you're mourning, anyway? The tragedies of the Jews, or me?"

Bloom looked at her without answering; he was mesmerized by her mind reading.

"We've had very happy times together." She moved closer to him, on her knees. "You've helped me feel good about myself and I've gotten a lot of good work done because of you, Arthur."

Bloom didn't like the final-curtain sound of any of this.

"There may even be something for me percolating at the *L.A. Times* . . . I'll feel terrible if I have to sit here and can't make you smile."

Bloom tried, but his jaw was locked tight against smiling. "Everything you're saying has the sound of farewell, of summing up."

"No," she said.

"I know what I hear."

"Maybe what you want to hear. What would be easy for you to hear, my little rabbi, a magic solution, a *deus ex machina*. Now come here." She put her arms around him tightly and she began to sing, "Dream along with me . . . I'm on my way to the stars . . . Dream along . . ."

"Perry Como," said Bloom, very quietly. "His theme song."

"That's better. Now sing!"

"But it's Tisha b'Av," Bloom protested.

"Not on my calendar it's not. Oh Arthur, snap out of it, please. So maybe something has changed between us, maybe our relationship has entered a new stage."

"Off stage," he muttered.

"I've never seen you like this. Arthur"—she turned his chin toward her—"a new stage, not off stage, you funny man. Now cheer up." Bloom shook his head. "Are you down in the dumps about that nut, Bernie Levitt? That *is* something to be upset about, Arthur. But I know you can handle him."

Bloom suddenly felt such warmth flowing from her to him that it was like food, energy, to his unfed system. "I need you very much," he said.

"And I need you too, Arthur. Unlike you, however, I also need a square meal."

"Not on me tonight, darling. Not tonight."

On his knees he slid across the floor to her, reached out, and in the process knocked over the dish that had held the eggs, flipping the ashtray as well. It was a mess, but he was overcome with desire for her, and they made love there, on the floor.

It was strangely backward, however, as if this were truly the first fumbling time together. When they were done, he held her tightly next to him. He did not want her to go, as if her leaving would cut him loose to float in a zone he now dreaded.

"What new stage are we in?" he asked.

"I'm not sure, Arthur. Maybe we're just finally getting around to knowing each other."

She stayed with him for an hour, until she thought he was asleep, and then carefully slid out from under his arm, put on her clothes, and left.

But Bloom had not been asleep. As soon as she was gone, he reached over, pulled nearer to him the stone he had brought in from the lawn, and, in keeping with what the pious among the Jews have done for centuries, he went to sleep there on the floor, with the rock as his pillow.

67

Temple Elijah's Tisha b'Av prayers began in late afternoon, so that a daily service could be combined with the reading of *Eicha*, the Book of Lamentations, which, customarily, is done in the evening.

"Broochim Ha-ba-im," Bloom began. "Welcome to you all, to your synagogue on this holy day. I hope you are holding up well, those of you who are able to and have been fasting. (The packed sanctuary would—thank God—mean that not too many people were going to be at the Japanese restaurant and the racetrack.) "I'm gratified to see so many of you here," Bloom went on, with a tired smile, "and with a group like you, I hesitate to use such metaphors very often, but today, let me say that it pleases me greatly to see such a full house. I might even say I'm flushed with pride that so many of you are playing it straight and have come through for me."

"You see," Lucy Leonard whispered to the woman sitting next to her, "he's deliberately being jovial on a solemn day. There's a meaning behind it!"

In fact Bloom had done so much pre–Tisha b'Av mourning, it was a great relief to be, finally, here. He and Panuzzi proceeded with the service, which was, until the Torah reading, uneventful. Then, at this crucial juncture, Eli Ginsberg could not find the proper place in the scroll, Exodus, chapter fifteen. "Who's been turning it?" Eli whispered angrily to the cantor. "We're ten miles away." Panuzzi signaled Bloom over, and the three of them frantically tried to find the spot, but the Torah scroll was turned so much, it was all the way into the fifth book, Deuteronomy. Bloom knew the scroll had been at the right place the day before because he had checked it himself. Someone had messed with it, and Bloom already had his suspicions.

"You see?" said someone behind Sarah North. "You see?"

Sarah turned around sharply, while the Torah was being rewound, and said, "What is it you see?"

It took nearly ten minutes to get back at the right line; then Eli Ginsberg read quickly yet emotionally, as the doleful text required. Afterwards, Panuzzi chanted the beautiful hymns: *Eli Zion V-oreha, Kmo Esha b'tzireha, vkivtulah, chagurat sak, al ba-al neyureha."* Bloom translated: "Here is Zion in her sorrow, like a woman in labor, like a virgin wearing sackcloth, the garment of mourning, as she remembers the one she shared her youth with . . ."

Three quarters of the way through the service, Brenda Weiner received a report, Bloom saw, from an unidentified person speaking to her from beyond the partition. When she finished, she walked back onto the platform, and whispered the news to Bloom before she resumed her seat.

The news was mixed. The good: only five people had attended with Bernie at Ted Kasuyama's. Only five out of the whole congregation! The bad news, however: At Santa Anita, all five had already picked long-shot winners in four of four races run. On two-dollar bets, they had already parlayed earnings of nearly $13,000, and the night was only half over. These were winnings of a new magnitude, as far as Bloom could guess, and there would be no way to keep a lid on such information.

Bloom felt his stubble (he had not shaved for three days—also a requirement of mourning), felt the dryness of his throat (no water in eight hours), and he thought of his mother and Zion and the defeat of Bar Kochba in the rebellion against Rome, and the disasters that had befallen the Jews, hiding from crusaders at York, at Worms, hiding from Russians and Germans and the Arrow Cross Hungarian police. Then he thought of Jews fighting Germans and fighting the British and the Arabs, and he made a mental note to right the balance of the day in his remarks, lest it be forgotten that Jews fight as well as die. Would he fight? he wondered. How is Nannette? he wondered. He ran his tongue over his parched lips, and now let his hand turn the page as he followed the concluding odes along with Panuzzi.

68

The next morning Bloom was seized by a panic that soon crystallized into a serious plan to convert Dawn. What did it matter that he had averaged C-minus in four years of Talmud at the seminary? For this task he felt eminently qualified, and was enthusiastic to begin. He felt that if only Dawn would consider converting, the chief problem would be solved, and he could deal with the seminary, Bernie Levitt, anything. And there was something else he could not explain: Somehow he felt her lack of interest in Judaism a sign that in spite of her obvious feeling for him, and in spite of his own principles, she just was not on his side.

That night, over a sole dinner at a harbor restaurant, Bloom felt Dawn was struggling to be patient with him. "If I don't become a Jew," she said to him, "you tell me it'll kill your mother, but if I *do*, that kills my mother. It looks like, either way, it's matricide. Now which of them is going to go, Arthur?"

She smiled at him tenderly, but they both felt the distance between them tonight as more than the table's three feet, as the full breadth of culture, history, and faith. "Actually, Arthur, your harping on this conversion business is no joke." She spoke to him quietly, in the tones of conviction. "The problem in our town is not Dawn Nakazawa, non-Jew, but Arthur Bloom, lucky rabbi."

They finished their desserts and coffee without further talk of conversion, but soon afterward he was at it again.

On the telephone the following night he pleaded with her to trust her instincts. "I can sense it underneath all your loyalty to your mother, your *gimu*, whatever you call all those obligations—I can sense a desire for us to work something out. Judaism is very versatile and attractive. We'll work out our own approach. We can have doctrine-free zones, you can have your library, I'll have mine; you have your sabbath, I'll have mine; we can have everything his and hers—from towels to Gods."

"This isn't funny, Arthur. I'm doing a story on a rent-a-wife agency in Arcadia. If you're interested, let me know." Then she hung up.

A day later, however, in bed with Dawn, and in spite of an alarmingly low lust level for her, Bloom still went on.

"What's gotten into you?" she said harshly. "I just don't understand, Arthur. You're making me feel less like your lover and more like a project you're working on. A short-range project, a long-range project! I can tell by the tone of your voice that you've set up this goal and you're going after it, and I don't like it one bit. Look at you, the proof is in the penis, Arthur. You don't like what you're doing either. Look at you. We never used to have this trouble before."

"A temporary condition, I assure you."

But neither of them was so sure any more. Dawn pulled the sheet tightly around her and rolled away from him to the edge of the bed.

69

Working on the vodka and scotch inventories in the store, Dawn was surprised to overhear Lucy Leonard and Ethel Axelrod gossiping just beyond the counter about the rabbi and some rock. Risking Ono's rage, Dawn invited the women aside, then into her office.

On the sidewalk, fifteen minutes later, Dawn hesitated as she waited for the green light so she could cross and see Bloom. No, she had a better idea. It was only a hunch, perhaps, but she was learning to follow them now. She wanted to find out more about this rock, and another source was needed. She knew precisely where to find it. Dawn turned down the street, jumped into the van, and drove west. As she pulled opposite the Cadillac showroom, she saw Bernie leaving the lot, easing a prospective buyer, it seemed, into the driver's seat of a shining new car. Dawn stayed in her van parked across the boulevard. Although she had intended to talk directly with him, maybe this would be an even better opportunity. She saw now that Bernie took his key out, and, after handing it to the customer behind the wheel, walked around and slid into the passenger seat beside him. The PR man for the Messiah, Dawn thought, was going on a test drive.

When the Cadillac left the lot and disappeared into traffic, Dawn walked into the showroom. It seemed empty.

"Is it going to be interviews or Cadillacs today, ma'am?" Dave Diamond had come up behind her.

"You startled me!"

"It's my new sales approach, Miss Nakazawa. I terrify people into buying. How can I help you today?"

"No cars and no interviews today," she told him. "I'm here for a straight spy job, on your boss. You want to help?"

"Not you, too! There's too much spying going on all over town. Of course I can't blame you for wanting to get in on the action."

Dawn knew Black Dave was an ally, and she hardly waited for his permission to begin looking for what she was hoping to find. She surveyed the large showroom, stopping finally beside a beige El Dorado that was near a long desk strewn with papers. "Is this where he works?" she asked.

"Yeah," Dave said. "It's a mess because he's never here any more. What with his charitable activities"—Is that what he calls them? Dawn thought—"Bernie just ain't around like he used to be."

"I hope you don't mind my looking around, Dave."

"Well, Bernie just left, and since he's not supposed to be back, I don't see why not. Be my guest. But what is it you're looking for?"

"Oh," she answered, "when I find it, I'll let you know. Let me have my fun, okay?"

"Sure, sure." Black Dave laughed. "You look hot and tired, Miss N. Are you sure you don't want to take a load off, or maybe I can get you a soda?"

"No, thank you." And then she saw it. There, across the desk, buried under some papers, which she removed, beside a Star-of-David letter opener and a pile of books, was the rock, the same one. There was no mistake about it, and Dawn touched the stone with a red nail.

Dave was watching her. "Funny guy, that Bernie," he said.

"Meshugeh, right?"

"Right, right." Dave laughed. "Absolutely, one hundred percent, not a full house up there lately, Miss N. Look, I work for the man, and let me say I was the first to tell him he's going too far this time. I'm in a delicate position, and, as you well know, I believe in making a buck. But I draw the line at false advertising—especially in matters of the Lord."

"May I quote you?"

"You can, you have, and you will." The sexton laughed.

"Why doesn't the rabbi feel the same way as you?"

"Oh but I think he does. He's just a little shy about stepping on people's toes. A rabbi in our tradition, Miss Nakazawa, is a teacher, a peacemaker, not a divider."

"You're getting more and more quotable," she said. She now walked slowly around Bernie's desk and peered at the spines of the books. The titles were in transliterated Hebrew and they didn't make any sense to her.

"I would hate to see Bernie come between you and the rabbi, Miss Nakazawa."

"Don't tell me we're a cute couple," she said, seated now at the dealer's desk, reading, note-taking, and wishing that Black Dave would not hover about her so.

"I won't tell you that," he said, "but you are. And if I can help the cause of interfaith, interracial, inter-everything love, just let me know."

"Okay," she said, "you can," and she asked him to tell her about the books Bernie had on his desk.

After a few minutes Dawn had learned enough, and she turned to go.

"Bernie'll be very disappointed he missed you," Dave said to her on the threshold of the showroom.

"You can tell him I wasn't," Dawn said. "Ciao."

"Shalom, baby." Dave waved her across the lot, and then reentered to close up.

Dawn drove back and found Bloom in his apartment. He was wearing his Bronx apron, doing the dishes. When she came in, he turned off the water and moved to greet her with still-wet hands outstretched. She stopped him and leaned against the bookcase and pointed to the window. "*He* was there, Arthur, right there. That crazy Bernie Levitt was right there all the time and he was probably watching us make love, too! He was taking pictures for all I know!"

"Hold on," said Bloom, untying his apron. "Whoa!"

"Don't 'whoa' me. I am not making things up."

She was angry and beautiful and he was so delighted to see her, nothing was going to make him mad at her. "How do you know?"

"The rock, Arthur, the goddamn magic rock everyone's talking about!"

"Yes?"

"Don't tell me you don't know about it!"

"Well, of course," Bloom guessed, "the rock."

"Yes, your rock of lamentations, the dumb old rock from the backyard, Arthur! He took it. He stole your rock from you, probably right after he got his own rocks off looking at us."

"I don't believe it."

"Look yourself. Where's your precious rock?"

Bloom circled around the bed, went down on his knees and reached under it. Then he looked up at Dawn. "It's not here."

"Of course it's not. I'm telling you he took it. He came in and he took it, and now it's sitting on his desk over at the showroom. For all I know it's for sale, along with the cars!"

He sat down on the edge of the bed, while she paced around the room. After a long interval, she said, "I don't know how long this has been going on, Rabbi Bloom, but everything we do now is observed. Not the occasional thing people see us doing when they spot us on the street or in the pool, Arthur. They're out after us like some weird permanent stakeout on our lives."

"You feel it's that bad?"

Dawn stood in front of him, crossed her arms over her chest, and said, deliberately, "I came to cover a story, Arthur. Now it's pretty clear to me I've become part of it. Maybe it's time I took myself off." She moved as if to go, but he held her by the forearm.

He felt it coming now, the storm about to be unleashed, and he held her there as if the contact would stop it.

"I just don't know," she said. "I just don't know."

"But I've spoken to Bernie." Bloom tried to reassure her. "I've spoken to him more than once; I've given him a piece of my mind, believe me. He certainly won't be asking you to convert me any more."

"Conversion, conversion! Is that the only thing you think about any more, Arthur?" But she was relieved, and sat down.

"Sure, he's nuttier than the rest. He's a real problem. I admit it. I'm no fool, in case you hadn't noticed."

"If you were that, Arthur, or anything closely resembling one, I would have let my mother handle your liquor order when you came over, and I would not be in your apartment now."

"Try to understand, then," he pleaded with her, "that these people are not these dangerous, diabolical elements you've imagined."

"Did I imagine we were being spied on? Did I imagine the rock just sprouted wings and flew from your bedroom to that Cadillac dealership? It's not my imagination that's in question here, Arthur, but your phenomenal ability to delude yourself. We differ here, Arthur. On this we have a serious difference."

"Look"—he was up now, gesticulating, walking around the room, trying to get through to her—"they follow me the way some people follow ball players, the way my mother keeps up with the details of Lawrence Welk's life. My mother knows more about the Lennon Sisters than they know about themselves. She knows all about accordionist Myron Floren, his wife, his kids."

"Arthur, you're being cute, and you're trying to charm me, and it's close to working. But there's a big difference between you and Myron Floren. No one is proclaiming that divine white light emanates from Myron Floren's accordion. No one's saying that, not even Lawrence himself. From them we get only bubbles, but from Rabbi Bloom, in the doctrine according to Levitt, we get the holy, hot, magical light of Jehovah's presence. Arthur, this is not a TV music show, this is very serious."

"Look, Bernie is a problem. I'm not denying that, but I'm convinced it's a problem of degree. It's the same as what I have to put up with when people go after my tie clip, my cuff links, dozens of yarmulkahs . . . you've seen all that, and you've reported it. So now it's a rock."

Dawn stood up. "You call it a rock. I call it our privacy, our acts of love, our life put on stage. And something else I've been meaning to ask you. . . ."

Bloom wanted to interrupt her. He pulled her near him and tried to kiss her as she talked. "Ask," he said passionately, "ask, seek, and you shall find."

"Arthur!" She pulled away from him, assuming the seriousness of a position in the center of Bloom's rug, which was the center of the room. "I want you to think about Bernie Levitt for a second. Not the slot machine ladies who find you so adorable. . . ."

"The way I find you."

"Arthur, would someone like Bernie Levitt have gotten as far as he has if he didn't somehow sense it all had your okay, if he didn't know you would just glide along with it all?"

Now Bloom stepped away from her. "I *don't* give my stamp of approval or whatever it is you're implying that I give. I absolutely don't."

"No," she said, "you only look the other way," and she turned and went toward the door.

"Where are you going?"

"I don't know." The screen door slammed on her last words. "I just don't know, out to get some air, out to see who's peeking on us now."

He followed Dawn out onto the veranda and came up beside her. "Don't go, please."

"Things are getting way out of hand, Arthur. Maybe you should go away with me until this blows over." But then she thought, *No, that's a terrible idea.* She moved across the veranda to the far bannister. "Anybody out there?" she shouted. "I hope your camera breaks."

"Sit down here with me," Bloom said as he took her arm and eased her onto the middle step. "No one can see us from here. No one can see you but me." He kissed her, but her lips were slow to respond.

"Arthur, what can we do that won't be grist for the crazy mill here? Everything's led so far to nothing but miracle rocks and kimonos in the synagogue, and you—look, I know you're on the verge of losing your job."

"It's also led to us," he said.

"Don't evade or charm your way out of hearing me. I say Rabbi A. Bloom, Class of 1971—and not Bernard Levitt—is still the laid-back master of ceremonies here, if you want to be."

"Dawn, I have spoken to him. I've taken seriously what you've said. I told you that, but you keep harping on it."

"But maybe, just maybe, the way you have of saying *No* to him and the others is a form of *Yes.* People feel, they intuit, Arthur. They're not dumb. I'm not dumb."

"What more can I do?"

"I just think you're coasting along too much."

"It's ironic," he said, without taking his eyes off her, "that you're now stopping what you started, what you inflamed."

"You're the lucky rabbi, Arthur. Not me."

"You wrote about it. You fanned the flames. You made it bigger than it ever deserved to be."

"I wrote a series of exposés. And, believe me, if there was one reader I wanted to get through to, I'm looking at him now."

"Get through to me now," Bloom said as he put his hands in the dark drapery of her hair. "Go off together with me, and you'll get through."

"No." She pulled away. "And I don't like how you are always

changing the subject. Kids do that when they want to avoid being criticized, when they know they've done something wrong."

"How's this?" Bloom pulled in his gut and slid down one step. "How's this for maturity and directness? And please notice I am on bended knee: Don't leave me. Marry me."

"You're totally out of your mind. You know what that would do to your synagogue?"

"Let's think about what it would do for us. It would make me very happy."

"We can't." She shook her head. "We absolutely can't."

Bloom, who hadn't planned on proposing, who surprised himself as much as Dawn, who hadn't thought it would come out quite this way, so casual, so jokey, so giddy, was now stunned by what he had done. It was a proposal, all right, and the first time he had ever asked anyone to marry him, and, he felt now, as he looked with longing and embarrassment at her, it well might be the last. Had she heard him, really heard him? "At the risk of making myself look silly again," he said, "are you aware you've been proposed to?"

"Yes, Arthur. You don't look silly to me at all, but I've turned you down."

"Oh God," he cried.

"For now," she added, and left him there alone.

70

August was a terrible month for Bloom. He stayed mainly indoors, lost his tan, and time seemed to gather around him like rising water. For nearly two weeks, he and Dawn did not speak, but one sad afternoon he reached into his bookshelf, caught an anthology of poetry, and opened it at random to find Auden's "September 1, 1939," that ominous poem written on the day the Germans invaded Poland. He read the final haunting line, "We must love one another or die," and on the impulse this provided he got on the telephone and renewed his proposal to her.

"But I can't marry you, Arthur, and it troubles me that you still don't seem to understand how impossible the request is now." (Still

that "now," that ray of hope!) "Don't you see," she went on with
nervous intensity, "that it's precisely what they want? We'd be
playing right into the hands of—"

"No, we would not. We would marry and leave this place."

"Impossible."

"Run away with me."

She refused him again. He sensed, however, something begin to
grow within him.

"We should stop seeing each other, Arthur. For good. It's the
only choice we can make now."

"A terrible choice."

"Yes, but people use love like anything else. They're using us."

"They! They! Who's they? I don't feel used. When I'm with
you, I feel great. I feel as I have never felt before in my whole
life."

"Let me help you burst the bubble, Arthur. Do you know that
they tried to organize a lottery on who could guess the place and
exact time you proposed to me? The winner was supposed to get five
thousand dollars. In the end I think it fizzled, but even so—"

"Did you tell anyone?"

"No. Did you?"

"No."

"Nevertheless, it's been found out—God knows how. I ask you,
Arthur, is this the sign of a healthy Jewish community?"

"It's a scandal, and I'll look right into it."

"Oh Arthur, Arthur! Forget it. We've just got to separate. It's the
only way. Don't you see that it is precisely marriage that they want?
Or even any continuing relationship. No matter what we do, even
if we wave to each other across the street, they're into it, they're
examining its meaning, its significance. Maybe we could somehow
have headed it off earlier. But not now. We just fuel it by being
anywhere together."

"There's got to be another way out of this."

"Tell it to me," she challenged him.

"I don't know it yet, but give me time, please."

"I know you're trying, Arthur. I know you by now. I've been
talking and writing and thinking about you. Sometimes I even feel
I know you better than myself, which maybe makes me harsh on you
the way I am on me. But this whole business is not in my hands any

longer; it's in yours. The hands of an ordinary man, an extraordinary ordinary guy, not any messiah—but a man who never even won anything himself except dinner for two at the Sun Luck East Chinese restaurant in New York. It's plain up to you, Rabbi, darling. End of sermon."

When she hung up, Bloom called Bernie Levitt.

71

On the following sabbath, the last before Rosh Hashanah, Bloom stood at his lectern just after the Torah reading, and, to the surprise of everyone and the horror of his mother, he resigned his post.

Then he made three announcements: First, the classical penalty for violating the sabbath is death; second, the classical penalty for gambling is banishment from the synagogue; and third, and most significant for this *shabbat* afternoon, the classical penalty for the proclamation of false messiahs is excommunication.

"We are devoting this morning to a debate on the subject, a kind of public disputation," said Bloom, "so that we as a congregation can clear the air and be done with it and be ready for the High Holy Days unblemished." Then he summoned Bernie and Brenda up to the dais.

"This can't be allowed," Sarah said as she stood in the first row. "You can't give that man"—she was pointing to the dealer, severe in his expensive pinstripe suit—"any sort of forum here, Rabbi. Anyway, what's to debate!"

"Come, come." Bloom took a step toward Sarah. "We are a people who believe in learning and education. You or anybody else is welcome to participate in the forum, and the truth will come out."

"No." Sarah raised her voice to castigate Bloom, but then realized, fully, that he had just resigned and in so doing had eliminated much of her leverage. "Let Brenda officiate, then, and not you," she said, more softly now.

"That's precisely the plan."

Brenda stood at a lectern Panuzzi had just now carried in, placed between Bloom and Levitt. The synagogue quieted. Sarah looked over the packed sanctuary, but finally, slowly, reluctantly, she sat, and the debate began.

Bernie made the opening statement:

"Because the time is now propitious, because the ten signs of the messianic age are now rapidly showing themselves"—he spoke evenly, coolly, a creature of conviction—"because of all this, I am happy to be here today. *Shabbat shalom!*"

"*Shabbat shalom,*" responded Bloom. He felt light, clearheaded, and not a bit angry. It was as if his resignation had freed his soul and made it possible to talk publicly about these matters in a way not permitted before. He nodded to the congregation, they "shabbat shalom-ed" him back; the atmosphere was positively congenial.

Bernie took his Bible from the lectern, held it high, and read from Isaiah: " 'Then the moon shall be confounded and the sun ashamed; for the Lord of hosts will reign in Mt. Zion and in Jerusalem.' This particular vision—a prophetic vision if ever there was one—combines the establishment of the state of Israel with the moon landings, that is, the shaming of the sun!"

"It probably refers to physical celestial events, eclipses," Bloom interjected.

"The times of trouble and turbulence that we are in," Bernie went on, unperturbed, "especially in the Fertile Crescent, known as the Middle East, are always events that precede the messianic coming. Take recent oil crises, those long lines at the pump, the chronic shortage of home heating oil, so that people back east are freezing by their own hearths . . . I say that all this is yet another sign."

"I want to point out"—Bloom raised both hands toward Bernie —"that this kind of messianic speculation is something few modern Jews engage in, although I suppose there are some in every generation. Perhaps we are host to our generation's in Mr. Levitt."

"Not in me," said Bernie, "but in you, Rabbi. *You*"—and he pointed his finger at Bloom and called out his name, B-LOO-OOM, making it three syllables, with each syllable carrying wind and thunder.

The atmosphere in the synagogue changed. There was a crackling silence.

Bernie continued: "I am not the subject of the debate, but Arthur Bloom is."

"No." Bloom raised his voice. "I am most certainly not the subject of this debate. The subject is the subject. The issue is whether according to Jewish history and cosmology sighting of the messiah has any more substance to it than the sighting of UFOs."

"Every Jew," said Bernie solemnly, "will have to choose whether what has happened in our little community, under the leadership of Rabbi Bloom, is yet another sign of the imminent arrival. As for me, I have chosen. I ask Rabbi Bloom now, before all of us, to make his claim."

"I have no claim to make," Bloom quietly said.

"Elijah is the prophet of Israel," Bernie boomed, "designated to proclaim the messiah. That means it's to happen here. This house of worship in which we sit today is named not Temple Ezekiel or Temple Beth Shalom but Temple Elijah."

"Eh? With respect to Bernard, these are not earth-shaking, conclusive arguments."

"The rabbi does himself, this community, and the world"—he raised his voice so he could be heard throughout the sanctuary—"a major injustice. Rabbi, you know better than any of us that you cannot escape yourself. And, if it's any comfort to you, neither could Jonah, Jeremiah, Joel, Obadiah, Habbakuk."

"You're the kook," an angry voice shouted.

"Shsh," cautioned Brenda.

"Every prophet of the Old Testament hesitated. What's the first thing Moses did after God spoke to him from the burning bush? What's the first thing Gideon says in the morning, by the river, after the Lord has spoken to him in a dream? Did Jeremiah answer, Right here, Your Honor? Did Jonah leap for joy and say, My pleasure to serve?

"No. In every case, they acted as you are acting, Rabbi. They say, No, not me. They say, Why me and not some other slob? I'm poor, they say, and ill-equipped, and some even run off and try to hide from the omniscient eye of the Lord. It wasn't easy for any of them to accept their selection. Why, God chased Jonah all the way to Nineveh. And I believe with all my heart he's after you, Rabbi, here in Gardena."

The congregation held its breath. Bloom shook his head slightly. It was as if a vessel had just passed, leaving unexpectedly large waves in its wake. Bloom had not expected such erudition, nor had he recognized that Bernie was a natural orator.

"Rabbi Bloom," said Brenda sweetly, "your response, please?"

Bloom fiddled with his hands, he rubbed the wooden slats of the lectern like a nervous hitter getting a grip on the bat handle to throw off the pitcher's rhythm. Finally, when enough time had elapsed, he said, "An early medieval rabbi, Judah ha Hasid, is said to have known when the messiah would arrive, but he died before he could tell anyone. I only wish our fellow congregant, Bernard Levitt, good health, but no man alive knows when the messiah—or his harbingers —will come."

"Or *her* harbingers," Panuzzi said aloud from his seat near Sarah.

"Thank you, Angelos"—Brenda smiled down on her cantor— "but let's not muddy the waters."

"Yes, let's look at the facts," Bernie said. "Have we won or have we not won? Have we or have we not accumulated"—he looked at the note card before him—"$98,524 in the special fund, not counting another $24,218 we have already distributed to charities—all because of our man, Arthur Bloom? Regardless of his denials, these are the facts. The question you all must ask yourselves is why this has happened. As for me, I have already asked, and I have my answer. He is standing across from me."

Bloom moved away from his lectern and stepped toward the dealer. "If I asked you to walk through fire, would you walk? If I asked you to put on a blindfold and stroll across the Harbor Freeway at rush hour, would you?"

"You may mock me, if you want, Rabbi, but you do not unconvince me."

"This is not mockery," Bloom retorted, "but history." Bloom paused when he thought he saw in the back of the sanctuary a familiar figure. It was, yes, just who he thought it was. But he was losing the line of his thinking. "Not mockery," he caught himself, "because throughout history many thousands of Jews have died chasing false messiahs. In the year 448, for example, a Jew appeared on the island of Crete and said on one not so fine day that he was Moses! He promised the Jewish inhabitants that he had powers to lead them across the sea to Judea, without ships! He fixed a specific date for this maritime miracle, and when the hour arrived, he ordered the believers to jump into the ocean. Some did, and drowned. What is it, Bernie, that you are asking people to jump into?"

"Nobody is asking anyone to jump, to act, but only to believe.

Those of us who believe our eyes see this: here are the rabbi's actions, and then here is all this incredible good fortune. Is this just a random occurrence, a coincidence?"

"That's the *post hoc, ergo propter hoc* fallacy," cried Bloom.

"Explain," said Brenda.

"Just because B follows A, it doesn't mean B was caused by A. Is the morning traffic jam caused by the rising of the sun? For all any of you know the reason you have won so big at the casinos is that the dealers have let you. Maybe they like the publicity it attracts, maybe it has nothing whatsoever to do with me. Maybe management just made the decision."

"Nobody believes that," a voice called up from the sanctuary.

"Every time you get the flu, the Dodgers or Angels win, and this *proves* your runny nose is the cause!" Bloom shouted back down. He did not like the way things were going.

"What's more," said Bernie, "we're way beyond money. I've had dreams and visions; I've seen the rabbi more than once surrounded by undulating sapphire light. The residue, the glory of the first light of creation! How many of you have looked carefully in the rabbi's eyes?"

"My eyes do not undulate, nor are they sapphire," Bloom protested. "They're brown."

"Directly from the head of primordial man, Adam ha Kadmon, lights shone out, after the cosmic catastrophe, and created the world. From that light letters of *loshen kodesh,* the holy Hebrew tongue, were configured. Light and language. That light—there in *his* eyes —is still the last best hope for the repair of the world. It is strong light, and when it mixes with the weak light, a bond is created helping to bring the universe back to the original design in the mind of the creator. When the rabbi and Miss Nakazawa have carnal relations, they create the glue that holds the bond. If we are courageous, we would copy these actions, for such activities are an expression of belief, and such belief will lead to the restoration of the world and the end of days!" Bernie stopped and wiped the sweat from his forehead.

Thank God, thought Bloom, I got him to say it. "If I may translate for our friend, he would like to see all Jews with Japanese girlfriends and boyfriends—Bernie would like you—all of us—*deliberately and calculatingly*—to go counter to customs and tradition, and thus bring messianic times closer. Isn't this your not-so-hidden intention? If it is, I proclaim it nonsense, utter nonsense!" cried Bloom.

"Intention is irrelevant," said Bernie.

"You're irrelevant," a voice shouted, off to the right of the sanctuary's main aisle.

"A servant serves," Bernie screamed back.

"Order," called Brenda, "order in the House of God, please."

"Those who believe," Bernie roared over the shouting below him, "should follow the rabbi's example"—he stepped dramatically to the edge of the dais—"and resign as he has! Withdraw from the synagogue! There were no synagogues, no rabbis, no rules, no yarmulkahs, no *tallises,* no sabbath, there was nothing but eternal light at the beginning of time, and there will be none of these artificial encumbrances at the end."

Bloom looked for Dawn but couldn't find her in the moiling back aisles.

"Order!" shouted Brenda.

But there was none, and the remainder of the sabbath service, including the return of the Torah, could not be conducted. When the commotion had died down and the sanctuary was cleared, Brenda and Panuzzi carefully rolled up the holy scroll of the law and returned it to its ark.

72

"Who's smoking?" Bloom heard Nannette's voice. "The rabbi is smoking on shabbos!" How could he? He crushed the cigarette out. "So now that he's an ex-rabbi, it makes it okay? Come eat some lunch, Arthur." Nannette was sitting at the head of the dining-room table. Leonidas was pouring her some tea. A platter of delicatessen sandwiches was the centerpiece.

"Don't hide behind the salami," Leonidas said. Bloom sat up in his chair and reached for a sandwich.

"So this was the surprise that you told me was in store! This is a surprise for the mother of a rabbi? This is why I dragged myself to the synagogue—to hear my son resign his job!"

"If he had held out a little longer," said Leonidas, "he would have been fired—no? That way, at least, maybe he could have gotten unemployment."

Nannette raised her voice at him. "Fine for you to joke!"

"I had to do it, mom."

"Why had to? You didn't have to resign!"

"It's been coming for a long time."

"You can fool yourself, Arthur, but you can't fool me."

"I'm not trying to fool anyone. Anyway, I was just thinking it didn't go so badly; the debate could have gone worse."

"Yes, you could have levitated yourself up over the holy ark," said Leonidas, "and floated over our heads."

"You shut up," said Nannette, "and serve him some tea." She shook her head at him, and Bloom looked across the table at his mother as if he were looking back across the expanse of their life together. He was a bad boy; he had done a bad thing. "Get me some of those cigarettes, will you?" she asked Leonidas.

When she had lit up and inhaled deeply, she turned her head toward him. "It's lucky for you I already had my stroke for this year because"—she whooshed a stream of smoke out—"if I hadn't, I'd sure be working on one now. You should have discussed this with me, Arthur. That's what a mother is for."

"It was my decision, mom. And you know something? I still think it was right. I was the center of too much conflict, I was being used, I had to state clearly my position. . . ."

"Who are you kidding, son?"

"What?"

"You resigned for her."

Bloom felt a little knot of fear on the right below the ribs. "Maybe a little, yes," he said, "but that wasn't all of it."

"How much did it represent, Arthur? Twenty percent? Thirty? Half the decision?"

"What are you getting at?"

"Are you getting ready to run off with the girl?"

"No."

"Oh, Arthur."

"What's going on, mom?"

"She has really made you dance to her tune, hasn't she?" Nannette was quieting down, her anger mellowed by sadness. "Maybe it's my fault. Maybe with your father around or another man around, this wouldn't have happened and you would have learned more about girls."

"Mom!"

"Her mother was right," said Nannette. "She's got you so tied up around her little finger, she moves just like this, and you jump, her rabbi, her little puppet."

"Just what are you talking about?" He stood up now. "What is it, ma?"

Nannette looked away from him. "Leo, my son has given up everything, absolutely everything in his life and all for a girl who, I have on good authority, is seriously involved with another man."

"Who?" shouted Bloom. "What authority?"

"The girl's mother told me, that's who!"

" 'The girl, the girl,' " Bloom erupted. "You can say her name, mother. Not saying her name isn't going to make her disappear."

"Arthur, did you hear me? She's involved with another man. A young man named Matsumoto. Arthur, you look surprised."

"I've heard his name before. I think your information is wrong." Bloom felt like running back into the den.

"Then you know he's a Japanese boy she's known all her life."

"I don't believe any of what you're saying."

"How could you be so blind? To have given up everything, and for what? For nothing! How couldn't you know!"

"I didn't know because it isn't true." He was up now and putting on his jacket. "I want to borrow your car, please."

"You didn't eat," Nannette said, watching him.

"Because I'm sick to my stomach," Bloom said. "Where are the keys?"

"On the bureau," said Leonidas. "Don't crash it. It's the only one we have."

At the door Nannette stopped him. "You resigned, but it hasn't been accepted yet. The board has to consider and accept it. You can change your mind and take it back."

"I don't believe it," he shouted, as he raced down the hall and out to the parking lot. "I just don't believe it."

On the freeway he drove recklessly and far too fast. He remembered Dawn standing there this morning in the back of the synagogue and then she was suddenly gone, not there for him to seek out any more when his labors were done. And now this! Running around with Matsumoto? Well, she had not concealed his name, but . . . My God, I had better slow down, he thought as he flew at seventy-five miles per hour through the interchange and now south on the Harbor Freeway toward Gardena.

73

The lights were all off in both the store and the house, and Dawn's van was gone. Bloom crossed over, walked quickly down to the Duplicating Room, but it too was closed. He stopped on the sidewalk, turned around, and bumped into Adolph Gruen. "Excuse me," said Bloom.

"Good shabbos, Rabbi. A wonderful service today."

"Thank you, but somehow I don't believe you."

"Wonderful." Adolph kept smiling.

Bloom wanted to get away, he wanted to find Dawn, to talk to someone, but not to Gruen, who now lay a hand across his arm. "Should I become a Shintoist, Rabbi? Should I? Would that help?"

"I forbid it!" Bloom looked into his eyes.

"But Bernie says . . ."

"Don't listen to what he says. Now please let go of me."

Bloom turned in under the willows, but the front doors were locked. He was locked out of his own synagogue. Then as he opened the side gate and walked down the driveway, he realized that it was no longer his synagogue: he had resigned. Nevertheless the side door was open, and he entered.

There wasn't a soul inside. His heels clicked on the linoleum of the foyer and then went silent on the carpet of the sanctuary. The scene of the uproar was now still, silence filling up the room as if a last and final service had just been held. Indeed, thought Bloom, maybe mine has.

Old habit, however, and a nostalgia for the present, gripped him and moved him down the center aisle and up to the dais. The two lecterns where he and Bernie had debated remained. He rotated them so that they faced each other, and now, moving behind one, he addressed his invisible interlocutor behind the other. Shortly after he began, he realized he was talking to Rabbi Karpf.

"First of all, I wanted to thank you for being here."

He heard Karpf's response as if the old rabbi were right there. "Not at all, young man. I felt both a professional and a personal obligation to come."

Resuming as Bloom, he said, "And I, sir, left New York with a feeling of respect for you, too. Because I respect and I like you, I want to speak plainly and say some things that I didn't get a chance to say in New York. May I? Thank you very much. If I'm a little outrageous, I hope you'll understand. I have a lot to get off my chest tonight."

Karpf would understand, Bloom thought, and he would have said, "That's precisely our purpose in speaking with you: to clear up your mind. But may I suggest that since we're in the house of God, you put a yarmulkah on before you start?"

Bloom went to get a yarmulkah and put it over his bald spot— it felt bigger than ever before—and returned. He felt anger bubble up, and he suspected that it had been there for years, brewing, waiting, building, and now it came out, waves of ironic anger for everyone and everything that seemed to stand between him and Dawn.

"Well then," he began, "I'm not making excuses or alibis, Rabbi, but you have to understand how tough Jewish life is out here, how different from New York, where you don't think twice about being a Jew. Back where you are, it's like Jewish life in Solomonic times —there's an established authority, hierarchy, do's and don'ts. Here in L.A. we're still in the pre–Ten Commandments days, we're still wanderers in the desert, only instead of Sinai it's the wastes of the Mojave. In Biblical times, in the hour of their need, the Jews gave in to the Golden Calf. Why should it surprise you that now they go for slots, dice, chips, endless youthfulness, you name it!

"It doesn't surprise me at all," said Bloom-as-Karpf. "In every generation . . ."

"Both situations call for," Bloom interrupted, "a special person to galvanize the population, to unite them, to disabuse them of the paganism of the hour, to keep them coming in so that at least we have a *minyan* on shabbos!"

"Well put, young man."

"Thank you, Rabbi. I'm sorry my tongue seemed to desert me this morning."

"Moses was like you, young and unproved. He also didn't know what to say or do."

"Yes, but then he hit the stone and water came out."

"And do you also intend to perform miracles, Bloom?"

He looked up, alarmed, and, of course, there was no Rabbi Karpf across from him. He wondered if, under all the pressure, he really was losing his mind.

"A ridiculous question!" he answered.

"I'm glad to hear that, son, because I think the entire Peer Review Committee would hold you in serious error if you thought yourself a miracle worker."

"It's not that I believe it," Bloom implored. "It's that people believe it *about* me. You heard Bernie this morning—a madman, a full-fledged Sabbatean. A Frankist! I've never held myself up as anyone other than who I am."

"And who might that be?"

"Look at me here. I'm clearly a man, just a man."

"Rabbi," said Karpf, "our profession is a difficult and often demanding one, and one which is not often held in as high esteem as it should be. This is known on occasion to lead to difficulties and to misreadings, misperceptions of the state of congregational affairs."

"Your meaning, counselor?"

"To be blunt again"—Karpf-Bloom cleared his throat—"there is a growing and high rate of mental illness among rabbis. Is there not the real danger that you are suffering under a delusion or two and need a good rest? Puerto Rico is lovely, they have a kosher hotel, and we'd be happy to pay your way."

Bloom raised his arms. "Rabbi Karpf, if you gentlemen want to know what makes people crazy, what warps perspective, you, with all respect, only have to leave your little compound. You have been hanging around the seminary far too long. It takes little effort to be a good Jew, at least some kind of Jew, in Manhattan. Where else but in New York do they celebrate, Jew and gentile alike, the giving of the Ten Commandments and, simultaneously, the lifting of alternate-side-of-the-street parking regulations?

"No," Bloom cried, "I haven't finished yet, Rabbi, because I am not talking about parking. No! I'm talking about you, about us, rabbis and ex-rabbis like myself. You know we have struggles, we have adaptations to make in Gardena and everywhere else in this country, but what ideas do you have to help us with? Can you imagine a lifestyle more historically unsuited for the Jewish religion, a religion of learning, piety, and long hours stuck in a chair than this lifestyle of surfers, barbecuers, beachcombers, and weekend gamblers? But instead of acknowledging and assisting, you pay lip service and you play a waiting game, hoping in your heart of hearts it all will just go away. You want to hold your breath and call it swimming. You want to send me to Puerto Rico, but I'm not going. Instead maybe you'll come with me on a little trip to see what a wasteland synagogue life is in danger of becoming in most parts of the country. Don't you see them— synagogues and school buildings without congregations and without students? Community centers without communities, a whole system growing emptier each year and dying on the vine with little harvest?"

"You were a phlegmatic young man as a student, and look what's happened to you! You're an exaggerater, an overdramatizer. Has this been the influence of California on you, Rabbi?"

Bloom sat down in the upholstered chair beside the ark, listening to the echoes of his voice. "I am not exaggerating, sir, when I tell you there is no longer any attendance problem at Temple Elijah. We could have a packed house three times a day every day. Every shabbos is like the High Holidays."

"Perhaps"—Bloom-as-Karpf wagged a finger across the podium— "but you have achieved this at a terrible price. Of the six hundred and thirteen commandments, you and your congregation are in violation of six hundred and fourteen."

"I'm just telling you that the Silver Dollar is potentially a fine and healthy synagogue, and, what's more, I love it there. It's well and good for you to sit and respond, Rabbi, with your *God Forbid*s, but precisely what America's synagogues now need is not a sage but rather a synagogue doctor to fix them up, spiritually, financially, in all ways. The Silver Dollar's an exciting place to be, and, frankly, after three days in New York I couldn't get back fast enough."

"Try to get hold of yourself, Rabbi Bloom." He was standing now, his hands on the lapels of his blazer, pulling at them, as if to rip them —a sign of mourning. "Maybe a long rest in Hawaii is desirable."

"I'm feeling okay. Not great, but okay. I don't need a rest. Anyway, I'm out, I've resigned. I don't work here any more! Would you try now to punish the synagogue even after I'm gone? But what could you do?"

"We can isolate your synagogue in many other ways, Rabbi. It would not be attractive or pleasant."

"I would fight you," said Bloom. "Even though I'm no longer rabbi here, I would fight you to keep this place the way it is. I would go on television. Oh, the talk shows here would be dying to get the lucky rabbi to come on and deal a few hands and talk. And I would talk, plenty."

"Please, son," Bloom charaded, pulling his imaginary beard, lowering his voice, all his rabbinical histrionics overflowing, mocking themselves. "Let's be conciliatory. Let us decide that we will keep the whole matter local and under control. Let us endeavor to settle it as if it were a family squabble."

"Then lay off," Bloom cried. "And no more threats, please!"

"Bravo, quite a performance. . . . Hello, Arthur."

It was her voice, but it was dark now in the sanctuary, the day having grown to night, and he could not see her.

74

Bloom stumbled over one of the lecterns and banged his shoulder on a doorjamb as he frantically tried to find the panel of switches. He flicked both rows. The sanctuary was flooded with yellow-white light, and he told Dawn all Nannette's accusations.

"Other people say those things about me," she said calmly. "You never have until this moment."

"I don't hear a denial yet. Is it true about you and Matsumoto? Is this it? Is this behind all your noble efforts to open my eyes? You're saying, Well, here's the rabbi I've sort of been interested in. He's under my belt now. Another notch, and now I'll go on to more elusive game."

"This is awful of you, Arthur."

Bloom felt himself growing dizzy. "You *are* going back to Matsumoto. I know you were in touch with him. Is that why you turned down my proposal? You're going to go back to him."

"I didn't date him, Arthur. I interviewed him."

"You've been interviewing me as well."

"Don't do this to yourself."

"But why did you have to wait until we were not seeing each other for the innocent interviewing to start?"

"Because I thought you might react jealously. I thought you might not understand, and it would hurt your feelings, and I didn't want that to happen."

"How thoughtful of you."

"You see, Arthur? You see how right I was."

"Panuzzi warned me, and others did too. They said, Arthur, don't fall so quickly for her. What comes up must come down. I guess it's down time, again."

"No, Arthur," she said, "you're dead wrong."

She sounded so final, so beyond his reach. "And I suppose you're giving swimming lessons to him, too. Oh, he's Japanese, he's probably into water the way you are and doesn't need lessons."

"You're getting nasty and ugly, Arthur. Yes, at first you were a story but I liked you too"—he heard the past tense, and never had a point of grammar been clearer to him—"and I am a person with needs and feelings, and so it's happened between us, and I don't have regrets. But I know when something is amiss, and it is, here and now!"

"What's amiss is that I think I've been used, lied to, led on, and taken advantage of. You're the one with more experience in these matters. Where's your sense of responsibility?" Bloom felt his head heavy, and his shoulders ached as if he had not slept in days. "This is bullshit. This is only the world's most cerebral, most protracted goodbye."

"My main reservation," she continued, her finger raised now and going at him as she could do, like a lawyer in court, "was that, yes, you had a fine brain and a strong body, and a sympathetic heart, but back inside you somewhere was this funny weak point, this blind spot about yourself: You felt yourself ordinary, or maybe a kind of failure in your career, which is not true, but it was a feeling you had and carried around with you and you still have deep inside you there at a depth where it will be hard to eradicate. Arthur the failed poet, that's what you considered yourself. The failed philosopher, the most irreverent and undistinguished rabbi ever produced in the whole history of the Jews! And because of this, Arthur, you've glamorized yourself, you've transformed an inferiority complex into this other business, the lucky rabbi. No, don't nod your head as if you know something about this I don't. Instead of accepting yourself for who you are—and are not—you've bought this lucky rabbi nonsense, and you won't give it up.

"Arthur, I just heard you up there at the great debate in the dark. I know what goes on inside you. I know what the big need of yours is to make you act out things the way you do. Yes, you've resigned, but so what! You're no longer the lucky rabbi. Now you're the lucky ex-rabbi, the lucky rabbi without a pulpit."

"No."

"Yes," she said quietly. "Remember John Milton: 'Fame, the last infirmity of a noble mind'? I think you've got it bad, Arthur—in spite of outward appearances. I think you feel you've just got to be somebody spectacular, somebody who will add his name to the Jewish hall of fame. You've spent so much time reading that you find it intolerable that you're not a Maimonides, or whoever. So you've gone and let yourself relax into being this local celebrity. Sure, you're trying to keep the synagogue from falling apart, but look at the consequences! If you would only let go of the notion, and be just your regular, cute, bookish, quotidian self without secret pretensions! I'm sorry, Arthur. I'm very, very sorry!"

Bloom wanted to shout Take Me, Take Me, but it was clear to him finally that he was a real puzzle to her. He was two Arthur Blooms—one, the humble man he thought he was himself, and this second Bloom, this danger to himself and the community, this naïvely self-deluding fellow she must either reform or avoid.

"I'm convinced, Arthur, that the lucky rabbi could not have continued in peace here. It's just too screwy. If not me, then someone else. Somehow, sooner or later, your life here would have reached a crisis."

"Come closer to me, please!"

"No, Arthur, this isn't easy for me, either. When I'm near you, even when you're loving to me, I can't help but get this feeling from you that you think I've done something to you, something wrong, that in your eyes I've committed some sort of crime." They looked at each other for a long moment, a painful note of music held and held. Then Dawn said, "And maybe I have."

"No," Bloom answered quietly.

"Arthur, maybe I have committed some sort of crime—the crime of trespassing in your life."

She held her hands out to him now, her arms straight and unmoving, waiting, it seemed, for the cuffs. Bloom took her by the wrists and held her there. He wanted to pull her toward him but couldn't; it was not her resistance or a lack of strength on his part, but a force that interceded between the two of them. He stood there, feeling her soft skin under his, the delicate bones of her wrists which he loved, and he recognized that for all his agonizing and his analyzing to get at it, she had put what had happened between them best, with truth's usual simplicity: they were trespassers, each a kind of beloved trespasser in the other's life.

He moved his hands slowly up toward her elbows, but she withdrew from him. He felt helpless and said, "I simply don't understand how we are allowing this to happen. I simply don't get it."

"You would," she said, "if you were the person I need you to be."

"I should demonstrate my regard, my love, for you by agreeing to separate and never see you again? This I should understand?"

"Yes."

"I don't get it."

"You'd understand," she said as her tears poured out, "if you wanted to."

75

MESSIAH OR PARIAH?

by Dawn Nakazawa

Mashiach, the Hebrew word for messiah, or saviour, is more and more frequently heard on the streets of Gardena, California, these days, where a member of the local synagogue, Temple Elijah, has recently proclaimed the synagogue's rabbi, Arthur Bloom, as, if not the messiah himself, then most definitely a kind of lieutenant in the messiah's advance guard.

Bernard Levitt stated in a recent forum at the synagogue that the signs of the messianic age were appearing, and in Gardena! "I've had dreams of the chariot of Ezekiel, I've seen wonders performed by the rabbi, and I know the messiah might be stuck in a traffic jam, but it'll be cleared up and he'll soon be on his way."

Mr. Levitt, a fast-talking man who is the owner and operator of the local Cadillac dealership, previously had a vision of the messiah right on his car lot. Now he feels that the temple's unusual young rabbi may have been in part responsible.

According to Levitt, "The rabbi is already imbued with emanations of divine light." This is the explanation, continued Mr. Levitt, of the remarkable good luck the rabbi is reputed to impart to his congregants when they gamble at Gardena's casinos.

In order not to fuel the flames of controversy, Rabbi Bloom has announced that he has quit his pulpit at Temple Elijah.

Mr. Levitt then urged all the congregants also to quit the synagogue, in emulation of the rabbi. Mr. Levitt believes that it is incumbent on every Jew to decipher the hidden indicators of the coming of the messiah and also to accelerate his arrival. Levitt believes that the best, truest, and most efficacious means to bring this about is to follow the rabbi's example.

The arrival of the messiah is an event which Jews, unlike Christians, believe has not yet occurred. Yet the arrival of the messiah remains an important element of Jewish theology. Mr. Levitt pointed to the Holocaust during World War II and the subsequent founding of the State of Israel as two signs of the messiah's imminent arrival.

Rabbi Bloom rejoined, during an exchange at the forum, that according to Biblical Jewish thought, the messianic age, if it arrives, will be characterized as an age when all strife is eliminated, as in the Isaianic vision of the lion lying down with the lamb and the transformation of swords into ploughshares.

Pinning such hopes on living individuals, however, does not sit well with the institutions of organized Judaism. In response to a telephone inquiry about whether the messiah is arriving in the person of Rabbi Bloom, the Rabbinical Association in New York stated through a spokeswoman: "This is a regrettable development, but a private one and part of a continuing dialogue between the Association and Rabbi Bloom. We don't want to grace it with a lot of attention."

The Rabbinical Association is the professional organization of rabbis in the Conservative Movement of Judaism (to which Rabbi Bloom belongs). It places Jewish clergymen in posts across the country.

The Academy of Judaism, one of the Southland's most prestigious colleges for Jewish studies, had no official comment. However, the Academy's librarian, a man familiar with the situation, commented, "I know Mr. Levitt, and I for one would not buy a used car from him!"

When asked specifically what was occurring in Gardena to convince him that the messiah was on the way, Mr. Levitt responded, "It would be a mistake to expect that suddenly, due to the rabbi's powers, traffic in L.A. will suddenly lighten up, or the smog will disappear, or the L.A. River refuse to flow on the sabbath."

Then he paused and added mysteriously, "Yet anything can happen."

76

During the week before Rosh Hashanah, Bloom went to stay at his mother's apartment, and his absence from Gardena created a vacuum into which rancor poured. Bernie Levitt, Lucy Leonard, Ethel Axelrod, Adolph Gruen, and a half dozen others began a kind of picket line along the sidewalk in front of the synagogue. People going in to pray with Brenda and Panuzzi were waylaid and urged to turn back. "The rabbi's quit the synagogue, and you should, too!"

"You are commanded to break the law," Bernie's voice boomed. "You are commanded not to pray on Rosh Hashanah. You are commanded to sin, because sinning will bring redemption."

Eli Ginsberg tried to strike Bernie with his duck-handled cane, but missed, fell on the sidewalk, and broke his hip.

As if the religious factionalism in the community weren't severe enough, people also began to lose at the casinos. The pattern seemed to be that the more you got involved in partisan religious imbroglios, the worse cards you got at stud, the more you busted at twenty-one, and the more frequently the dice rolled out of your hand like a pair of cursed bricks.

This was an uncanny turn of fate, whose meaning depended on the interpreter. Bernie proclaimed that the rabbi's separation from Dawn and his seclusion at his mother's in L.A. had caused it. "History teaches," he said over his megaphone, "that some persecution, some price, must be paid for our ideas. Sanctify God," he proclaimed, "by violating Rosh Hashanah this year. Sanctify God through your sins, and you expedite the end of days!"

After two days of the shouting and shoving under the willows, Sarah North retained a lawyer, the police were called, and Bernie and company were hauled into court for disturbing the peace.

The more trouble there was, the more Bernie deciphered in it the contractions of the world as it readied itself for the birth of the messiah. Bloom's resignation was an omen of even more mysteries to be unlocked. With resignation in the bag, said Bernie, surely marriage to Ms. Nakazawa and then conversion to another faith could not be far off. Would it be one of the Christian varieties— perhaps a Japanese version—or a yet unnamed and undiscovered new abomination? Moreover, OPEC was just now meeting in Caracas, the PLO was shooting it out with the Israeli Defense Force on the Litani River, calamitous events seemed to be brewing. "Watch the rabbi," Bernie urged. "Watch him and learn!"

As more of these disturbing and bizarre claims reached Bloom at Nannette's apartment, he realized that, resigned or not, he could not resign from this predicament. He might leave town, the state, the country, or even the hemisphere, but no matter where he went, until a resolution was reached, he was going to be a refugee from his own life. But what resolution?

True to his commitment to himself, however, he would help Leonidas take care of his mother, and he would stay out of Bernie Levitt's fishbowl. Never again would he offer himself up to be touched, petted, pawed. How glad Bloom was that he no longer had to listen to congregants' tales of gambling woes, and he was also relieved from the responsibility of considering himself anybody's spiritual advisor but his own. He refused to talk religion, and he most emphatically refused to discuss his supposed talismanic qualities with Leonidas or anybody else. And he also refused to reconsider his resignation.

Bloom paradoxically also suddenly felt free to become a more observant Jew than he had been as a practicing rabbi. He began to pray with feeling, with *kavanah,* an untranslatable quality of integrity and longing combined, which he had not experienced since he had said *kaddish,* the mourner's prayer, on the death of his father. He prayed, and he worked hard to become conscious of the wonder of life around him.

He did not return to Gardena, however, for the whole week, leaving the Rosh Hashanah service entirely to Brenda. With pleasure he heard that she had done a creditable job. More than creditable, it had been at times inspiring, especially those moments when she herself had taken the extra ram's horn and generated, along with Panuzzi, a trumpeting duo of mighty *teruas.* She and Panuzzi had been a great hit—so Panuzzi told him, anyway—and Bloom responded to the news not with envy but with relief. What disturbed him, Brenda, Panuzzi, Sarah North, and the whole anti-Levitt faction, however, was that the synagogue had been only one third full; or to put it more truly, the sanctuary had been two thirds empty. A great many people, far too many, had heeded Bernie and stayed away. Even the rabbi-and-cantor-in-love attraction of Brenda Weiner and Angelos Panuzzi had not drawn the usual High Holiday crowd to Gardena. Without the lucky rabbi, Bernie had been able to lure most of the congregation away. This success, Bloom could not help but feel, was his personal failure. He began to feel that his refuge in L.A. was more like a hideout, his resignation a less than noble retreat.

After Rosh Hashanah, Bloom's concern heightened. The ten days between Rosh Hashanah and Yom Kippur were the Ten Days of Repentance when one was supposed to prepare the heart for contrition. For on Yom Kippur itself, the last of the ten days, one's fate, according to the tradition, was permanently sealed, irrevocably engraved in the Book of Life for the coming year. The choices were all laid out in the liturgy that Bloom now read on his mother's couch, high over the park: whether you lived or whether you died, whether in good health or in traction, whether rich or poor, happy or miserable. If there was a time to make a move, that time was now.

To stay away from the synagogue on this day as well, as Levitt was now urging, was serious business indeed. And yet Bloom's intelligence was that many people were thinking of doing precisely that. Confusion and disarray reigned at the synagogue. What was a sin and what was a *mitzvah?* Bernie Levitt had turned them inside out and tagged the results with Bloom's name. What's more, the betting fortunes of temple members, including the car dealer himself, continued to erode. But this only encouraged and confirmed Bernie in his kabbalistic speculations. Arthur was separated from his Japanese love, living with and taking care of his mother, no longer even physically close to Dawn or the casinos; all of these facts Bernie interpreted as indicators that Bloom was making a turn to become a well-behaved, well-meaning, conventional young man. In other words, Bloom was doing the right thing, and as a result gamblers were losing, which was just another "proof" for Bernie Levitt. To do right was a sin, he continued to proclaim, to do wrong was a commandment of God. People argued heatedly, because if your luck continued to be lousy at cards, dice, and at slot machines, and if you lost with every hand, then weren't you liable to lose as well on Yom Kippur, in the celestial casino, in heaven, as the Manager checked His Book and found your credit all gone?

So Bloom watched and waited in the wings and wondered what, if anything, he might do. He tried to make chicken soup for his mother, but it came out too thin and full of bones; he helped her with her facial exercises, and he agonized over what his life had become.

Although few people noticed it, the tension on Sarah North had been more than she could bear. In spite of all her apparent success, she sensed she might be losing. She had an inexperienced girl as acting rabbi, a synagogue that, to her thinking, had become a mockery, and by now there was reporting on each new debacle in the sleazy L.A. papers. What's more, the distance between her and Abe had grown even wider. He had left the temple board, which, for all practical purposes, now ceased to exist; as to Bloom's resignation, Abe thought it the most regrettable development in Gardena in ten years, and he laid the blame for it squarely on his wife.

"You forced him to do it," he told her. "You drove him until he had to."

"I'm proud of it," she said shakily. "It's you I'm ashamed of now, my own husband."

"There's too much shame in you, Sarah."

The nearly empty synagogue on Rosh Hashanah may have been what did it, the trigger. For two days later, in the morning, she got up early and drove to Nero's Grotto to play. There were only four other people at the low-ball table—none of whom knew her. It was unusual of her to have gone to Nero's, since her regular place was the Silver Dollar, so she must have chosen Nero's precisely to be among strangers. They said she didn't look bad—no worse than themselves—had said little, and made no complaints about feeling sick.

They had played maybe two dozen hands when it hit, a heart attack so massive that it flung Sarah's glasses off her head as it flattened her against the chair, made her extend her legs rigidly out in front of her, as if she were in a vehicle about to crash and she were trying to protect herself. Then the force of it twisted her body as she reached across, her fingers clawing at the upper rib cage, and left her draped over the arm of the chair like a thin forgotten coat.

"Bring us a live one," the player directly across said. But it was no joke. Sarah North was dead.

The funeral was held the next day, but not in Gardena, and it was not conducted by Rabbi Bloom. Although he had called immediately to offer his condolences and his services, Abe declined. "You understand, Rabbi, I'm trying to do what she would have wanted, and I don't believe she would have wanted you even to attend. Please, no hard feelings? When I die, you can have the job."

Leonidas, Nannette, Angelos, Brenda, and a dozen others from the synagogue drove to the Mt. Zion Cemetery in the San Fernando Valley, where they heard a rabbi even younger than Bloom, they said, say the usual things over the body of this woman whom he had never even met. Then Abe threw the first shovelful of dirt on the simple casket, and she was gone.

Alone in the apartment in L.A., Bloom felt desolate, and responsible. Heart attacks derived, in part, from tension and pressure, and he certainly had contributed to raising pressure in Gardena enough to shatter one, probably far more, hearts. His mother had had a stroke—thank God, a minor one—and now Sarah was dead, gone just like that; who would be next? He had quit, he had resigned in the hope that the mania would abate. His resignation had turned out to be not beneficial, but lethal.

He heard the tumblers turning in the lock, and then he sat up on the sofa. Nannette and Leonidas, wearing dark clothes of mourning, entered. She came up to him and put her hand on his forehead. "You're wet, Arthur. You're sweaty." Her hand felt so good there, his mother's hand.

"I think I might have been dozing, talking in my sleep. Tell me how it was."

"How is a funeral?" Leonidas dropped onto the chair next to Bloom. "A funeral is a funeral."

"Tell me what happened, Leo."

"Nannette and Arthur," the Greek said, "I have, unfortunately, seen plenty more people die than you. It does make a difference the way you die and are buried. It's better to die on your feet than on your knees, that cliché is true. It is also true that it is better to have your own grave than a mass grave. Sarah had her own, a simple grave, a simple box, a simple ceremony. It wasn't bad."

Bloom sensed a cover-up. "What gives? Something happened."

"Nothing."

"Something."

Nannette came over and sat on the arm of the chair next to Leonidas and smoothed the Greek's unruly cowlick. The funeral had put Nannette into a smoothing, soothing frame of mind; with Sarah under the ground, and no longer touchable, Nannette wanted to touch her living and her loved ones. "He was there," she said, after much attention to Leonidas's hair. "That horrible man was not wanted, but he came anyway. We didn't see him in the chapel, but when we walked outside, during the procession across the grass to the grave, there he was as if he'd been waiting there. It's a huge cemetery, I don't even know how he knew the spot."

"It's easy enough to find out," said Leonidas. "You just ask."

"Or you follow people in your car," said Bloom quietly.

"Anyway," Nannette went on talking, and grooming, "he's all wrapped in his *tallis*, when nobody else has one on, not even the rabbi, and he comes up to people during the procession, when you're supposed to be quiet and respectful, and he says, even before poor Sarah is in the ground, 'It's a sign from God,' he says. 'It's a victory! God struck her down because He is removing obstacles. God doesn't want anyone to be in the way of the rabbi. Her dying was another birth pang of His messiah!'"

"The man has no decency," said Bloom, "no sense of where to stop."

"Leo, tell Arthur what you said you would."

"I'm supposed to give you an apology," Leonidas said to Bloom. "Your mother's making me do it, but I would anyway." Leonidas paused, and Bloom waited. "I played along with him for a while, but it was a mistake. Listen, son, Levitt is an earnest but very troubled man. *Meshugeh* makes it sound too nice. He's sold his share of the business—there's a lot of money involved. He and Adolph Gruen and that poor misguided Lucy and some others are going to gamble it all on Yom Kippur. Deliberately on Yom Kippur, and they're after everyone to join them."

"I told you, Arthur," Nannette said, "I told you none of this would come to any good. Staying away from the shul on Rosh Hashanah was bad, but now staying away isn't enough for them. Now everybody's supposed to gamble twelve hours straight instead of praying. From Kol Nidre on, at the craps tables, at blackjack, the biggest bets for the biggest holiday, the biggest sins they can muster."

"It won't happen," Bloom said calmly.

"What did you say?" Nannette had left the room to change shoes, and now was quickly back, in moccasins and her blue housecoat.

"I said it won't happen. I said the jig is up."

Leo put his hand on Bloom's arm. "I tried to stop him at the funeral, you know, but he's strong and totally convinced that what he is doing is right. He's a zealot who's on fire. He keeps going and going, faster and hotter, gathering momentum. He doesn't care if six people come with him or sixty or six hundred. He intends to gamble in the casino, to flout the holiday, to tempt fate, to do whatever it is he's doing. I told him by the grave, after Sarah was covered, I told him that if Arthur Bloom has anything to do with the messiah, then I am Johnny Carson. He laughed and kept on praying."

Nannette moved over to sit beside Bloom on the couch. "You know, Sarah, may she rest in peace, liked you. She really always liked you, even when you started up with Naka-whoever, she liked you and was very hurt. She was such a sad lonely woman!"

"I know, ma."

"She never wanted you to resign, Arthur. I talked to her and she told me." Nannette moved to the edge of the cushion. "It's very sad."

"A heart is not a foot," said Leonidas. "You cannot break it on purpose, quickly like that. It takes years of dedicated self-destruction, time."

"No matter," said Nannette, "I think she willed it."

"So," said Leonidas as he stood up and clapped his hands together, "what are we going to do?"

"You're going to do nothing," Bloom quietly said. "It's all up to me. I'll do what I have to do."

"The man does not want to stop. Nothing will stop him," Nannette said. "I know, I tried, too. I went to him and told him to leave my son alone, and he went right on, as if I hadn't been there at all, and now it's come to this. In everything he sees the reverse, in the terrible he sees blessings. A death is a sign, an arrest is a sign. Bad is good, there's no sense, no logic."

"Oh, there is," Bloom said, as his plan crystallized. "Again, you

might not like how I go about it, ma"—he turned to them both—
"but I know what I have to do to stop him."

"No violence," said Nannette, "please."

"No violence, ma."

"What then?" Leonidas was finally slipping off his coat and hanging it in the closet. "A lawyer?"

"No. With logic, of course," Bloom answered. "The logic of the
man's own mysticism. I'm going to out-kabbala our local kabbalist."
Bloom was up now and putting on his shoes. "There are only a few
days left before Yom Kippur. No time to waste."

"Where are you going?"

"I'm going." Bloom stopped, and then he said, "To pay my
respects to Sarah's grave, and then I'm going to Gardena."

"To Levitt?"

"Yes. I'm going to make him a deal he absolutely can't refuse."

"Take a jacket—it's chilly," said Nannette. "The messiah
shouldn't catch a cold."

79

As agreed, they met beneath the weeping willows in front of the
synagogue.

"We've been expecting you to contact us, Rabbi. We've been
waiting for you a long time, our revered rabbi!"

"Wait no longer." Bloom smiled. "I'm all yours."

Bernie struck Bloom as having somehow grown bigger, having put
on some weight, a man who has absorbed and enlarged himself on
a sudden new eminence. They walked around the synagogue building toward the side, intending to enter there, but since the evening
was so pleasant and inviting, and because what he had to discuss with
the man was the very definition of the profane, Bloom suggested
they stay outside. They drew up two chaises longues near the diving
board. Bernie stretched himself out in Bloom's chair, and Bloom
lightly and reverently lay upon the one Dawn used to sit in. Venus,
the evening star, appeared, along with Jupiter, right above the roof
of the synagogue.

"I've been doing some studying and some thinking," Bloom began. "Actually, a great deal of thinking and reading, as I know you have."

"I've been praying and hoping, Rabbi. I never for an instant lost faith in you. I knew you would join us!"

"Well, Bernie, you see, you drove Dawn from me with your surveillance and your phone calls, and I suppose with your faith in me, which all of your tactics were somehow an expression of—am I right?"

"She's not so far away," he said contentedly. "I know she's in your thoughts, and I trust all of us are in your thoughts, as well. We need to be, Rabbi. It is very important as the holiest day of the year approaches."

"Exactly," said Bloom. "I could not agree more." Then he rested his hands on his stomach and said, "Actually when I was informed you had sold your business and were urging people to take all their assets and play along with you the highest stakes they could afford on Yom Kippur, that's when you entered my thoughts in a new way, a startling new way."

"Yes?"

"I can't let it happen."

"Yet it will, it must."

"Why must it? Listen, I'm going to tell you a little story. It slipped my mind when we debated. Is it all right with you?"

The car dealer raised his legs onto the diving board and said he was always eager to hear and learn from the rabbi.

"You see"—Bloom leaned toward him—"there was this messiah in Yemen back in 1172, around that year, I might be off a little. Anyway, he told people just what you're telling people now: to sell all their property, to turn their property into portable wealth. He told them to join him because they wouldn't need furniture or houses or livestock much longer. He told them they should ready themselves instead to book passage on ships for Jerusalem, for the messianic age, the return of all peoples to Israel, was upon them. This fellow made speeches up and down the country for months. When he was finally arrested, the messiah was asked by his Arab captors for proof of his divine claims. 'Cut off my head and I will come back to life' is what he said. And that is precisely what the Arabs did."

Bernie Levitt took his feet carefully off the diving board.

"The head and the body, to the best of the chronicler's knowledge, were never reunited."

"Rabbi, we play the hand we're dealt. You're my hand, and not any Arab captors, and not Yemen in the twelfth century. I choose to play my hand this way. Other generations, who will have to play their hand with the Lord, can judge me when the time comes."

"But that's precisely it," Bloom said. "Let me play the hand for you! Isn't that what you've really been after all along? You attribute great power to me, so why not let *me* be the lightning rod? Why not let me play?"

Bernie crossed his arms over his chest, and Bloom continued. "Let's understand each other. You feel the messianic age is upon us, is near, perhaps a hair's breadth away. But a hair's breadth measured against eternity can be a lot. So you want to give it a helping hand. You're an impatient man."

"As you are," said Bernie.

"Right, so you are looking to expedite, to move the contractions along to the crisis? And the chief means you have been using to do this is to act *as if* the end of days has arrived."

"Maybe not the end of days, but at least its heralder is here—you!"

"Me, of course." Bloom smiled. "But to really wrap it up and to demonstrate your conviction to others, you urge people to sin, to break laws, for in the end of days, or even in the era of the heralder of the end of days, laws no longer are binding, injunctions are unnecessary, the Torah is revealed to be not the jewel itself, but the box containing the real jewel, the light of redemption. Right?"

"We have no misunderstanding, Rabbi, only a lack of conviction on your part."

"Not any longer," said Bloom.

"No?"

"Yes, I too want to gamble on the holiest day of the year."

"Rabbi, I'm astonished. Is this really true?"

"Yes, sir."

"How wonderful! How fantastic!" Bernie grabbed Bloom's hands, drew them near, and wrapped them in his, a great nest of palms. *"Boruch ata Adonai, elohenu melech ha-olom,"* Bernie chanted in enthusiastic, joyful whispers, *"asher kid-shanu ba-mitzvotav (she ayn od olaynu likayame) vi-hi-gi-yanu lasman hazeh!* Blessed art thou, O Lord our God, King of the Universe, Who has sanctified us with His commandments (which are no longer binding) and has brought us to this day!"

Bloom joined Bernie on his feet and said, quietly, "Amen."

"We'll meet here," the dealer said, "and with you at the head of our procession, we should be able to draw off a dozen more people at least. What about Brenda? If we could get her, both rabbis?"

"I don't think so," said Bloom. "I don't think you can count on that."

They were slowly circumnavigating the pool. "Are you sure, Rabbi? Even with your influence?"

"I'm sure."

"And what of the cantor?"

Bloom shook his head.

"I know Leonidas has gotten cold feet, but what of your mother? The rabbi's mother? Now that would be a stroke."

"I don't like that choice of words," said Bloom.

"Forgive me. What about her?"

"I'm not sure I've made myself clear," he said. "No one else is going to gamble on Yom Kippur, Bernie."

The dealer stopped suddenly. They were at the shallow end. "No one else?"

"No one." Bloom's eyes did not leave his. "Not even you."

Bernie stared at Bloom. Bloom's back was to the pool, his shoe just one large stride from the water. For a moment Bloom thought perhaps Bernie was about to put his hand on his chest and lightly tap him in. Levitt raised a hand, but it hooked Bloom at the elbow and pulled him along. "Just where did you have in mind, Rabbi, that we, the rest of us, should be?"

"Why, in the synagogue, praying, of course! Every last one of you."

"And you where?" Bernie laughed.

"Right there, next door." He pointed to the Silver Dollar Casino, with its glittering sign peaking just above the roof line. "If you all pray hard enough and loud enough, I'll probably be able to hear you!"

"Rabbi, you don't know how to gamble. You've never played."

"What difference does that make?" said Bloom. "If I've got it,

I've got it, right? Don't tell me you have any doubts about my powers, my ability to win?"

"Rabbi, you don't know the first thing to do. You don't know where to sit, what to open with, how to raise, to pass—"

"I'm sharp," Bloom interrupted him. "I'll learn."

"You'll lose thousands before you know what's happening."

"Money's not the point, anyway, is it? Are you forgetting I'm the lucky rabbi? I'll recoup, and then if you're right, that is, if we're right, then we'll win big, tremendously big, with all that money to invest. Then we take all the winnings and do what our people has always done at moments like this throughout history. We'll arrange a charter flight to Israel, for the whole congregation, for whoever wants to go, whether they've been for or against us, right or wrong, we all up and go." Bloom pointed to the diving board beside them. "The jumping-off place for the kingdom of heaven!"

"No," said Bernie, growing a little more solemn. "That's not the way I see it. I say you lead us, you go with us into the casino. Inside you *bless us*, maybe, if you want, but I don't like the idea of your playing."

"But if your theory is correct—bad is good—it'll work; God will find a way and I'll win big."

"No."

"Yes," said Bloom, "and here's something else. I want to play only with *your* money—your assets, plus what's left in the synagogue fund you set up. I don't want anybody's money but yours. I've got maybe two thousand dollars in my savings account. That's all my money, and I'll throw that in, too, if you like. What's two thousand dollars compared to the fate of the world?"

Bernie scrutinized him in silence.

"About how much do you have, all told, the dealership proceeds included?"

Bernie hesitated and then slowly said, "About a quarter of a million dollars, Rabbi."

"That's not much either, measured against eternity, is it?"

"And you want to gamble with it all?"

"With it and all my savings, too. And while I gamble, you will all pray, together, all of you, with Brenda and with Angelos and my mother, you and Lucy and Adolph and Ethel, and it'll be just the way it used to be on Yom Kippurs past when we've been together as a congregation. You remember, don't you?"

"I remember."

"The differences will be just two: I'll be next door, giving your messianic hopes the ultimate test, and the second difference is that you'll be saying mourner's *kaddish*, I hope, for Sarah North."

Bernie shook his head. Bloom, in the gathering darkness, was not sure if it was yes, no, or both.

"And these ground rules will apply as well: Nobody, none of you, can come in; you all must pray and fast and not jangle the change in your pockets and stay in the shul until services are over. And I will stay and gamble until I double the money, or have lost it all for you, every last penny. But that's not likely to happen because I am, after all, the harbinger of the end of days."

"What if I say no?"

"Are you thinking 'No'?"

"Yes, I am, Rabbi."

"Then I'll tell everybody what I have offered, and you won't have a leg left to stand on the day after Yom Kippur. You've always said it was a question of belief, of conviction, and demonstration of that conviction through action. Now you have a chance to prove it, to put your money, all of it, where your conviction is. Think of it this way," Bloom said, as they arrived back at the chaises, "if you win, you win very very big. I'm absolutely yours. You are, in the following days, a wealthy and influential man and you can take your movement beyond Gardena. I'll lend myself to whatever you want. I'll be convinced, or I'll act that way in public for you.

"As for me," Bloom went on, "I win what? I win nothing. Dawn is gone, my job is gone, my mother's had a stroke, Sarah is dead, I'm practically expelled from the Rabbinical Association of America, and for this particular deed that I am offering to perform on your behalf, I will probably be excommunicated, or will deserve to be. I will never be able to return to this crazy synagogue, or any synagogue."

"So why do it, Rabbi? Why offer?"

"Because you've driven me to it. Because it has to end this way. If we are commanded to be redeemed through sinning and violations, I'm giving you the biggest sin I can come up with."

"But you'll *try* to lose," Bernie said. "You may try to lose on purpose."

"No, you can arrange it with the floor manager if you want to watch me. I'll try to win. I'll learn at the cheap tables, and only when I have some understanding of the rules will I go to the more expensive tables. I'll give it a true, honest shot; otherwise the experiment has no validity, and that's what we are interested in, isn't it, Bernie? The truth of your claims?"

Bernie was slowly shaking his head. "No, no, no . . ."

"I am offering you me, the lucky rabbi, gambling on Yom Kippur, a sin punishable, I believe, by death. I'll probably throw in a few additional sins as well, if you want. I'll smoke a joint—I'll probably need it to go through with this—and I'll eat some cheeseburgers."

"You do, anyway."

"But I'll do it in public. In a big way. Double cheeseburgers! French fries, the works! Hey, man, we'll really see what God's made of, won't we?"

But Bernie Levitt was unamused. He had counted on Bloom's resistance, and this sudden all-embracing compliance had thrown him.

"Rabbi," he finally said, "I'd prefer you leave the gambling to me. I'd prefer you convert instead. Sabbatai Zevi did. Jacob Frank did, a whole handful of false messiahs did, so you can, too."

"But Bernie," Bloom cried, "I may not be false! Isn't that what you're all about? And I am not going to associate myself with false messiahs unless I have to. If I'm the real article, we'll find out in the casinos, with your money and my money, where it's safe, where nobody's head is going to be chopped off, and where nobody's life savings—except yours and mine—are at stake. Nobody's life and future are on the line but ours."

"No," said the dealer. "I don't buy it!"

"Let's compromise," said Bloom. "I'll play first. If I play and win, as should happen, if you're right, then I'll convert at that point." Bloom's heart beat rapidly. "That's a promise. I'll convert to anything you say. You name it—Buddhism, anything; at that point I won't have to be particular."

Bernie pulled out a pack of cigarettes from his vest pocket, offered one to Bloom, who declined, and then lit up. "Let's say you *lose*, Rabbi. What do you foresee then?"

"In that case, it's over and done here. Your movement, as you call it, is over with, totaled. If I lose, the lucky rabbi is no more. No explanation, no excuses. I'm not saying you should leave town—I don't even know where I'm going to end up when this is over—but I don't want you to dog me. Done will be done. Because if you don't, I'll take you to court, and I don't mean the Sanhedrin. And I'm sure I can get witnesses—Dawn and others—and I'll have you up on invasion of privacy and criminal trespass, which is a felony, and on charges relating to your nasty phone calls and to voyeurism, and I haven't finished yet."

"Let me think about it."

"If by tomorrow at two, when I check with my bank, you haven't deposited that quarter million in my account, there is no deal, and I squeal. I squeal that Bernard Levitt is a charlatan, a false proclaimer, who when the lucky rabbi offered him *the great* proof, *the* desecration nonpareil, he turned it down."

Bernie walked slowly away, and Bloom watched him stop and then stare up at Venus, and then start again. He opened the gate, and when it creaked shut, he halted and placed his hands on the top of it. "One thing I don't get," he said. "Why, if you feel this way, after all, don't you just take me to court even if it's against your inclination? Why put yourself through this test? I can see you don't really want to do it, which could—you'll agree—sabotage the whole thing, undermining the means, coloring the outcome—so why are you doing it, Rabbi? Why?"

"Because," said Bloom, approaching the gate, menacing Bernie for the first time in his life, "because what if I win?"

"Yes," said Bernie, "there is that."

"What if I win?" Bloom repeated. "What if I win?" he said aloud, even louder, and then, not caring if Bernie was still there in the driveway or anyone else was looking, he slipped out of his shoes, inched toward the edge, and let himself fall, saying, "What if I win? What if I win?" as he dropped, fully clothed, into the water.

80

He surfaced near the shallow corner, where his old inner tube, now partly deflated, was barely afloat. He pulled himself up the slippery steps and then, wringing wet, up to the veranda, where he stripped before entering.

When he turned on the light, the old mess greeted him, a familiar friend. He took a bath towel he found draped over the stereo and dried off, slipped into his jeans, pulled the *machzor*, the High Holiday prayer book, and three other books off the shelf, and began to study. There was much to prepare, he felt, even though he wasn't going to lead prayers or even pray himself. Perhaps because of that, he found himself mumbling all the the hymns, doxologies, blessings, and pronouncements of faith, all to himself in a low voice, surrounded by the congregation of his books and a full bag of potato chips that he had found in the fridge.

He read and reread the chapter in Genesis on the binding of Isaac, the Akeda, the story of the human sacrifice of Isaac by Abraham, stopped in the nick of time by an angel of God. This was the traditional Yom Kippur portion of the Torah, which people would be reading while he played seven-card stud. He wondered if a little ram would appear for him, as it had for Isaac and Abraham—a substitute sacrifice sent by God—or whether he would have to go through with the plan he had set in motion.

He rose and went into the kitchen to look for a glass of wine; something vaguely sacramental appealed to him now, but he was out of wine, and practically everything else.

As he stood behind the sink and looked out through the screened window, the overhanging branches of the eucalyptus moved in the wind, revealing lights on at the Nakazawas'. Every impulse told him that he should not go across, so he turned away and went back to lie on his bed. But after a quarter of an hour he was up again at the window. No, he should not go, he should not try to see her, but, after all . . . he did need some wine for the holiday.

As he put on his shoes, he had another thought: He called a florist not far from MacArthur Park and ordered a dozen carnations for his mother, to be delivered immediately.

By the time he was at the curb, he knew by the absence of the van and an icy intuition that, although the lights glowed in the store and the house, Dawn was not there.

"Rabbi Bloom," said Ono as he entered, "we thought we would not see you here again."

"I only came to buy some wine, some Israeli wine for the holidays."

"We don't want you," she said. He could not fault her for not being clear. "We are very busy, can't you see? It is inventory time. I have much work."

As he looked around he remembered, then, a Japanese saying that Dawn had taught him: No matter how hungry he is, no matter how many days he has gone without a morsel, a samurai picks his teeth, as if he's just eaten, whenever he walks by a restaurant. Yes, Bloom decided, he would not even ask about her.

"I would like this." He rested his hand on a bottle of Kedem. "Only this. This is all I've come for, and, oh yes, this too." It was a bottle from Schapiro's, a small kosher winery in New Jersey, whose product had somehow reached the Nakazawas' shelves.

"Take what you want and go," she said harshly. It was as if she didn't even care if Bloom paid or not.

"Mrs. Nakazawa, I've come in your store as a customer, not a suitor."

"You're a troublemaker," she said from her stool behind the counter. "You've come here to butter me up. But I don't butter so easy."

"I've just come to buy these." He tried to be casual and at ease.

"You stay on your side of the street, okay?"

"Mrs. Nakazawa, how much do I owe you?"

"A lot," she said. And then, as he was opening his wallet, she said, "More than money, more than all the money you could find, you owe me . . ."

Bloom looked around the store. "What's the problem, Mrs. Nakazawa? What's wrong?"

"Gone," she said to him, as if he were the cause of it, "just gone!"

"You mean she's in L.A.? She's traveling?"

"Do you know what 'gone' means? She hasn't called in three days. She drove off—but she doesn't tell me where, and I don't ask."

Bloom felt that if this was a request for help, it was a strangely remote one. Yet Ono Nakazawa seemed, oddly, to want him to stay.

"You listen, Bloom. It is hard to be a parent. Maybe someday you will find out, and your children, if you are luckier than me, will not be heartless."

"She is not heartless."

Ono seemed not to hear him. "You're in a long line, Bloom, remember that. And now I join that line with you. My daughter collects and discards. Boyfriends I am used to seeing her do this with, but now she is discarding the one parent she has left."

He took another step toward the door, and then stopped. "With all due respect, Mrs. Nakazawa, in everything she's said to me about you I never once got the impression that she's doing anything like discarding you."

"Really! You know someone for a few months, and you are an expert?" Ono looked up from the papers that lay before her on the counter, her eyes glanced off Bloom's, and then she looked away as if embarrassed. She reached under the counter and held out to him the little silver spice box he had given Dawn as a gift. "She left this when she packed her things; I don't want it under my roof."

Bloom took it, put it in the brown bag with the wine, and handed her ten dollars.

She took the money, rang up the sale, and, as she dropped the change into his hand, she said, "From now on, no more Israel wine —okay? Discontinue! New policy, from now on, the synagogue can go elsewhere."

Back in his apartment, in the thickening darkness, Bloom put on his yarmulkah, opened the Kedem, and had a good long drink. In the top drawer of the desk he also found his cantor's stash—four joints and a little ball of hashish. He had another glass of wine, put Dawn's spice box on the table beside him, and made his first call, an explanation to Panuzzi and Brenda. He told them to save their words, that it was all set, that there was no sense trying to argue with him about it, and they should simply run the service as they had discussed it, as if nothing were happening with him at all. Levitt and all the others must be seated in the front, and not allowed out or to send runners to the casino, or to disrupt, or to interfere in any way. On the contrary, Bloom urged Brenda to give Bernie, Adolph, Lucy, all of them, *aliyahs*, Torah readings, *haftorahs*, the job of opening and closing the ark, of carrying the Torah around the sanctuary, the *gelilah*, all the honored functions during the service, anything they could think of that would work. "Bring them back," Bloom urged Brenda, "bring all of them back."

"Are you sure you're going to go through with this?" she asked. "I am."

Then Panuzzi took the phone from her. "Arthur, I think excommunication will suit you well, after all. You'll have Baruch Spinoza and all those other intellectuals, all the highbrow company you've been yearning for."

"According to the tradition," Bloom replied, under the incipient influence of the cantor's marijuana, "a Jew spends a maximum, an absolute maximum—no matter what the offense—of twelve months and a day in hell."

"For you, Arthur, that last day is going to be a killer. Good luck."

"Goodbye, Angelos."

Bloom now checked his watch and called L.A. Yes, the carnations had arrived. Bloom alerted Nannette to prepare for a little shock in three days, when Yom Kippur would begin. He told her not to pay heed to what people would say, that he would be trying to feel holy on the inside even as what he was doing on the outside was obviously blasphemy. "And don't listen to talk of excommunication either, mother. It's a joke, it can't be serious. Ask Brenda, and she'll explain to you that when Jewish communities had power and loyalty and their own courts—"

"For a mother, it's no joke," Nannette said to him quickly as if she wanted to get it over with, her patience at its limit. "Embarrassment and shame are not joking matters. Arthur, it's not the stroke that keeps me from holding my head up high. It's you. You and Leonidas and that loonie car dealer. I only hope Angelos and Brenda have twenty children, all good, normal Jews, to make up for you!"

"Anger's good for you, mom. It keeps the blood flowing smooth."

"That's beside the point."

"The only point as far as I'm concerned is your getting completely well."

"If getting me furious would cure me, I'd be better already. If shame and anger had the power to make me feel strong and young again, I'd already be well. I'd be twenty-one and kicking. You're a fool, an idiot, forgive me for talking this way to a rabbi, but you're my own son. You could have gone with Brenda. You could be going

out with her, *you*. That's what she was there for. You could have
saved yourself, and now, look at you. You're in up to here"—she
raised a shaking, quivering hand to her neck—"and you're going
under."

"No, I'm not."

"Better that I should die before I see the outcome."

"No."

She pulled the table toward her, reached the vase, and grasped the
carnations by their red heads. "And don't send me flowers. Bring me
apologies. Bring me reforms in your behavior, not crazy solutions like
you're telling me. That's all I want from you, that's all. Is it too much
to ask?"

"That's my mom."

But she violently threw the flowers on the floor and hung up on
her son.

81

By the afternoon of the eve of Yom Kippur, the most sacred day on
the Jewish calendar, Rabbi Bloom had succeeded in smoking a joint
and a half of Panuzzi's Acapulco Gold; it was very good but Bloom
deliberately rationed himself so that his head would be clear. He also
drank a little more Israeli wine and he did not forget to say, as he
stared into the mirror, "Blessed art Thou, O Lord our God, King of
the Universe, Who in His wisdom multiplies forgiveness in the
world." It would be a blessing Bloom would be much in need of
today.

Since his return to Gardena he had been studying: the tractate
Yoma in the Talmud, replete with the laws and sanctions surrounding Yom Kippur; his file on Dawn Nakazawa, full of notes, unfin-
ished haikus and love poems, and a photograph of Dawn in the
yellow bikini astride the diving board; and his worn sheet of notebook paper, the one that bore the outline of his life. Another ending.

Under the influence of this study, the marijuana, the wine, and
something intangibly more, Bloom sensed that he was at a point of
understanding himself in a new way. Of course he was on the verge

of despairing, but paradoxically he felt on the verge of exaltation as well. He felt a wave rolling under him, fast and fascinating, and he was on the top, cresting and leading. The shore was now not too far away, and all he had to do was make one or two more moves, delicate and risky to be sure, but if he executed them properly they would bring him in.

Then again, he had no choice in the matter; it was not up to him. For on Yom Kippur, according to ancient Biblical law, the priest, and only the high priest (and surely I am high, giggled Bloom) must enter the holy of holies and perform a ritual in which he takes on to himself, and thereby symbolically absolves, the sins of his people. At no other time in the year can the priest enter, and he must do so completely alone, in absolute solitude, to seek the face of God.

Bloom rose from his desk, knowing precisely what had to be done. He took from the bottom drawer of his bureau the *kittel*, the long white prayer robe, that had belonged to Nannette's grandfather, and he wrapped himself in it. Over his yarmulkah he threw his baseball hat, over his eyes his sunglasses, and then, washed, shaven, and in thongs, he descended the stairs.

It was far too early for people to start assembling for services, so Bloom passed unnoticed into the deserted synagogue. He walked up the center aisle, paused at the midpoint, and looked up toward the podium to experience the vantage of those who looked up to him. His eyes wandered to the admonition written in bold black Hebrew letters above the holy ark: Know Before Whom You Stand. Bloom then walked up and took the ram's horn, the shofar—the temple's extra one—from underneath Panuzzi's lectern, and left the sanctuary.

By the time he had walked a block beyond the willows, and certainly by the time he reached the bank at 2:20, a small group of people had already begun to trail him. Bernie's deposit, which he had arranged two days before, had cleared. Bloom ordered a cashier's check in the amount of $252,213, representing Bernie's assets, and the full $2,428, all of Bloom's own. Then, leaving the bank, and stopping every few blocks to blow the shofar, he retraced his steps. In front of the synagogue Bloom gave a brief sermon to those who had gathered; it was a sermon so observant of homiletical proprieties, Bloom felt even Rabbi Karpf would have approved. He began as well as ended with the story his father had once told him, a memory of

Arthur's grandmother from a distant, faraway Yom Kippur. How, for the *kapores* ceremony, the ancient custom of atoning for sins, she had brought home a live chicken from the market, and then she whirled it up over and around her head three times, carefully pronouncing each of these words: This fowl is my substitute, my vicarious offering, my atonement. This fowl shall meet death, but I shall enjoy a long, pleasant life of peace. Then the chicken had its neck stretched across the sink, and its throat quickly cut by the gleaming butcher knife.

"You can understand," Bloom told his rapt listeners, "how the entire custom, so bloody, so tinged with not-so-faint Christian influences, was ultimately dropped, and is today frowned on by many rabbinical authorities. Nevertheless, ladies and gentlemen," he said as he bowed politely out toward the crowd, "today you may consider me your chicken."

Bloom now took out the shofar, delivered a respectable *terua*, and then a dozen very short blasts. The loud outdoor trumpeting soon brought a Gardena Police patrol car up to the crowd, and, Bloom noticed, a slow parting of the drapes in the Nakazawas' store. Bloom raised the shofar and blew one long, final note across the boulevard.

He told the police, No, he had no permit for a parade today, and they told him that there had been a few too many processions and religious assemblies lately, and that he should get his people inside or disperse them.

Bloom tipped his Yankees hat to the police and crowd, and then surprised them all by walking not into the synagogue but away from it. At the driveway, he turned toward the crowd, hesitant and trailing behind, took off his cap, and, like a bride with a bouquet, tossed it toward outstretched hands. As people scrambled for it, Bloom crossed the driveway and entered the Silver Dollar Casino through its main door.

He sunk into the deep carpet and thought: This moment has been waiting to happen all my life. This is it, my desecration and maybe my redemption all wrapped up in one. *Hakol tzafui*, says Rabbi Akiba, *va harishut nituna*. Yes, he and Dawn had talked about this once, a long time ago. Everything is preordained, but there is still free will, or at least the incredibly palpable illusion of it that Bloom was now experiencing. Somehow he'd known it was there, his rebellion, this volcanic fist gathering tighter and tighter from adolescence on through rabbinical school, not unflexing itself until now. But then again he had chosen to spring it, because there was no alternative.

Bloom looked around this new habitat and thought, Thank God for this place! In other epochs, people gave up everything, often including their lives, to find out what he was to find out in the next twenty-four hours. Thank God for this casino, he thought, thank God for this place, history's safe eschatological laboratory. Here no lives were being gambled with, except perhaps Bernie's and certainly his own; here only plastic chips, red, blue, and white, would be risked. Chickens a substitute for real sacrifice, the priest for the congregation, chips for money, and he for Temple Elijah. It all seemed right enough, symmetrical, all bases touched.

Bloom stepped away from the gilded front doors to the dim alcove on the right, where he solemnly offered his sofar to the coatcheck girl. Was there a *bracha*, a blessing, for entering the casino? "If there is," he said to the gawking hostess in her little white miniskirt, "consider yourself blessed."

A few gamblers looked up to see him, but most of the house kept their eyes on the cards. "What'll it be, Rabbi?" Kavanaugh, the floor manager, was speaking. "You sure you don't want to just go home? You don't look very good."

"I'm fine." He showed the bank check to the manager. "And I intend to invest all this today in your fine institution."

"I figured I'd see you here sooner or later." Kavanaugh extended the rabbi a pen. "Endorse, please."

"Fine," said Bloom. "Now bring me chips, my son. Chips, chips, chips."

"How much to start, Rabbi? Two, five, twenty-five, or a hundred, to open?"

There was a swirl of voices, dense smokiness, lights, and no clock on any wall. "Seat me anywhere."

In a quarter of an hour Bloom was staring into the faces of six low-ball players. He had seen none of them in the temple; and apparently they did not know him. "I never played poker with Jesus Christ," said the fat man beside Bloom. Bloom barely knew the game, but he had chips, he had hands, and he dealt the cards as he saw the others do. Within fifteen minutes he had lost several hundred dollars, but he was learning, he was being drawn in. Bloom fumbled with the cards, but the woman next to him, a red bouffant on her head the height of a milk carton, helped him out. He lost, but then he began to concentrate. He played the next dozen hands very carefully. He dropped out twice with eight-threes. Then, right before his own deal, he was dealt a six-four. He upped the betting modestly and stayed pat. He was called, and he showed them. He won. He ordered coffee and a whiskey and a pack of cigarettes. He was settling in. He had a run of good cards, then bad, he strove for his seven or eight highs, but he hit the deck. Then several times he decided to bluff, and on a half dozen more hands he simply got confused, bet, raised, and folded; summarily he was down $4,000.

"Better fix it, young fella," said a man in overalls, the man who had just beaten him.

"Rabbi, honey," said the red bouffant lady, "you got to know when to hold 'em and when to fold 'em."

"How do you know who I am?" he asked.

"Everyone does."

Bloom decided to take a break, to walk around. Instantly he was staring at Angelos. "Arthur, I'm watching your act, and I've reconsidered. I know you don't want me or anyone else here, but I think you should call it quits now and come with me. You don't even have to be in the shul. Stay with me if you want. Open the store if that's the kind of thing you want to do. Arthur?"

Bloom looked up and said simply, "A deal is a deal. Also consider Numbers 29:7: 'On Yom Kippur, on the tenth day of the seventh month you shall have a holy convocation and ye shall afflict your souls.'"

"It's not my soul's being afflicted, Rabbi. It's my checkbook." This was Lucy Leonard, who stepped out from behind Panuzzi. "Please, Rabbi, let's discuss this whole arrangement. I know Bernie has made lots of mistakes, but this is a bad thing, and I don't want you to go through with this."

"It is *my* arrangement, not Bernie Levitt's," Bloom said emphatically. "Now back to the synagogue with both of you." And then to Lucy, "My dear Ms. Leonard, today is a day of prayer and reflection. Try to make it so for you, and don't worry about me, Bernie's money, or anything earthly. Go and pray."

Down now $8,000, Bloom recognized one of the dealers. He went up to the blackjack tables and waited until middle-aged, short, brown-haired Audrey Axelrod, Ethel's sister, recognized him.

"Oh, Rabbi," she said, "I don't know if I ought to."

Bloom sat down heavily on the stool opposite her. "Please deal," he said, "thou daughter of Israel, and then get out of here and go pray. I'm here today as your surrogate."

Bloom was gambling heavily now, moving from a break for blackjack back to the poker table with the highest stakes. He was mainly losing; occasionally he won, but he was going to stay. He would not be moved from the pit, and as the hour of Kol Nidre approached, and with that the official beginning of Yom Kippur, his resolve increased. Audrey left when her shift was through, pleasing Bloom, for she was going to the synagogue. But Bloom remained. Thirty minutes before sunset, the moment of the onset of the Day, Abe North came over to Bloom. He was wearing a dark gray suit. From his dwindling tower of chips, Bloom looked up and said, "My condolences, Abe."

"Rabbi, for the love of God, come."

"No," said Bloom. "On these, the High Holidays, I have become your high roller. Sarah would have wanted it this way. She always was after me to lead, and now I am leading. One big experiment, then over and done with."

"It's Yom Kippur." Abe put a slightly trembling hand on his shoulder. "We'll delay the service so you'll have time to run upstairs to shave and shower."

Bloom looked up from his cards. "In ancient Biblical law," he said, "the penalty for violating Yom Kippur is excommunication. Abe, technically that's a penalty more severe even than death. I am aware of things."

"Will you please shut up, friend," said the player opposite Bloom.

"Arthur," Abe whispered, "Brenda is waiting. She'll take care of everything. Just come. Wash your face and sit up there with us."

"*Gmar chatima tova*, Abe. May you be sealed in the Book of Life."

Bloom kept losing, with just an occasional win. He was down nearly $18,000, and Kol Nidre hadn't even started. He played on. In defiance of the agreement, other representatives were sent to cajole Bloom back. To them all, he quoted Psalms. The casino emptied and then filled up again, in waves; Bloom thought he could hear, when the doors were flung open, the long, lugubrious melodies of the Kol Nidre service. But he played on. He took breaks, went into the lounge, smoked, watched the basketball game, and then, when he got hungry, he had a double cheeseburger at the grill. Then he returned to the table. The same timeless lights and flicking drone of chips moving across felt-covered tables. He had no idea of the hour. He moved back to low ball and then to blackjack again. His eyes were tired, and then he took another break when he must have slept several hours, and he rose, and went down the steps into the pit once more to play. He was exhausted, but so grateful that in spite of an honorable effort, he was very definitely losing. The lucky rabbi was already down by nearly half his stake, and the other half was beginning to be in danger. People stood behind him to watch him lose, a knot of two or three staring unabashedly until the floor manager chased them away. What a pleasure, though, to lose, to be so unlucky.

His *kittel* was by now heavily spotted with ashes, coffee, whiskey, cheeseburger, and rice pudding stains. Bloom's sense of time was now completely shot; he wondered if this was the sense of time in eternity, in the world to come. He was about to return to a game where the pot had grown on a single hand to $5,000, when he heard someone entering hail someone else, "Good Morning."

"Good morning." Bloom beamed happily. In spite of the pit boss's best efforts to disperse them, spectators continued to gather wherever Bloom was playing. No higher pots had ever been played for at the Silver Dollar Casino. And never had there been a sprightlier, happier, or bigger loser than the fellow in the white toga. The rabbi was down already $113,000.

Bloom played on, and then the morning prayers came to him as he played and lost and then lost again. He hummed the melodies, he stood up and stretched at the gambling tables at those moments when, according to his internal service, it was time to rise. He looked up now, and Brenda Weiner herself had come. Her long blond hair fell over the black rabbinical robes. In her hands she held the *machzor*, the special High Holiday prayer book. "If you must be here, I brought you this." Then she kissed him.

"Very kind of you," Bloom said, and then he handed the prayer book back to her. "Best of luck on your sermon."

In fact, as Bloom gambled on, losing $10,500 on a single terrifi-
cally ill-judged hand, he was sure he could hear Brenda delivering
the sermon; he was sure he could make out her words, her expatia-
tion on themes in Jonah. When a chip girl came by, a Mexican
whose name was Xiomara, Bloom reached out and took her hand,
saying, "Do you hear Brenda? What she's saying? That forgiveness
and repentance is for all nations, black, brown, white, and yellow,
and for all ethnic groups, and for people of all beliefs, and in all of
this, gender is to be discounted. Xiomara, that means you."

"May I get you a coffee? Something to eat—on the house—along
with your chips, sir?"

"Yes, God, more coffee, Xiomara. More coffee."

Bloom drank, dropped several thousand more, got up and uri-
nated, and returned to low ball. In spite of two good runs—he *was*
trying—he was soon down to his last $15,000. He sensed it was time
for the Confession of Sins. He was losing even faster than he expected, at a spectacular, wonderful rate that could only belong to the
utterly luckless. While he played his cards, Bloom beat his breast
once for the sin of pride, once for the sin of speaking rashly, once
for the sin of not having respect for elders, and for the sin of bearing
false witness; one strike for the sin of slander, one for the sin of
gluttony, and for the sin of impatience; for these, and for everything,
for every sin. . . . Bloom thought he might try opening this time with
a pair of queens.

The game wore on, and the red bouffant lady showed up again,
went out, and came back. Bloom thought he saw Bernie once at the
table in the corner of the pit, the high roller table where he had spent
so much time lately—where you opened with a thousand—but he
no longer could be sure of what he was seeing. No, it was not Bernie,
he realized as he went and got some more chips and dragged himself
by the corner table. Levitt had kept his part of the bargain, just as
Bloom had. The floor manager urged Arthur to keep the few remain-
ing chips. He offered him a room at Gardena's best motel, and a car
to drive him there. But the rabbi did not want to be moved. He lost
everything, and then stood, kissed each of his adversaries at the
table, men and women, on the cheek, saying, "May God bless you
and keep you, may He cause His countenance to shine down upon
you, and give you peace."

"Same to you, Rabbi."

"Happy Yom Kippur, kid."

"I'm gonna buy an Israel bond with this dough, Rabbi. In your name."

"Shalom, kid."

Bloom stumbled out of the pit, lay down in the lounge, and immediately fell asleep. Xiomara covered him with a spare tablecloth against the breeze from the air conditioners.

Hours later Bloom awoke, felt his stubble, and got up and parted the curtains of the small windows in the lounge; he had not known these windows gave such an unobstructed view of the synagogue pool, his balcony, and the eucalyptus by the gate. It was late afternoon, it was growing toward nighttime, and the hour of Yom Kippur's final service, the *Neila,* the closing of the gates; the last chance was at hand for additions and deletions to be made in the Book of Life. The last chance, before the shofar would be blown one final time, and the gates locked shut, with God having made His judgments as to whether you got in the Book of Life for the righteous, the Book of Life for the wicked, or the Book of Life for all those in between. And then, of course, thought Bloom as he rubbed his eyes and stretched, there must be some just plain left out, some people like himself who fit nowhere, who float, are lost, or hide, beyond all registration.

Bloom stretched again, looking up to where he had been living these three years, then wearily checked his pockets, where he found three hundred dollars in chips. With this he went to the dice table and began to lose immediately. After the last bum roll, after all the chips before him had been swept away, he returned to the dark lounge and fell into a dream-tossed sleep: He saw the darkened shul, the Torah draped in deep black, the room palpitating in the light of a dozen candles. A *minyan* slowly gathered. And the leader of the service stepped out from the crowd, obscured still by shadows. Then from beneath the shrouded prayer shawl the leader—a rabbi, Bloom assumed—read the writ of excommunication: You, Arthur Bloom, are hereby ordered to have no social intercourse with the Jewish community. You may neither buy nor sell, you may not live within its precincts or be buried in its cemeteries according to its rituals. In life and in death, you are cut off, broken, severed, from the holy community of God!

At the end of the reading, the rabbi stepped forward, and Bloom saw it was Dawn.

He woke in a sweat, lifted himself up to look through the window again toward the synagogue. He heard Panuzzi's blast on the shofar as he fell back to sleep again, quickly, with the high piercing *t-kee-yah gdolah* in his ear: the High Holidays had ended.

82

Bloom awoke fourteen hours later, sat up, rubbed his face, and realized that, having lost, he had won: Dawn was there in his bedroom. "Good morning, my darling rabbi," she said. He pulled up his sheet in automatic modesty—he was naked—felt his stubbled face, and then watched Dawn doing this incredible thing: She was pulling out the drawers from his bureau, folding his clothes, and packing them in the Gladstone. "Angelos brought you here, in case you were wondering," she said. "I've come to congratulate you and then take you with me." Bloom continued to study her in her reddish-brown sunglasses and her floppy white hat with chin strap that altered the shape of her face. Yes, he had not seen her in these yellow shorts either or wearing this T-shirt with a bright red parrot design, but it was unmistakably Dawn Nakazawa.

"You're not running from me any more?"

"Right." She smiled. "We're running together now. I think that we belong to each other. I've decided to accept your proposal too, if it's still standing."

With a groggy coyness, he said, "Which proposal is that?"

"That I become your wife."

"Oh."

"Well? Do you accept my acceptance?"

Bloom sensed his heart beating in a kind of slow motion as he answered her, "I suppose I do, but where are we going?"

"We're headed for my cousin's beach house; she's away in Europe for at least six months and it will do until we find something better." Bloom listened in amazement. She continued to speak as calmly as if she were reporting the most ordinary weather. "You really can't stay here since you're no longer working for the synagogue, and I've decided my mother and I are better to each other when we don't live cheek by jowl."

"So it's off to the beach with us?" He sat up straight in bed.

"Right! Now that you can swim, you'll be safe, and I know you like the beach."

"Where is this house?" He still could not believe what was happening.

"I've mentioned it to you, Arthur. It's just south of Long Beach. It's small but cozy. For people who like being close."

"I do like being close to you."

"I know you do, Arthur."

"I'd like to be close to you now," he said.

She continued to pack, his socks now, and here she took out an old prayer book that somehow had found its way into the sweater drawer.

"Dawn, you know what's happened, don't you?"

"Of course."

"I didn't do it for you."

"Nevertheless"—she threw his extra sheets and pillowcases into a laundry bag—"I'm very proud of you, Arthur."

"And that's why you've decided to become my wife?"

Now she stopped. She walked over to the bed and slowly put her hand on his chest, over his heart. "This is why," she said. "It's my personal opinion you've got the very best one that's ever been made." She moved her hand to his face, his chin. "And your smile, that's another reason I'll marry you. I like the way it comes not from the lips or even the eyes, but from some hidden smile source deep inside. Those are two reasons. I could come up with many more if you needed them. Do you need to hear more?"

"I'd like to, but since you've said yes, and are now packing all my belongings and taking me with you, I suppose reasons for doing this are a little after the fact."

"Good boy! You're learning." And then she leaned down and kissed him.

"Are you familiar," he said softly, his lips touching hers, "with the great Buddhist teaching that desire is the source of all suffering?"

"I suppose I will be."

"I propose we suffer splendidly together."

She was on his lap now, kissing his mouth, cheeks, his unshaven grubby face. He pulled up her T-shirt, and her breasts sprang out to him. He touched them gently and then rested his face on the shiny fossa at the base of the sternum, then her stomach, her scar, all her history. On his knees he kissed them all.

She returned his kisses, on the arms, legs, his feet, and while she ministered to him, he reached over to his nightstand and read to her from Talmud Nedarim, the section dealing with relations between men and women. My mother should forgive me, he thought, for he had the place again marked with a sweat sock:

> Rabbi Johanan ben Dahabai said: Four things were told to me by the Ministering Angels: Why do people become lame? Because they have intercourse from the rear; why do people become blind? Because they gaze at the female genitals; why do they become dumb? Because they kiss "that place"; why do they become deaf? Because they talk while having intercourse.
>
> Said Rabbi Johanan: These are the words of Rabbi Johanan ben Dahabai, but the Sages say, "The law is *not* according to Johanan ben Dahabai; but anything a man wants to do with his wife, he may do. It is just like meat that comes from the butcher's; if he wants to eat it with salt, he may do so, if he wants to eat it roasted, or boiled, or seethed, he may do so; and the same applies to fish."

"What I like about that," Dawn said, laughing, "is 'and the same applies to fish.'"

"I love it all," Bloom said. "One of the things I realize now that I've left it in a way is how much of it I so love, how much of it is simply part of me."

They stretched out now beside each other, leg to long leg. "Arthur, I never left you, you know. Not really."

"I think I know that."

"There was no question, not ever, of not coming back to you. Only of waiting for you. A question mainly of when. And now you're here, now you did it, and you're here."

"Yes"—he pulled her to him—"I'm here, all right."

"And there's something else. We're not alone, Arthur. I'm pretty sure there is someone else quite close and listening." Bloom raised his head. His eyes darted about the room. Not Bernie again, not any more, no!

"Not that." She ran her fingers across the little inlets of his hairline. "No, thanks to you, that's gone, forever, I hope. But we're still not alone." She paused and drew his hands to her stomach. "Are you ready for this?"

"You're kidding?"

"No."

"When?"

"In about seven months. Are you pleased, Arthur?" Bloom rolled toward the cradle of her neck. He buried his head there in the darkness. "Arthur?" But he was too overcome to speak and he wanted to stay there hiding like a child, like their child—*their* child —might do someday soon, with his hands over his face blocking out the world and the light. "Arthur, are you okay in there?" She could feel his tears streaming down her chest, and moistening her shoulder. And as he cried and hid there, the questions rose up to him and he combated them, so that when he asked himself in the silence and the darkness so that only he could hear, Is it my baby? Are you sure? How do you know? he answered, Of course it is, you idiot! She loves you.

"You didn't come back to me because I'm the father of your baby?"

"I told you, Arthur. I never left you, not really."

He snuggled closer to her now, at her shoulder and her neck, where he spoke to himself again, asking—now that he was going to be a father—whether she might consider converting, be Ruth to his Naomi and declare, Wherever you go, I go, your people will be my people, your God my God. And then he answered himself: Shut up! For godsake, just shut up! He just remained there now, eyes closed, nuzzling at Dawn's clavicle like a man dangling from a ledge, full of power in his arms, just waiting for the moment to gather his strength and pull himself up.

"Arthur?"

"Yes," he said, his face still hidden. "I am very happy."

They rested like this in the echo of their resolve to take the next step in their lives together. The sun streamed in through the bedroom window, their bodies felt elegant, long, noble, fertile. "Pardon my ignorance," Bloom finally said, "but will intercourse bother him?"

"No"—Dawn smiled—"it won't bother her at all."

"In that case," Bloom whispered, "the rabbis say it's a *mitzvah* if the woman has her orgasm first."

"Bless the rabbis," Dawn murmured. "Bless all the rabbis, and, in particular, you."

83

Bloom's marriage to Dawn took place a month later. It was held not at the synagogue and not at the Japanese community's cultural center but at Gardena City Hall. In attendance were Brenda and Angelos, Nannette, Leonidas, and Ono Nakazawa. Both Nannette and Ono had at first declined, but when they were informed Dawn was pregnant, the future grandmothers reconsidered and came. Acquiescing to her daughter, Ono brought Akira along, too, carrying the urn of his ashes in her arms, as they entered the chapel for the ten-minute ceremony. When it was explained to Nannette who, what, was in the urn, she found it, at first, grotesque. However, by the time the vows had been exchanged and they had all driven to L.A. and sat down to the wedding lunch set out on her table, she and Ono were getting along famously. Not only did they have their dead husbands, but a future grandchild to discuss as well.

During the course of the lunch, Nannette and Leonidas had offered to work part time in the store. After a week of thinking about it, Ono accepted. Being behind the counter and talking to all kinds of people, helping Ono shlep boxes, all of this, they decided, would help to keep them young. If Nannette or Leonidas wanted to go and play cards, Abe North often filled in. While working, they all discussed Bloom, Dawn, and especially the baby-to-be.

The beach house proved to be the right idea at first. Dawn's cousin was extending her travel by three months, but as the birth grew nearer, Dawn and Bloom realized they needed more room and a space that was their own.

"My old place?" Bloom offered one afternoon as they read together on the sofa. But it was more than a question.

"There's hardly more room there."

"Oh sure there is," he said. "A whole extra bedroom, the veranda is the size of another room, and then, of course, there's the pool. You remember the pool, don't you?"

She put down her book, moved to his side of the couch, and turned his head toward her. "Arthur, you don't want to go back just for the space?"

"No."

"And not just for the pool, wonderful as that will be?"

"No," he said sheepishly, at first. "I want to go back, I think, because I want to go back, if they'll have us. And I promise, Dawn, I promise on—as we used to say as kids—my Jewish honor that I won't try to convert you."

Dawn wrote one more piece, and then called it quits at the *Eye*. In the fourth month of the pregnancy, before she really showed at all, she got the break she'd been waiting for: she had two more interviews at the *L.A. Times*, and was offered a job. She took it immediately. Bloom agreed he would stay home with the child and while fixing bottles, changing diapers, and getting to know his offspring, he would think about his rabbinical career. Everyone agreed it would take a lot of thinking.

In Dawn's fifth month Bloom formally wrote to Abe North, the acting president of Temple Elijah, asking for his job back.

"Speaking personally," Abe said when he telephoned him, "you've only been on honeymoon leave and it's always been yours to reclaim. But in my august new capacity, I will have to take your request under advisement."

"Which means what?"

"I'll run it by the others one at a time—probably when we draw seats at the same poker table."

"I feel I should warn you," Bloom added, "in case you aren't fully aware already, that you'll probably be cut off from a lot of the major organizations who don't want to be tainted by association with the Southland's first and foremost intermarried rabbi."

"What association? What support?" Abe laughed. "Nothing from nothing is nothing."

"You really think it'll be okay?" Bloom was timorous.

"A camel without its hump is a plain ordinary horse, Arthur. That's what Leonidas has been saying, and he's right. Without you we're just a little hole-in-the-wall place. But with you, we're the Silver Dollar Shul, Casino, and Temple Center Incorporated."

"I don't come alone any more, Abe."

"With you and your wife we'll really stand for something important. Not to worry, Arthur."

In Dawn's sixth month, with objections continuing only from Eli Ginsberg (who was rehospitalized when the pin failed to repair his hip fracture), Bloom and Dawn repossessed the apartment over the synagogue garage. But because the synagogue had been financially drained, Bloom could have only the apartment and little or no salary for his sermons and his work. "I'll do it," he said to Abe North, from whom he took the keys, "I'll do it for love."

Even before they moved back, life in town and at the synagogue had returned to what, for Gardena, was normal. Bernie Levitt had quietly left Southern California for Israel. The number of people attending services had dwindled with Bloom's departure, but with his return there always seemed to be at least the ten needed for a *minyan*, so services could be held every day. They were led by Bloom and sometimes by Angelos Panuzzi in preparation for the time when the rabbi would be busy with a morning bottle or diaper and might not be able to make it down for services. Brenda, whom Panuzzi was now engaged to, was no longer at the shul because she had returned to New York for her last year of rabbinical school. She flew out often, however, specifically for holidays, which she presided over at the synagogue with Bloom. Panuzzi did all the maintenance work around the synagogue, too, because Black Dave, though still active, was now busily engaged in restarting the car business as Dave Diamond Cadillac. He had found a new location just off Paradise Road, and, of course, Dave had his angle: Although the new location was off the main drag, he'd heard that a Long Beach–based oil company was sinking exploratory holes in the area, and Dave wanted to get in on the action.

Bloom and Dawn read, wrote, made love, barbecued, and swam. As Dawn grew bigger, Bloom concentrated and wrote an article— turned down by every journal—about a rabbi in a mixed marriage. But Bloom was not discouraged; articles were to read and write, but life was to live. He spent a great deal of time living now, touching Dawn's expanding abdomen. Together they charted the baby's changing positions, the elbows, the head, and the exquisitely tiny feet and toes.

One evening, as they lay in bed and saw together a dozen rapid kicks, the last of which seemed to pinch a nerve in Dawn's back, Bloom put his head to Dawn's belly button and yelled, "Hello in there, hello! We all know you're in there," Bloom went on. "We know you have important work to do," he joked, "but the time's not right. Not yet. Take it easy. Don't hurt your mother so. There's another two months. If you hear me, kick."

Instantly the baby kicked. Bloom and Dawn looked at each other and began to laugh.

As the delivery date approached, anonymously generated rumors did float into Gardena: If the rabbi had been the harbinger, surely his offspring will be the true article. Other signs abounded: Syria experienced a coup; Yasir Arafat, on the eve of an important U.N. appearance, came down with a painful gallbladder attack; a little-known third baseman, Aurelio Levi, made the Yankees as backup utility infielder; the fiery chariot of Ezekiel was supposedly spotted again in the night sky above L.A.—flames from the wheels allegedly grazing the dry grass and starting a small brushfire below Mulholland Drive. All these signs could only mean that . . . Bloom and Dawn even received a letter from an eccentric and wealthy Hollywood producer inquiring if he could film the birth.

Only the immediate family was allowed in Gardena Hospital. Ono, Nannette, and Leonidas waited in the lobby, while Panuzzi, singing old Ladino—Judeo/Spanish—melodies, paced with Bloom outside the door of the labor room.

The baby was a boy. Of course he was beautiful, if wrinkled and tired from the fight to be born into the crazy world. He had eyes like melting chocolate drops, and Bloom took one look and fell in love with his son immediately and, he was sure, forever.

The child was named Akira Samson—Akira Sam, for short—after his grandfathers. He proved normal and average in every way, came forth with no prophetic pronouncements on his lips, and experienced very non-messianic gas and colic that lasted three months. The birth had been only the usual miracle.

Two weeks after the birth, as Bloom and Dawn floated on twin

inner tubes across the surface of the synagogue pool, with Akira Sam
bellowing on his mother's lap, Black Dave rushed up the driveway,
through the creaky gate, and was just able to stop short of falling in
at six feet. "They found it," he shouted. "They found oil, Rabbi.
Right here under the pool, under the whole place!"

"Come again?"

"Oil, man. That's right, through this exploratory well down the
end of Paradise Road near me, they found this field that runs apparently up the entire east side of the boulevard, spreads out under the
shul, and then turns north for a few hundred yards. Unfortunately
it stops at my property line, but, Rabbi, look!" He handed Bloom
a sheaf of legal papers, with appendices and many dotted lines to sign
one's name on. "The money's not spectacular," Dave said, "but it
sure is secure. I figure the synagogue's got at least $2,000 a month
coming to it in fees for leasing the ground rights, and that money
means you—hi there, Miss N.—and the little family."

Bloom read quickly and realized that the income generated by the
oil would indeed be enough to pay him his former salary plus perhaps
even a little more; it also would guarantee maintenance of Temple
Elijah in perpetuity. *"Vay iz mir,"* said Bloom, but he had a big grin
on his face and he dropped himself through the inner tube and was
now swimming to his wife and child.

When he surfaced near her, Dawn said to him with a wry smile,
"Maybe you're the lucky rabbi, after all!"

Akira Sam, who'd been howling for twenty minutes, suddenly
went quiet and fell asleep, seeming to have no opinion, yet, on the
matter.